# Can You Lose the Unibrow?

## Book One

### In the

## *Ladies in Lab Coats Series*

### By

## *Sally Burbank*

*Sally Burbank*

# Books by Sally Burbank

## Non-fiction

*Patients I Will Never Forget*
*The Alzheimer's Disease Caregiver's Handbook: What to Remember When They Forget*

## Fiction

### The Ladies in Lab Coats Series:
*Can You Lose the Unibrow? (spring 2019)*
*More Than a Hunch (To be released late 2019)*
*Hearts Heal in Haiti (To be released 2020)*
*Love Has No Color (To be released 2020)*
*Squeakers Meets His Match (To be released 2021)*

## Anthologies

### Chicken Soup for the Soul:
*— Miracles Happen*
*— Power of Positive*
*— Hope and Miracles*
*— Reader's Choice 20th Anniversary Ed.*

# Dedication

This book is dedicated to Dorothy Willard, whose sixty-plus years of happy marriage to my father, Everett Willard, as well as her passion for all things Shakespeare, inspired this book. As the great bard himself once said,

*"O, Lord, that lends me life, lend me*

*a heart replete with thankfulness."*

~William Shakespeare~

# Can You Lose the Unibrow?

## Winner for Best Romance in the ACFW 2017

## First Impression Contest

For inquiries and speaking engagements, contact the publisher at:

## Woodmont and Waverly Publishing

## 207 Woodmont Circle

## Nashville, TN 37205

## Salburbank@icloud.net

This book is a work of fiction. All characters, places, names, and events are either a product of the author's imagination or are used fictitiously. Any likeness to events or persons, alive or dead, is entirely coincidental.

"I Can't Make You Love Me" is written by Mike Reid and Allen Shamblin. © 1991 Almo Music Corp., Brio Blues Music, and BMG Songs, Inc. All rights reserved.

Cover Designer: Najla Qamber Designs

Editor: Candie Moonshower

ISBN-13: 978-0-9983206-0-1 (paperback)

ISBN-13: 978-0-9983206-1-8 (eBook)

*"How sharper than a serpent's tooth*
*it is to have a thankless child."*
~William Shakespeare~
*King Lear*

# Chapter 1

Tall, dark, and handsome — that's what twenty-year-old women want. By age thirty, they lower their standards to tall and dark. Age forty? *Please, God, let him have a job.*

Sheri Morris scrolled through the unsavory characters displayed on her laptop and grumbled to her mother, perched behind her like a vulture waiting for roadkill, "A year's subscription to *Losers Looking for Love.* You shouldn't have, Ma."

Linda Morris harrumphed. "Excuse me, but the website is called *Christian Professionals Looking for Love.* It's time you found a husband." She wagged a scolding finger. "And now that you're forty, you can't afford to be too choosy."

*Choosy?*

Sheri eyed the cigarette dangling from the lips of one morbidly obese contender. "I'll need an oxygen tank to keep this one alive." She gestured toward the screen. "Look at these guys. Duds, all of them."

Linda brushed her off with a dismissive wave. "Nonsense. You don't need a whole battalion — just one nice man."

One nice man? In your dreams, Ma.

Sheri heard enough stories about online dating disasters to write a book — a very depressing book. Talk about an ego-busting, budget-bloating demoralizing waste of time — and that's if she didn't wind up dead in a dumpster.

Oblivious to Sheri's musings, Linda prattled on. "I've always dreamed of a Christmas wedding." Her eyes grew dreamy, and she extended her arm. "Picture it, Sheri. You in an elegant velvet wedding gown. The bridesmaids in festive cranberry red. The church adorned with fragrant evergreens, holly berries, and flickering white candles. Poinsettias will circle the altar, and the shimmering lights on a Douglas fir will make the church magical."

Sheri snorted. "You're planning my wedding when I haven't even had a first date?"

"With all the men to choose from on this website, you'll have a husband in no time." She snapped her fingers.

*Right.* Her mother made finding a husband sound as simple as ordering a Weed Wacker off Amazon. Not wanting to hurt her feelings, however, she forced herself to say nothing—until her mother insisted, "Cupid is computer savvy these days."

Sheri rolled her eyes. "Shakespeare says, 'Some Cupid kills with arrows and some with traps.'"

Linda waved a scolding finger. "None of your Shakespeare foolishness with me, young lady. You can laugh all you want, but website dating is how it's done these days."

"Except I wouldn't marry any of these guys. Look, I know you meant well, but honestly? I wish you'd just bought me a terry-cloth bathrobe and slippers instead of this line-up of lunkheads."

"I was trying to be nice. A year's membership for this website was expensive, and you don't seem very grateful for my generosity." Her eyes pooled with tears, which she made a point of brushing away dramatically with the back of her hand. Then, to drive in her nail of shame, she reached for a tissue and blew her nose with the volume of a foghorn. "I try so hard to be a good mother to you and Tess, and what's my reward? Ingratitude, that's what."

*Here we go again: guilt, gift-wrapped with a giant bow. Happy Birthday to me.*

Her mother picked up the framed photo of Sheri's sister standing with her husband, Colton, and son, Jacob, from Sheri's desk. "Tess and Colton are so happy, and they have little Jacob to boot." She dabbed her eyes with a tissue. "I just wanted you to be as happy as your sister. Is that too much for a mother to ask?"

6

Sheri was about to apologize when she heard Tess trill from the living room, "Did I hear my name?"

Mrs. Perfect-in-Every-Way breezed into the study and hooked a blond curl behind her ear. She eyed the smoke-stack-of-a-man displayed on the screen and snickered. "Is that future lung cancer victim the guy Ma picked out for you?" She elbowed Sheri. "Just the man any doctor would want to marry—a smoker."

*Thank you, Tess.*

One glance at her mother's crossed arms and thunderous glare, and Sheri forced herself to say, "I'll keep browsing, Ma. There's bound to be one decent guy."

*Just not this one or the last thirty I checked out.*

She grabbed her mug of coffee and gulped a hefty swig. She'd need all the caffeine she could get to whittle through this sorry passel of deadbeats without wanting to inject herself with cyanide.

*Please, God, let there be one tolerable man in the bunch.*

Somewhere out there was a smart, funny, and principled man—her soulmate—and she wouldn't settle for less, no matter how much her mother cajoled her.

She clicked to the next candidate and groaned. Definitely *not* said soul mate—a sixty-seven-year-old banker seeking a forty-year-old woman.

Tess skimmed the man's profile over Sheri's shoulder. "Gross! What gives that old geezer the right to play in the sandbox? He's old enough to be your father."

Sheri scooped up another bite of cake and ice cream and stuffed it into her mouth. Surely stress would burn off the calories. Besides, it was her birthday.

She clicked to the next guy—Jeremy—a forty-year-old heavy metal guitarist with scraggly hair and enough tattoos to cause a worldwide ink shortage. Jeremy wanted a supportive helpmate. Sheri shook her head in disgust. "Interpret that to mean he needs someone to pay his electric bill."

Tess laughed and nudged her, but their mother's sour expression suggested she wasn't amused.

Sheri clicked to the next screen. A guy with five ex-wives.

*Next.*

She spooned in another mouthful of carrot cake and wiped the luscious cream cheese frosting from her lips before clicking onto an attorney who bragged about how many lawsuits he'd won in the last ten years. One of those "1-800-BAD-DRUG" sharks. Wait! Hadn't she seen this guy's picture plastered all over Nashville's buses? Just the man every physician wanted—a lawyer who got rich suing doctors.

"Face it, Sheri," Tess said. "While you were slaving over textbooks in college, medical school, and residency, the rest of us snagged up all the decent guys like bargains at a Macy's Midnight Madness sale. Looks like you're left with the dregs."

Sheri squelched the temptation to asphyxiate her sister with cake. The cruelty of Tess's words, however, rang true.

"Theresa Morris Peterson, you take that back this instant," her mother demanded, jabbing a finger in Tess's direction. "That was mean and uncalled for, and I won't stand for it."

Sheri suppressed a smile. You'd think they were still squabbling six-year-olds from her mother's reaction.

Tess raised upturned palms. "Just saying…"

Sheri had always told herself she'd find a husband once her internal medicine practice was up and thriving. Her mantra? Focus on your studies and worry about husband hunting later. Unfortunately, "later" had come and gone nine years ago, and now, her twelve-hour workdays left little time to meet a smart, likeable guy the natural way. Hence, her mother's birthday gift.

How degrading to expose her picture and profile to hundreds of strangers as though she were some worn-out nag at a horse auction one step from the glue factory. But after eight years without a date, she needed to kiss her pride goodbye before she wound up dying in a nursing home all alone.

Resolve renewed, she ignored Tess's barb and clicked to the next man on the website. A CPA named Greg Palmer.

Hmm. He might prove useful around April fourteenth.

Friendly brown eyes stared back at her, and his smile would make a dentist do a happy dance. At least the guy wasn't morbidly obese or holding a Marlboro. Even better? No boastful display of a shotgun and dead deer carcass draped around his shoulders like two previous contenders.

Before she could comment on the encouraging lack of mutilated animals, her sister pointed at his eyebrows—or eyebrow—to be specific. "Get a load of that unibrow! It's as bushy as a squirrel's tail!"

"Those eyebrows could easily be fixed with a simple tweezing," her mother pointed out.

Tess jabbed Sheri with her elbow. "Just think—you could spend your first date plucking his eyebrows."

Sheri burst into laughter until her mother's scathing glare made her clamp a hand over her mouth.

"Bushy eyebrows are no reason to reject an otherwise acceptable man," Linda insisted.

Tess's eyes nearly fell out of their sockets. "Acceptable? Are you kidding, Ma? Look at that butchered haircut and those awful horned-rimmed glasses. And check out the nerdy bowtie." She snorted. "He'd be as much fun as a tax audit."

"Speaking of tax audits, what if he works for the IRS? Would he audit my tax returns before agreeing to take me out?"

"Don't be ridiculous," Linda snapped.

"I don't know, Ma," Tess countered. "Accountants are known for being neurotic about minutia. What if the guy finds some obscure mistake Sheri made and then reports her for tax evasion?"

Sheri's heart lurched. *Tax evasion? Yikes!* She hastily mashed on a key to exit the man's profile. *Why chance it?*

Sheri glanced at her watch then up at Tess. "I thought Jacob had a two-o'clock T-ball game."

Tess eyed the wall clock and jolted. "Holy moly, we're supposed to be on the field in thirty minutes." She dashed out of the study hollering to her husband and son to hightail it to the car—and make it snappy.

Never one to miss her grandson's games, Linda grabbed her purse and bolted toward the front door. "Meet you at the ball field, Tess." When she reached the door, she turned and shouted back to Sheri, "Good luck with the husband hunting," then dashed out.

Sheri signed off the website, drained and demoralized from her depressing exploration of available men.

She attempted to distract herself from the misery of husband hunting by tackling her favorite piece—the Moonlight Sonata—on the piano. When Beethoven failed to cheer her, she ambled to the bedroom and grabbed an overflowing basket of dirty clothes. Even laundering dirty socks beat rummaging through a hopeless line-up of men she'd never want to meet, let alone marry.

*Have I waited too long to find love?*

*"Cupid is a knavish lad, thus to make poor mortals mad."*
~William Shakespeare~
*A Midsummer Night's Dream*

# Chapter 2

After an afternoon of laundry, cleaning the bathroom, and paying umpteen bills, Sheri couldn't help herself: she signed onto the dating website in hopes her Fairy Godmother had downloaded Prince Charming while she'd squirted Ty-D-Bol into the toilet. When she scrolled down to the email section, her eyes did a double take. The rock guitarist, Jeremy, had invited her out for coffee.

She promptly typed a polite "no way" and was about to push send when she thought better of it. Since she hadn't had a date in nearly a decade, it might not hurt to freshen up her rusty dating skills with a guy who wasn't a serious candidate—a practice date, if you will. On impulse, she sent Jeremy her available times. One minute later, he responded, "How 'bout right now? I ain't got nothing better to do."

*He sure knows how to flatter a girl. And speak proper English.*

A gentleman would have fabricated an enchanting lie claiming he was enthralled with her photo and profile and couldn't wait to meet her. She would have nothing in common with this guy, but against her better judgment, she agreed to meet him at a nearby coffee shop in thirty minutes.

She closed her computer and dashed to her bedroom to change. What had possessed her to meet with a guy who probably listened to Metallica at deafening decibels? What if he showed up stoned?

*Well, at least this way I can tell Ma I had a date.*

She yanked off her ripped jeans and pulled on her only pair of khakis. Or *tried* to pull on her only pair of khakis. They must have shrunk two sizes since she'd last worn them because the zipper would *not* C-L-O-S-E no matter how hard she sucked in her gut.

She tugged and pulled and yanked on the zipper until she finally had it zipped — provided she didn't inhale.

*So much for size twelve.*

Hamlet, her Maine Coon cat, brushed against her leg and stared up at the flabby muffin top that drooped over her waistband.

"I know, I know. I need to join Weight Watchers, don't I?"

He rubbed against her again, reassuring her he'd love her no matter how much she weighed. She squatted down to pat him. R-I-P! The pants were so tight they'd torn. Swell.

"Guess I won't be wearing these," she informed the cat, as she tugged off the skin-tight khakis and pulled out her trusty black elastic waistband pants. Not much of a fashion statement but at least they fit. Maybe a colorful shirt would jazz things up. She pulled on the emerald green blouse her mother once claimed made her hazel eyes look vibrant green.

Dread crept up her spine like the whispery legs of the brown recluse spiders that her mother feared so much. Sheri had no appreciation for heavy metal music, so why was she meeting with an acid rock guitarist?

She shushed her inner fusspot and buttoned her blouse then grabbed a fuchsia and green-striped scarf and twisted it around her neck. She twirled in front of the mirror and frowned. "It'll have to do," she muttered to Hamlet.

Most women would now apply lipstick and eyeliner and mascara, but the few times Sheri attempted to apply make-up, she ended up looking like a raccoon with lipstick on its teeth. Her feminist claims that she'd rather be accomplished than pretty were great for admission into Johns Hopkins Medical School, but not so great for charming a date — or fixing her hair.

She stared in the mirror and wanted to weep. What could she do with the foot-long Brillo Pad that grew from her scalp? Her hair was like a malfunctioning Tesla electric ball — exploding in all directions. She'd always told herself her untamed hair made a statement: I am a smart, independent woman who does not define

12

her identity by her appearance. Interpretation? I am smart *except* in all things cosmetic.

Pulling her hair back with a pearl barrette, she glanced at the clock. Yowser! She was supposed to be at the coffee shop in two minutes. She slipped on her black clogs, grabbed her purse, and dashed for the door.

Once she arrived, she glanced around for Jeremy but saw no one who matched his online photo. She secured a table and waited. And waited. After drumming her fingers for eighteen minutes, she purchased a decaf and fumed. He was the one who wanted to meet right now.

*I'll give him two more minutes, not a second more. A girl has to have some standards.*

Just then, in walked a longhaired beatnik garbed in an Aerosmith T-shirt. He eyed her up and down. *"You're Sheri?"*

She nodded, ignoring his incredulous tone. "Jeremy?" She extended her hand and smiled.

*At least he doesn't reek of marijuana.*

He ignored her outstretched hand and continued to stare. "Man, I barely recognized you. You seriously need to update your online photo."

She felt her cheeks burn. In truth, the picture her mother submitted to the website *was* outdated, but still...

He grinned. "You don't miss many meals, do you?" He then snickered as though he'd said something hilarious. Ha, ha, ha.

She must have looked ready to smack him because he raised a hand and insisted, "I was only kidding. Can't you take a joke?"

Since she wanted to clobber him with her purse, apparently not.

Just because her online picture *was* taken ten years and twenty-five pounds ago, was no reason to be rude. Besides, in *his* online profile he claimed a height of 5'10". No way! He was at least two inches shorter than Sheri's 5'9" frame. If he could stretch the truth about his height, why couldn't she wiggle on her weight?

13

He gestured toward her belly. "I'm surprised a doctor would let herself go like that. Or did you lie about the doctoring thing, too?"

Rage rocketed through her. Yes, she *had* been lax with diet and exercise lately, but she did *not* need this cocky midget bullying her. She glanced around and noticed other diners watching them—and snickering.

*Swell! The laughingstock of Starbuck's.*

She snatched up her purse ready to bolt, but Jeremy grabbed her arm. "Don't get your granny panties in a wad. I thought you'd appreciate my honesty."

She'd never been so tempted to fling scalding coffee in a man's face before. "I need your honesty about as much as I need a consult with Dr. Kevorkian."

He scratched his brow. "Kevorkian? Is he that doctor on TV who pushes spinach smoothies?"

*Swell. Stupid and rude.* "Oh, never mind." She would not waste one more second on this jerk, or she might insist on a consult with the infamous Doctor Death—for him!

"You women are so touchy." He gripped her arm and refused to let her pass by. "Look, I'm sorry if I hurt your feelings. Let's start over. Why don't I let you buy me a caramel latte and a blueberry scone, and then we'll sit down like civilized human beings and get to know each other." He wore the grin of a used car salesman trying to unload a lemon. "Sound like a plan?"

*A plan for disaster.*

Sheri yanked her arm free and hissed, "Let go of me, you infuriating little twit."

He blocked the door with his arms. "Don't leave. Let's grab a bite and talk." He opened his arms wide and smiled in a manner he no doubt thought was disarming. It worked all right—she wanted to *dis*-arm him.

Shoving him out of the doorway, she stomped to her car. He trotted after her like a relentless Chihuahua nipping at her heels.

"Hey, I don't suppose you'd help a struggling musician make his rent payment this month? I'm two hundred bucks short."

*Is this guy for real?*

"Come on, Sheri. I know you can afford it. We all know you doctors roll in dough. Besides, isn't giving to the poor the Christian thing to do? If you see your brother in need and don't help, where is the love of Christ, and all that?"

She climbed into her car and slammed the door in his face.

*I should run him over and rid the world of a menace.*

She squealed out of the parking lot with Jeremy's humiliating comments reverberated in her brain like a pinball gone berserk.

*Never again. I'll rot in a nursing home before I will ever subject myself to another mortifying date like that one.*

Once home, she slammed her purse onto the kitchen counter, kicked off her clogs, yanked off her scarf, and flung it on a chair. She opened the pantry and searched for something to soothe her bruised ego. Crunchy? Salty? No, this kind of disaster called for chocolate—the more, the better.

*"I'd rather hear my dog bark at a crow,
than a man swear he loves me."*
~William Shakespeare~
*Much Ado about Nothing*

# Chapter 3

Sheri's phone rang as she pulled a carton of French Silk ice cream from the freezer.

"Hello?" she said, trying her best to disguise her rage.

"Is this Sheri Morris?" asked a pleasant male voice.

"Yes. Who is this?"

*Knowing my luck, the Unabomber.*

"Greg Palmer."

*Greg Palmer?* Was he that nerdy accountant with the unibrow? The one who might audit her? She'd declined his invitation...hadn't she?

"Are you that accountant with the bowtie?" she asked, unable to disguise her barbed tone.

"Yes, and according to the website, you invited me to call."

*What? No way!*

Then she remembered how quickly she'd clicked off his profile in her attempt to avoid a tax audit. Had she accidentally clicked on the wrong key in her haste?

She stifled a curse. She didn't have the patience for this — not after her disastrous date with Jeremy the Jerk.

She cradled the phone to her ear, so she could scoop out a hefty portion of ice cream into her bowl. "Look, I must have accidentally pushed the button that said I wanted you to call. Trust me — it was a mistake. The last thing I need is a tax audit."

A warm chuckle percolated across the airwaves. "A tax audit? You think I audit women before I ask them out?"

She'd used up her last drop of self-control when she'd refrained from running over Jeremy with her car, so she snapped, "Why not?

16

My last date wasn't above begging for rent money. We hadn't even shared a cup of coffee—that he wanted *me* to buy—when he hit me up for two hundred bucks."

She returned the carton of ice cream to the freezer and sank her spoon into its chocolaty deliciousness. Time to indulge her bruised ego.

"That's awful. And I thought I had it bad when my last date told me I was as much fun as an undertaker."

She couldn't help it—she burst out laughing. "Wow! That must have stung."

"In more ways than one. I'd forked out ninety bucks for a fancy dinner and flowers, and what was my reward? Being told I belong in a morgue."

She savored another creamy bite of ice cream before confessing, "My date practically threatened to sue me for false advertising because I'd gained a few pounds since my online picture was taken."

"On a positive note, at least he *told* you why he rejected you. I rang the doorbell of one woman, and as soon as she opened the door and took a look at me, she claimed the woman I'd come to take out no longer lived there. Give me a break—I recognized her from her profile picture."

*Apparently, frumpy women aren't the only ones who get dissed.*

"Ouch," she offered sympathetically.

"I'm tempted to join a monastery, and I'm not even Catholic."

She shifted her phone to her other ear, surprised at how much better she felt after talking to this guy. No doubt the old misery loves company thing. "Sounds like we've both been burned by online dating."

"I don't get it. I've built up a prosperous accounting practice, I don't drink or gamble or do drugs. I go to church, and I try to be a nice person, but women won't give me the time of day. Another accountant in my firm, who's been married three times, never lacks for a date. What's up with that?"

*Maybe the co-worker doesn't have a shrub growing above his eyes.*

She kept her thoughts to herself and had to admit, despite his ghastly unibrow and nerdy bowtie, she kind of liked the guy. Plus, who was she to point fingers at someone with a lackluster appearance?

"Try digging up a date when you're a plump, forty-year-old woman doctor. Apparently, men think I'm only good for free medical advice and rent money."

"Ditto for accountants. One date asked me to do her taxes as a favor. When I calculated that she owed the IRS four hundred dollars, she had the nerve to ask *me* to pay it!"

"You're kidding." Maybe Jeremy wasn't so bad—he'd only hit Sheri up for two hundred.

"Do I have SUCKER written across my forehead?" Greg lamented.

"Moocher magnets, that's what we are."

"Moocher magnets, huh?" He chuckled then asked, "Do you ever feel like intelligence and stability are a detriment when it comes to online dating?"

She nibbled the last bite of her ice cream. "People assume we're boring."

"Or an interest-free bank."

She noticed Hamlet staring up at her with expectant eyes. "That empty bowl is mine. I'm the pre-wash cycle, remember?"

Sheri placed the bowl on the floor, and Hamlet began to lick. She patted her chubby kitty.

*Hamlet needs those ice cream calories about as much as I do.*

"You know what I'd like?" Greg said, interrupting her thoughts. "I'd like someone to date me four or five times and tell me, with honest constructive criticism, what I'm doing wrong. Tell me what I need to do to make a woman fall in love with me."

"Kind of like that movie, 'Hitch' with Will Smith."

"Yes! I loved that movie."

"Me, too. Especially the part where Albert wants Hitch to teach him how to kiss. Wasn't that a hoot?"

"Hilarious." After a pause, Greg said, "You know, we could do that for each other."

Sheri's heart jolted. *Teach each other to kiss?* No way! She clenched her jaw. *I should have known he was a creep.*

"I am so not teaching you to kiss. Drop dead, scumbag," she shouted into the phone.

She was about to disconnect when Greg shouted, "Sheri, wait! That's not what I meant. Not at all."

"Then what did you mean?"

"I meant, we could be critique partners to each other—like Hitch was to Albert."

"Critique partners? Meaning...?"

"Meaning, we go out on a couple of dates together and then outline what needs fixing in each other. We'll mentor and encourage each other along the way until we each find our soulmate."

"Accountability partners, in other words." She chewed on the idea. "Just friends, right?"

"Absolutely." He released a loud sigh. "As long as you promise not to tell me I'm as dull as a tombstone. I still haven't recovered from that one."

She laughed, ambling into the living room. "I'm in, so long as you promise not to audit me."

"What's up with you and your tax audit phobia? Have you been cheating on your taxes?"

"Of course not! But I file them with a cheap computer software program, and I'm paranoid I may have broken some obscure tax law without even knowing it. What if the IRS clobbers me with back taxes and penalties claiming, 'Ignorance of the law is no excuse?'"

He chuckled. "I love paranoid people like you—they keep my accounting practice booming."

"I know what you mean—there's no shortage of hypochondriacs, either."

When the conversation lulled, Greg asked, "Were you serious about the accountability partner thing? Truth is, I don't relish life in a monastery—Gregorian chant isn't my thing."

"I'm game, if you are. What have we got to lose?"

"Not a thing. How about I pick you up this Saturday night around six? We'll share our first impressions of each other, and then we'll assuage our egos with steaks and baked potatoes. After we eat, we'll outline a self-improvement strategy for each of us. We'll call this venture Operation Soulmate."

They set the ground rules: No emotional involvement—just honest, objective feedback. They'll mentor each other until they each find the perfect life companion.

She provided her address and ended the call with a mixture of horror and excitement. She had just agreed to let a complete stranger nit-pick everything about her. Could she handle the criticism? She pictured Greg's botched haircut and unibrow.

*Could he?*

*"Though this be madness, yet there is method in it."*
~William Shakespeare~
*Hamlet*

# Chapter 4

"Wait! You agreed to let that nerdy guy with the unibrow give you beauty advice?" Tess stared across the restaurant table as though Sheri had lost her mind. "Isn't that like asking Kim Kardashian to tutor you in physics?"

"I know it sounds crazy," Sheri said, slicing through a pepper ring. "But he asked me to mentor him, so what could I say?"

"How about, 'No, I won't mentor you because I'm a complete dimwit on all things cosmetic', or, 'I can't attract a mate myself, so who am I to give advice?'"

"Hey!" Sheri slammed her knife onto the table and glared across the table at her sister. "Be nice!"

The table next to them turned and stared at the raised voices.

Tess sawed into her chicken breast and lowered her voice. "It's true, Sheri, and you know it. When it comes to hair, clothes and makeup, you're a complete disaster. Now medical things — that's a different story — you're brilliant. But the reason you haven't had a date in over ten years —"

"Eight years, thank you very much," Sheri corrected, buttering her roll with a vengeance.

"Whatever," Tess said, with a dismissive wave of her hand. "You haven't had a date *in a very long time* because — let's face it — you've completely let yourself go. You've gained a good thirty pounds since high school, and your hair is a frizzy mop. You don't wear any makeup, and your clothes —" She clicked her tongue and shook her head. "Even a bag lady has more style. No man is attracted to a frump, you know."

Sheri sawed into her steak wishing it was her sister's neck. Was there a guillotine anywhere on the premises?

21

*Here we go again — put-downs disguised as helpful advice.*

Why did Tess always have to make her feel as unappealing as a used colonoscope?

Tess's expression softened, and she grabbed Sheri's hand and squeezed. "Look, I'm not saying this to be mean, but *somebody* has to be frank with you, or you'll never find a decent husband. You don't want to wind up with that nerdy accountant, do you?"

Sheri wiped her mouth with her napkin, remembering all the rude comments women had made to Greg. Even though she hadn't met him yet, a wave of protectiveness came over her. Tess made Greg sound no better than swamp bilge just because he didn't dress like some GQ model.

"Internal qualities and character are more important than external appearance," Sheri pointed out, stabbing a cherry tomato with her fork.

Tess scowled, as though marriage to a nerd equaled a fate worse than beheading. "I suppose — if you're not embarrassed to be seen with the guy in public. Personally, I'd stay an old maid like you before I'd marry a nerd like Greg."

Sheri slammed her water glass onto the table more harshly than she'd intended, and water sloshed onto the tablecloth.

"Oh, I get it. 'Get thee to a nunnery', huh?"

Tess's face puckered in confusion. "What?"

"It's from Hamlet." Sheri crossed her arms in disgust. "Oh, never mind."

Tess rolled her eyes. "You and your Shakespeare! No wonder you can't get a husband."

Sheri clenched her jaw shut to refrain from hurling an ugly retort. The two sisters glared at each other.

With a kinder tone Tess said, "Look, if you ever want beauty or fashion advice, I'm glad to help." She reached across the table and grabbed Sheri's hand. "Colton and I both think you could be *pretty*, if you put forth a little effort. Why don't you let me help you?"

Sheri snatched her hand away.

How nice! Miss Altruism had offered to rescue her poor, pitiful sister from winding up in a convent.

*Well, forget it!*

She'd sooner take advice from an accountant with a unibrow and a bad suit than a holier-than-thou younger sister.

She motioned for the waiter to bring the tab. *This meal is over.*

*"Thine face it not worth sunburning."*
~William Shakespeare~
*Henry V*

# Chapter 5

What do you wear to your own dissection? Should she try to impress Greg and wear Spanx and a fitted black dress, or should she go au natural and obtain his honest feedback on her normal, everyday appearance? Opting to glean the most advice as possible, she pulled on the same outfit she'd donned for her disastrous date with Jeremy the Jerk.

The doorbell rang promptly at six. Sheri ignored her pounding heart and opened the door, muttering to herself, "I need my head examined for agreeing to this."

She glanced up into the large, brown eyes of a tall, not completely unattractive guy—if you ignored the huge furry caterpillar growing straight across his brow. She found herself staring at his unibrow. It was even more pronounced in real life than in his picture.

*Good grief! Why didn't he trim the thing?*

She stuffed her initial repulsed reaction, introduced herself, and invited him in for iced tea. As they passed by her baby grand, he commented, "Wow! That's a gorgeous Steinway. Do you play?"

"I do. Music and academics were my two claims to fame. I used to sing and play solos in our high school music productions." She ran a hand over the piano's smooth surface. "Unfortunately, with my heavy work schedule, I don't have the time to practice as much as I should, so my skills aren't what they used to be."

She escorted him into the living room, and they sat on the couch and sipped tea, awkwardly avoiding eye contact.

Hamlet waddled in and eyed Greg. When Greg extended a hand, Hamlet jumped onto the couch and frisked his fluffy tail across Greg's face. After circling umpteen times, he flopped onto Greg's lap.

"I hope you're not allergic to cats."

"No, I like cats." He scratched the delighted kitty under its neck. "Though this guy could pass for a baby cougar. Guess I better stay on his good side, huh?"

Hamlet purred contentedly, as Greg stroked his back. "Is he your guard cat?"

Sheri chuckled. "He'd flunk out of guard cat school, I'm afraid. He'd purr for anyone—including a burglar, no doubt."

Greg continued to pay undue attention to the cat, as though procrastinating the real reason for his visit. Finally, he suggested they share their gut reaction to each other.

"You first," he said diplomatically, gesturing toward her. His thigh began to thump.

She gripped the arms of her chair, not believing she was about to fling a cruel zinger at an otherwise nice man. Before she could chicken out, she blurted, "Can you lose the unibrow? It's so bushy, I can't help but stare at it."

His shoulders slumped, and he released a loud sigh. "I've been told that before, of course, and I even tried a nose hair trimmer on it once, but it felt like my whole face was getting sucked into a corn auger. Talk about painful."

"Can't you get it professionally waxed off?"

He winced and pulled back. "I hate pain, and I've read about waxing. Don't they literally rip the hairs right off your face? Why would I pay good money to be tortured?"

"Because you want a wife?" she suggested with a smile.

"On second thought, I could adopt a sheepdog instead. She'd be far less discriminating about the bushy eyebrows. I mean, who would she be to point paws?"

"Ah, but with a dog, you might wind up with fleas."

"Touché." He stroked Hamlet as though mulling over her advice.

After an awkward pause, she said before she lost her nerve, "Okay, now it's your turn to critique me."

She held her breath as he sized her up. She dreaded what he would say. When he hesitated, she insisted, "Out with it. What was your first impression?"

"You want me to be brutally honest, right?" His thumping thigh increased in both velocity and height.

*That's not a good sign.*

"Totally," she insisted, though she secretly wished he'd flatter her with lies.

He sucked in a breath and hesitated before informing her, "Your hair is awful—a cross between Janis Joplin after a heroin fix and Bozo-the-clown. Can't you straighten it or *do* something with it?"

*Had he been talking to Tess.* Talk about a time-consuming nuisance—and expense.

Embarrassed, she quipped, "Perhaps I should enroll in clown school. I'm bound to find a husband there."

"The auburn color is pretty, but the texture is so. . ." His brow furrowed as he struggled to come up with an appropriate word.

"Frizzy?" she suggested.

He rubbed his chin in thought. "No, it worse than that. More…crazed—like what you'd expect from a lunatic in an insane asylum. Or the Joker, perhaps."

Her mouth dropped. "I look like I belong in an insane asylum?" She released a nervous laugh. "That's discouraging. I'll take clown school over a looney bin."

His face brightened. "You know what? I have a cousin who's great with hair. Roxie owns one of those over-priced hair salons where women pay a fortune for a haircut. What do you say we go there together? I'll get her to tone down my eyebrows, and I'm sure I can sweet talk her into straightening your hair for a huge discount since I do her taxes for half price."

"I guess it's worth a try." She dreaded the extra time straightening her hair would require. Besides, when it came to hair styling, she was all thumbs.

Greg pulled out his phone, called Roxie, and scheduled them an appointment for Sunday afternoon. After he ended the call, he chuckled. "Roxie said she's been plotting to trim my eyebrows in my sleep for years. She insisted on tomorrow — before I chickened out."

He glanced at his watch and suggested they head to the restaurant, so they wouldn't be late for their reservation.

On the drive, Sheri couldn't help but ask, "If you thought I looked like a lunatic, why did you call me?"

He glanced over at her and his Adam's apple bobbed. His eyes widened with an expression that said, "Busted!" After a long pause he said, "I don't think you really want to know."

*That doesn't sound promising.*

Too curious to let it go, however, she said, "It couldn't be any worse than what you've already told me. Come on — spill."

"Well, since my previous dates all flopped, I figured I needed more dating practice to improve my skills. Since you'd only had one other guy — some scruffy rock musician — give you a thumbs-up, I figured you couldn't afford to be too choosy."

Her mouth dropped.

*He sounds just like Mom!*

Bile boiled up her esophagus. *Dating practice? How dare he use me like that!*

But then...who was she to talk? Isn't that exactly why *she'd* agreed to meet up with Jeremy — to practice dating with someone who wasn't a serious contender? How demoralizing to make the same loser list as Jeremy.

"I'm sorry." Greg's eyes took on the guilty look of a Bassett hound caught chewing the remote control. "I never would have told you, if you hadn't insisted."

When she admitted she'd done the same thing to Jeremy, they laughed. "Online dating is a real ego buster, isn't it?"

"It's definitely a sport for masochists." He pulled into a parking place at the steakhouse. "Let's go assuage our bruised self-esteems with a delicious dinner, shall we?"

*"The tartness of his face sours ripe grapes."*
~William Shakespeare~
*A Comedy of Errors*

# Chapter 6

Greg shut off the engine and ran over to her side of the car to open her door.

*Charming, old-fashioned manners.* Apparently, they still existed.

"So even Bozolina-the-clown is entitled to chivalry, huh?"

He raised upturned palms. "What can I say? My Mama raised me right." He bowed at the waist. "I even open car doors for clowns and lunatics."

The hostess seated them at a quiet booth and after much deliberation between the chicken cordon bleu and a rib eye, she settled on the steak. Within minutes, the waiter returned with two bowls of Caesar salad.

They munched their greens in silence before Greg asked, "What else did you think about me?"

She chewed a pepper ring slowly to buy time to come up with a tactful way to tell him she hated his haircut. She swallowed and stalled further by sipping her water.

*Here goes...* "So many men are bald, but you could have a gorgeous head of hair. That buzz cut makes you look harsh—like Sergeant Carter."

Greg choked on his water and reached for his napkin. "From Gomer Pyle?"

She nodded. "Buzz cuts went out with the jukebox."

His shoulders sagged. "But they're so easy. With a buzz cut I don't have to waste time on my hair every morning."

She pointed at her hair. "Like me not wanting to waste time straightening *my* hair?"

He grinned. "Touché." He grabbed a roll and began buttering. "I'm sure your time *is* limited, with you being a doctor."

29

"True, but excuses aren't winning me a husband."

"We'll just have to do whatever it takes, no matter how time-consuming," Greg said, stabbing a crouton. "It sure seems like a waste of time, doesn't it?" His shoulders drooped, and he released a loud sigh. "Don't you wish you could find someone who would love and accept you exactly the way you are?"

"Absolutely, but then the course of true love never did run smooth."

She instinctively covered her mouth with her hand. *Did that come out of my mouth?*

She could hear her mother's admonishing words: "Quoting Shakespeare all the time will turn men off as much as picking broccoli out of your teeth with a toothpick at the dinner table."

Normally, she had better control over the Shakespeare muse that played in her head.

Greg stopped chewing mid-bite, grinned, and pointed his fork at her. "Lysander. *A Midsummer Night's Dream.*"

She nearly dropped her fork. *Greg knows Shakespeare?* "I-I'm impressed—a fellow fan of the Bard, I see."

"Let's just say I mastered five soliloquies before I graduated from high school. I doubt anyone knows more Shakespeare than I do."

She raised a brow. "Oh really? You're going to have to prove a boast like that. How about, 'All that glitters is not gold.'"

"Easy. *Merchant of Venice.*"

"Okay, what about, 'Cowards die many times before their death, but the valiant taste of death but once.'"

"*Julius Caesar.*"

"Some are born great, some achieve greatness, and some have greatness thrust upon them."

"*Twelfth Night,*" he said, without missing a beat.

*Drat! He does know his Shakespeare.*

She'd have to resort to trickery. With a poker face, she said, "How about 'Oh! What a tangled web we weave, when first we practice to deceive?'"

He stared up at the ceiling as though lost in thought, and then grinned and waved his fork at her. "Nice try. You thought you could fool me, didn't you? But I didn't fall for your tangled web of deception, Missy. Sir Walter Scott, and not Shakespeare at all."

She crossed her arms in defeat. "Okay, you win." She eyed him suspiciously. "How come an accountant knows so much Shakespeare?"

He smirked. "I probably should have told you before you challenged me that I majored in British Literature until I realized I couldn't make a living quoting sonnets. Finance can be dull, but I knew I could support a wife and kids with a business major." He frowned. "For all the good it's done me. I may as well have stuck with British literature."

"Maybe so." She drummed her fingers on the table and forced herself to say, "Well, it's your turn to insult—I mean, critique me."

He wiped his mouth with his napkin and studied her face. "Get contacts. Those granny glasses make you look bookish and dowdy. Barney Google, even."

The waiter, who had returned to fill their water glasses, overheard Greg's comments, and his eyes bulged as though shocked at the rude comments.

Sheri instinctively pushed her glasses up the bridge of her nose. Are they that bad? So far, Greg had found nothing positive about her appearance except her hair color, which could easily be duplicated with a bottle of Clairol. Janis Joplin after a heroin fix? A lunatic? Barney Google? She may as well join a freak show and spare herself the time of online dating. Perhaps she could charge admission to come gawk at her freakishness.

The waiter returned with their steaks and baked potatoes. He plunked the plate in front of Greg with a decidedly frosty demeanor.

Sheri forced herself to cut up her steak, but a wave of hopelessness ruined her appetite.

*Everything about you spells dowdy old maid. Tess said so, and now Greg. I'm a hopeless case.*

As though sensing her glum mood, Greg reached across the table and touched her forearm. "Sheri, there's nothing wrong with you that Roxie can't fix. You have a pretty smile, you're smart, funny, musically gifted, and you seem like a nice person. More important? You love Shakespeare."

She shrugged, unconvinced.

He grabbed her hand and shook it. "Listen to me. What I've criticized about you is just window dressing. Don't get discouraged—it's far easier to change a hairstyle than a personality."

She mashed her baked potato as though on autopilot. "I haven't faced the truth about my appearance in a long time. I'm thirty pounds overweight, and I've let myself completely go." She sucked in a deep breath and released a sigh. "If I'm serious about attracting a decent husband, I've got to lose weight and gain some confidence. She pointed at him with her steak knife and announced, "As of today, I am getting in shape and bursting from my cocoon."

The waiter returned a few minutes later and described a sumptuous dessert menu of raspberry swirl cheesecake, death-by-chocolate cake, key lime pie piled high with whipped cream, and a hot apple cobbler with vanilla bean ice cream.

Before Sheri could respond, "One of each, please," Greg said, "No thanks. Sheri needs to lose thirty pounds, so just bring us some decaf."

The waiter's eyes widened in shock, and then his lips tighten. He walked away shaking his head.

As soon as he disappeared into the kitchen, they burst into laughter. "He thinks you're a tactless jerk," she said.

"That's me—smart, tactless, and homely."

A wave of compassion coursed through her. No wonder he didn't groom his eyebrows. He saw himself as homely and hopeless, so why bother?

*Like you — you quit trying years ago.*

"Greg, you're not homely. You just need… pruning."

"Pruning?" He smirked. "You make me sound like a rose bush."

"Underneath that bushy unibrow and butchered haircut is a potentially handsome man. You've got the bones to be a knockout."

"As in Knock-Out-Roses? As in, 'A rose by any other name would smell as sweet?'"

She grinned. "*Romeo and Juliet,* and it appears I'll need to tackle your lame jokes as much as your unibrow."

He pinched his belly. "Unfortunately, I've got a lot more than bones on this frame. Ten extra pounds, to be exact."

"Stand in line." She pinched a thick roll of her own spare tire. "Luckily, nothing we can't fix with strict diet and exercise. Are you going to join me?"

His shoulders slumped. "Sounds awful. I dread it already."

"We need to walk an hour a day to lose this flab."

His eyes bulged. "An hour a day? I don't have time for that. I'm at the office twelve hours a day."

"As am I, so that excuse won't fly," she retorted with crossed arms. "We'll just have to *make* the time. Meet me at six in the morning at the trailhead for Radnor Lake. If we walk around the whole lake, it's four miles, and if we power walk, we can do it in an hour."

He offered a military salute. "Yes, Sir! Look who's leading the troops now, Sergeant Carter?"

Of course, the waiter chose that exact moment to return with their decaf. He shook his head but said nothing. After he stomped away, Sheri said, "More fodder for your Jerk-of-the-Year award."

They finalized their plans to hike early Sunday morning before church. He drove back to Sheri's house and walked her to the door.

"See you bright and early at Radnor," she said.

He waved goodbye as he headed for his car.

She strolled into the house with a lightness in her step. Greg was definitely no Prince Charming, but she instinctively knew she could trust him. Like her, he had let himself go and had given up on love. Now she had a game plan and an accountability partner. Maybe she wasn't doomed for a nunnery after all.

She changed into pajamas and tried to envision a year from now, when a slim, attractive Sheri would gaze into the eyes of a handsome man who would adore her. Who knows? Maybe Ma's Christmas wedding could come true, after all.

For the first time in years, she snuggled up to a new bedtime companion — hope.

*"The tender leaves of hope, tomorrow blossoms."*
~William Shakespeare~
*Henry VIII*

# Chapter 7

Sheri's bedtime companion, hope, ran away the second her alarm clock jarred her out of a deep sleep at the ungodly hour of five-thirty a.m. She groped the nightstand for her glasses then crawled out of bed, stretched, and shuffled to the bathroom.

*What possessed me to commit to a four-mile hike this early on a Sunday morning?* Even God rested on the Sabbath!

Should she call Greg and cancel? No doubt he was sputtering about her ridiculous hike as well. She reached for her phone to cancel but thought better of it when she noticed her underarms jiggling in the process. Besides, it would be rude to cancel when the lousy idea had been hers in the first place.

She frowned at the mirror. Even a lunatic's hair looked tamer than hers this morning, but she had no time—or ability—to fix it. She pulled it back with a scrunchy and yanked on some gym shorts and a T-shirt. No point worrying about her flabby thighs since Greg had made it clear last night what he thought of her saddlebags. Surprisingly, his already negative view of her as a bespeckled Bozolina with cellulite liberated her. She didn't have to try to impress him because he was merely her accountability partner.

She tugged on her Nikes and bolted for the door. Luckily, it would only take ten minutes to reach Radnor Lake this early on a Sunday.

She pulled into the parking lot and crawled out of her car. Greg stood stretching his calves against an oak tree. Dressed in fluorescent chartreuse plaid shorts and an orange tank top, she had to wonder if he'd bought the hideous duo at a rummage sale. She eyed his thermos of coffee and kicked herself for not setting up her own coffee pot with a timer.

"Good morning," Greg said pleasantly. "I brought you some coffee." He lifted a spill-proof cup from the ground and handed it to her. "I had them add skim milk and two packets of Splendas since I noticed that's how you drank your decaf last night."

*How thoughtful — and observant.*

She took the cup with a grateful smile. "That was sweet of you. Thanks, Greg!" She sipped the much-needed brew then lifted her cup. "Here's to getting in shape and finding our soulmates." She tapped her Styrofoam cup against his thermos in a mock toast.

After swallowing a few sips, Greg said, "I figured we'd need the caffeine lift until we mastered these early morning hikes — unless you're one of those morning larks who beats the sun up.'"

She laughed. "Only when a patient *makes* me beat the sun up. Trust me, I prefer to sleep in, especially on a Sunday morning."

He responded with a friendly smile.

*At least his teeth are nice.*

They strolled down the woodsy trail to the trill of chickadees and the melodic "cheer, cheer" of cardinals. Graceful ferns and vibrant violet wildflowers dotted the edge of the trail. A gentle breeze fluttered the birch leaves.

"If we have to hike four miles a day, you couldn't have picked a prettier spot," Greg said.

As they rounded a corner, a doe and her white-spotted fawn glanced up and stared at them, ears perked up, eyes wide. Greg and Sheri froze. Clearly accustomed to people, the deer resumed their breakfast. After several minutes of admiring the duo, Greg and Sheri resumed their hike.

Greg matched her pace easily, a delightful thing, since all her friends whined they could never keep up with her. As though reading her mind, Greg commented, "It's nice to walk with a woman who can keep up with me. I hate trudging at the pace of a slug. I once had a woman accuse me of being rude because I walked way ahead of her."

"You left her in the dust, huh?"

He grinned. "Pretty much, and she turned down my request for a second date."

"You think?"

The miles zipped by as they reminisced about their childhood and college experiences. After graduating from Vanderbilt, Greg stayed in Music City to complete his MBA and to live near his college sweetheart, Jodi.

"She dumped me for my roommate," Greg confided. "A month after graduation."

Greg stooped down to toss a fallen limb off the trail. "I was so smitten with her, I would have moved to the moon to be near her. But as I look back on it, our breakup was probably a blessing in disguise."

Sheri stepped over a large tree root. "Why?"

"Jodi always had to be out and about. Shopping, dancing, attending concerts, hanging out with friends. I wanted to spend time alone with her and only go out with friends on weekends."

"Sounds like you weren't compatible."

"In hindsight, we weren't." He chuckled. "Plus, Jodi had no appreciation for Shakespeare. She claimed he wasn't the Great Bard, he was the Great Bore."

"No!" Sheri covered her mouth in mock horror. "You certainly couldn't marry a woman with such scandalous taste!"

"It would be heresy, right?" His lips tightened, and he increased his pace, now striding like a man possessed. They were quiet for several minutes as Sheri struggled to keep up. As though sensing he was being rude, he slowed down again so Sheri could catch up. "Sorry. Didn't mean to take off like that."

"That's okay. You were clearly thinking about your breakup."

He sighed. "Despite her disdain for Shakespeare, I was crazy about her, but she married my ex-roommate within a year. We weren't meant to be, I guess."

Sheri smirked. "As in, 'To be, or not to be?'"

He rolled his eyes, his lips twitching in amusement. "Do I need to add dreadful sense of humor to your growing list of flaws?"

"Sorry, I couldn't resist." She placed a comforting hand on his shoulder. "I'm sure Jodi's rejection stung."

While Sheri had never been deeply in love herself, she could imagine how painful a break-up would feel after a four-year relationship.

Greg wiped the sweat off his face with his tank top. "Unfortunately, I internalized that since Jodi found me boring, I must be a bore. And what woman wants a bore? I never dared to date after that until I hit forty, panicked, and signed up for the dating website."

"You're just more of a homebody than Jodi. It doesn't make you a bore—it just makes you introverted."

"I suppose," he said, though his tone sounded unconvinced. He stopped dead in his tracks. "Be honest—do *you* find me boring? Am I really as dull as a tombstone?"

"Not at all. I enjoy that you read and stay abreast of world events instead of plopping in front of ESPN for hours on end like my sister's husband. All he does is watch sports. Now *that's* boring."

"When I'm nervous, I tend to drone on about financial planning because it's an area I'm confident about. Jodi once told me I could put an insomniac to sleep when I got started on investment opportunities."

She smiled. "My mother says I gross her out with my medical stories at the dinner table. She scolds me with, 'Sheri! Nobody wants to hear about putrid green mucus and oozing bedsores while eating.'"

He winced. "I agree with your mother, I'm afraid. Besides, your stomach-turning stories might help me stick to our diet."

Greg reached down and grabbed her hand to help her step up onto a huge rock in the trail. "Maybe we're both too weird for love," Sheri lamented.

"Speak for yourself." He flaunted his chest and bent his arms at the elbow to reveal his unimpressive biceps. "I intend to morph into a dashing, irresistible stud-muffin. Women will stand in line," he said, his wry grin belying his words.

"Stud-muffin, huh? Didn't that word go out with bell-bottoms?"

He shrugged. "Probably, but don't worry. The new me will know all the cool lingo."

She chuckled. "Sure you will."

When they rounded the corner to the parking lot, Greg asked, "You still up for our appointment with Roxie this afternoon?"

She lifted a brow. "Since *you're* the one getting plucked like a chicken, the bigger question is, are *you*?"

His face blanched. "You're a doctor—can't you administer general anesthesia and knock me out first?"

"I'm an internist, not an anesthesiologist, so unless you want to end up like Michael Jackson, you best grit your teeth and bear it like a man."

"On second thought, I have an emergency load of towels to wash this afternoon." He snapped his fingers. "Guess I can't make it to the eyebrow waxing."

Sheri wagged a finger at him. "You are so getting those ridiculous eyebrows plucked before a den of rodents takes up residence."

"Yeah, yeah. I've heard it before." He waved her off with a dismissive hand. "I'll pick you up after lunch."

She climbed into her car and prayed Roxie was as skilled as Greg claimed. What if the woman leaned toward punk or the freakish styles sometimes displayed in hairstylist books? Square

Afros, tiny ponytails that stuck up every which way like Pippi Longstocking, or streaks of fluorescent turquoise or garish green?

The more likely scenario? Her hair would look great in the beauty shop when *Roxie* styled it—but then frizz out like a mad scientist when Sheri tried to replicate it at home.

Well, if it's too atrocious, she could always buy a wig.

*"The toad, ugly and venomous, wears a precious jewel in his head."*
~William Shakespeare~
*As You Like It*

# Chapter 8

Greg pulled into Sheri's driveway tempted to turn around and speed home. What had possessed him to agree to an eyebrow waxing? He'd read about the dreadful procedure online, and it sounded more befitting a torture chamber than a beauty salon. Forget waterboarding. Just threaten to pluck the eyebrows of terrorists one hair at a time, and they'd tell all in no time.

Despite his trepidation, he forced himself to turn into Sheri's driveway. He knew his eyebrow shrubbery was off-putting to women, and he'd been alone long enough. In the years since Jodi dumped him, he focused solely on his career, and in most ways, it paid off. He had completed his MBA, purchased and paid off his house and car, and maximized his 401K. Trouble was, he couldn't snuggle in bed with a Roth IRA.

Was it too late to find someone special? For fifteen years he'd stuffed his longing behind spreadsheets and accounting software. But time was running out if he wanted a wife and children. Call it a middle-aged crisis or an epiphany. He only knew he didn't want to spend the rest of his life alone, and if that meant devoting more time to exercise and personal grooming, he'd just have to suck it up and do it. As Sheri locked up her house and strolled toward his car, he gripped the steering wheel and told himself, "You can do this."

Sheri climbed into the car, her wild hair flying in all directions.

"Ready for your pruning?" she asked with a smirk.

"If you're ready to pull your finger out of the electric socket," he retorted without missing a beat.

Despite her cruel insistence that he wax his eyebrows, he couldn't help but wish he could find a woman with Sheri's friendly personality and wit. Her intelligence could rival Einstein's—if only her hair didn't, as well! He couldn't imagine kissing a woman he found as unappealing as a pile of bounced checks.

To be fair, Sheri had potential. Her hair color reminded him of sun-kissed copper, and her eyes matched the greenish-blue of a stormy summer sea. Her full lips framed a lovely smile. Unfortunately, her granny glasses and matronly polyester pants would have to go if she wanted to attract a man.

Shallow of him? Totally. But who wanted to marry the winner of a Miss Frumpy America contest? Certainly not him.

Could Roxie help her? For Sheri's sake, he hoped so, because despite her unimpressive appearance, he genuinely liked her.

*"Mirth cannot move a soul in agony."*
~William Shakespeare~
*Love's Labor's Lost*

# Chapter 9

Foxy Roxie's Beauty Spa located in an upscale East Nashville community ranked as the ritziest hair salon Sheri had ever visited. Then again, since she usually settled for low-budget stylists at Cheap Cuts, it didn't take much to impress her. Stained-glass panels featuring purple irises in the front door, an intricate star-patterned black and white marble floor, Boston ferns in ornate white urns, and a modern fountain where water gurgled over a polished block of black granite joined together to create an opulent but relaxing reception area. Apparently, many of Music City's most famous stars patronized Roxie, as Sheri counted twelve signed and framed photographs of some of country music's top stars hanging on the wall.

Roxie herself resembled Loretta Lynn, with her slight frame and curly black hair. Arms extended, she rushed forward and hugged Greg then introduced herself to Sheri. "I've been scheming to wax off those hideous eyebrows of his for years now." She eyed the offensive unibrow and wagged a finger in his face. "Mark my words, when I'm through with you, you'll be a lady-killer."

"I believe stud-muffin was the word *he* used," Sheri said.

"Stud-muffin?" Roxie scratched her forehead. "Didn't that word go out with hula hoops and peace signs?"

Greg crossed his arms. "All right, you two. No ganging up on me."

"Then let's get this show on the road." Roxie rubbed her hands together in a display of feigned evil delight. As they walked to the waxing room, Greg lagged behind Roxie, as though heading for his own execution. Roxie gestured with her hand for Sheri to join them. "If I know Greg, he'll need all the moral support he can get."

Greg climbed onto the table and lay stiff as an ironing board, his hands gripping the edges of the table. Roxie combed, shaped, trimmed, and snipped off as much of the overgrown parts as possible with special brow trimmers, but the stubble of his unibrow above his nose remained.

As Roxie lifted the cover of the hot wax, his eyes widened to the size of moon-pies. He turned to Sheri. "This isn't going trigger a heart attack, is it? Because it won't matter what my eyebrows look like if I'm dead." He eyed the door as though ready to bolt.

"Don't you want to look good for your funeral?" Sheri quipped.

"To use one of your Shakespeare quotes, Greg, it's time to 'Screw your courage to the sticking place,'" Roxie said. "Now buck up and quit acting like a wuss."

Greg scowled at her. "Good thing you never became a nurse. Compassion is definitely not your strong suit."

She ignored the comment and wiped his brow with alcohol and then smeared hot wax on the bridge of his nose. She applied strips on top of the wax and pushed the strips into the wax. "Pardon my pun, but unlike your courage, this wax will stick just fine." She laughed at her own humor.

"Ha, ha, ha," he sputtered, his face scrunched in anticipated pain. "Hurry up and get it over with." He gripped the sides of the table, eyes wild with fear.

"For two seconds, this will hurt like nobody's business, but before a scream can exit your mouth—"

"Scream?" He bolted to a sitting position and turned toward Sheri. "You ought to change the name of this joint to 'Roxie's Sadist Shop.'"

Roxie pushed him back down. "Hush. It won't be that bad." She smirked and added, "For me, that is."

Hoping to defuse his anxiety with humor, Sheri said, "Consider it a free cardiac stress test. And the good news? If you *do* go into cardiac arrest, I'm licensed in both Basic and Advanced Cardiac Life Support."

He glowered. "Just you wait, missy! Roxie probably has some diabolical potion in her witch's cauldron for you, too."

He wiggled his fingers as though casting a witch's spell. "Eye of newt, and toe of frog. Wool of bat, and tongue of dog."

Roxie ignored his reference to the witches in *Macbeth* and grabbed the edge of the waxed strip. "One, two, three." With a quick, firm tug, she yanked off the strip above Greg's nose.

"Ow!" He grabbed her wrist as she reached for another strip. "Why don't you set up a guillotine—It'd be quicker."

"A guillotine?" She touched her lip in thought. "Nah, too messy and definitely not good for repeat business."

Unfazed, Roxie painted hot wax above his left eyebrow, and repeated the procedure.

Greg yelped in pain. "I ought to finagle your next tax return so you get audited."

She snorted. "Like Greg Palmer would risk his stellar reputation as one of Nashville's top accountants over an eyebrow waxing." She gripped her face as though terrified. "I'm scared."

He failed miserably in his attempt not to smile at her snarkiness. "You are so doomed for a scathing review on Yelp. Here's my tag line—'Sadist hair salon owner tortures clients.'"

Roxie rolled her eyes. "And here's my rebuttal—'Big baby client needs to grow a backbone.'"

He lasered her with a glare.

"Only two more strips, and we're done." She painted wax to shape under his brows, applied the strips, and ripped off the outliers. Before he could howl, she patted his shoulder and said, "Okay, handsome, sit up and see the new you." She grabbed a mirror and handed it to him.

While Greg checked out his new eyebrows, Sheri couldn't help but check out the new Greg. Besides the obvious redness, she immediately noticed how the waxing enhanced his large brown eyes. His brow—once scraggly and off-putting—now looked strong and masculine, neat and professional. She blurted out, "Wow, you have no idea how much better that looks, Greg."

He shrugged. "I don't see why eyebrows are such a big deal."

Roxie grinned. "Then you'll have to trust me, because I *do* see why eyebrows are a big deal. That one simple waxing improved your appearance ten-fold."

Roxie transferred Greg to a swivel stylist chair and pulled out a men's hairstyle book. She browsed through the pictures looking up occasionally to appraise a certain haircut with Greg's facial structure.

"This is it." She thumped on a picture with her index finger. "This gorgeous specimen of male has the same bone structure and hair texture as Greg." She handed the book to Greg while Sheri peered over his shoulder. "We'll let your hair grow for a couple months, and then I'll style it to look like this."

The male model in Roxie's stylist book was movie star handsome with thick hair curling around his ears. If Greg ended up half as handsome, women would be flocking.

"What do you think?" Roxie asked.

Sheri pointed at the picture and wiggled her eyebrows. "Can you clone him for me?"

"What's so great about that guy?" Greg asked, glowering at the picture with crossed arms

Roxie and Sheri made eye contact and laughed.

"Definite eye candy."

"Almond Joy and Snickers rolled into one," Roxie agreed.

Greg inspected the picture more closely and shrugged. "Well, if styling my hair like that will make women drool over me as much as you two are drooling over that picture, count me in."

"Just you wait," Roxie said, patting his shoulder. "Two or three months from now, when I'm through with you, I might even be willing to admit you're my cousin in public."

He whacked her arm. "That, dear Cuz, was not nice, and if I wasn't desperate, I wouldn't put up with your verbal abuse."

46

"Why not?" Roxie retorted. "It'll be good practice for marriage." She then turned to Sheri and gestured toward the swivel chair. "Next victim, ah, I mean client."

Sheri hopped into the chair, and Roxie evaluated the bone structure of her face and profile. She rolled a lock of Sheri's hair in her fingers to assess its texture.

Sheri's cheeks burned with shame. No doubt Roxie had to bite her tongue to keep from announcing, "This is the worst hair I've ever had to work with. I can't do a thing with it."

Thankfully, Roxie said nothing. Not a word. Instead, she circled Sheri like a judge at the Westminster Dog Show, her lips pursed in thought. Sheri rubbed her perspiring palms on her slacks. If Roxie announced her hair was hopeless, she might be tempted to dive into that vat of hot wax and melt into oblivion.

Roxie chewed on her bottom lip and then pulled out a couple of stylist's books. She turned the pages slowly, her eyes narrowed in concentration.

*Will she tell me to shave my head and buy a wig?*

Roxie thumbed through several of her styling books before finding a style she thought would be perfect for Sheri. She thumped the picture and beamed, "This is it!"

She placed the book in Sheri's lap and gestured toward a style that framed the face gently but lengthened in the back. "This will look perfect on you."

Sheri stared at the picture then glanced up at Roxie in disbelief. "Except this woman's hair isn't frizzy."

"Yours won't be either when I'm through with you. First, we'll condition your hair for a couple of months, and then we'll use this miraculous straightening solution I've developed. Once I cut and style it with a detangler, you'll have body, not frizz."

"Detangler?"

"A trick of the trade." Roxie pulled out bottles of shampoo and conditioner and tucked him into a Roxie's Beauty Spa bag. "In the meantime, apply this coconut and avocado oil conditioner after

47

you wash your hair, and leave it on for a full ten minutes. If we rid your hair of its dryness, it won't frizz so badly. Also, quit pulling your hair back with elastic bands—they make your hair break off at the jawline. That's what makes it frizz. We want your hair full and beautiful and sexy."

"I doubt my hair will ever look sexy," Sheri lamented.

Roxie slammed her stylebook shut. "Oh, ye of little faith. When I'm through, Greg won't be able to keep his hands off you."

"Roxie! We're not dating," Greg scolded. "We're just accountability partners."

"Friends," Sheri agreed, nodding like a bobble-head.

"Besides, even if we were dating, you know I'm a man of high moral standards and impeccable integrity—an upstanding member of society." He blew on his nails and raised his nose in mock snobbery. "Above reproach."

"And I'm the Shah of Iran," Roxie retorted, in her thick Southern twang. She turned to Sheri. "Don't believe a word of it. Greg once rigged up a bucket of water to pour down on the head of our math teacher as he entered the room. The poor man nearly drowned."

Sheri's mouth dropped in shock. "Greg!"

"I was twelve!" Greg protested with raised palms.

"And now you're forty, but you're still incorrigible," Roxie insisted, jabbing a finger onto his chest. "Devilish to the core."

Sheri enjoyed the playful banter between the two cousins who obviously shared a brother-sister relationship. If only she shared the same closeness with Tess, but it was hard to feel close to a sister who incessantly rubbed in how much prettier and slimmer she was.

Roxie scheduled a two-month follow-up appointment. This would allow their hair time to grow. She also provided the tools and instructions for Greg to keep his eyebrows trimmed. "You better keep that thing contained, or you'll have my wrath to contend with."

"And more waxing in the torture chamber," Sheri added.

He responded with a grimace. "I'd thank you for your services today, Roxie, but frankly, on a pleasure barometer, it ranked right up there with a root canal with no Novocain."

Roxie patted his back. "You done good, Cuz, and keeping it trimmed will be a lot easier than what you endured today, I promise."

"That's a relief. Hey, are you coming to Aunt Sadie's birthday party in two weeks?"

"Wouldn't miss it." She smirked. "It'll provide the perfect opportunity for me to make sure you're keeping up with your eyebrow hygiene." She mimed plucking his eyebrows.

Greg seared her with a glare. "I suggest you bring a veggie platter and leave your tweezers and hot wax at home."

Roxie walked them to the door and trilled, "Just warning you."

As Sheri and Greg climbed into his car, Greg said, "I swear that woman loves tormenting me. She practically salivated with every rip of my eyebrows. I felt like a chicken being plucked."

"She seems like a lot of fun to me. I like her."

Greg pulled out of the parking lot. "I've known Roxie since we were both in diapers."

When they reached Sheri's house, she invited Greg in for iced tea. They lounged on the couch and perused a photo album of her family, while Hamlet purred contentedly between them. Greg stared at Tess's high school graduation picture and commented, "Wow, your sister is gorgeous, isn't she?"

*Why didn't he come right out and say it — and you're an ugly dog.*

To her horror, Sheri's eyes suddenly pooled with tears. She quickly turned her face away.

Seeing her brush tears from her eyes, Greg said, "I'm sorry. That was tactless of me. I didn't mean to upset you."

She shrugged, hating her obvious display of vulnerability.

He glanced around for a tissue box, grabbed a couple, and handed them to her. "I'm sure it was hard growing up with such a pretty sister."

"All I ever heard growing up was, 'Tess, is so beautiful,' or 'You're Tess's sister?' as though no one could believe I came from the same gene pool as the beautiful Tess. She was a cheerleader and homecoming queen, and I was the bookish Valedictorian. Beauty queen and nerd."

She twisted her damp Kleenex in her fingers and stared into her lap as the unwelcomed memories flooded her. "Tess never missed an opportunity to rub it in, either."

After a minute, she wiped her eyes, feeling vulnerable and mortified that Greg knew her deepest wounding. "Sorry for the waterworks. Just once, I wish someone thought I was pretty, too." She wiped her eyes with her tattered tissue before adding, "I mean, having a photographic memory is great, but it sure gets lonely."

Greg reached for her hand. "Tess might be prettier on the outside, but you're beautiful on the inside. And when Roxie finishes up with you, you'll be pretty—inside *and* out." He squeezed her hand. "Wait and see—things will get better."

Somehow his blunt honesty meant more than if he had conjured up a lie and told her he thought she was already pretty. No amount of sugarcoating would change her frumpy appearance. She had invested all her time and energy into expanding her medical practice, and none whatsoever on her appearance. The results spoke for themselves. She longed to feel pretty, loved, and desirable. If losing thirty pounds, buying new clothes, fixing her hair, and replacing her glasses with contacts helped her reach that goal, she'd just have to make herself do it, because marriage to her stethoscope no longer filled the void.

*"Lord, we know what we are, but not what we may be."*
~William Shakespeare~
*Hamlet*

# Chapter 10

Over the course of the next ten weeks, Sheri and Greg hiked at Radnor Lake every day, except when it rained. On rainy days, they substituted free weights and crunches at Greg's house. Broccoli and salmon became her new best friend, and a bowl of blueberries replaced her beloved French Silk ice cream for dessert. Each week they celebrated their weight loss with a Saturday morning splurge of Mexican omelets and toast.

"Dora" and "Bambi," the white-tailed doe and fawn who greeted them at the same bend in the trail most mornings, became the highlight of their daily hikes, along with the ever-changing array of purple, yellow, and pink wildflowers as late spring evolved into mid-summer.

By the end of ten weeks, Greg had lost ten pounds, and Sheri couldn't help but notice that with his weight loss and trimmed brows, Greg's face now etched a handsome masculine profile. Plus, with ten weeks of hair growth, his chocolate-brown locks now curled on his forehead and around his ears, softening his previously harsh military cut. How could she not notice his enlarging biceps and triceps—thanks to their weight lifting routine? His smile, already attractive before his shape-up efforts, added the final touch. Even his boxy Henry Kissinger eyeglasses had been replaced with contacts.

Inspired, Sheri exchanged her granny glasses for contacts, and she had to admit, while time-consuming, they improved her appearance. The temptation to indulge in ice cream and tortilla chips challenged her on a daily basis, especially after a long and trying day at the clinic. To re-train herself not to eat when stressed, she indulged in a luxurious bubble bath or trudged around the neighborhood listening to audiobooks until the urge to binge on junk food passed. The improved self-control paid off, as she could now look at herself in a full-length mirror without wanting to sob into her fat-free, sugar-free yogurt. While still twelve pounds from her ideal body weight, the eighteen-pound weight loss had definitely paid off. If Roxie could cast a spell on her untamed mane so it didn't look like she'd been electrocuted, she might transform into a halfway decent-looking woman.

While the coconut oil hair conditioner *had* calmed the frizz, only a miracle could make her hair match the picture in the stylist's book, however.

Thus, on the morning of their hair appointments, Sheri strolled into Foxy Roxie's salon anxious but eager to see what Roxie's magic wand could accomplish. After Roxie oohed and ahhed over their weight loss and new contact lenses, she ushered Sheri to a chair and attacked her hair with a potent relaxer. While the relaxer sank in, she clipped and styled Greg's hair until she stepped back and said, "Am I good, or what?"

"Good at bragging," Greg retorted.

Roxie handed him a mirror, so he could inspect her work. After eyeing his new cut, Greg shrugged. "Not bad."

"Not bad?" Hands on her hips, Roxie snapped, "Did that eye doctor botch up your contact lens prescription? This cut is perfect, you ninny."

Curious, Sheri peered over her magazine and then nearly dropped it. Wow. She couldn't stop herself from staring. "Your hair looks just like that model in the stylist book."

Greg made no further comment but continued to gaze in the mirror as though adapting to his new appearance. Sheri could tell by the way he avoided eye contact that he was both flattered and embarrassed by all the attention. "Well, I'm glad you ladies like it." He smirked at Roxie. "Will I have to beat women off with a stick now?"

Roxie smacked his upper arm with a comb. "You better lose that fat head of yours real quick, or I'll beat *you* with a hairbrush! Better yet, next time you come in, I'll give you a botched-up Mohawk to put you in your place."

Greg heaved out his chest and jutted his nose in the air with a feigned show of snobbery. "You can hardly blame *me* if women start finding me devastatingly handsome and utterly irresistible."

Roxie pointed toward the door. "Get your conceited tush out of my chair and don't return until I text you that Sheri's done with her hair treatment." She pushed on his back to shove him out of the chair. "Skedaddle."

He laughed and strolled toward the door. "Bossy little thing, aren't you?"

Roxie chuckled and commented to Sheri, "I hope I haven't created a monster. He used to be sweet."

Sheri transitioned to the rinse station where Roxie washed out the relaxer. She slathered on a rich conditioner with the exotic aroma of mango and coconut.

"We'll let this conditioner soak into your hair for a few minutes, then I'll rinse it out and start cutting."

Sheri thumbed through a People magazine while she waited, but she couldn't focus on celebrities when her mind stewed about the unintended consequences of Greg's chic new look. Would his personality change now that he was toned and handsome? Would he no longer want to hang out with a plain Jane like her once gorgeous women started clucking over him?

She had agreed to help him find a wife, but he'd quickly become her best friend. Would that friendship sink like a jalopy in quicksand as soon as Greg had a girlfriend? Of course, it would.

Heaviness settled over her chest. Even though he'd only been in her life ten weeks Greg had become the brother she'd never had and the friend who shot straight with her. She'd learned oodles about world events, history, and retirement planning, and he'd encouraged her to stick with their diet and exercise plan. She could be herself with him, and his dry humor always left her laughing.

When had their morning hikes become the highlight of her day?

She forced herself not to think about it. To quote her mother, "No point borrowing trouble."

Roxie rinsed out the conditioner, then parted and pinned Sheri's hair into small sections. She snipped and styled and feathered and trimmed with a confident eye, adding wispy bangs for a final flourish. "Bangs add a feminine touch." She leaned in and whispered, "And they cover wrinkles. It'll make you look ten years younger."

Roxie demonstrated how to use large rollers and how to blow-dry to prevent frizz when she didn't have time to let it dry naturally.

When Roxie finished, she handed Sheri a mirror. Sheri took a deep breath and stared at herself in disbelief. Smooth hair now framed her face in a soft, flowing style. Thanks to the sleek new haircut and contact lens, she barely recognized herself.

"Girlfriend, I got you looking pretty as a dogwood in April."

Roxie then taught her how to apply eyeliner, mascara, and the slightest touch of shadow to enhance her hazel eyes. When done, Sheri gazed into the mirror, shocked at the transformation. Dare she say it? *I love...almost pretty!*

Roxie beamed. "Wait 'til Greg gets a peek at you. He'll thank his lucky stars he discovered you first."

"We're not dating, remember?"

"Not *yet*. But Prince Charming won't know what hit him when he walks in here and sees Cinderella all dolled up." She wagged a finger at Sheri. "Mark my words."

Roxie texted Greg she had finished with Sheri's haircut. She then made Sheri hide in the bathroom until Greg was seated with his eyes closed.

Sheri's stomach churned in anticipation. Would Greg be as thunderstruck as Roxie claimed he would?

"Okay, Cinderella, time to make your grand entrance," Roxie hollered into the bathroom. Sheri strolled out, head held high and stomach sucked in. She tried to ignore her pounding heart.

Roxie flung out an arm and declared triumphantly, "Ta-da!"

Sheri held her breath, not wanting to admit how much Greg's favorable opinion mattered to her.

His eyes widened, and his mouth dropped. He broke into a huge grin and turned to Roxie and high-fived her. "Wow, I barely recognize her. You're a miracle worker, Cuz."

*Miracle worker?* Sheri's ego plummeted. Must Greg claim Roxie had performed a *miracle* to get her looking decent? Like she was some dilapidated shack on the Home and Garden channel that needed a complete renovation? Sure, *she* had said those very words, but that was different—*she'd* said them. The more Greg inspected her as though he were some rancher choosing a heifer at a cattle show, the more she wanted to clobber him with a curling iron.

*Would it have killed him to merely say I look pretty?* It wasn't as though Roxie had turned water into wine or healed a blind man.

She grabbed her purse and hair styling supplies.

*Who cares what Greg thinks? We're just accountability partners. He isn't the one I need to impress, anyhow.*

Somewhere out there was her soulmate—the man who would find her beautiful and irresistible. Obviously, Greg was *not* said man.

Roxie interrupted her thoughts with promises to take them both to the mall to purchase stylish clothes. "Greg has the fashion sense of a 1960's flower child. Or with those dowdy black suits he wears, an undertaker."

Remembering the hideous chartreuse shorts and orange muscle shirt he'd worn on their first hike, Sheri had to agree.

"And you, Cuz, have the retirement-planning skills of Bernie Madoff."

Roxie laughed. "Point taken."

They paid Roxie then strolled to Greg's car and hitched on their seatbelts.

"Can you believe how much better we look in only ten weeks?" Greg enthused as he backed out of his parking place. "I think we're finally ready to check out the dating website again."

Sheri's stomach lurched from memories of her disastrous encounter with Jeremy the Jerk.

Greg merged onto the highway unaware of the roils of dread churning in her stomach at the thought of another online date. "We'll download our updated photos and check out who's available. I'll bet we get some bites this time."

"Don't you think I should wait until I reach my ideal body weight? I still need to lose twelve pounds."

"Nonsense. You look fine at this weight. Besides, it's not too early to at least explore who's out there. Why don't you come over to the house and help me check out women?" He grinned. "You can help me pick out a hottie."

She secretly hoped every candidate looked like a cross between Eleanor Roosevelt and Mother Theresa, only without their brains and compassion. The longer Greg took to find a girlfriend, the longer she'd keep him as her best friend. Selfish? Absolutely!

She glanced over at Greg's glowing face. She couldn't let him see how disheartened she felt. After all, their original agreement said nothing about staying lifelong friends. Even with Roxie's best efforts, he still viewed her as a nothing but a pal and a fixer-upper project who Roxie performed a miracle on.

How ironic. She'd always thought beauty would remove the inferiority complex that clung to her like a medicinal leech, but now, if she were honest, if she were forced to choose between homeliness *with* Greg in her life, or beauty *without* him, she'd choose Greg. She loved their walks in Radnor Lake, their crossword puzzle competitions, and sharing their deepest feelings. He shared her love of Shakespeare and British literature—an almost extinct trait in today's world. But Greg clearly found her lacking, even after the makeover, or he wouldn't be so eager to check out other women on the website – or palm her off on some other guy.

Deflated and depressed, she released a heavy sigh then declined Greg's offer to check out other women. "Thanks, but I need to clean the house."

Greg's eyes narrowed, as though he didn't believe her, but he didn't press the issue. They rode in silence until he reached her house. "It's probably just as well. I've gotten way behind on a couple of big accounts because of all the hours I've wasted exercising."

*Wasted? Gee, thanks!*

"I didn't mean to get you behind," she said, unable to hide her defensiveness.

"I didn't mean it like that. Trust me – I *needed* to lose weight and get in shape, and thanks to you, I've succeeded. But as a consequence, I've put in fewer hours at work, and now I need to play catch up."

She unbuckled her seatbelt, hating the stiffness between them. "See you tomorrow at six," she mumbled.

"Bright and early, coffee in hand."

She jumped out of the car and was about to slam the door when Greg said, "Sheri? I love what Roxie did with your hair. You won't have any trouble finding the perfect guy now."

Must he be so hasty to get rid of her? If she looked so great, why didn't *he* want her? Not that she wanted him, mind you – she just didn't want anybody *else* to swipe her best friend.

She knew she was behaving like a petulant child. Greg had meant his comments as a compliment, but her old nemesis – rejection – had reared its ugly head. She couldn't help it. She'd wanted Greg to say she was beautiful. But he hadn't.

"Thanks." She closed the car door and dashed up her front steps, so he wouldn't see the tears in her eyes.

*Why should I care what Greg thinks, anyhow?*

She trudged up the front steps reminding herself he was just her accountability partner and hiking buddy. Nothing more. She would now need to search in earnest for her true soulmate.

If only she could convince herself of this.

As she unlocked her front door, she could sense Greg staring at her.

*Fine! Stare all you want, you clueless Neanderthal!*

*"Women speak two languages — one of which is verbal."*
~William Shakespeare~

# Chapter 11

*What was up with Sheri?*

Here Roxie had made her all beautiful — just what she claimed she'd always wanted — and yet she seemed mopey. Snippy. Angry with him for some reason. Maybe she hated her new haircut but didn't want to hurt Roxie's feelings. Was she bummed out about the extra thirty minutes she'd have to invest on her hair and makeup each day? He'd have to convince her it was time well invested, as her hair looked soft and inviting now — the kind of hair a man might want to run his fingers through.

Greg merged onto the interstate mulling over Sheri's sour mood. She had cried on his shoulder about wanting someone to find her attractive, but when he and Roxie bragged about how great her hair looked, she didn't seem thrilled at all. He'd told her she'd have no trouble finding the man of her dreams, but instead of elation, she acted dejected. What was up with that? Women!

If something was bothering her, why hadn't she shared it with him? Didn't they share everything with each other? He'd told her about Jodi jilting him, and she'd shared about her strained relationship with her sister. Those weren't things you shared with the trash man.

He drummed his fingers on the steering wheel as he drove into the parking garage of his office building.

Had he said or done something to offend her? Probably. "You have the sensitivity of a bear in a beehive," Jodi once told him when he hadn't picked up on one of her supposedly obvious body language cues. Apparently, he was supposed to know that when she said she *didn't* want a slice of Death by Chocolate cake, it really meant she *did* want one. If she wanted the cake, why didn't she just *say* so, he'd asked her. She had rolled her eyes and insisted he should have figured it out by her wistful tone.

*Wistful tone?* Men were supposed to be mind-readers?

He could only hope his new look would make up for his apparent social ineptitude. He glanced into his rearview mirror to inspect his new look. It was hard to get used to—the trimmed eyebrows, the sophisticated haircut, the contact lenses—he barely recognized himself anymore. He had to admit, he loved the new Greg.

Unfortunately, the new Greg wasn't without his faults. He certainly hadn't improved in his ability to understand the baffling nuances of the female brain. Something was bothering Sheri, and he hadn't a clue what.

*"Love is a smoke made with the fume of sighs. When the smoke clears, love is a fire burning in your lover's eyes."*
~William Shakespeare~
*Romeo and Juliet*

# Chapter 12

Sheri put off perusing the dating web site with Greg for as long as possible, but after three weeks, she could come up with no more excuses.

"I need your help so I won't pick a dud," Greg insisted. Thus, she came over after dinner to help him sift through all the website profiles of available women in their age bracket.

Hunched over Greg's shoulder as he clicked through the women, Sheri was amazed that several women sent photos dressed in clothes so hideous even Goodwill would reject them. Greg immediately axed these women. "You'd think they'd put forth a little more effort for a dating website photo. I mean, I wore a suit and bowtie for mine."

Sheri remembered Tess's reaction to Greg's photo wearing the nerdy bowtie and undertaker black suit. Nope! She and Greg had no business casting stones at others for lousy fashion sense, but she kept her opinion to herself.

He eyed the next candidate's photo and raised an eyebrow. "Blue hair? I don't think so."

They clicked onto someone who was morbidly obese and nearly bald. Sheri's heart squeezed in sympathy. *That poor woman. She probably has polycystic ovary disease or lupus.* Cushing's disease, maybe? Or what about Alopecia areata? She should email her and encouraging her to seek medical attention since most of these conditions were treatable.

Too late—Greg had already clicked onto a blonde with huge cornflower blue eyes. Vanessa Bigelow. Sheri stared at the beauty, and her stomach sank. The woman was drop-dead gorgeous and as buxom as Dolly Parton.

A stab of jealousy quickened Sheri's heart. She knew it was wrong, but she couldn't stop herself from insisting, "Nix her — she looks high maintenance. I'll bet she spends an hour every day on her hair and make-up."

Greg's eyes narrowed. "I thought you told me your new haircut and makeup took forty minutes a day."

Sheri felt her cheeks flush. "Well, yes, but that's only *forty* minutes. I'll bet Vanessa spends at least an hour."

Greg's brow furrowed. "So, forty minutes is fine, but sixty minutes is high-maintenance?"

"Absolutely." Sheri nodded emphatically. "Besides, I never *used* to be a forty-minutes-a-day kind of girl, so that makes me different. Primping is not my baseline personality, but Vanessa is bound to be frou-frou."

Greg thumped the computer screen with his finger. "If twenty extra minutes is the price she pays to look like that, I say it's twenty minutes well invested." He continued to gape at the woman like a dog drooling over a T-bone.

*How shallow! All he cares about is looks.*

She crossed her arms and glared at him. "Stick your eyeballs back in their sockets, will you? She's probably stupid — your classic blonde bimbo."

"Good point. I sure don't want a dummy, no matter how pretty she is. Let's check out her profile." He scrolled down and then broke into a huge grin. "Says here she received a Nurse Practitioner degree from Vanderbilt, and she's a charge nurse on the hospital oncology ward. That hardly qualifies as a bimbo."

Drat! Smart *and* pretty. It wasn't fair.

"A nurse?" Sheri scowled. "You don't want a nurse."

"Why not?" Greg raised exasperated hands.

"You'd have to compete with all those hunky Vanderbilt doctors."

When he stared at her dumbfounded, she added, "If you're smitten with her, I'll bet half the physicians at Vanderbilt are scheming to date her, too. She'll break your heart, just like Jodi did."

A hurt expression crossed Greg's face. "Are you saying I'm not attractive or good enough to compete with doctors?"

Her cheeks warmed.

Yikes! That *is* what she'd said. Time to back pedal.

"Not at all. But why risk it? It took you a decade to get over Jodi."

Greg jabbed his finger at Vanessa's photo on the screen. "Because she's worth it! She's gorgeous, she's smart enough to be a charge nurse, plus, it says here she's active in her church and even goes on medical mission trips to Haiti." He stared at her picture clearly entranced. "She's worth the fight."

Sheri grabbed the mouse and clicked to the next profile. "You asked for my assistance, so I say she's out. Too frou-frou and too much competition."

"Out? Says who?" Greg roared. He grabbed the mouse back from her and clicked on Vanessa's profile again. Glaring at Sheri he commented, "'The lady doth protest too much, me thinks.' I'll have you know, when I was in the grocery store yesterday, a woman in the produce aisle asked if I was married, and when I said no, she handed me her phone number and told me to call."

*What?* Sheri's mouth dropped. "Wow! That was bold."

"I'll admit it was a bit brazen, but my point is, women are beginning to notice me. Even though you still think of me as a unibrowed chunk of lard with a botched haircut and a bad suit, not everyone shares your opinion anymore."

Her cheeks flamed at the accusation. "Wait a minute! I never said you're unattractive."

He crossed his arms. "You just said I wasn't attractive enough to compete with hunky doctors."

How could she tell him it had nothing to do with *his* attractiveness and everything to do with *her* insecurity? What was she supposed to do? Admit she was greener than Kermit the frog? If she helped him find his perfect Mrs. Palmer, it would leave her all alone. Well, forget it! She didn't want to lose her best friend.

Guilt crept in, and her heart constricted. She claimed to be Greg's best friend and mentor, and the whole point of Operation Soulmate was to help him find a wife. Now she was selfishly finagling things to keep him for herself. Who did that?

*A selfish conniver, that's who.*

Convicted, she forced herself to say, "Greg, you're right. You should email Vanessa. She's clearly the one you like best, and if things are meant to work out, they will. If she's too frou-frou, you can always break it off."

"Except I probably shouldn't put all my eggs in one basket. A woman that gorgeous is bound to have a zillion guys after her. Let's see who else is out there."

"What about this one?" Sheri pointed to a bespeckled, black-haired geologist.

Greg eyed the woman, and his face puckered as though he'd sucked on lemons. "Newsflash—I am not attracted to mustaches." He pointed to the woman's hairy upper lip.

She leaned in to inspect closer. Okay, maybe she *was* a tad mustache-challenged. But was that any reason to reject an otherwise intelligent woman?

"That teeny bit of upper lip hair could easily be removed." She gestured toward his forehead. "Just like your unibrow. A little hot wax, and poof—gone!"

Greg leaned back in his chair, eyeing her skeptically. "So, on the first date I say, 'Love the dress, love the shoes, but can you shave off that revolting mustache?'"

She rolled her eyes heavenward. "First of all, she probably would have already used a depilatory cream *before* your first date."

He raised an unconvinced brow. "And if she hasn't, instead of a bouquet of roses, I'll gift-wrap a razor and can of shaving cream?"

She whacked his arm. "Don't be a dunce. Once you *know* her well enough, you kindly, but gently, tell her she needs to bleach or wax off her mustache."

He frowned. "But if she looks like a man, I don't *want* to date her long enough to get to know her. To be honest, that mustache is a real turn-off."

*What a cad!* He would write off a perfectly nice woman over something as trivial as a mustache? He should be ashamed of himself! Sheri shot him a scathing glare.

Greg ignored her glare and stared at the photo. "Besides, if she's got a mustache, she probably has some kind of hormone imbalance, and if her hormones are all screwed up, she's probably crabby and moody all the time. Who wants a woman who's PMS-ing 24/7?" He pulled a magnifying lens from his desk drawer and leaned in closer to inspect the woman's hairy upper lip. He gestured toward the screen. "I'll bet her testosterone level is higher than mine."

"Oh really, Dr. Palmer? And you know this from your vast years in medical school, do you?"

He ignored her sarcasm. "Worse, I'll bet a woman dripping with testosterone can't get pregnant. I want to have a child someday."

Unexplainable anger surged through her. He would reject this poor woman just because she had a minor mustache and might be infertile? Never mind that she might be brilliant, kind, talented, and funnier than Carol Burnett. The sneaker fit a little too well, and the underlying message? Homely women don't deserve love.

She hissed through clenched teeth, "Are you saying if she can't have children, you don't want her? Just like that?" She snapped her fingers and glared at him.

Greg's eyes widened as though finally figuring out he'd hit a nerve. "No, if I truly loved a woman, and she turned out to be infertile, I would accept it, or we would adopt or take in foster children. But why go out of my way to *pick* a woman with infertility issues?" He held his magnifying lens at the screen again and examined the woman's chin. "Look—she almost has a mini-beard, too. I'm telling you, this woman produces enough testosterone to start her own pharmaceutical company. I want a woman who looks like a woman, and ideally, one who can bear a child. Is that so terrible?"

She sucked in a deep breath in an effort to contain her fury. "You sound like a caveman with a club. A male chauvinist pig who only wants his wife barefoot and pregnant."

Greg pulled back in his chair, eyes wide.

Sheri continued her verbal berating. "I despise men who pick women based solely on looks."

*Because they've ignored me my whole life.*

His lips thinned. "When did I say I pick a woman solely on her looks? I don't want a dummy, a slut, a snob, a bore, or an atheist, no matter how beautiful she is. I want a woman who is intelligent, fun, compassionate, and, yes, at least *somewhat* attractive. I don't want to kiss a woman with enough facial hair to scratch my face. Is that so terrible?"

*Okay, maybe I've overreacted a teeny, tiny bit.*

Perhaps her frustration from years of men rejecting *her* had reared its head out of the muck. She knew her attack on Greg was unfair—probably because she pictured men scanning *her* photo online with a magnifying glass and offering derisive comments about her hair or weight in the same dismissive manner Greg had rejected this poor woman.

She couldn't stop herself. "You say you want a woman who is intelligent. This woman has a Ph.D. from Emory—in geology, no less. I'll bet she's brilliant."

"Geology?" Greg scratched the back of his head and sighed, as though unimpressed. "So, we'll engage in a lively discussion about tectonic plates? Or spend our date night analyzing rocks?" He rubbed his hands together in feigned delight. "Ooo—I can hardly wait!"

Sheri couldn't help but laugh. "All right, I get your drift. I guess we should eliminate the geologist from your potential wife list, huh?"

"Definitely." He clicked off the woman's profile with the speed of a video game champion.

They clicked onto another candidate, a dental hygienist named Theresa who had already sent a message to Greg stating she'd be open to a relationship. She didn't have the drop-dead beauty of Vanessa, but at least she wasn't upper lip-challenged. Greg shrugged. "She's okay, I guess. I suppose I could give her a call." He responded with the enthusiasm one would use to contact an exterminator to rid the house of termites.

"Just because she isn't as voluptuous as Vanessa Bigboob—"

"Bigelow," Greg corrected. "Vanessa Bigelow."

Sheri thumped her forehead with the palm of her hand in an exaggerated fashion. "Oops, Freudian slip." It was mean, but she couldn't help it. "I'll bet you a hundred bucks Vanessa's bust is all implant. Silicone city. Boob job."

Greg cleared his throat. "I believe the correct medical terminology is breast augmentation, is it not, Doctor Morris?"

"Oh, shut up, wise guy! She's probably as vain about her bust as she is about her hair."

Greg swiveled around in his chair, crossed his arms, and studied her. "What's up with you tonight? You're normally not vicious and catty and mean." His eyes narrowed, and then he broke into a huge grin. "You're jealous!"

*"Beware of jealousy; it is a green-eyed monster*
*which doth mock the meat it feeds on."*
~William Shakespeare~
*Othello*

# Chapter 13

"Don't be ridiculous," Sheri snapped far too quickly, crossing her arms in protest.

"You're jealous because I may have found my someone special before you found yours. That's why you're acting all snippy and unreasonable."

She looked away. "Well, to be honest, I do fear being left behind."

Greg put a hand on her shoulder. "Is that what this is about?"

She turned her face away, disgusted by her traitorous tears.

"Look at me," Greg said, softly.

She forced herself to meet his gaze then confessed, "I don't want to lose the friendship we have. When you get a girlfriend, I'll be toast."

*There — it was out.* She didn't like hiding things from him, anyhow.

"Come here." He pulled her into a warm hug, his arms cradling her. "We're in this together, remember? I won't abandon you. As far as I'm concerned, any girl I get serious with will have to accept our friendship, or it's a deal breaker."

"You really mean that?" Her spirits lifted slightly.

"If it weren't for you, I'd still be using work as an excuse to not shape up or meet anyone. You're not just my best friend — you've made me a better man." He cupped her face with his hands. "I won't ditch you, Sheri, I promise." He pulled his hands away and then frowned. "Unless you keep accusing me of being a male chauvinist caveman pig."

"With a club," she added with a chuckle.

He grinned. "You're stuck with me." He squeezed her shoulders and forced her to look at him. "Feel better now?"

She nodded. Worries assuaged, she said, "You should contact Vanessa. She's clearly your top choice."

Greg thumped his head. "Ah, the woman finally sees reason. But believe it or not, I'm actually going to email that dental hygienist first. My dating skills need work, so since Theresa has already expressed an interest in me, I'd like to have a trial run with her before I ask out my dream girl." He patted his heart and raised his eyes heavenward. "Darling Vanessa."

Sheri rolled her eyes. "Oh brother! I will laugh so hard if Vanessa's profile picture is ten years old, and she's now as hairy and pot-bellied as an orangutan."

He ignored the snide remark. "I don't suppose you'd sit at the restaurant table next to mine and eavesdrop on my date with Theresa?"

"You mean I'd hide behind my menu and critique your conversational skills?"

He shrugged. "Something like that. We'll work out subtle hand signals, so you can let me know if I need to change the subject, or if I have broccoli in my teeth."

"That might be fun." She grinned. "I could accidentally pour a pitcher of ice water down your shirt if you babble too much about index funds. Is that subtle enough?"

His eyes widened. "Leave the ice water in the pitcher. If I need to change the subject, rub your mouth with your index finger."

"Shucks! That's no fun."

"Maybe not, but I forbid you to douse me with ice water." He pointed at her. "I mean it."

She offered him a crocodile smile. "Since you're hiring me as your dating consultant, you'll pay for my dinner, of course," She stared at her nails and tossed out, "I'll probably order lobster tails and scallops. Oh, and a doggie bag of filet mignon for Hamlet."

He frowned. "Gold digger."

"Hey! The new clothes Roxie made me buy cost a fortune."

"Tell me about it. She sure delights in ringing up our credit cards."

"She gets the fun, and we get the bills."

Greg gestured toward Sheri's new apricot top and scarf. "I do like what she's picked out for you. That color looks great with your hair color."

"She's got you looking spiffy, too. More tailored and sophisticated."

"My newest suit coat ought to be made with gold thread for the price I paid for it." He scowled and added, "If I don't snag up the perfect woman before this thing is over, I'm dumping the whole kit and caboodle of overpriced duds on Roxie's doorstep with a hefty bill."

"Speaking of perfect women, let's get back to our computer search, shall we?"

They browsed through a few more women but rejected them all—smoker, too old, too young, or downright weird. I mean, why would anyone raise rattlesnakes for a hobby?

Sheri swiveled in her chair to face Greg. "So, it looks like we're down to the dental hygienist and Vanessa, right?"

Greg patted his heart. "Sweet Vanessa—heart, be still."

"Hey, I can manage that. A potent beta blocker, and flatline, here we come," she offered with a grin.

"I'll pass on your cardiac cocktail, thank you. Let's send Theresa a message and see if she's up for dinner this weekend."

Once he'd sent his request, Greg said, "Okay, now it's your turn to find Mr. Right."

She raised hands of protest. "No way! I need to lose ten more pounds before I look for a guy."

He eyed her up and down. "You look great at this weight. Don't lose any more, or it might come from the wrong place, if you get my drift." He wiggled his eyebrows.

She whacked him in the arm. "Roxie's right—you're incorrigible."

"I'm merely protecting the interests of your future husband. Can I help it if God gave women breasts to attract men?"

Her mouth dropped. "Did you really just say that?"

He raised unapologetic hands. "Just saying…"

"God gave women breasts to nurse babies, you Neanderthal," she snapped, unable to contain her contempt. "We're mammals."

His brow cocked. "Ah, but if a man isn't *attracted* to a woman, there's no baby to nurse, right?"

She blew out an exasperated sigh. "Cave man, Neanderthal. We need to get you a wife, so you can get over this fetish of yours."

"No fetish. Just a healthy appreciation for the feminine beauty God created."

"Right!" She felt her face warm as an image of Greg giving *her* body some appreciation slipped into her mind. She instinctively gripped Greg's computer desk to steady herself.

She imaged herself in Greg's arms kissing tenderly, then passionately. Her arms would wrap around his neck, and he would pull her closer. His kiss would intensify and—

"What are you thinking?" Greg asked. "You zoned out on me."

His blunt question dropped her back to earth like a skydiver with no parachute. Thud! She'd rather be pickled in formaldehyde then have Greg know the direction her thoughts had taken. She had suppressed her sexuality for so long, her sudden desire for Greg shocked her.

*How can I be attracted to a Neanderthal chauvinist pig? Besides, Greg wants Vanessa.*

She could never reveal where her thoughts had roamed. It would ruin their friendship, and she'd rather have Greg as a friend than not at all—even if he could turn into a caveman with a club.

How had this happened? When had geeky, unibrowed Greg transformed into a man for whom she harbored fantasies? Unthinkable—and unwanted! He was her accountability partner!

Greg's eyes narrowed, waiting for her to answer, but she felt so overwhelmed, she couldn't speak. "I, uh… I mean, um…"

"Are you okay?" he asked, inspecting her.

"I, uh, spaced out for a second. No biggie."

Like a pesky mosquito at a picnic, he wouldn't let it go. "It's like your mind was somewhere else."

*Must he badger me?*

Wanting to escape before he pried it out of her, she grabbed her purse and bolted toward the front door. "I've got to head home now. I need to tackle the laundry before tomorrow."

He charged after her. "Wait! We haven't found a guy for you yet."

*I don't want another guy – I want you.* But she could hardly tell him that.

"When I lose these last ten pounds, it'll boost my confidence."

"I'm telling you, you look fine the way you are." His questioning eyes met hers, but she shook her head.

He shrugged. "If you're sure, I'll walk you to your car."

She hustled to her car with Greg trailing wordlessly behind her. Disturbed by her sensuous thoughts only moments earlier, she didn't trust herself to look him in the eyes. She pretended to fumble through her purse in pursuit of her car fob.

"Thanks for your help tonight," Greg said, hands in his pockets. "If Theresa agrees to dinner this weekend, I'll make a reservation for both tables and let you know."

"Sounds good." She opened her car door, desperate to scurry home where she'd be safe from his probing eyes and disturbingly inviting lips. She was about to crawl into her car when Greg touched her arm. "Sheri?"

She peered up at him. He leaned close, his face mere inches from hers, and she held her breath.

"Thanks for everything. I wouldn't be where I am without you."

She offered a hasty, "You're welcome," then dove into her car.

As she backed out of the driveway, she reminded herself Greg would fall in love with another woman soon, and no matter how much he reassured her, she knew no girlfriend would tolerate Sheri hanging around like a pesky younger sister. She needed to program her mind back to their original deal—accountability partners only. No emotional involvement. Greg didn't want her as a girlfriend. Once he'd won over Vanessa—or some other woman—his friendship with Sheri would end, no matter how much he insisted otherwise.

*Let it go. He's your accountability partner and nothing more.*

Once home, she crawled into her pajamas and flopped into bed, too depressed to brush her teeth, wash her face, or put on the overpriced wrinkle cream Roxie had insisted she purchase.

*Why bother? Who will care if I'm toothless and wrinkled?*

Cinderella had dolled up for the ball, but Prince Charming hadn't even noticed, because Prince Charming wanted Vanessa.

She punched her pillow in frustration then forced herself to pray. "God, help Greg find his soulmate, and help me let him go."

This was one prayer she secretly hoped God wouldn't answer.

*"Time goes on crutches 'til love has all his rites."*
~William Shakespeare~
*Much Ado about Nothing*

# Chapter 14

"Ma, what are you doing here?" Sheri asked, as her mother strolled into her medical office with a plate of roast beef, mashed potatoes, and green beans. Sheri glanced at her watch. Not even eleven o'clock and she still had four more patients to see.

Linda Morris laid the plate on Sheri's desk. "Does a mother have to have a reason to visit her daughter?"

*At eleven in the morning on a hectic Monday? Yes!*

"First, I wanted to remind you about the annual Claiborne family reunion coming up." She gave Sheri the date with an admonishing, "No flimsy excuses to get out of it this year. Matilda needs to see how slim and attractive you've become. I'm so sick of her belittling you."

*You and me both.* Linda's snobbish family made Joan Rivers seem sweet. Sheri penciled the date and time of the reunion into her planner, secretly praying her appendix would rupture a few hours before the event, so she would have a non-flimsy excuse to get out of the dread affair.

Linda continued. "Second, I brought you a nice, healthy lunch, so you'd have the stamina to finish all your patients and paperwork. I know Mondays are always your busiest day."

"Thanks, Ma, that's sweet of you."

*Now out with it — what's your real agenda for being here?*

Her mother eyed her up and down with a furrowed brow. "You've lost weight awfully fast. You aren't becoming anorectic, are you?"

Sheri forced herself not to roll her eyes. "No, Ma. I'm only aiming for my ideal weight. No lower, I promise."

As though not listening to a word Sheri had said, her mother continued her interrogation. "You aren't vomiting up your dinner, are you? I've read about bulimia and eating disorders."

Sheri sucked in a deep breath and released it slowly in a failed attempt to remain calm.

*I don't have time for this — I'm already half an hour behind schedule.*

She forced herself to count to ten, so she wouldn't snap something ugly. *"Honor thy father and thy mother that thy days may be long."* Her least favorite of the Ten Commandments.

Linda prattled on. "I read in one of my women's magazines that anorectics are usually high achievers just like you. The article mentioned an excellent treatment facility called Anorexia Alcoves in New Mexico." She tapped her lower lip. "Or was it in Arizona? No, I remember, it was in Colorado."

*Lord, grant me patience.* "Ma, I promise you, I don't have anorexia. I weigh 154 pounds, and my ideal body weight is 145. You're borrowing trouble."

Linda sat on the edge of Sheri's desk examining her nails before finally revealing the real reason for the impromptu visit — maternal inquisition. "You've been so busy with your work and exercise these days, I haven't heard a word about how the husband hunting is going."

Groan and double groan.

*Say something to shut her up and make her leave.*

Sheri pasted on a huge grin. "You'll be delighted to know I'm going to a steakhouse this Saturday with a very handsome man."

She hoped that would be enough to divert her mother from her favorite lecture topic: You're-A-Ticking-Clock-and-I-Want-More-Grandkids.

"Really?" Linda's face lit up. "Did you meet him because of the website I gave you?"

Sheri nodded. Her mother needn't know her Saturday night "date" would consist of hiding behind a menu gesturing

75

frantically at Greg to quit his financial planning lecture as he attempted to woo Theresa.

"You think he likes you?" her mother pried, eyes aglow.

"I *know* he likes me." Sheri smiled deceptively.

Linda patted Sheri's face. "I won't keep you since the waiting room is full of patients." She frowned. "You really should try harder to stay on schedule. Patients hate waiting, you know."

She slid off Sheri's desk and headed toward the door. "I *knew* you'd be a December bride." She sauntered out of Sheri's office humming, "Here Comes the Bride."

*"All the world's a stage. And all the men and women merely players.*
*They have their exits and their entrances.*
*And one man in his time plays many parts."*
~William Shakespeare~
*As You Like It*

# Chapter 15

Sheri sipped iced tea and perused the menu of the steakhouse Greg had selected for his date with Theresa.

She glanced around the restaurant and eyed Greg's empty table. Talk about weird—spying on someone else's date? How lame was that? She had to remember to avoid eye contact with Greg and rely on the subtle hand signals they'd worked out earlier this week.

If she yawns, he should change the subject because he is boring. If she pulls out her compact mirror and applies lipstick, he has food in his teeth. If she drums her fingers on the table, it means the girl is a total nutcase, so he should cut his losses and end the date early with no dessert or coffee—why waste time and money on a dud?

While Sheri munched on the tossed salad she'd ordered as an appetizer, the hostess escorted Greg and Theresa to the table directly in front of hers. Sheri chomped on a carrot curl as she sized up Theresa. The woman had a beautiful smile—no surprise there since she worked for a dentist—and she styled her raven black hair into a becoming bob. Her turquoise earrings and necklace coordinated nicely with her black pants and white tailored blouse. She did have an eagle's beak of a nose and an unusually high forehead. Overall, though, the girl was pretty enough—or at least she wasn't homely. Sheri had secretly hoped Theresa would show up blubbery as a manatee and dressed in a gunnysack.

She watched Greg pull out his date's chair—no surprise there. Hadn't he told her his Mama raised him right? Sheri peeked over her menu to see how Greg looked. His open-necked tailored white shirt with sleeves rolled halfway up his forearms looked relaxed and yet sophisticated. His thick hair curled invitingly around his ears, and his eyebrows were thankfully plucked to perfection.

Looks? He'd nailed it.

Conversational skills? Well... Though a brilliant man, Greg, when nervous, sometimes displayed the social IQ of a toenail fungus.

Squashing her selfish desire that the date would flop, Sheri called upon her inner angel voice and prayed, "Lord, keep Greg from babbling about mutual funds, and give me the discipline not to douse him with ice water if he does. Amen."

She held her breath as the couple sat primly in their chairs and glanced shyly across the table at one another. Neither ventured a word.

*Come on, Greg. Say something—anything! Don't sit there like a tombstone.*

After an embarrassingly long pause, Greg feigned undue interest in his menu and mumbled something about craving prime rib. Sheri already knew what Greg would order since his menu choices on their weight loss plan were as predictable as Old Faithful—fish or chicken, steamed broccoli or asparagus, and a tossed salad with low-fat dressing.

After the waiter took their orders, Theresa and Greg snatched furtive glances across the table at one another, but neither said a word. Greg cracked his knuckles, and soon his thigh jiggled. Her heart quickened, and she silently encouraged him.

*Come on, Greg. Ask about her job, her family, her hobbies.*

Theresa fared no better. She hadn't muttered a single word other than, "Iced tea," and, "Grilled salmon and broccoli." Wow! This date had stalled out like a 1983 Yugo.

Greg glanced up at Sheri with panic etched across his face. Sheri pulled a pad of paper and a magic marker from her purse and wrote in big black letters, ASK ABOUT HER JOB. Since Sheri sat behind Theresa but facing Greg, she could hold up her sign like a tour guide at the airport without Theresa seeing it.

Greg scanned the message and responded with a slight nod. "Theresa, tell me about your job."

Sheri rolled her eyes. Had she seriously pined for this conversational lug nut?

Theresa swallowed several sips of tea and wiped her mouth with her napkin. "I'm a dental hygienist," came her less than chatty response.

Duh—that was on your website profile. Help him out here, Theresa!

Greg cracked his knuckles again. His leg now thumped so forcefully under the table their tea glasses rattled. Thankfully, the waiter rescued him by returning with a basket of rolls. Greg eagerly grabbed a dinner roll and buttered it with undue fascination. After he'd buttered and chewed for a solid two minutes, Sheri scribbled another sign in bold letters and waved it at him. ASK ABOUT HER BOSS AND CO-WORKERS.

"Tell me about your boss and co-workers," Greg parroted.

*Okay, he gets an A for following instruction and an F for creativity.*

Miss Monosyllable eked out, "Dr. Nelson is nice," and, "My co-workers are nice, too."

No wonder the woman was single—she could barely string five words together. She must be either painfully shy or so nervous she was paralyzed. Judging from the bead of sweat dripping down the side of Greg's face, Theresa wasn't the only one who was nervous.

Sheri gestured with a sweep of her hand across her forehead for Greg to mop the sweat off his brow. Greg complied and offered her another look of panic.

She scribbled on the backside of her paper: SIBLINGS AND PARENTS.

Theresa was an only child, and her mom and dad were, you guessed it, nice.

Yeesh! Would the woman declare Hitler nice?

Sheri stuck up another sign. HOBBIES??

Theresa loved to knit.

Swell. Now there's a riveting conversation starter for any red-blooded American male. Knit one, purl two.

Greg glanced up at Sheri with such a look of desperation she thought he might bolt.

She held up one last sign: FAVORITE FOODS AND VACATION SPOTS. If the mute creature couldn't come up with more than five words on this one, Sheri would drum her fingers on the table—their agreed upon signal to end the date early. If that didn't work, she would hustle to the bathroom, call Greg on his cell phone, and rescue him with some trumped-up emergency.

Unfortunately, a snooty waiter chose that exact moment to strut up to Sheri's table with arms crossed and a haughty frown. "What on earth are you doing?" he demanded.

Before Sheri could utter a word, he continued his scolding. "This is not a kindergarten class where one waves little notes to one's friends from across the room. Displaying hand-scrawled notes hampers the dining pleasure of our other discriminating patrons."

She wanted to crawl under the table, but the last thing she needed was for Theresa to discover her conspiracy with Greg. Thus, she had to trump up a plausible excuse...and quickly. She motioned with her index finger for the waiter to come closer.

She whispered in his ear, "We're actors rehearsing a play that takes place in a restaurant. When Greg forgets a line, I hold up a sign to prick his memory. He's supposed to know all his lines for tonight's dress rehearsal."

She held her breath as she waited for the waiter's response. Her excuse was lame, but what else could she do—tell the waiter she'd been spying on Greg's table because he was such a dating dimwit he needed flash cards like some third grader memorizing multiplication tables?

Amazingly, the waiter instantly warmed to her explanation. "How positively mar-velous! I simply *adore* the theater." He clapped his hands in glee. "And what play are we rehearsing?"

Sheri felt a wheelbarrow's worth of sweat ooze from her pores. *What play? Darned if I know.*

Her mind went blank. She racked her brain to think of a play — *any* play — that took place at dinner. He stared at her, his eyebrow raised in anticipation.

"*Guess Who's Coming to Dinner.*" The words spilled out before she could stop them — it was the only thing she could think of under pressure.

His face lit up. "How delightful. I simply *adore* Sidney Poitier, don't you? He totally deserved that Academy Award for *Lilies of the Field.*"

"Absolutely!" she gushed, nodding like a bobble-head. What she really adored was the waiter falling for her ridiculous story.

"And what role is your gentleman friend playing?"

"The lead — that's why it's so critical for him to know his lines."

The waiter turned to study Greg, and his brow furrowed. "If you don't mind my asking, how will he play the role of a black man?"

Sheri's heart lurched. Of course. Sidney Poitier was black. She should have known her attempt to lie would fly like an ostrich.

The waiter stared at her eagerly.

She'd have to wing it. "Ah, we're doing an avant-garde version of the play. A racial switcheroo, if you will."

The waiter clapped his hands in delight. "How positively clever! I simply must see the production. Where is it playing?"

*Oh, what a tangled web we weave, when first we practice to deceive.*

The irritating quote permeated her mind, and her heart pounded like a kettledrum. Any faster and she'd need an Adenosine drip to slow it down.

*Come on, think!*

81

"Ah...we're with a small theater company out of Bowling Green, Kentucky."

He glanced at his watch. "Kentucky? It's nearly eight. Aren't you late if the dress rehearsal is tonight?"

Sheri felt her cheeks warm. She hadn't thought of that. Shoot! Like a performer in an impromptu comedy club, she'd have to improvise. Unable to make eye contact, she inspected her nails. "Oh, you know what night owls we thespians are. The rehearsal starts at nine, so we'll make it."

He leaned in close and whispered, "You know, I was once a theater major myself. Unfortunately, there were no acting jobs to be had when I graduated, so I was reduced to waiting tables. But every now and then, I land a role in a local production."

"I'd love to see you perform someday." It didn't hurt to humor the man.

He beamed. "Well, I did make a *mar*-velous Professor Higgins in *My Fair Lady*." He winked at her. "I'll get that blackened salmon out straight away. I wouldn't want you to be late for your dress rehearsal."

The waiter returned with her plate of fish, then sauntered over to Greg and Theresa's table and served their entrees, as well. "Here's your salmon and broccoli, Sir." He grinned at Greg and added conspiratorially, "I'm sure you'll need all the protein you can get for tonight's performance." He winked with a knowing smile, as though they shared a secret. He then rushed back to the kitchen.

Greg's brow furrowed as if to say, *"What performance?"*

Theresa's eyes narrowed. "What 'performance' was that waiter talking about?" She etched imaginary quotation marks around the word performance with her fingers. "Did you think you were hitting a home run with me tonight?"

Greg's face blanched. "What? No!"

She ignored his response. "I thought this was a dating site for *Christian* professionals." She yanked her linen napkin from her lap and slapped it next to her dinner plate. "This was our very first date, and to be honest, not a very good one, so if you have any funny ideas about making the moves on me or getting fresh, you're in for a rude awakening."

Greg's eyes bugged in alarm at her sudden verbal barrage.

"Wait! You've got it all wrong!" He waved his hands in protest like a railroad crossing sign. "I would never get fresh with you. I have no funny ideas. None!"

She crossed her arms and her eyes bore into his. "Then what 'performance' was that waiter talking about?"

Wow! Sheri watched Theresa in shock. Miss Mouse had suddenly turned into a hissing tabby raring for a catfight.

Panic was written all over Greg's face. "What performance?" He squirmed in his seat before claiming, "My performance on a huge accounting test."

"You're taking an accounting test—tonight?" She shook her head. "Give me a break! It's Saturday night."

Greg wiped his mouth with his napkin, his desperate eyes meeting Sheri's across the tables. Torn between horror and amusement, Sheri could do nothing but see how this thing played out.

"My boss is a real stickler, and since he'll be in Atlanta at a conference next week, tonight is the only time he had free to administer the test."

Theresa scowled. "Come on! You expect me to believe you're taking an accounting test tonight—after our date?" She glanced at her watch. "It's already eight o'clock."

"My boss is a total night owl."

Her head cocked, as though considering his lame excuse. "How would that waiter know you had an accounting test tonight?"

Greg froze then managed to recover. "Oh, I eat here all the time. I mentioned my accounting test to him the last time I came in."

Sheri noticed Greg's underarms were now soaked with perspiration.

*Nice to know telling lies doesn't come easy for Greg, either.*

Theresa then made the fatal mistake of asking, "And what exactly is he testing you on?"

Greg *should* have responded with a generic answer like new tax laws or retirement planning. But no, Greg was incapable of short answers on financial anything, even on a good day. When stressed, or, in this case, desperate, all bets were off.

He cracked his knuckles then launched into his speech. "One of the most important things to know about retirement planning is avoid hidden fees. One of the worst profit drainers is the 12b-1 fee which rewards intermediaries for picking a particular fund. This fee..."

Sheri dropped her head into her hands.

*Here we go...*

After completing his dissertation about 12b-1 fees, he droned on about front-end load and back-end load funds.

Remembering their signals, Sheri yawned and stretched her arms over her head. Greg never even looked in her direction. In fact, he seemed to have forgotten that Theresa was on the verge of walking out on him five minutes ago. To be fair, Theresa must have forgotten as well, as she now was leaning on her elbows, probably struggling to stay awake.

On and on, he droned. "Beta measures how an asset moves up or down compared to its benchmark index fund. Alpha, on the other hand, is a historical measure of an asset's return on investment compared to the risk adjusted expected return."

Theresa's head snapped forward, as though she'd nodded off.

Sheri yawned even more dramatically. No luck. She stretched her arms overhead, arched her back, and opened her mouth wide enough to swallow a grapefruit. Mr. Excitement remained oblivious and blathered on.

*Diversify, diversify, diversify!*

Greg had previously warned her he could launch into financial planning monologs when he felt overwhelmed in social situations.

She now knew what he meant. Boy, did she know what he meant! She yawned again—her mouth so open it practically hit the floor.

Greg may as well be blind.

She shook her head in dismay. How could Greg have graduated number one in his class at a top MBA program and yet be so clueless about social cues? At this rate, they'd all be retired before he finished his lecture.

She impulsively picked up her uneaten dinner roll and flung it straight at Greg's head. With any luck, Theresa's eyes would be closed in slumber when the roll jolted him out of his lecture.

*Thump!*

The dinner roll hit his forehead and then landed onto his half-eaten salmon fillet. Jolted by the errant roll, Greg turned and looked her way, thus ending his mind-numbing dissertation. He glared at Sheri and without thinking snapped, "Hey! What'd you do that for?"

She snapped back, "It was that or a pitcher of ice water. Your twenty-minute monolog was putting me to sleep. Apparently, this roll slipped from my hand when I fell into a stupor."

His face flushed the color of his salmon fillet. Theresa turned around with a startled expression. "Do you two *know* each other?"

Greg sucked in a noisy breath and cracked his knuckles, as though debating whether to lie further or 'fess up. He finally looked Theresa in the eyes, lowered his eyes in shame, and confessed, "Sheri is my dating tutor."

"Your WHAT?" Her glare swiveled from Greg to Sheri and back to Greg again. She looked madder than a grumpy goose.

Greg's leg now thumped like a bass drummer on cocaine. "I know it sounds idiotic, but I haven't had a successful date in years, so Sheri came along tonight to critique me and help me get through our date."

Theresa glared at Sheri. "You've been *eavesdropping* on our conversation?"

From Theresa's incensed tone, you'd think Sheri was Squeaky Fromme after her assassination attempt on President Ford.

"Actually, I didn't *hear* any conversation," Sheri retorted. "I only heard Greg's mind-numbing monolog about diversifying retirement portfolios."

Her eyes bore into Sheri's. "Is smacking someone in the head with a dinner roll part of your tutoring package, or do you charge extra for that?"

Sheri's cheeks burned. "Only when scribbling notes, yawning, stretching, and glaring at him don't do the trick."

Theresa's lips thinned, and she shook her head in disgust. "I should have known better than think I'd meet a decent guy online. My mother warned me the men would all be losers." She gestured toward Greg. "Exhibit number one!"

She snatched up her purse and shoved back her chair. She couldn't resist a last zinger. "You two are the weirdest people I've ever met, and trust me, you meet a lot of weird people in a dental office." She glared at Greg. "I'll take a cab home."

Just then, the waiter moseyed back over and inquired how the play rehearsal was progressing.

Greg's brow creased, and he opened his mouth to say something, but Sheri, who had seen the waiter coming their way, bolted over to Greg and punched his back with the force of a cannonball. "Our rehearsal for *Guess Who's Coming to Dinner* is progressing fabulously, isn't it, Greg?"

"Ah, splendidly."

Theresa, who had overheard this exchange, spat out, "First a test? Now, a play rehearsal? You two are certifiably crazy! Looney tunes." She circled her index finger at her temple then stormed out of the restaurant without looking back.

Thinking Theresa was part of the play rehearsal, the waiter enthused, "My, my! Isn't she's talented! What a convincing display of anger."

*Convincing indeed!*

The waiter smiled bashfully and placed his hands into a "pretty please" prayer gesture. "Would you mind doing a few lines from the play? I'd love to see how you've varied the script to account for the racial switch."

Greg glanced at Sheri with a deer-in-the-headlights look.

*We are so busted.*

Thankfully, Greg rallied and saved the day. He glanced at his watch and feigned a startled expression. "Oh, my goodness! It's getting late. We've got to hustle, or we'll be late." He turned to the waiter and raised apologetic palms. "I'm sorry. We'd love to run lines with you, but we really need to skedaddle. Can we get our check, please?"

The waiter bowed. "Certainly."

Greg pulled out his wallet and handed over his credit card.

As soon as the waiter left to process the card, Greg and Sheri looked at one another and burst into laughter.

"Well, that date was a booming success, don't you think?" Sheri said through her titters.

By the time the waiter returned with their receipt, they had laughed so hard they had to wipe tears from their eyes.

As they strolled out of the restaurant Sheri said, "Can you believe Theresa thought the waiter told you to eat all your fish, so your sexual performance would be up to par tonight?"

Greg's shoulders sagged. "I've never been so embarrassed in my life. She must think I'm a complete boar."

"Which kind? The fat, snorting pig, or the kind that drones on and on about stock funds until you fall asleep into your salad?"

Greg flicked her arm. "It isn't funny. My first date as the new me—a complete disaster."

"You think?" She burst into laughter. "Poor Theresa. She'll probably kiss online dating goodbye forever."

"Who could blame her? I need to email her an apology. Lord knows she deserves one." After a pause, he added, "I'm glad that wasn't my date with Vanessa." He wiped the back of his hand across his brow with a "Phew" gesture. "I knew I needed a practice run before I contacted my dream girl."

As they neared the parking garage elevator, Sheri said, "In fairness to you, surely Vanessa will be easier to talk to. Theresa didn't help in the conversation department one bit."

Greg's shoulders wilted. "Tell me about it. Getting her to open up was like pulling teeth, pardon the pun."

"She barely said a word."

"Maybe she's used to clients whose mouths are numbed up with Novocain," Greg conjectured.

"Or minds doped up with nitrous oxide. No wonder she couldn't string a full sentence together."

"Until she accused me of planning to make the moves on her tonight. Then she wouldn't shut up."

"And then that waiter thought her outrage was all part of our play rehearsal." Sheri snorted with laughter.

As they reached the parking garage elevator, Greg pushed the up button, his expression glum.

Sensing his discouragement, Sheri said, "On a positive note, your next date can only go better."

He whacked her arm. "Be nice."

"Hey, if you want 'nice,' maybe you should make up with Theresa. She seemed to think everybody was nice. Her boss, her co-workers, her mother."

"Everybody except *us*. We're weirdos."

"Certifiably crazy."

"Looney Tunes." Greg circled his index finger near his head like Theresa had. "No wonder I degenerated into a financial planning lecture—the woman gave me no help whatsoever."

The elevator dinged, and the door opened. They walked in and Sheri pushed the button to the third floor. "What floor are you parked on?"

"Same as you. I'll walk you to your car."

They walked in silence until Sheri asked, "Didn't you see me yawn and stretch to get your attention? I only resorted to flinging my dinner roll at you because you ignored all our agreed upon signals."

Greg's head dropped, and he stared down at his shoes. "I guess I wasn't paying attention."

"You think? I practically performed a rain dance to try and get your attention."

He hung his head in shame.

When they arrived at Sheri's car, she reached into her purse for her fob and turned to say goodnight. Before she could turn away, he reached for her arm and their eyes met. He leaned forward and for a fraction of a second, she thought he was going to kiss her goodnight. She smiled and licked her lips trying to suppress her unbridled joy.

Except...he didn't. He stood there like a Buckingham Palace guard and stared at her. Was the romantic pull between them all in her head? Probably.

"Well, goodnight," he said, then ambled toward his car.

Cheeks flaming, she mumbled goodnight and dove into her car. She squealed out of the parking garage like an Indy 500 contender.

*Could this night get any more embarrassing?*

*"The course of true love never did run smooth."*
~William Shakespeare~
*A Midsummer Night's Dream*

# Chapter 16

After subjecting herself to another ten weeks of dietary drudgery, sweaty hikes, considerable angst and self-denial, Sheri *finally* reached her ideal weight. She thought this day would never come. For the first time in a decade, she looked slim and sexy in her new — and thanks to shopping sprees with Roxie — expensive clothes. She'd even mastered that dratted detangler attachment on her hair dryer and could style her hair in under twenty minutes.

Greg claimed she now had no excuse for not exploring the available men on the dating web site. While flattered, she had to wonder if she looked so great, why didn't *he* want her? Why was he so anxious to palm her off on some other guy?

If she had to hear one more word about Vanessa Bigboobs, she'd clobber him with her hair dryer. For all his *talk* about precious Vanessa, Greg had yet to drum up the courage to shoot the woman so much as a one-line email. By now, the woman was probably planning her honeymoon! Greg clearly suffered from PTSD (Post-*Theresa* Stress Disorder) and was too shell-shocked to risk rejection from his dream girl.

If only to shut him up about Vanessa, Sheri promised she would select and email several dating contenders for herself *if* Greg would *finally* send Vanessa an email. Ready or not, tonight, she would plunge into the shark tank of online dating.

After dinner, Greg hunched over her shoulder as she scrolled through the available men.

"What's with all these old geezers robbing the cradle?" she grumbled after twenty minutes of fruitless searching. "Look at this guy!" She jabbed a finger at the picture of a gray- haired man, old enough to be her father. "He'll be in a nursing home before I even qualify for AARP!"

Greg agreed. "He definitely belongs in the 'Senior Singles' category."

"Clarence. Even his name sounds old," Sheri sputtered. "I had a great-grandfather named Clarence."

Greg wagged a scolding finger at her. "Now, now. Don't be a name snob."

"Maybe I should match him up with my mother. Since Dad died, she's been lonely and aimless. I think that's why she's become obsessed with meddling in my life—she's bored."

"Unfortunately, if Clarence is a cradle-robber, he probably won't go for your mother. But you could sign her up for the Senior Singles website."

Sheri pointed at him. "You may be on to something. Two can play this game."

Greg snickered. "The last laugh will be on us if she has better luck finding a soulmate than we do."

"Hey, if it gets her off my back, I'm all for it." She clicked to the next candidate, hoping this one wasn't ready for adult diapers.

After reading the man's profile she fumed, "This one is unemployed." She crossed her arms in disgust. "The website is called Christian *Professionals*. What is he? A professional moocher? They're even worse than the cradle robbers. At least Clarence has a job."

Greg reviewed the guy's profile more thoroughly. "Technically, he's not *unemployed*. It says here he works part-time as a comedian and magician."

Sheri rolled her eyes. "Right! In other words, unemployed."

"Comedian *and* magician?" Greg rubbed his chin. "You suppose that means people laugh when he bungles up his magic tricks?"

"That's assuming he can even dig up a gig to bungle."

She clicked onto the profile of a man who initially looked promising—her age and employed—but then discovered he smoked.

*Forget it!*

She spent too many hours lecturing patients about the risks of lung cancer and emphysema as it was. No way would she waste what precious free time she had nagging a nicotine-addicted husband.

Next came a morbidly obese man holding a triple-scoop ice cream cone. The ice cream looked far more appealing than the man. Plus, he would no doubt sabotage the diet and exercise lifestyle she desperately needed to continue, if she hoped to maintain her weight loss.

Then came the weirdoes—grown men who played Dungeons and Dragons or who spoke in bizarre Lord of the Rings elfin languages. "If they're going to learn a foreign language, why not pick a practical one—like Spanish?"

Now a line-up of Peter Pans who squandered every free second on video games. They published their scores for shooting imaginary aliens and terrorists using make-believe weapons as though the scores were college GPA's. She wanted to email each and every one of them a scathing message: GROW UP!

No doubt about it—the pickings were slim. Slim, indeed.

Just as she was ready to surrender and call it a night, Greg pointed over her shoulder at a man she'd already written off. "What about this guy?"

She clicked on Tom Harbinger, a baldy with bulldog jowls. At least he was her age and held a respectable job as a pharmacist. He didn't smoke, and he was active in his church. No mention of Dungeons and Dragons or video game scores. Not even a shotgun or deer carcass wrapped around his shoulders.

*Just no fireworks—not even a firecracker.*

She shrugged. "To be honest, I've never been attracted to men who are completely bald."

Greg crossed his arms and frowned. "That's awfully shallow, don't you think? You'd reject a perfectly acceptable man over something as trivial as a lack of dead protein growing from his scalp?"

Sheri turned and cocked a brow. "Excuse me? You, who picked a woman based on her bust size, are criticizing *me* about judging someone's hair?"

He pounded the desk. "For the hundredth time, I did *not* pick Vanessa because of her bust size. She's a charge nurse at the hospital, so she's smart. She goes on mission trips to third-world countries, so she's kind." He smirked. "It's merely my good fortune that she also happens to be endowed with appealing physical attributes."

She rolled her eyes. "Oh, brother! If you get to pick someone who's smart, compassionate, *and* gorgeous, why should I get lopped with a guy I'm not the slightest bit attracted to?"

"Because he's a pharmacist. You'd have lots to talk about."

"Seriously? You think after a twelve-hour day in the clinic I want to come home and talk about decongestants and hemorrhoid suppositories? I can see it now." She raised her hand toward the sky. "He will expound on the half-life of fluoxetine, and I'll discuss the renal metabolism of tobramycin." She pierced him with a glare. "Now there's a date I'm dying to have."

Greg raised his hands in surrender. "Yeesh! You don't have to bite my head off. I'm only trying to help."

"It's just that you've found this blond bombshell with a brain but then want to palm me off on some bowling-ball-of-a-man because we can discuss the cytochrome P450 excretion of simvastatin."

His face contorted. "The what?"

"Oh, never mind."

She clicked on another unpromising candidate and wanted to punch a wall. Here she'd lost thirty pounds, wasted thirty minutes every morning on her hair and make-up, spent a small fortune on stylish clothes, *and for what?* There wasn't a single man on the website that excited her in the slightest. In fact, she'd rather spend her Friday nights soaking in the tub with a good book than dating any of these men who were, as far as she was concerned, a waste of a Y chromosome.

She slammed down the lid of her laptop. "I refuse to look anymore. It's too demoralizing." She stood up and wandered to the kitchen for a glass of diet green tea.

Greg sat down in the chair and raised the computer lid. "Not so fast. Your dream man might be floating in cyberspace just waiting for you to discover him."

"I doubt it," she shouted from the kitchen, as she dropped three ice cubes into her glass.

"Don't give up so easily. *You* might be a quitter, but *I* intend to look until we both find suitable life companions. That was the goal of Operation Soulmate, remember?"

She filled her glass with tea and sputtered about the futility of looking any further. "Nothing but dregs and men twice my age."

"Hey! I found three new listings," Greg yelled from the study. "Just added today, in fact!"

Sheri wandered back to the computer, fully aware she was behaving like a spoiled brat. Greg deserved better than grouchiness. She released a loud sigh. "Alright. You win. My pity party is over." She leaned over his shoulder and sipped her tea. "Anyone promising?"

Greg clicked on the first new listing, and Sheri nearly dropped her tea glass. A luscious specimen of male with a physique like Adonis smiled back at her with perfect teeth. His classy haircut could grace the cover of one of Roxy's stylist magazines, and his large, expressive, brown eyes penetrated straight into her heart. Sheri stared until her jaw fell slack.

Greg glanced up at her and scowled. "Quit drooling like some Pavlovian dog—you'll get my shirt wet. Besides, you shouldn't judge a man based solely on his looks."

Ignoring him, she grinned and pointed at the screen with her index finger. "There's my future husband. I want him."

Greg stared at the screen and pursed his lips. "I'll admit, on the surface, he seems promising, but for all you know, he chops up his dates and stores them in the freezer." He leaned back in his chair. "Better run a criminal background check. Anyone who looks that good is bound to have serious psychological issues."

*Huh?*

"Why do you say that?"

Greg raised upturned palms. "He's probably your classic narcissist."

Sheri grabbed the mouse from Greg. "Give me that." She scrolled down to skim the man's profile. "Nicholas Carr. Age forty-one. His wife died three years ago after losing a five-year battle with ovarian cancer. Only now ready to date. Works as an attorney for a medical malpractice company that *defends* doctors." She glanced up at Greg, beaming. "Listen to this—graduated magna cum laude from Vanderbilt Law School, and he's a deacon in his church. His only daughter, Maddie, is a freshman at Stanford."

Greg shrugged. "He sounds okay, I guess."

"*Okay?*" Sheri shouted, arms akimbo. "He's way more than okay, you ninny!" She clicked down and read more of the profile. "Says here he runs and hikes in his free time. He could help me stay fit." She grinned. "Here's *my* Mr. Right—Nicholas Carr. He's perfect."

"Too perfect, if you ask me," Gregg muttered. "Remember Ted Bundy? A dozen women wound up dead thanks to that good-looking, smooth-talking attorney."

"You're jealous!" Sheri exclaimed, eyeing his addled demeanor.

His eyes widened. "Jealous? Not at all. I'm merely concerned for your safety. Did his wife *really* died of cancer? He could have strangled her, for all you know."

Sheri rolled her eyes. "That's ridiculous. Besides, I'll only meet him in public places until I get to know him better."

Greg then spouted a litany of potential dangers that rivaled the length of Santa's naughty list—stalkers, Mama's boys, murderers, rapists, control-freaks, tax evaders, hoarders, identity thieves, and wife-beaters. Sheri tuned him out and insisted on sending Nicholas a friendly email suggesting they meet up for coffee.

Unlike Greg, Sheri refused to dawdle. After reviewing all the deadbeats and cradle robbers on the website, this Nicholas Carr would fly off the shelf faster than a vial of penicillin in World War II.

If Greg was too clueless to realize Sheri liked him, she'd best move on to greener pastures in the form of one gorgeous and brilliant Nicholas Carr. Besides, Greg was obsessed with Vanessa Bigboobs, so Sheri shouldn't waste one more second pining after a man who didn't want her.

Emboldened, Sheri shot off an email to Nicholas and then insisted Greg now had to email Vanessa—tonight—before she married one of her countless other admirers at the hospital. "She's bound to have a dozen suitors vying for her affection by now, Greg. You need to contact her before you end up reading her wedding announcement in the Tennessean."

After forty minutes of writing, editing, analyzing, agonizing, deleting, re-writing, and revising, Greg managed to pull off the following email:

*"Hi, Vanessa. I'm Greg Palmer, a Nashville CPA. I'd love to take you out for coffee and scones sometime. Interested? Shoot me an email. I look forward to meeting you!"*

Sheri snapped her laptop shut, unable to contain her glee. "This has been a most productive evening, don't you think? We've both found our perfect person. Operation Soulmate is bearing fruit."

Greg grabbed his keys. "Wonder who will hear back first."

"I hope it's me," she said, unable to suppress her devilish grin.

Greg turned and wagged a finger at her. "If you wind up at the bottom of the Cumberland River with cinder blocks on your feet, don't blame me."

"Since I'll be dead, I couldn't blame you. Besides, how do you know Vanessa isn't a slit-throat? You ever heard of the movie *Fatal Attraction*? I'm told the femme fatale in that movie was a bunny boiler."

His head jerked up. "A what?" He raised a hand to stop her. "No, I don't want to know. Besides, Vanessa's a nurse, and nurses are known for being nurturing."

Sheri snorted. "Not all of them. And trust me, I know. Ever heard of Nurse Ratchet from *One Flew over the Cuckoos' Nest?*"

He didn't seem the slightest bit worried. In fact, he grinned. "You wait and see. Vanessa will be sweet and nurturing and totally crazy about me."

She decided not to burst his bubble. Now that she had a potential love life of her own, why rob Greg of his dream girl?

Now all she could do is wait—and pray Nicholas Carr would contact her.

*"But O, how bitter a thing it is to look into happiness
through another man's eyes."*
~William Shakespeare~
*As You Like It*

# Chapter 17

Each morning before her four-mile hike with Greg, Sheri checked her emails, praying for a response from Nicholas. Two long weeks had passed since she'd sent the email and not a word. Not even a "Thanks, but no thanks." Had he taken one glance at her photo and tossed her into the "No way" pile the way she and Greg had rejected so many others? How demoralizing. After all the catty comments she'd made about other contenders on the website, perhaps she deserved rejection. The old, "What goes around, comes around," thing.

As she trudged around the trails with Greg, she tried to downplay her disappointment. "Nicholas is probably on vacation."

"But most people check their emails on vacation," Greg pointed out.

He sounded just like her internal doomsday crier. Must Greg *and* her inner worrywart rub it in? It was obvious—Nicholas had no interest in her. Nada.

She stepped over a rotting log in the trail and then had to run to catch up with Greg. Again.

*What's up with him today? He never walks this fast!*

Hoping to save face, Sheri raised the possibility that perhaps Nicholas *couldn't* email her. "Maybe he's backpacking in some remote location—like Mongolia—where there isn't any Wi-Fi. He said he likes to hike."

Greg's dubious expression suggested he didn't buy it, but he refrained from comment and charged ahead with a silly grin on his face.

"Something has you beaming like you won the Tri-State lottery. Out with it."

Greg grinned. "Okay, if you insist. Guess who emailed me last night?"

Before Sheri could open her mouth to respond, Greg burst out, "Vanessa! She's agreed to meet me for coffee."

"Really?" Sheri opened her arms wide, pulling him in for an impulsive hug. "So that's why I couldn't keep up with you this morning—you're walking on air."

He practically glowed. "Can you believe it? Our date is this Thursday at seven. I've set up an emergency salon visit with Roxie two hours beforehand to make sure I look my best. I cannot blow this date."

"That's wonderful news," she said, surprised at how excited she was for him...if only Nicholas would call.

Greg winced as Roxie tweezed two errant hairs from his eyebrows. "Ow! That hurt, sadist!"

Ignoring him, Roxie spun his chair around to better assess his profile.

"So how are things between you and Sheri these days?"

"Sheri?" He shrugged. "She's upset because this lawyer she's taken a shine to hasn't responded to her email. She's pretending it doesn't bother her, but she wears a perpetual pout when she thinks I'm not looking."

Roxie trimmed the sides of Greg's hair. "Is she upset about your date with Vanessa tonight?"

"Not at all, but I've tried not to talk about her too much, since I don't want to rub it in that Nicholas hasn't called her."

"She must be disappointed."

Greg nodded. "I don't get it — Sheri's smart, funny, likable, and now that she's fixed herself up, she's easy on the eyes. So why isn't Nicholas biting?"

Roxie pulled the hair on each side of Greg's ears to ensure the two sides were even in length. "If Sheri has cleaned up so well, why don't *you* go after her? You two seem to get along great."

"Sheri?" He shrugged, not bothering to cover up the surprise in his voice. "Our agreement says we must remain as accountability partners only. I mean, she's a great friend, and we share a lot of laughs but..." He frowned. "I'll be brutally honest with you. I didn't find her attractive at all when we met. Truthfully, she was kind of homely."

"She's not homely now." Roxie impaled him with a penetrating gaze. "Is she?"

"No, she's not," Greg agreed, hoping Roxie would buy his less than enthusiastic response. No point taking a shine to Sheri if she was gung-ho about Nicholas now.

Roxie's brow furrowed. "If you now find her attractive, why aren't you pursuing her?"

Greg shrugged. "It's too late now. She's got her heart set on this hot shot lawyer now. Heck, the guy defends doctors in lawsuits, and she practically drooled when she saw his picture. I can't compete with that."

"Maybe not." Roxie snipped off a couple of errant hairs then checked her work with a critical eye. "I suppose it's for the best since you've got your big date with Vanessa tonight." She grinned impishly. "Now that you've let me have at you, you're no longer homely as a hyena yourself. But then, I get lots of practice turning some surprisingly homely celebrities into hunks."

He chuckled. "Gee, thanks. I appreciate the comparison."

"Anytime." She handed him a mirror to inspect the back of his head. "What do you think?"

Greg gave the mirror a cursory inspection. "It looks fine."

"Fine? She put her hands on her hips. "It looks great, you ninny! I am the Great and Powerful Foxy Roxie, and don't you forget it."

He pretended to bow in her presence with an outstretched arm. "Is that obsequious enough, or do you need me to prostrate myself on the floor?"

Laughing, she ripped off his plastic cape and patted him on the shoulder. "Go charm the pants off this dream girl of yours. But if things don't work out, don't blame me, because I've got you looking hot."

"Let's hope Vanessa thinks so, too." He glanced at his watch and jumped from the chair. "Yikes! It's already six-thirty, and I'm supposed to meet her at the coffee house in thirty minutes."

"Well, then. Skedaddle!" She waved her hand toward the door

"Thanks, Roxie. Wish me luck."

*"Friendship is constant,*
*save in the office and affairs of love."*
~William Shakespeare~
*Much Ado about Nothing*

# Chapter 18

Greg would wring Sheri's neck if he knew she was spying on his date with Vanessa, but as his dating mentor, Sheri told herself she was merely fulfilling her obligation to monitor how their evening progressed. She shushed her inner critic who scolded, "Have you degenerated into a sneaky, low-down stalker?"

*"So, sue me,"* she hissed back at her conscience.

She disguised her hair by cramming it into a cowboy hat she'd borrowed from Tess, and she covered her eyes with large, mirrored sunglasses. She rimmed her mouth in bright red lipstick—a color she never wore—and tugged on Tess's cowboy boots and too-tight skinny jeans. No way would Greg recognize her in this getup, but just in case, she planned to sit somewhere behind him and camouflage her eavesdropping with an open newspaper.

At a quarter to seven, she ordered a venti skinny latte and escaped to the women's bathroom. She peaked out every five minutes, and sure enough, at five minutes before seven, Greg wandered in and grabbed a seat by the window. She stealthily slithered to a table behind him and opened her newspaper. She could tell he was nervous—his knee thumped like a bass drummer, and his fingers drummed the table as though typing a letter. Every couple of minutes he eyed his watch, glanced out the window, and cracked his knuckles. Seven o'clock. Five after seven. Ten after. Quarter after. The longer he waited, the more frenetically he thumped, drummed, and cracked.

Poor Greg. Had his heartthrob stood him up? He would be devastated.

Finally, at twenty minutes after seven, Greg pulled out his phone and called Vanessa. Sheri overheard, "Okay, I understand, Vanessa. I'll see you in fifteen minutes."

Back to the frenetic thumping and typing.

Sheri couldn't help but smile. Vanessa had at least one flaw—tardiness—and that would drive Greg bonkers if they ever became an item. In the four-plus months Sheri had known him, Greg had never been late. Not once—not even by two minutes. She tried to suppress a smirk as she envisioned Mr. Punctuality stuck waiting thirty minutes every time he went on a date with Vanessa. Hey, she tried to warn him beautiful women were high-maintenance.

At seven fifty, Vanessa breezed in and apologized for her tardiness. Greg's cheery reply revealed all was forgiven.

Sheri clenched her teeth and shook her head in disgust. *Gorgeous women get away with everything.*

Vanessa touched his arm and gazed up at him with huge cornflower blue, heavily mascaraed eyes. Sheri could tell from Greg's nervous laugh that he was utterly bewitched by the woman.

Even more striking in real life than in her photo, Vanessa's perfectly manicured nails, sexy legs, and long, thick, blond hair styled with soft curls would captivate any man. But the real draw? Her bust. She wore a snug-fitting blue top that accentuated her eyes and displayed just enough cleavage to entice a man without looking trashy.

Sheri forced herself to relax her mouth before the green-eyed monster gave her permanent lockjaw. Or TMJ.

She hunkered down behind her newspaper, so she could shamelessly eavesdrop.

*Maybe she'll be painfully shy like Theresa...*

But no, unlike Theresa, Vanessa launched into easy conversation about how much she loved her job as a nurse practitioner at the oncology clinic. She then expounded on her family, and even the décor in her living room.

*Okay, definitely not shy.*

In fact, Greg had offered little more than encouraging nods.

Vanessa confessed to one vice — shopping. "It's not as bad as it sounds, though. I try to shop at sales, and with one of my credit cards, I save ten cents a gallon on gas."

Of course, the save-ten-cents-per-gallon-of-gas claim spoke Greg's love language, and he complimented her on her excellent financial sense.

Give me a break! He would have a stroke if he knew how much money Vanessa squandered for that Louis Vuitton purse and Gucci heels.

After she recounted a marginally humorous story, Greg laughed as though Vanessa deserved her own comedy hour.

*She isn't that funny.*

Peeking over the top of her newspaper, Sheri witnessed Vanessa touching Greg's arm with her perfectly manicured fingers. Sheri's insides twisted. She couldn't grow inch-long nails like Vanessa and still practice medicine. What patient would subject herself to a pelvic exam performed by a doctor with inch-long claws? Plus, how could she play the piano with nails clicking on the keys?

Meanwhile, Greg's tone of voice — the few times he managed to get a word in edgewise — revealed a man besot. Mesmerized. Completely bamboozled.

Sheri, however, was completely bored by the woman. On and on she prattled — Nashville needs sidewalks, blueberries provide anti-oxidants, her church choir sang the most awesome rendition of Amazing Grace last Sunday, she loves vacationing on the beach, and wasn't it awful about that recent school shooting? Had Greg read the latest John Grisham thriller?

With such skills at filibustering, perhaps Vanessa should run for the U.S. Senate. On a positive note — Greg would have no need for his 401K dissertation tonight.

After eavesdropping for an hour, Sheri couldn't stop yawning.

When Vanessa finally stood up to leave, Greg jumped to his feet and eagerly asked her out for dinner the next night. And if that wouldn't work, he could do Saturday night. Or Sunday after church. Or Sunday evening. Or Monday lunch—whenever Vanessa could make time for him.

*How pathetic — he's groveling! Show some pride, Greg!*

As Greg and Venessa left the restaurant, Sheri swallowed her last sip of latte. A wave of despair overtook her. Greg was bewitched by Vanessa, and yet Nicholas Carr hadn't responded to Sheri's email, and probably never would.

She refused to torture herself any further by watching Greg fall in love with Vanessa. She slunk out of the restaurant, her shoulders sagging. No matter how hard she tried, prettier and flirtier women—like Vanessa—would snag up all the decent men and leave her with the old geezers, unemployed country music wannabes… and magicians.

*Well, forget it! I'll remain single before I'll settle for a moocher like Jeremy.* She repeated her new mantra—I *am not a Moocher Magnet.*

Vanessa had reeled in Greg like a Mississippi catfish—in one hour flat. Greg claimed he'd never give up his friendship with Sheri, but if Vanessa ever felt threatened by their relationship, Greg would ditch Sheri in two seconds flat.

She pulled into the parking lot of the nearest grocery store and trudged to the ice cream freezer to purchase French Silk ice cream—her first indulgence in four months.

*Why not? What do I have to show for all my effort?*

A wardrobe full of over-priced clothes and a lousy detangler attachment, that's what. No boyfriend, no husband, not even a guy willing to buy her a measly cup of coffee.

Roxie claimed she was attractive now, but if she was, why didn't men fawn over her the way Greg went gaga for Vanessa? Greg said she was pretty now, but he said it with the same detached tone one would use when selecting a paint color for the guest bedroom. "Yes, this sage green will complement the new curtains nicely, don't you think?"

She stomped into the house and slammed her borrowed cowboy hat and sunglasses onto her bed. She tugged off the way-too-tight cowboy boots and flung them against the closet door. She peeled off her skinny jeans and changed into baggy sweats and a tattered oversized sweatshirt.

*Why not? Nobody cares what I look like.*

She snatched a cereal bowl from the cupboard and loaded it with French Silk ice cream. She pulled a spoon from the utensil drawer and ignored the imaginary angel on her shoulder shouting, "Don't do it! Don't do it!"

"Oh, shut up!" she snapped at her irksome conscience. "I'm having a pity party, and you're not invited."

She crammed the remaining carton of ice cream into her overstuffed freezer and slammed the door. She plodded into the living room and was about to spoon in a luscious mouthful when she heard car tires crunching over the gravel of her driveway.

*Go away! I'm not in the mood for company.*

*"The mind of guilt is full of scorpions."*
~William Shakespeare~
*Macbeth*

# Chapter 19

Sheri whipped open the kitchen curtains and prayed it wasn't her mother. Eying Greg's familiar MINI Cooper, she hung her head in shame.

Even worse—Greg. Had he come to gloat?

*Buzz off! I'm not in the mood to hear about your precious Vanessa.*

She yanked the curtains shut, sputtering about uninvited guests.

She glanced down at her huge bowl of ice cream, and a bolt of panic zapped through her. Greg would be so disappointed in her if he saw such gluttony. She ran into the kitchen and tried to jam the bowl into the freezer. Try as she might, the evidence would not fit, no matter how much she rearranged the frozen broccoli and green beans.

The doorbell rang. Frantic to rid herself of her incriminating bowl, she yanked out three bags of frozen broccoli and tossed them into the refrigerator. She crammed her bowl of ice cream into the freezer and ran for the door. She glanced down at her dumpy sweats and sweatshirt and groaned. She was dressed like the winner of a bag lady competition, and right after Greg had spent an hour in the presence of a blond goddess.

Too late now. Since the house was lit up, and her car was parked in the driveway, she couldn't pretend she wasn't home or had gone to bed. She released a frustrated sigh.

*Might as well get it over with. He isn't attracted to me anyway, so what difference does it make?*

She could answer the door wearing an army tent for all Greg would notice.

She unlocked the door, and there stood Greg, glowing like a lightning bug at midnight. The happiness radiating from his eyes sent her heart fluttering.

Greg pulled her in for an impulsive hug and then danced a silly victory dance. "She likes me! She likes me! She agreed to go out for dinner Saturday night. Can you believe it?"

Sheri tried to force herself to be excited. At least one of them would find love. Hadn't that been their game plan all along?

She forced herself to sound excited for him. "That's great, Greg. I told you things would go smoothly tonight."

He gripped her shoulders and squeezed, his face radiant. "You would have been so proud of me. I didn't say a single word about retirement accounts or tax loopholes — not one."

*You didn't get a chance to — you barely got a word in edgewise.*

Greg's smile exuded such unabashed joy she impulsively pulled him in for another hug. "You've worked hard for this, and now you've got the woman of your dreams."

He shrugged, but the grin plastered across his face revealed hope. "Well, I haven't got her *yet*, but it's a start."

"It beats being labeled certifiably crazy, right?"

"Vanessa is even prettier in real life than in her picture. I don't think I took my eyes off her the whole time."

*Trust me, you didn't.*

"She's the most beautiful creature I've ever seen." He gripped Sheri's upper arms and squeezed again. "Can you believe she agreed to a second date?"

"She's lucky to have you."

After she invited him into the living room, they sat on the couch, his knee thumping with excitement. "I'm so pumped. I bet I won't sleep a wink tonight."

Hamlet jumped onto Sheri's lap and batted her arm with his paw — his signal that he wanted to be stroked. As she patted her demanding kitty, she inquired innocently, "What's she like?"

In the midst of his mesmerized stupor, Sheri wondered if he'd noticed Vanessa never quit talking.

Face aglow, he said, "She's so friendly. What a wonderful change to go out with a woman who helps carry the conversation."

*Helps? Try a verbal coup d'état!*

"So, she talks a lot?" She avoided eye contact as she scratched under Hamlet's neck.

"Truthfully, she did most of the talking. But she's not a snob or a dimwit, and I'll take super friendly over shy any day."

Sheri nodded and said nothing. Greg rose from his chair and wandered toward the kitchen. "I'm thirsty, so I'm going to grab some ice water."

As he reached the kitchen, her heart suddenly lurched.

*No! Don't open the freezer door!*

She jumped off the couch, knocking Hamlet to the floor. She raced toward the kitchen, but before she could stop him, Greg opened the freezer door to pull out an ice cube tray, and there, staring him in the face like an incriminating stash of enriched uranium, sat her huge bowl of French Silk ice cream.

Greg stared at the contraband and then turned toward Sheri with widened eyes. Sheri hung her head.

*You are so busted!*

Her face flamed in shame, and she wanted to crawl into the bowl of ice cream and hide behind a chunk of chocolate.

"Sheri? Have you been cheating on our diet?" he inquired gently. Surprisingly, his tone didn't sound accusatory, just concerned.

She lowered her eyes and mumbled, "I was about to have a pity party when you drove up."

He shut the freezer door and pulled her into a hug. "Nicholas still hasn't contacted you, has he? I'm sorry." He rubbed soothing circles on her back. "If he's passed up a great woman like you, he's an idiot."

She released a sigh of relief. Greg understood her moment of weakness and didn't judge her. Instead of scolding her, he seemed to understand how a bowl of French Silk ice cream might soothe a damaged ego. Somehow his care and concern unleashed an emotional levy. She burst into tears. "I'll never find anybody."

He hugged her again and then wrapped an arm around her shoulders. "Just because things with Nicholas didn't work out, doesn't mean there's not some other great guy out there."

*There is — you. But you don't want me.*

The depressing thought brought on a fresh wave of water works. Embarrassed, she pulled away and reached for a tissue. "Sorry, I didn't mean to spoil your special night. You caught me in a weak moment, that's all. I'll be okay—I promise."

She wiped her eyes, blew her nose, and tried to pull herself together. How inconsiderate to fall apart when Greg was so pumped up about his date with Vanessa. Talk about a soggy blanket! She crumpled up her tissue and flung it into the trash. "Thanks, I feel better now."

He tilted her head up and met her gaze. "I wish I had a magic wand and could make Nicholas fall head over heels in love with you." He reached for her hand and squeezed it. "You wait, though—before this year is through, we'll both have found our someone special. With all the time and effort we've devoted to looking like something the cat *didn't* drag in, we deserve it, right?"

"Gee, thanks, Greg. Nice to know my looks now marginally top road kill. I suggest you avoid that line with Vanessa."

He chuckled. "Vanessa? I'll be quoting sonnets to her." He cleared his throat and spoke with dramatic flair, "Shall I compare thee to a summer's day? Thou art more lovely and more temperate."

"How about this one?" Sheri asked. "'Let me not to the marriage of true minds admit impediments. Love is not love which alters, when it, alteration finds, or bends with the remover to remove.'"

Greg kneeled down on one knee and flung an arm over his heart and melodramatically recited the next line of the sonnet. "Oh, no! It is an ever-fixed mark that looks on tempests and is never shaken."

Before she could stop herself, she joined him on the floor with bended knee and outstretched arm. They finished the sonnet with a few glitches then burst into laughter.

"If Vanessa and Nicholas could see us now, they'd both race for the exit ramp," Greg insisted.

Sheri feigned surprise. "What? You don't think *all* their dates recite poetry?"

Greg smirked. "Face it, Sheri. Theresa was right—you and I *are* weird."

She crossed her arms in mock protest. "Speak for yourself!" She raised her nose with a condescending air. "I can't help it if my brain operates on a higher sphere than your common guttersnipe."

"Guttersnipe?" Greg rose from the floor and chuckled. "Now there's a word I don't hear every day." He picked up her copy of *Great Expectations* on the coffee table. "Ah, reading Dickens, I see. That explains the guttersnipe."

She shrugged and offered him a sheepish smile.

After a pause he added, "Well, I won't keep you. I just wanted to share my good news."

She walked him to the door. "Thanks for coming. Vanessa's a lucky woman."

He grinned. "Now all I have to do is convince *her* of that." He suddenly turned back around. "Wait a minute! Hand over that contraband."

Her eyes bulged. "My ice cream?"

He nodded and feigned a stern expression. "Give it up, Morris!"

"My French Silk?" she eked out in a squeaky voice. She pasted on her most pathetic pout. "You know it's my favorite."

"Precisely." He touched her nose. "Which is exactly why I'm taking it away. A depressed woman and a carton of chunky chocolate ice cream make a deadly duo."

He followed her back to the kitchen, and she reluctantly opened the freezer door and handed over the carton.

"Meanie," she hissed.

"The bowl," he added, with a hand-it-over gesture.

She snapped her fingers as though disappointed he'd remembered it. "Hope you're happy, spoilsport." She slammed the bowl into his hands with undue force. "I was looking forward to my pity party tonight."

He pulled a package of frozen halibut from the freezer and plunked it on her palm. "Here — if you're hungry, eat this."

She eviscerated him with a scowl. "Just what a depressed woman *doesn't* crave — more fish! So help me, I've eaten enough fish these last four months to sprout fins."

He chuckled. "I know what you mean." He reached for a spoon to scoop the ice cream from the bowl back into the carton, and then stopped himself. "Tell you what. Let's celebrate my successful date with Vanessa. You and I will *split* this bowl of ice cream. We can walk a couple extra miles tomorrow to burn it off. Deal?"

She grinned. "Deal!"

While Greg stuffed the ice cream carton and fish back into the freezer, she retrieved an extra spoon, and they sat at the kitchen table. Salivating over her first bite of ice cream in four months, she said, "Let's savor every bite."

Ten minutes later, after oohing and ahhing over each delectable nibble, Greg declared, "I'd forgotten how delicious French Silk ice cream can be."

"Definitely beats celery sticks."

He rinsed the bowl in the sink and loaded it into the dishwasher. "Tomorrow, bright and early, we pay for this treat with a six-mile hike."

She groaned. "Ten minutes of taste bud bliss, and thirty extra minutes of grunting and sweating. What a rotten deal!"

He grinned, heading toward the entry hall. "I'm so pumped tonight, I think I could run a marathon."

She rolled her eyes and pushed him good-naturedly toward the door. "Yeah, yeah. Enough with the happy guy routine. You're making me sick."

He chuckled. "Whatever you say, sourpuss."

Greg's cellphone trilled. He tugged it out of his pocket and glanced at the caller ID. His forehead creased. "It's Vanessa." He glanced over at Sheri with a worried look. "I hope she isn't calling to cancel our date, or I'll be grabbing that carton of ice cream."

Sheri gestured toward his phone. "Only one way to find out. Answer it."

He answered the phone and after listening several minutes said, "I thoroughly enjoyed our date, as well."

She offered him a thumbs-up sign. Vanessa hadn't called to wig out on him. In fact, she launched into some kind of long, drawn-out story that left Greg mumbling an occasional, "Uh-huh," and "Oh, really?"

He switched the phone to his other hand and strolled back into the living room and settled into the couch. "I wanted to tell—"

Before he could finish his sentence, Vanessa butt in.

*How rude! Does the woman ever come up for air?*

He flopped onto the couch. "I'll bet!" After another five minutes, he was back to his obligatory, "Uh-huh" and "You don't say." He tried to say something, but after five words was cut off.

She noticed Greg's eyes drooping. He shifted his position on the couch to stay awake. Hamlet, capitalizing on a captive audience, settled onto Greg's lap and began his loud, contented purring. Greg stroked him idly.

After another ten minutes of watching Greg on the couch with a phone glued to his ear, Sheri retired to the bathroom and washed her face, brushed her teeth, and changed into her flannel pajamas.

When she returned to the living room with her dental floss, she found Greg now lying on the couch, his eyes closed, his ankles crossed. Clearly, his enthusiasm for the monolog had dimmed. She knew it was time to take action before Greg went into rigor mortis. She shook his shoulder and pointed at her watch. She then opened and closed her hands in a "Yakity-yak-yak" gesture.

Greg told Vanessa, "Well, it's been great talking with you, Vanessa. I have to go now. See you Saturday night."

After several more minutes of trying to get off the phone, he finally managed to end the call.

He looked shell-shocked. "She's a bit of a talker, isn't she?"

"You think? I've attended slumber parties with six teenaged girls that had fewer words spoken."

When Greg's face fell, a pang of guilt stabbed her. Must she burst his bubble so soon? Hoping to bolster his spirits she offered, "Don't worry — she'll settle down once you get to know each other. There's so much to learn about each other in the beginning, right?"

"That must be it." Greg nodded in agreement.

"So, what did she say?" Sheri sawed dental floss methodically through her teeth.

He squirmed and avoided eye contact. "I'm not really sure."

She stopped flossing to stare at him. "You were on the phone for twenty minutes, and you don't know what she said?"

He chewed his lower lip. "Apparently, there's a fabulous shoe sale at Nieman-Marcus this weekend Fifty percent off."

*Now there's news any red-blooded American male is dying to know.*

Not wanting to burst Greg's enthusiasm, she forced herself to respond, "Good to know. I'll have to check it out."

Greg rose from the couch and strode toward the door. "I really am leaving this time." He gestured toward her floss and grinned. "I wouldn't want to keep you from your dental hygiene, or you might be forced to see Theresa."

She grimaced. "I'd sooner go toothless."

"See you bright and early tomorrow for our six-mile hike."

"Same bat time, same bat station. Coffee in hand." She lifted an imaginary thermos, already dreading the extra two miles she'd agreed to hike to burn off her ice cream splurge. Too late now. She'd committed to it. No doubt she'd be forced to listen to six-mile's worth of glowing endorsement for Vanessa's beauty, charm, and effervescent personality.

*God, grant me patience!*

*"Frailty, thy name is woman."*
~William Shakespeare~
Hamlet

# Chapter 20

Over the course of the next three weeks, Greg and Vanessa dated nearly every night—that is, if listening to non-stop chatter counted as a date. Boy, could Vanessa talk. And talk. And talk. While still enamored by her huge blue eyes and flowing blond tresses, Greg dreaded her phone calls. Did he really need to know her co-worker's favorite color was lavender? Or whether Vanessa ate Special K or Raisin Bran for breakfast that morning?

He finally resorted to speakerphone, so he could put down his cellphone to pay the bills, fold the laundry, and empty the dishwasher while she jabbered. As long as he mumbled, "Uh-huh," every few minutes, she babbled on, not seeking his opinions about anything. In fact, she didn't seem to notice whether he was listening or not.

*A stuffed effigy would suffice.* He tried to stifle the unflattering thought.

While he knew every detail about Vanessa—down to her brand of mouthwash and toilet paper—she had learned almost nothing about him. The one time he'd tried to kiss her goodnight, she couldn't shut her mouth long enough to pucker up.

He was hesitant to tell her the non-stop talking wore him out. God had clearly wired all forty-six of her chromosomes to chatter. The real question? Could he stand a lifetime with a motormouth? Would he be reduced to long nights at the office if he felt the need for a taste of peace and quiet?

When he found himself getting annoyed with her, however, he reminded himself of his depressing days with no girlfriend—the lonely years after Jodi ditched him. Truthfully, it still flummoxed him—and flattered him—that a woman as gorgeous as Vanessa gave him the time of day. Everywhere he went, men turned to stare at her. His ego — smashed to smithereens by Jodi — was beginning to recover. Plus, wouldn't chattiness rank low on a list of vices? It wasn't like she kicked kittens or stole money out of the church offering plate. In fact, except for chronic tardiness and constant jabbering, Vanessa epitomized womanly perfection. He *should* be thrilled.

Vanessa was already tossing out hints about a future together — how many children she wanted, what part of Nashville they should live in, which church to attend, and even what color bridesmaid dresses she dreamed of — a buttery lemon. It appeared all she needed was an engagement ring. And yes, she even knew the size and shape of the diamond she wanted.

Despite years of desperately wanting a wife, the more interested she became in him, the more Greg wanted to hop on a plane for Bora Bora — *alone* — and never return.

He hadn't shared his jumbled thoughts with Sheri, as it seemed traitorous to Vanessa. As his girlfriend, Vanessa deserved loyalty, not bad-mouthing. Besides, Sheri was still sulking about Nicholas not calling. Greg complaining about his beautiful new girlfriend would equate to eating French Silk ice cream in front of a Biggest Loser contender. Plus…

*What if the problem isn't Vanessa? What if the problem is me?*

He'd lived his whole life as a bachelor. He was accustomed to peace and quiet. And didn't a lot of men complain their wives talked too much?

Did Vanessa babble when she was nervous in the same way Greg launched into financial planning dissertations? She might simmer down once she felt more comfortable with him — once she'd said everything there was to say. Oh, what a joyous thought!

Maybe a candlelight fondue dinner for two would help her discover another use for those succulent lips of hers besides babbling. If she were half as good at kissing as she was at talking, he'd be a lucky man — a lucky man indeed.

*"This above all: To thine own self be true."*
~William Shakespeare~
*Hamlet*

# Chapter 21

Sheri spooned French Silk ice cream into her mouth, but the guilt of cheating on her diet ruined the delight she would normally experience from the luscious treat. She had gained back five of the thirty pounds she'd lost yet couldn't motivate herself to stop.

*Don't sabotage yourself. So what if Nicholas hasn't called? So what if Greg has a girlfriend? That's no reason to undo all the progress you've made.*

She spooned another bite into her mouth.

Why not eat ice cream? She wasn't pretty enough to entice Greg, and Nicholas wasn't interested in her either. Ice cream was the only sensual pleasure she would ever know.

*All my efforts have amounted to nothing more than a maxed-out credit card.*

"Find joy where you can," her devilish inner voice crooned. "And that's ice cream."

"No!" With a sudden burst of self-control, she plunged the bowl, still mostly full of ice cream, into the kitchen sink and covered it with hot water.

*I will not sabotage myself. I deserve better.*

Just because Greg and Nicholas didn't want her, didn't mean she should let herself go. From now on, she would eat healthy and look good for her, and her alone.

*I deserve to be healthy and confident. I deserve to feel good about myself. I am not doing this just to get a guy.*

She offered up a prayer seeking self-acceptance and inner peace and reminded herself of a quote she'd read once on Facebook: "Contentment is not getting what you want but appreciating what you already have." Or something like that.

Still sorely tempted to dish up another scoop of ice cream, she reminded herself of a diet tip she'd read in a magazine — distract yourself from your cravings by doing something active — preferably outside. She glanced out the kitchen window and eyed crabgrass overtaking the begonia bed. She would weed the flowers — that would get her out of the kitchen.

She changed into her rattiest jeans and a stained sweatshirt, pulled on some garden gloves, and tackled the crabgrass with a vengeance. Somehow stabbing at the irksome pests with a trowel dissipated some of her frustration.

After she watered her wilted begonias and tidied up the bed with fresh mulch, she admired her work. Weeding definitely beat gobbling down four hundred calories of ice cream.

She tugged off her gloves, washed her hands, and settled into her computer chair. Against all reason, she still checked the website daily to see if Nicholas would leave a message.

Besides, maybe some other perfect man had joined while she was weeding.

With renewed resolve, she scrolled down the array of men. When she came to Jeremy the Jerk still seeking a "supportive helpmate", she nearly bee-lined back to the freezer. She scrolled through all the men in her age group, but neither Nicholas nor Prince Charming had emailed her while she was out gardening. She signed off with a frustrated sigh.

The doorbell jolted her from her doldrums. Startled, she opened the door to find Roxie with a surprisingly sober expression.

"Is this a good time for me to come visit?"

"Sure." Sheri gestured toward the living room couch.

Roxie plopped onto the couch and with no attempt at pleasantries, she blurted, "Are you gonna let Greg fall for that megaphone-in-stilettos without so much as a fight?"

"I beg your pardon?" Sheri stammered, shocked by the blunt question.

Roxie crossed her arms. "Oh, come on! I can tell you're sweet on Greg, and if I have to listen to that blabbermouth, Vanessa, at another family gathering, so help me, I'll hang myself with a hair dryer cord."

Sheri couldn't help but smile. *Roxie doesn't like Vanessa.*

But unfortunately, Greg did, and *he* was the one who mattered. In fact, the man seemed more than smitten — he practically glowed on their hikes when he talked about how pretty Vanessa was.

"How I feel makes no difference," Sheri reminded Roxie. "Like my favorite Bonnie Raitt song says, 'I can't make him love me, if he don't.'" She raised her hands in defeat.

Roxie waved a dismissive hand. "Oh, fiddlesticks! What he needs is some competition to make him realize how much he'd miss you if you found somebody else. Threaten him with the prospect of losing you."

Sheri snorted. "I don't think he'd feel the slightest bit threatened."

"That's because he's overconfident he can have you anytime he wants — that he can drool over Vanessa but still chum around with you." Her lips tightened, and she shook her head in disapproval. "He takes you for granted, and it isn't right."

"But in our original deal, we agreed to keep our relationship strictly platonic. We're supposed to mentor each other to fall in love with somebody else."

"Oh, pooh!" Roxie waved her off. "Rules are meant to be broken. Now we need to take drastic action before he marries that chatterbox. We need to make him jealous."

Sheri shifted in her chair. "How do I make him jealous? Men aren't exactly beating my door down to date me."

Roxie grinned devilishly. "Funny you should ask. Come to my salon right now, because I've got a client you need to meet."

"Now?" Sheri glanced down at her filthy jeans and ratty sweatshirt. "I can't go anywhere looking like this."

Roxie eyed the dirt-smeared garden duds then pointed to Sheri's bedroom. "Go throw on some clean clothes and come on."

"I'm not fit to meet the trash man, let alone a prospective boyfriend. One whiff and he'll head for the hills."

"What you look like won't matter."

*How could it not matter...unless?*

"Is he blind?"

Roxie rolled her eyes. "Of course, he's not blind! And FYI? Caleb is gorgeous."

"If he's gorgeous and he's not blind, why won't it matter what *I* look like?"

Roxie let out an exasperated sigh. "Enough with the pesky questions. Just trust me."

"But—"

"No buts." Roxie grabbed Sheri's hand and pulled her off the couch. She pointed toward the bedroom. "Change your clothes and meet me at the salon in fifteen minutes. We need to threaten Greg and make him jealous before he gets the harebrained idea to propose to Madam Jabbermouth."

Sheri feared *Roxie* was the one with the harebrained idea, but before she had time to protest, Roxie pushed her in the direction of the bedroom. "Mark my words. Someday, you'll thank me for this."

Before Sheri could protest further, Roxie was gone.

*"God made him, and therefore let him pass for a man."*
~William Shakespeare~
*Merchant of Venice*

# Chapter 22

Sheri pushed open the door to Roxie's salon and froze at the sight of the drop-dead gorgeous man leaning against the counter laughing with Roxie. He sported a sleek haircut that reminded her of a young Tom Cruise in *Top Gun*. Piercing ice-blue eyes, a toned physique, and a smile so perfect it must have cost his parents a fortune in orthodontia completed his "stud muffin" credentials. Sheri had to hand it to Roxie—Mr. Sophistication *could* make any man jealous—maybe even Greg.

Except…he looked younger than Sheri—by at least five years. Maybe even ten. Would Greg believe this handsome—and younger—man would give her the time of day? Doubtful. Sheri's faith in Roxie's cockeyed scheme plummeted like the 1929 stock market. Embarrassment flooded over her as she glanced down at her dullsville khaki pants and Tennessee Titans T-shirt.

*Why would such a handsome man want to squander five seconds with me? He could have his pick of the litter.*

Roxie rushed forward and gave her a warm hug, then Mr. Dreamy extended his hand with a smile. "Hi, I'm Caleb."

After they shook hands, Roxie gestured for Sheri to sit, and she offered her a diet soda. Once Sheri popped the tab and swallowed a swig, Roxie launched into her game plan. "Here's the deal. Caleb works as a model and actor. His agent thinks he has a good chance of landing the lead role as a trauma surgeon in a new medical drama that will air on NBC."

"Wow! That's great," Sheri said, impressed. "But how does this involve me?"

Roxie and Caleb made eye contact. "There's one teeny, tiny, problem," Roxie said, measuring an inch with her thumb and index finger. "Caleb can't handle anything medical. Needles, blood, odors, you name it."

"Just *talking* about gross stuff makes me woozy and weak. Sometimes I even faint."

*Okay. Not good.* "That could pose a problem if you're playing the role of a surgeon."

"You got that right." Caleb shook his head in disgust. "It's so embarrassing. I've been this way since I was a kid. I had to be hospitalized after a major car accident, and all those needles and smells and IV's traumatized me." He smirked. "Pretty funny that I'm now trying to land the role of a trauma surgeon, isn't it?"

"It *is* ironic. I'm still confused how you think I can help."

Caleb and Roxie made eye contact again and smiled.

*What are they scheming?*

"Since his audition is a month away, we were hoping maybe *you* could slowly build up Caleb's tolerance to gross stuff," Roxie explained. "Desensitize him so he doesn't pass out on the set."

Sheri chewed her bottom lip. "Do a progressive immersion program, in other words?"

"That's exactly what I need," Caleb said, pointing at her. "I asked Roxie if she knew anyone who could work with me intensively over the next four weeks until I can handle a surgeon role without passing out. Landing this job will launch my career, but not if I faint in every episode."

Turning to Sheri, Roxie said, "This will benefit you, too, Sheri. You can show Greg pictures of you and Caleb together. Tell Greg you and Caleb are 'seeing a lot of each other.'" She made quotation marks with her fingers. "Just leave out the minor detail of *why* you're seeing a lot of each other. If you repeatedly toss out Caleb's name and photos, Greg will turn greener than the Grinch." She raised upturned hands. "It's a win-win proposition. Caleb lands the role of a lifetime, and you make Greg so jealous he ditches Madam Motormouth and comes running to you." Roxie grinned as though she'd discovered the cure for Ebola virus. "What can I say? I'm a genius."

Sheri turned toward Caleb to gauge his reaction to the preposterous scheme. Was he comfortable feigning he was Sheri's boyfriend?

He gripped her hand, his eyes pleading. "I know it's a lot to ask, but I'm desperate. If posing as your boyfriend in a few photos can benefit you in some way, I'm all in."

Sheri stared at him skeptically, trying to think of a tactful way to bow out of this half-baked scheme. Something in her gut told her she would end up regretting it, but Caleb's pleading eyes made saying no impossible.

She pursed her lips in thought. If Greg only saw *pictures* of Caleb—and never actually *met* him—it might work. Caleb *was* incredibly good-looking. Besides, wasn't helping a struggling actor land the role of a lifetime the charitable thing to do? Who knows? He might become famous!

The stakes were high. If Greg found out she'd willingly deceived him, he might never trust her again—let alone speak to her. And who could blame him? It was a rotten thing to do. But if she did nothing, she would lose him forever to Chatty Cathy.

*All's fair in love and war, right?*

Convinced, she squelched her conscience and nodded. "Sure, why not? I'd be happy to help you, Caleb."

"Wonderful!" He gripped her hand and flashed a grateful smile. "I am so relieved. You have no idea!" He invited Sheri to join him for coffee so they could plot out their strategy to build up his tolerance for all things medical.

Before they left for the coffeehouse, Roxie snapped photos with Caleb's arm wrapped around Sheri's shoulders. Sheri emailed the pics to Greg, but he made no response except to agree Caleb was indeed handsome. He even congratulated her on finding such a good-looking guy! Hardly the green-eyed monster gnashing his teeth in a fit of jealousy that Roxie had promised.

While sipping coffee, they brainstormed a progressive exposure program to extinguish Caleb from his vasovagal reaction to the sight and smell of blood, pus, and needles.

First, she would merely *talk* about gross cases, but with no actual pictures. When he passed that test, she'd expose him to YouTube videos of various procedures. Then, she'd see if her dermatologist friend, Dana, would allow Caleb to join her in some mole and skin cancer appointments. That shouldn't be too gooey or gross, but it would expose him to actual scalpels.

Next, Sheri would bring him into her office when Mack Clements, a patient with a perpetually infected diabetic foot ulcer, came in for his weekly debridement, if Mack was okay with an observer in the room. Since he was totally non-compliant to her outlined treatment program and had no-showed for his last appointment, the foot would likely be dripping with pus. If anything would trigger Caleb, the pungent reek of *Pseudomonas aeruginosa* ought to do the trick. It even made her noxious at times.

For his final test, Sheri would ask a surgical intern, Allison Smith, who she'd befriended at her Tennessee Women in Medicine group, to let Caleb scrub up and observe a couple of surgeries from a distance. Perhaps he could also join her on post-op afternoon rounds. Of course, the patients would all have to give their consent for him to be in the room, but in Sheri's experience, most patients were fine with observers when asked. If Caleb reached the point he could handle observing surgery, he'd be ready for his audition.

Pleased with their methodically planned desensitization program, they decided to jump right in. They ordered a platter of veggies and hummus at a restaurant next door.

"I will describe, in detail, what it's like to drain an abscess, but you will only be looking at hummus, not actual pus."

Caleb cracked his knuckles and stared at her with wide eyes, as though she'd suggested he separate Siamese twins.

She scooped up a golf ball-sized blob of hummus and placed it on her plate. "Pretend this is an abscess." She picked up her knife and stabbed into the creamy chick pea pseudo abscess. "Now pretend I have lanced the abscess with a scalpel. Next, I'm going to extract out all the pus." She glanced up to see how he was handling her fake abscess incision and drainage so far.

His face was whiter than his dinner plate.

"Caleb? Are you okay?"

*Thunk!* His entire torso collapsed onto the table.

*O-kay! Perhaps too ambitious for a first lesson. Yeesh! It was only hummus.*

She reached forward, grabbed his wrist, and felt for a pulse. Forty. Yup—classic vasovagal attack with its slow pulse and clammy, cold hands. How to perk him up... Hmm.

Sheri glanced around then grabbed her glass of ice water and threw it in Caleb's face.

Jarred by the ice water, he jerked into a sitting position. "Hey! Why'd you do that?"

"Adrenaline. You needed it to trigger a fight or flight response. Ice reverses the parasympathetic release of the vagus nerve by triggering an adrenergic response."

He stared at her as though she'd spoken Hungarian. "What?"

*Oh, forget it.* No point repeating her Biology 101 answer. Caleb was an actor, not a medical student. She would simplify. "Ice water was a handy antidote for your spell."

He grabbed his napkin and wiped the dripping water from his face. "Isn't there a less... frigid way to reverse it?"

"Yes, but I didn't have a loaded gun handy."

He pulled back in his chair as though he'd just discovered he was dining with a serial killer. "Look, I'll admit shooting me would put me out of my misery, but surely you aren't serious."

126

She laughed. "I wouldn't *shoot* you, silly. Any loud sudden noise will trigger adrenaline, and that can often startle someone out of a vasovagal attack.

Eyeing the worry lines etched across his brow, she added, "Relax! I was kidding about the gun. Next time, I'll keep ammonia pellets handy."

"Ah, smelling salts!" His face lit up and he pointed at her. "Now we're talking." His shoulders slumped and he released a discouraged sigh. "This wasn't a very promising first lesson, was it? If I can't even handle hummus, how will I ever handle an OR scene with a gunshot wound squirting blood everywhere?"

She reached forward and patted his shoulder. "Baby steps, that's how." Tomorrow night, you'll come to my house, and we'll *repeat* my lecture about draining abscesses. We'll do it every night until you are desensitized. Then we'll move on to the next step. Have faith."

Secretly, Sheri wasn't convinced she *could* cure this guy in under thirty days, but she'd give it her best shot—and *without* a loaded gun!

Caleb glanced at his watch and jumped to his feet. "I'm afraid I have to go. I'm meeting up with some friends for dinner, and I'm already late." He bid her a hasty adieu and bolted for the door.

Over the course of the next two weeks, Sheri re-exposed Caleb to hummus and disgusting medical talk. While he still became ashen, at least didn't faint. She then exposed him to YouTube clips with progressively ickier medical conditions. He handled videos of suturing lacerations and swabbing strep throats without incident.

Last week he managed to remain conscious while watching Dana, her dermatology friend, excising moles and skin cancers.

Tonight's lesson? They would watch a YouTube video of a woman in active labor—*without* the benefit of an epidural, as the woman had insisted on natural childbirth.

Caleb hunkered down on the couch and cracked his knuckles. "Are you sure I'm ready for his?"

"We'll find out soon enough," she responded evasively, mashing on the remote-control button that started the film.

He handled the panting and timed breathing fairly well. While pale-faced, he remained conscious and even asked a couple of questions about what was going on.

*So far, so good.*

Unfortunately, the baby's head must have moved until it mashed on the mother's pudendal nerve because all of a sudden, she started screaming with the blood-curdling shrieks of a woman in unadulterated agony. Between howls of pain she hissed at her husband, "This is all your fault, you no good son-of-a-*****."

*Yowser! Let me rethink my desire to have a baby. Adoption, anyone?*

Sheri clicked off the video and glanced over at Caleb to see if it was too much for him. He gripped the arms of his chair as though it were a roller coaster whipping down a steep incline. "No, keep going. We've only got one more week to work together, so I've got to push myself to work through this."

She resumed the video, and Caleb practiced the relaxation breathing exercises Sheri had taught him to do—ironically, the same Lamaze breathing technique the pregnant woman was attempting during her horrendous contractions! Suddenly, the woman's water broke, and fluid squirted everywhere, soaking her hospital gown, bed, and the poor delivery nurse posed between her legs about to measure how far dilated she was.

*Thunk!*

Caleb collapsed unconscious falling sideways on the couch. Sheri pulled out her smelling salts and wafted it under his nose. No luck. She rushed to the kitchen and returned with a bag of frozen peas and flopped it down the neck of his polo shirt.

*Let's hope this works, or I may have to buy a gun, after all!*

Thankfully, the ice did its magic, and he stirred enough to sit up. After swallowing a glass of ice water, he perked up enough to stand without shaking.

"Let's call it a night," he said dejectedly, looking as drained as the poor woman who'd endured a nightmarish childbirth. They never did get to see if she'd delivered a boy or a girl.

Sheri better cure Caleb of this particular phobia before he married, as any future wife would *not* appreciate him passing out during childbirth when *she* was the one enduring all the pain.

Today's lesson? Mack Clement's infected foot ulcer. The gregarious but obese diabetic was delighted to let Caleb sit in on his doctor appointment. "Just think? I could be meeting a future television star," he enthused.

Caleb sat rigid as a tombstone next to Mack's exam table. Sheri first scrubbed Mack's foot ulcer with Betadine three times. She then scrubbed her hands with Hibiclens and donned sterile gloves.

Using a disposable scalpel, she trimmed off the necrotic debris and whittled down the unhealthy fibrinous and purulent tissue until she uncovered the healthy granulation tissue below. To keep Caleb engaged, she kept up a running dialogue about what she was doing and why. While paler than the pus oozing from Mack's ulcer, Caleb at least remained vertical—a good thing since the medical assistant student, who was *supposed* to be diligently standing ready with ammonia pellets and ice watching for any signs of a vasovagal fainting spell, was, in fact, ogling Caleb like an Elvis-obsessed groupie.

Sheri was proud of Caleb. Even the noxious reek of *Pseudomonas* had not unglued him.

After packing and wrapping the foot, Sheri admonished Mack yet again to quit walking on the foot and to use the crutches she'd provided him two months ago. Oh, and quit eating all those Little

Debbie cakes! Even with three diabetic medications and 200 units of insulin a day, his sugars were atrocious.

Sheri pulled off her gloves and stashed them in the red contaminated waste disposal container. She scribbled out a script for Cipro and told Mack to take it twice a day.

After she and Caleb exited the room, she high-fived him with a grin. "You did it! You're now officially ready for your final exam—watching Allison Smith in the OR."

Caleb ran a relieved hand across his brow and grinned. "I can't believe I made it through anything as disgusting as that nasty foot debridement without fainting."

Mack Clements hobbled out of the exam room and stopped long enough to request, "Can I have an autograph—just in case you hit the bigtime?"

Caleb offered Mack a movie star smile. Sheri rustled up a piece of paper, and Caleb scribbled his signature with a flourish.

After Sheri confirmed the day Caleb would shadow Allison, Caleb said, "I would love to celebrate today's victory by treating you to dinner at a really nice place. You've been so helpful that it's the least I can do. Plus, I want you to meet the love of my life, Morgan. We've been together for two years now."

*Caleb had a girlfriend!* She smirked. *What Greg doesn't know won't hurt him.* Besides, Caleb would be leaving town in a week for his audition, anyhow. She'd just tell Greg that Caleb had moved to LA for his acting career, so their relationship was over. In the meantime, she'd enjoy throwing it in Greg's face that she had a dinner date at a pricy restaurant with a gorgeous actor.

She turned to Caleb. "I'd love to. When are you free?"

Caleb promised to make reservations for Friday night and let Sheri know where and when to meet him.

Sheri made sure to mention her upcoming date the next day on her hike with Greg. He insisted he wanted to meet this Caleb and give his seal of approval. "The guy sounds too good to be true. I want to make sure he isn't some con artist trying to pull one over on you."

Sheri bit the insides of her cheek to keep from smirking. If Greg only knew... Caleb was a con artist trying to pull one over on *Greg*!

She trumped up excuses to prevent the two men from meeting for fear Caleb would accidentally mention his long-term girlfriend, Morgan, or that Sheri was nothing to Caleb than a free desensitization therapist.

Her conscience goaded her for deceiving Greg, but she had plunged in too far to back out now. Since Caleb would fly off to California for his audition next week, the relationship would be over soon, anyhow.

The more she tried to blow Greg off, however, the more insistent he became. "Sheri, you *need* someone with objective eyes to check this guy out. You're too smitten to be rational. It sounds like it's becoming serious, if he's taking you to such an expensive place."

Okay, maybe Greg *was* becoming a tad jealous—she could only hope.

*"Expectation is the root of all heartache."*
~William Shakespeare~
*All's Well that Ends Well*

# Chapter 23

Sheri carted her fold-up lawn chair to the edge of the T-ball field and opened it next to her mother and Tess. Linda had roped Sheri into attending Jacob's final T-ball game for the year by serving up a hefty bowl of guilt pudding. "He's your only nephew, and he and Tess came to your birthday party."

While Sheri adored little Jacob, she *wouldn't* adore spending time with her mother and Tess at pipsqueak T-ball. Who enjoyed roasting in the sun for an hour to watch kids strike out? Each time Jacob came up to bat, the three women jumped up and cheered, "You can do it, Jacob!" Then he'd strike out, and they'd yell, "Good try. You'll get it next time."

*Or not.*

Noting the absence of Jacob's father, Sheri asked, "Where's Colton?"

Tess averted her eyes. Through clenched teeth she mumbled, "He's watching the Tennessee-Georgia game." The sharp edge to her voice suggested they'd had a fight about him missing his son's final game.

Sheri glared at her mother.

*Aunts are required to bake in the sun as a display of family loyalty, but fathers can lounge in an air-conditioned man cave watching football?*

Linda shrugged. "His loss."

Sheri reminded herself she had only come to support Jacob.

Toward the end of the game, however, Linda couldn't stop herself from interrogating Sheri about the progress—or lack thereof—in her search for a husband. "What happened to that handsome man you said liked you the day I brought lunch to your office? The one who took you out for a steak dinner."

"Things didn't work out," Sheri replied evasively. She quickly zeroed in on her smartphone to avoid eye contact with her mother. Yes, a Facebook posting of a cat tormenting a Great Dane couldn't be missed.

Like a Great Dane with a treasured bone, however, Linda refused to let it go. Hands gripping the arms of her lawn chair, she demanded, "What do you mean it didn't work out? What happened?"

Sheri shrugged and focused on her Facebook postings again—this time a parrot pestering a cat.

Using all techniques except Chinese water torture, Linda wore Sheri down and dragged out the truth about Greg and Caleb. Linda peered over the top of her eyeglasses. "If Greg is in love with Vanessa, and Caleb has a girlfriend and is moving to California soon, how does spending time with either of these men land you a husband?"

She had no answer, of course, because it *wouldn't* land her a husband. She swallowed a swig of her Diet Coke to buy time to dredge up a response. She then feigned watching Jacob's game—which had degenerated into a cacophony of whiny children poking each other with sticks as they stood in line waiting for their turn to bat. One little boy was picking dandelions in the outfield, oblivious to the ball rolling straight past him.

"I don't get it," Tess said, leaning forward in her lawn chair. "You've lost all this weight, fixed your hair, purchased stylish clothes, and you *still* can't snag up a guy who isn't taken or a complete nerd? What's the deal? Have you turned them off with your gross medical stories?"

Linda gripped Sheri's wrist with the force of handcuffs. "Please tell me you haven't mentioned that story about the oozing bedsore on your dates."

"Of course not!" Sheri yanked her arm back. Not on a *date*, but she may have mentioned it to Greg on a hike… and to Caleb, as a part of his desensitization program, but still, what did they take her for?

"You aren't babbling Shakespeare quotes at them, are you?" Linda persisted. "Men aren't into that hoity-toity stuff."

Tess snorted. "Women either. Shakespeare's a bore." She formed her hands into a pillow and feigned snoring.

*Is this a family outing or a verbal execution?*

Sheri counted to ten, so she wouldn't say something ugly.

"The only person I talk Shakespeare with is Greg, and that's because he was a British literature major." She glared at her mother and sister and crossed her arms. "Greg happens to love Shakespeare."

Tess rolled her eyes. "No surprise there. You two are peas in a pod — both nerdy and dull."

Linda swatted Tess's arm. "Theresa Morris Anderson! You apologize this minute! That was mean and uncalled for."

Tess mumbled, "Sorry," but her petulant tone suggested otherwise.

Linda wagged a scolding finger at Sheri. "No more fooling around! I gifted you with that dating website so you could find a husband. Quit wasting time with men who are already spoken for. We're aiming for a Christmas wedding, so you've only got three more months."

*Dream on, Ma. Try three decades.*

She glanced at her watch. Ten more minutes before the Family Inquisition Tribunal — disguised as a T-ball game — ended.

Ten lo-oong minutes.

*"Oh, what a tangled web we weave,*
*when first we practice to deceive."*
~Sir Walter Scott~

# Chapter 24

Sheri stood at the hostess desk of the swank restaurant Caleb had selected for their victory dinner and scanned the restaurant for Caleb and his girlfriend, Morgan. At first glance, she saw no couples. Then her eyes did a doubletake. There, nestled cozily together at a corner table, holding hands and with their knees touching, sat Caleb, not with his *girl*friend, Morgan, but with his *boy*friend, Morgan.

Sheri gripped the hostess station and stared, her mouth ajar.

*O-kay. Did not expect this.*

Since she'd had no idea Caleb was gay, she'd wrongly assumed Morgan, the significant other he had mentioned wanting her to meet, was a woman.

*My bad. Morgan is a unisex name.* She sucked in a deep breath to mentally regroup. *Thank God Greg isn't here! Wouldn't he love to rub it in my face that my new boyfriend has a boyfriend.*

Recovering quickly from her shock, she strolled to the table with a smile on her face and a hand outstretched toward Morgan. "Hi, I'm Sheri."

While Caleb was a hunky, muscular leading man type, Morgan was a tad chubby, and Sheri couldn't help but notice his slightly effeminate hand gesture when she shook his hand. His friendly smile and affable chuckle immediately put her at ease, however.

She took a seat, and Caleb handed her a menu. "The Oyster Rockefellers are to die for. Morgan and I order it every time we come here."

Morgan raised a conspiratorial hand to his mouth and whispered, "We hear oysters are a fabulous aphrodisiac." He winked at Caleb.

*O-kay!* Sheri nodded politely but said nothing.

*Oysters? Barf! I'd sooner eat cow dung. Thank God I won't have to eat the disgusting little buggers!*

After the waiter filled their glasses and placed the order for the oysters, Sheri happened to glance around the restaurant. She nearly dropped her water glass when there, waiting at the hostess desk, stood none other than Greg and Vanessa! She instinctively ducked behind her menu, leaned toward Caleb, and whispered, "Greg just walked in with his girlfriend."

He sucked in a breath, his eyes wide. "The guy you're trying to make jealous with my pictures?" he whispered back.

"Yes. And he thinks you adore me." She hunkered further behind her menu, practically crawling under the table.

*Why had she told Greg where they were eating tonight? Please, God, don't let Greg see me.*

Despite Sheri's best effort to stay hidden, Greg immediately recognized Caleb from the umpteen photos she'd flaunted over the last three weeks. He dashed straight to Sheri's table with a smile on his face and introduced himself and Vanessa to Caleb. He then turned quizzically toward Morgan. Sheri held her breath fearing Morgan would announce he was Caleb's boyfriend, as he hadn't heard Sheri's whispered comments to Caleb.

*"Please God, don't let Morgan expose me,"* she prayed, choosing to ignore the irony of beseeching the Almighty to aid and abet her attempt to deceive Greg.

She seared Caleb with a *don't-you-dare-let-me-down* look. He smiled reassuringly.

Ever the consummate actor, Caleb stood, puffed out his chest, and pretended to eye Greg competitively. He stuck out his hand and shook Greg's firmly. "So, you're the lucky guy who walks with my Sheri every morning. Thanks for keeping my girl so sexy and toned." He then reached for Sheri's hand and kissed it, his eyes adoring.

Greg's mouth dropped and Vanessa's eyes widened.

Meanwhile, Morgan crossed his arms, a scowl on his face.

Sheri's breath caught. Swell! Clearly Caleb had only told Morgan about Sheri's role in desensitizing him, and not *Caleb's* role as Sheri's make-believe boyfriend. Morgan *said* nothing, but his sour expression made it clear he didn't appreciate Caleb's flattering comments and romantic gestures toward Sheri.

"So, who is this?" Greg asked, gesturing toward Morgan.

Caleb thumped his forehead. "Forgive my poor manners. I want you to meet my, uh, my agent, Morgan."

Morgan's back straightened and he scowled. "I'm not your agent. I'm your—"

Caleb butt in and patted Morgan's shoulder patronizingly. "Now, now. Don't be modest, Morgan. You've done so much to advance my career. I'm so lucky to have you as *my agent.*" He lasered Morgan with a play-along-with-it glare.

Morgan stared back at Caleb with a deer-in-the-headlights expression. Thankfully, he said nothing further.

Vanessa saved the day by changing the subject. "Greg tells me you have a big audition coming up for a role in a major medical drama. You must be thrilled."

Caleb grinned. "Thrilled, excited, nervous. It's the leading role for a trauma surgeon in a Los Angeles ER. I'm terrified I'll blow my big chance."

"I'm sure you'll do great," Vanessa said.

The waiter neared the table with the platter of Oyster Rockefeller. Seeing the two standing guests he asked, "Do we have more guests joining the table?"

"No!" Sheri shouted, before realizing how rude she sounded.

Five sets of eyes turned and stared at her, shocked by her unfriendly outburst.

She scratched the back of her neck nervously. "Uh, what I mean is, uh, tonight is Greg and Vanessa's date night. I'm sure they'll want their privacy in such a romantic restaurant."

She hoped Greg would take the hint and find a different table. Better yet? Find a different restaurant on the other side of Nashville. Or Memphis.

Of course, Greg, who had been itching to check out Caleb for three weeks now, would hear none of it. "No, I've been wanting to meet you. That's why Vanessa and I came here tonight."

Sheri inwardly groaned. *Of course, you did.*

Offering a friendly smile, Vanessa heartily concurred and touched Sheri's shoulder. "Greg mentions you so often I'm dying for us to become friends."

*Of course, you are.*

There was no polite way out of this debacle, short of feigning cardiac arrest — or a grand mal seizure. Since she lacked Morgan's acting talent, she'd just have to wing it and hope for the best.

She eyed Caleb and Morgan. Could they possibly keep their relationship hidden for an entire evening if Caleb hadn't *told* his partner he was supposed to be acting as Sheri's boyfriend? This evening had disaster written all over it. Sheri's intestines churned, but what could she say when everyone but her seemed thrilled with the arrangement?

As Greg and Vanessa took their seats, Caleb suggested, "Let's celebrate together with a nice bottle of wine."

Even the waiter seemed delighted to have two additional patrons at the table. No doubt he envisioned a larger tip. He promised to notify the hostess of the change in seating.

"Have you guys eaten here before? What's good?" Greg asked, glancing up from his menu.

Caleb gestured toward his platter of oysters. "I always order Oysters Rockefeller as an appetizer." Parroting what Morgan had said earlier, he said, "I hear they're an aphrodisiac." He winked at Sheri.

She nearly spat out her ice water. Meanwhile Caleb was ogling her as though they shared some dirty little secret.

*What must Greg think?*

She glanced with dread in his direction. Greg visibly pulled back and stared at Sheri with his mouth dropped. Right now, she wished she could crawl into an oyster shell and slam the lid. Apparently, Morgan also wished she would crawl into an oyster shell and slam the lid, as he looked ready to shove a fishing pole down Caleb's gullet.

Greg made no comment except, "I'm not much of an oyster guy. Too chewy for my taste. I'll probably just order my usual salmon and broccoli."

As the others deliberated on their entrée choices, Caleb debated with the waiter on the best white wine to complement his oysters. His mastery of fine wines exuded sophistication.

Once the wine order was placed, Caleb rubbed his hands together in glee and grinned at Sheri. "Let's dig into our oysters, shall we, honey?" He then placed two of the oysters on her plate.

She offered up an Oscar-worthy performance not to gag at the sight. Why couldn't Caleb have ordered crab cakes? And why had he made it sound as though they ate the nasty little bottom dwellers as some kind of kinky foreplay? Now she'd be forced to eat one and pretend she liked it. She took her time cutting the oyster into pieces. *Maybe no one will notice if I don't actually eat one.*

After they placed their entrée orders with the waiter, Vanessa launched into a story about the gorgeous outfit one of her coworker's had worn today. The scarf was a lovely hunter green, and it complimented her black suede boots and pencil skirt. Sheri tuned out somewhere between the silver hoop earrings and bracelet.

Caleb, however, remained at full attention to every fashion detail and even inquired if the co-worker's boots were Dolce Gabbana or Gucci. Greg stared at him wide-eyed.

*How does he know so much about women's shoes?*

Then horror flooded her. Would Caleb's fashion savvy be a red flag to Greg? Hopefully not, since Caleb worded as a model and actor.

She kicked Caleb under the table. "Caleb, I need some coffee—right now. *Strong* and black." She hoped he'd take the hint to man up and knock it off with the fashion talk.

"Sure thing, babe." He squeezed her hand then flagged their waiter and ordered coffee. "As strong as you can make it," he insisted.

She glanced serendipitously at Greg to see if he had figured out Caleb and Morgan's relationship yet.

Greg glanced at his watch and commented, "You sure you want to drink strong coffee at eight o'clock at night? Won't it keep you up all night?"

Before she could answer, Caleb gripped her hand between his. "A little caffeine to energize our night won't be a bad thing, will it, babe?" He wiggled his eyebrows suggestively.

*Shoot me now!*

She felt her cheeks flame with embarrassment.

Caleb massaged the back of her hand seductively with his thumbs. "I want my kitten wide awake and fully engaged tonight."

*Shoot Caleb while you're at it.*

One look at Greg's narrowed lips and crossed arms, and she knew exactly what he was thinking. Instead of making Greg jealous, Caleb made Sheri look like a floozy. She and Caleb had been dating less than three weeks, and Caleb implied they'd be doing the naughty all night. She hung her head in shame.

*Why did I ever agree to Roxie's diabolical scheme? It serves me right for willfully trying to deceive Greg. Oh, what a tangled web we weave...*

She wiped her sweaty palms on her skirt. While riddled with guilt over her deception, she didn't want to confess in front of Vanessa. She somehow had to salvage her reputation before it was too late. "It's not what it sounds like, Greg. We're watching, uh, *War and Peace* tonight, so I'll need all the caffeine I can get to stay awake until the end of the movie."

"*War and Peace?*" Greg's forehead creased in disbelief. "What brought on your hankering for the Russian revolution?"

"*War and Peace?*" Morgan protested. "That's the first I've heard of it. Couldn't you pick a better flick than that?"

"Ah, I uh…" Caught off-guard she couldn't dig up a plausible explanation. She feigned a coughing spell and grabbed her glass of water.

Why, oh why, had she picked *War and Peace*? Talk about a mind-numbing bore—she'd sooner tour a nuclear dump. And apparently, so would Morgan!

She glanced over at Greg to gauge his reaction. He knew her well enough to know hours of tedious battle scenes on Russian soil were about as palatable as Morgan and Caleb's platter of Oysters Rockefeller. Just as she suspected, Greg stared across the table at her with a skeptical expression. Her hand shook as a wave of panic shot through her. She lowered her water glass to the table before she sloshed it everywhere.

*Think! Think!*

Thank God—the waiter chose that exact moment to bring out their salads and breadsticks, thus relieving Sheri of the need to trump up an explanation. She immediately commented on the savory smell of the garlic and reached for a breadstick.

She sighed in relief when Vanessa piped in with another tale about her fashion-challenged boss, thus diverting the conversation away from the Russian Revolution.

Five minutes into Vanessa's story, Sheri covered a yawn with her napkin. Caleb, however, nodded encouragingly and seemed fully engaged. She hoped Greg attributed his avid attention to politeness or his theatrical bent.

Sheri forced herself to swallow a swig of the strong, bitter coffee without grimacing. Yuck! It was potent enough to invigorate the entire Russian army. Any more of the vile stuff and she'd be able to stay awake through *Crime and Punishment,* too. Why had she chosen strong coffee as her unspoken signal to Caleb to "man up" and quit with the fashion talk? Yuck!

"You haven't eaten your oyster," Morgan said, gesturing toward Sheri's plate. "I thought you two adored them." His eyes narrowed with a "Touché" glint.

*Wicked, wicked man!* After one look at the slimy oyster, Sheri's stomach roiled, and she wanted to lace his salad with rat poison.

Everyone turned and watched her as though daring her to eat one. *I could wring his neck. Now I'll have to eat one and pretend I like it.*

Caleb forked an oyster and exclaimed, "I love oysters. Don't you?" He stuffed the entire thing into his mouth and began to chew and moan in ecstasy. "Delicious! Come on, honey, eat one," he coaxed, patting her hand.

She sliced off the teeniest morsel, popped it into her mouth, and swallowed it whole. Disgusting! To get the attention off her no doubt grimacing expression, she said, "You know, oysters have always reminded me of little gall bladders. I mean, their squishy but rubbery texture is identical to that of a freshly excised surgical specimen."

Caleb's eyes widened, his face turned white, and he spat out his oyster into his napkin as though it were a freshly excised surgical specimen. He suddenly slumped forward in his chair like a ragdoll holding on to the table as though struggling to remain conscious.

Oh, no! A vasovagal attack, and she hadn't brought any ammonia pellets with her. Curses! Apparently, Caleb hadn't passed his final exam on handling gross medical talk, after all.

When Caleb slumped forward like a ragdoll, Morgan jumped to his feet and ran to Caleb's side. "Is he okay? He looks like he's going to—"

Before the word "faint" could exit Morgan's mouth, Caleb flopped onto the table, his face nearly missing his salad bowl.

"Oh my gosh!" Morgan cried. He gripped Caleb's hand and squeezed. "Hang in there. I'm right here, honey. I won't leave you,

I promise." He turned to Sheri and hissed, "You're a doctor, do something!"

Without thinking, Sheri picked up her glass of ice water and flung it in Caleb's face. As expected, the adrenaline surge jolted him from his spell.

"Will you quit with the ice water?" Caleb snarled, though still slumped on the table. "It's really getting old!" O-kay! The ice water may had aroused him from unconsciousness, but it sure hadn't improved his mood.

Greg's brow furrowed. "Wait. This has happened *before*?"

Before Sheri could trump up a plausible explanation, Morgan piped in. "Yes. Didn't you know? Sheri's been tutoring Morgan in hopes he can overcome his aversion to medical stuff before his big audition next week."

Greg turned to Sheri with a crocodile smirk plastered across his face. "Oh, really! Sheri *didn't* tell me that." He eyed Caleb still sprawled like a bag of IV fluid on the table. "Looks like the lessons aren't going very well."

Caleb rose slowly into a sitting position, still looking glassy-eyed and pale. "No, actually, they're going great. This was just a minor setback."

"You're really auditioning for the role of a trauma surgeon?" Vanessa asked, her tone suggesting serious reservations.

"Yes." As though trying to get the attention off his embarrassing spell, Caleb picked up the platter of remaining oysters. "Have another oyster while they're still warm, Sheri." Before she could protest, he scooped three more onto her plate. He circled the plate to the others at the table. "Anyone else want a gall bladder?" He offered Sheri a good-natured wink.

Sheri's stomach twisted into a cramp. She eyed the oysters, and a wave of nausea coursed through her.

Sheri noticed Greg staring at Caleb with suspicious eyes, as though trying to piece together his schizophrenic personality changes. One minute, Caleb seemed a committed, adoring boyfriend to Sheri, and in the next, another man was calling him "honey" and holding his hand as though they were lovers. Plus, Greg now knew the real reason she was meeting up with Caleb. She could almost see the wheels turning in Greg's head.

*How can I possibly face him tomorrow? Maybe I should hop on the next plane out of Nashville — preferably one flying to Borneo.*

Unable to look anyone in the eyes, Sheri picked at the spinach and breadcrumb stuffing that surrounded the oysters on her plate. Her stomach nosedived like a Kamikaze B2 bomber.

She forced herself to slice off a tiny piece of oyster and pop it into her mouth. *Chew, gag, swallow, choke, repeat.* This oyster tasted even worse than her last one had — almost spoiled. *A gall bladder would taste better than this.* After two more revolting bites, when no one was looking, she stealthily dropped her remaining two oysters onto the floor next to her chair.

*Where is Hamlet when I need him?*

The waiter brought out their entrees, and everyone focused on their meal and wine while Vanessa droned on with a third non-story — something about her recent trip to the mall and the amazing bargains on handbags she'd found.

*What does Greg see in this woman?* Could he honestly stand to live with a conversation hog for the rest of his life?

She glanced over to see Vanessa touching Caleb's arm as she babbled on as though they were the only two people at the table. Was Vanessa flirting with Caleb? Sheri could understand why. It must thrill her to the tips of her overpriced stilettos to find a gorgeous man with a knowledge of fashion. After a lengthy discussion about name brand footwear, they burst into laughter when they both came up with the name Prada at the same moment. Sheri hesitantly met Greg's eyes across the table and offered only a shrug at his bewildered look.

She kicked Caleb under the table, and taking the hint, he informed Greg, "The only reason I know so much about women's fashion is because I once dated a model. She drove me crazy with all her talk about shoes and clothes, but I learned a lot by osmosis." He reached over and squeezed Sheri's hand. "That's why I'm dating a sensible, down-to-earth girl like Sheri now."

Morgan glared at her, arms crossed, lips thin.

Greg grinned. "She's down-to-earth, alright. Did she tell you her story about that foul-smelling abscess that ruptured and squirted pus in her face?" Greg winked at Sheri good-humoredly.

Yes, she *had* shared that story with Caleb, but for a very good reason! It was part of his therapy.

Caleb nodded. "Right over a plate of hummus and crackers. Talk about revolting!" Caleb made a gagging gesture with his index finger. "That one was right up there with tonight's gallbladder fiasco."

Greg and Caleb laughed conspiratorially then turned to gauge her reaction. Right now, she'd like to squirt putrid pus at both of them for making her look bad in front of Vanessa. She yanked her hand out of Caleb's grasp.

Registering Sheri's acerbic response, Caleb reached for her hand again. "Oh, come on, honey. Don't be a sorehead. We're only teasing you."

"Yeah, we *love* stories about gall bladders and fecal impactions. Especially at the dinner table, right?" Greg elbowed Caleb.

Caleb snickered. "Except when they're so gross I pass out and nearly land my head in my salad."

"Hey, keep dating Sheri and you'll end up with more head concussions than an NFL defensive lineman."

"I'll have to wear a helmet on our dates," Caleb agreed.

As if Caleb and Greg's taunts weren't bad enough, Morgan now felt entitled to hurl his barbs, as well. "Maybe you should enroll her in charm school. They might be able to teach her some table manners."

Greg chuckled. "Nah, I wouldn't waste my money. She'd wind up expelled."

The whole table, with the exception of Vanessa, chortled at her expense.

*Ha, ha, ha, and a barrel of laughs.*

Her face burned with humiliation as another stab of pain and a wave of nausea coursed through her. *Ow!* She instinctively grabbed her belly.

*Am I getting food poisoning, or is it just my nerves?*

It didn't help that Vanessa sat across from her with perfect posture and grace. No wonder Greg didn't want Sheri as his sweetheart. Apparently, real women talked about shoes, purses, and scarves, not bursting abscesses and fecal impactions.

*Face it, you can't compete with a woman like Vanessa. Men want flirty, sweet, and girlie — not nerdy, blunt, and squirty.*

Their taunting reminded her of being back on the playground in fourth grade, shamefaced and crying, while boys circled her yelling, "Four-eyes!" and, "Nerd!" Only this time, Caleb, Greg and Morgan were the schoolyard bullies. Tears filled her eyes at her humiliating memories.

*I'm an adult now, not a defenseless child. I don't have to put up with verbal abuse. I will not allow myself to be bullied.*

She slapped the table and jumped to her feet. "Fine! I get it. I'm sorry I grossed you all out." She turned to Greg. "Maybe we should quit our morning walks — that way, you don't have to listen to any more of my revolting medical stories, if they bother you so much."

Head held high, she planned to strut to the bathroom with what little of her dignity remained — her grand exit. Instead, she slipped on one of the slimy oysters she'd dropped to the floor earlier. Inexperienced with her new high heels, she flipped into the air and landed straight on her back with her legs sprawled out like the Wicked Witch of the East pinned underneath Dorothy's house.

*That's what I get for attempting to look sexy in heels.*

Intense crampy pain gripped her abdomen.

"Are you okay?" Vanessa asked, bending over her with a concerned voice.

"I'm fine," she replied, wishing she would just drop dead.

*Can this night get any worse?*

After Vanessa helped her up, Sheri brushed off her bottom and what was left of her pride. "If you'll excuse me."

Doubled over with belly pain and embarrassment, she bee-lined to the restroom.

With bitter coffee, oysters, wine, and a gigantic portion of bruised ego all churning in her stomach like a washing machine, she barely made it to the commode before she lost the entire contents of her stomach.

*"Must I hold a candle to my shame?"*
~William Shakespeare~
*Merchant of Venice*

# Chapter 25

*I can't face any of them ever again.*

She'd take a cab home, lock the door, bar the windows, and hide under the covers—forever.

Better yet, she would claim she suffered from a gangrenous gallbladder and then describe her revolting symptoms in lurid details—just to spite them.

She heard knocking on the door of her bathroom stall. "Sheri? Are you okay? I heard you vomiting," came the concerned voice of Vanessa.

Sheri suppressed a groan. *Go away! Can't you leave me with even a sliver of dignity?* Not wanting to be rude, she croaked out, "I'm okay."

"Are you pregnant?" Vanessa whispered through the stall door. *Pregnant? That was laughable!*

"Of course, I'm not pregnant!" she snapped before she could suppress her ugly tone. "You have to have sex to get pregnant."

"Oh. I-I'm sorry. I assumed from the comments Caleb made that you two were, you know, intimate."

"Caleb is all bluster and bravado." Sheri wiped her lips with toilet paper and added, "We aren't sexually involved."

"Oh," Vanessa responded with a happy lilt that irritated Sheri. Did Vanessa have plans to go after Caleb? How dare she! Caleb was *her* boyfriend. Well, okay, *pretend* boyfriend, and right now she wanted to wring his neck. But still! And besides, what about poor Greg?

Except after his snarky comments, she was furious with poor Greg. In fact, Vanessa could throw him into a meat grinder for all she cared.

Reality walloped her with a shot of adrenaline. If Vanessa went after Caleb, discovered he was gay, and then shared the news with Greg, he would uncover Sheri's role in Roxie's scheme.

"I'll bet those oysters were spoiled," Vanessa said through the stall door. "You probably got Staph food poisoning."

"No doubt," Sheri agreed, still too weak to stand.

"To be honest, I thought they smelled bad—that's why I didn't eat any."

*All oysters smell bad, so how would I know? And thanks for warning me!*

Sheri gripped the commode, her hands shaking and her head spinning. She couldn't spend all night in the restroom, so she may as well face the firing squad.

*Pick yourself up, hold your head high, and get it over with.*

With wobbly legs, she rose from the floor and clutched the walls of the stall until her lightheadedness passed.

Once her legs quit trembling, she stumbled to the sink and rinsed out her mouth. She glanced into the mirror and wanted to throw-up again—her face looked ashen, and her hair flew in all directions like the tentacles of a deranged sea anemone. Then she noticed a huge wad of vomit right at the bust line of her blouse.

Next to her stood beautiful, concerned Vanessa—without a drop of vomit on her clingy red sheath.

Sheri's eyes brimmed with tears. Men were visually wired, and whether she liked it or not, appearance mattered. Right now, compared to Vanessa, she looked as appealing as that platter of spoiled oysters.

She gripped the sink, a wave of complete exhaustion and defeat overwhelming her.

*I wish I could wake up in bed and find out this whole thing was a nightmare.*

She splashed water on her face to perk herself up then said, "Could you call a cab for me? I want to go home and crawl into bed. I feel too weak to drive."

"There's no need for a cab," Vanessa insisted. "I'm sure Caleb and Morgan will be glad to drive you home." Vanessa draped an arm around Sheri's waist to support her as she edged toward the bathroom door. "I'm sorry the guys picked on you about your medical stories. It wasn't very nice of them. And I'm sorry those awful oysters made you sick."

*If only it were as simple as bad oysters.* She'd take food poisoning any day over tonight's platter of humiliation.

Vanessa offered encouraging words as they inched toward the table where the guys were sitting. "You can do it. You're doing great." Sheri could understand why Vanessa was such a popular nurse. She found herself warming up to Vanessa's genuine concern and encouragement.

As they reached the table, the guys hung their heads like guilty basset hounds caught in the act of rummaging through the trash.

"Sheri, I'm sorry," Greg said. "I only meant to tease you, but I obviously hit a nerve. Please forgive me."

She nodded but couldn't make herself look at him. "It's okay."

Morgan showed far less sensitivity. He eyed her up and down. "What happened in there? You look awful!"

Vanessa glared at him. "Those oysters made her sick."

"It's probably Staphylococcal food poisoning as it's too soon after eating the oysters for *Vibrio parahaemolyticus*," Sheri informed them.

"Come again?" Morgan said with a furrowed brow.

"*Vibrio parahaemolyticus*. It causes projectile vomiting and explosive diarrhea."

"Enough!" Caleb stuck out his hand like a stop sign, his face blanched. "No more gross medical talk, or I'll flatline again."

Greg glared at Caleb and crossed his arms. "*You're* the one who ordered those blasted oysters and insisted Sheri eat them. I know for a fact Sheri *hates* oysters."

*Drat!* He remembered that from when she'd told him on one of their morning hikes. Oysters and liver. Her two aversions. So much for Caleb's aphrodisiac! Barfing over a commode didn't exactly heighten the mood for romance!

Vanessa, sensing the tension, took charge. "Greg, stop it. Bickering won't fix a thing. Now I'm going to ask the valet to retrieve Caleb's car. Sheri is too sick to drive home. Caleb needs to drive Sheri straight home, so she can crawl into bed. She's sick."

Eyes wide, Caleb pointed at Sheri's chest. "Is that puke all over your blouse?" His voice boomed loud enough to inform the cook.

*Why don't you announce it with a megaphone?*

Vanessa ignored Caleb's question and touched Sheri's arm. "Want me to call in some Zofran for the nausea? Give me your car keys and I'll pick it up at the pharmacy and bring it to your house. Greg can meet me at your house and drive me home."

"I hate to put you out," Sheri said, embarrassed at all the fuss. "Maybe I can drive..."

Even though she was woozy and weak, she probably wouldn't drive any worse than half the drivers she'd witnessed on Nashville highways.

Vanessa waved her off. "Absolutely not. It's not safe with you feeling so dizzy. It's no bother at all. I'll pick up some ginger ale, too."

"I'm fine," Sheri insisted, unable to look anyone in the eyes. Not wanting the evening to drag on one second longer than it had to, she said, "Caleb, get your car. I want to go home."

His face blanched. "You won't vomit all over my car, will you? Cause I don't want my car smelling like the day after a frat party." He laughed with a nervous, high-pitched laugh. "Besides, I might pass out again. I don't *do* vomit, remember."

*So much for the hunky trauma surgeon. The guy can't even handle a little vomit after three weeks of intensive therapy? He needs a backbone transplant!*

Greg's lips thinned. "How about showing as much concern for your supposed girlfriend as you do your precious car, Caleb?"

She noticed Greg's hands clenched into fists.

*Dear God, don't let Greg punch Caleb in the face. His audition is less than a week away.*

Morgan came to Caleb's defense. "Hey, he's already passed out once tonight, thanks to Sheri's disgusting, and I might add, completely *inappropriate* dinner conversation. He doesn't need to pass out again. He could bash his head on the dashboard and get into an accident." Morgan wrapped his arm protectively around Caleb's shoulders. "I forbid it. And frankly? The reek of your blouse is making even *me* queasy. I don't blame Caleb for not wanting you in his car."

"Fine," Vanessa snapped, lips thin. "*I'll* drive Sheri home in *her* car."

"No!" Sheri insisted. "If I'm such a piranha. I'll just call an Uber."

Caleb made a "Phew" gesture across his forehead. "Thank you!"

Greg shook his head. "No way!" He gestured toward Sheri. "Look at her. She looks terrible and doesn't need some unknown Uber driver dumping her off on the curb when she's sick like this."

Four sets of eyes simultaneously turned and stared at her vomit-drenched blouse and ashen face.

"Well, *I* can't do it," Caleb whined. He rubbed his neck nervously. "I'm just not the medical type. If Sheri throws up in my car, I'll faint. I know I will."

Greg mumbled to Sheri, "Is this guy for real?"

Vanessa clapped her hands and transitioned from fashion diva into charge nurse again. "People! Here's what we're going to do. Greg, *you* drive Sheri home, since you know where she lives, and you can handle her being sick. Caleb, you and Morgan are free to go. *I'll* drive Sheri's car to the drug store and pick up some ginger ale and Zofran, then I'll meet Greg back at Sheri's house so he can drive me home."

Caleb squeezed Vanessa's arm. "Thank you! You are my goddess divine for sparing me a trip with the vomit queen."

*The vomit queen?*

Sheri would have smacked him — if she'd had the strength.

Morgan had the audacity to add, "I sure hope this isn't contagious. Caleb *cannot* be sick for his audition."

*Thanks for the concern, Morgan.* She could be dying of Bubonic plague, but Morgan and Caleb would be more concerned about his precious car and audition. And after all she'd done for him!

Vanessa pulled a plastic makeup bag from her purse. She dumped her cosmetics into her purse and handed the empty bag to Sheri. "Use this if you feel sick on the drive home," she whispered, patting her on the back. "Take a Zofran as soon as I bring it to you, and sip on ginger ale so you don't get dehydrated." She giggled. "I don't know why I'm telling *you* all this — you're the doctor, for pity's sake."

Sheri thanked Vanessa for her concern. Feeling woozy, shaky, and worn out, she slumped into a chair and rested her head in her arms on the table.

Vanessa turned to Greg. "Give me your valet ticket, and I'll get yours and Sheri's car while you pay our tab." She obtained Sheri's valet ticket, patted her on the back, and cooed, "You rest here. I'll text Greg when his car is out front. Greg, make sure you support Sheri around the waist on the way out. She may get vasovagal and faint."

As Vanessa, Caleb, and Morgan dashed to the entrance of the restaurant to retrieve the cars, Sheri marveled at Vanessa's managerial skills — and her ability to run in four-inch heels. In a crisis, Vanessa became the perfect blend of compassion and authority. No wonder she had worked her way up to the prestigious role of charge nurse.

After several minutes, the waiter wandered over with the bill for the entire table and inquired who would be responsible for it. That's when Sheri realized Caleb and Morgan had taken off without paying for their share, let alone hers. Caleb was supposed to be treating *her* tonight as a thank you for all the hours she'd spent tutoring him! *He'd* been the one to pick a pricy restaurant and order those blasted oysters and an expensive bottle of wine. Now *she'd* be stuck paying the bill? Some thank you gift! She wanted to charge after the two cheapskates and demand they pony up. Except they would no doubt be gone by now. And she might pass out on the way to the entrance.

She forced herself to sit up enough to retrieve her wallet from her purse. As she sputtered under her breath about Caleb and Morgan, Greg touched her arm. "It's my treat tonight. Call it a peace offering for embarrassing you. I truly am sorry."

She mumbled thank you, her anger ebbing away. Greg hadn't *meant* to be hurtful, and normally, his teasing didn't bother her. In fact, she usually dished it out at him as much as he teased her. She had overreacted. Deep down, Greg was a loyal friend.

*Unlike Caleb.*

The jerk hadn't even bothered to say, "Hope you feel better," or "Thanks for treating me to dinner tonight," or even a cursory, "Goodnight!" The self-centered brat had the depth of a mud puddle.

Greg signed the credit card receipt and handed it back to the waiter. He reached for Sheri's glass of water. "Take a few sips so you don't get dehydrated." She forced herself to swallow several swigs then rested her head back on her arms, still feeling woozy.

After Greg received Vanessa's text that the car was out front, he wrapped his arm around her waist and slowly escorted her to the entrance of the restaurant. He tipped the valet and then assisted her into the car.

As soon as he shut her passenger car door, she slumped against it like a sack of potatoes.

*I feel awful. Is there a coffin handy?*

Greg raced to his side of the car as though sensing her urgency to get home and crawl into bed.

They exited the parking lot, and after several minutes of awkward silence, he inquired, "You warm enough?"

She drummed up enough strength to nod, though the temperature in the car was the least of her concerns right now. She shifted positions to stretch her abdomen, hoping to untangle the den of boa constrictors squeezing her intestines right now.

They rode in silence another five minutes before Greg cleared his throat and asked, "So other than his looks, what did you see in that guy? I've never met anyone so self-absorbed in my life."

She shrugged, too miserable to respond.

"He was a total jerk, if you ask me," Greg added.

*So much for making Greg jealous.*

When she didn't respond, he repeated softly, "What did you see in him, Sheri?"

She couldn't think of a credible response, so she just stared out her passenger window and ignored the question. Finally, she mumbled, "I was flattered someone that handsome was willing to spend time with me."

Greg's posture stiffened and he white-knuckled the steering wheel. "Please tell me you won't go out with him again — not after the abominable way he treated you tonight."

Her hands fisted. "Go out with him again? Never! I hope he chokes on an oyster."

Greg did a double take. "O-kay then!"

"Caleb bolstered my ego. You had Vanessa, and I had no one. I guess I felt left out."

He reached for her hand and squeezed. "There's *somebody* out there who will be perfect for you, Sheri. You just have to be patient. Don't settle for a scalawag like Caleb."

She couldn't help but smile. "Scalawag? I don't think I've heard that term in decades."

"Maybe not, but it suits Caleb perfectly. When it comes to character, Swiss cheese holds more water than he does."

Her fists clenched. "I wanted to punch his lights out. Still do, but I don't have the energy."

Greg chuckled and merged onto the interstate.

He glanced over at her with a smile. "You weren't really going to watch *War and Peace* tonight, were you?"

Sheri couldn't stand lying to Greg. They'd shared everything with each other, so games to make him jealous seemed wrong. Plus, they hadn't worked!

"No, I made that up, so you and Vanessa wouldn't think Caleb and I were sleeping together. Trust me—there's been no hanky panky with Caleb. None. He tossed out all those innuendos because he was intimidated by you."

Greg's eyebrows shot skyward. "The guy might become a movie star, and he's intimidated by *me*?"

She smirked. "Maybe he's jealous because your character is made of cheddar instead of Swiss."

He laughed as he pulled into her driveway. After running around to open her door, he helped her out of the car. "Let's get you inside and curled up in bed while we wait for Vanessa."

Once they reached her bedroom door, Greg said, "Change into some warm flannel pajamas, and toss out your blouse, so I rinse out that spot of vomit before it settles in. Do you have a stain stick?"

"In the laundry room," she mumbled, as she closed her bedroom door and tugged off her clothes.

Once in her pajamas, she handed Greg her blouse, marveling at his willingness to tackle such a nasty job. Since he knew how much the clothes Roxie made them buy cost, he no doubt didn't want the blouse ruined after one wearing. But still...it *was* thoughtful of him.

Sheri used up her last two drops of energy to brush her teeth and wash her face.

*I am so tired.*

Too exhausted to wait for Vanessa's return, she crawled into bed and turned out the light, grateful the intestinal cramps had dissipated somewhat—at least for now.

Hamlet jumped onto her bed, and after circling to find the perfect spot, nestled next to Sheri.

She rubbed his soft fur, and he purred with his soothing kitty motor.

*At least you love me, Hamlet.*

Eyelids heavy, she tugged up the covers to her chin and fell into a deep sleep.

*Maybe tomorrow will be a better day.*

*"The miserable have no other medicine, only hope."*
~William Shakespeare~
*Measure by Measure*

# Chapter 26

Sheri woke up Saturday morning surprisingly healthy—no nausea, stomach churning, or head spinning. After a refreshing hot shower, she changed into jeans and a T-shirt and wandered into the kitchen. Eyeing the bottle of Zofran next to her car keys on the kitchen counter, thanks to Vanessa's run to the pharmacy last night, she opened the bottle and swallowed one down.

*Better safe than sorry.*

She grabbed a can of ginger ale from the frig, opened it, and swallowed a couple of swigs. *Probably best to make sure I can keep fluids down before attempting crackers or toast.*

She settled onto her computer chair with Hamlet curled in her lap and forced herself to gulp down a couple more swallows of ginger ale. After she perused emails, Facebook, and the headline news, she clicked onto the dating website to see if, by some miracle, someone wonderful had joined since yesterday morning.

*That's about as likely as winning the Megabucks lottery when I've never even purchased a ticket.*

She scrolled through the usual moochers, old men, and weirdoes then clicked onto the "You've got mail" section. Her heart lurched when she noticed a new email—from Nicholas! Dreamy, handsome Nicholas! She had a fairy godmother after all.

Over two months had passed since she'd sent him her original email, but he had never responded. She assumed he wasn't interested. Had God answered the depressed monolog-of-a-prayer she'd dumped on heaven's door last night?

*Don't get your hopes up—he may say, "Forget it, lady!"*

Heart pounding, she clicked on his message. She read, reread, and triple read the note and then couldn't stop smiling— or doing a happy dance. With trembling hands, she read his email again:

*I apologize for not responding sooner. I attended a work convention for a week and then took a three-week vacation in Europe. (Prague is spectacular, by the way.) I then came home to a Mt. Everest of paperwork on my desk, so I haven't had time to think about dating until now. (You, as a doctor, no doubt understand what the first several weeks after a vacation are like.) Anyway, I finally climbed my way down from my summit of paperwork, and if you haven't already married someone else, I'd love to meet you at my favorite bakery for some blueberry muffins and coffee. Email me your response, and again, I sincerely apologize for my embarrassing delay.*
*~ Nicholas Carr ~*

Joy bubbled up inside her like a root beer float. He *hadn't* blown her off. He wanted to meet her! Happy, happy day!

She whisked off a friendly response. "Sure, let's get together." Though tempted to write, "Pick a day—any day. Pick a time— anytime," she mustn't appear overeager or worse, desperate. He needed to think she'd forgotten all about him. *Nicholas who? Oh yes, I remember now.*

Truthfully, she'd have cancelled a week of patients and flown to Prague in the baggage compartment along with cages of hissing cats and tumbling luggage, if that's what it took to link up with him. But to Nicholas, she must exude a detached sophistication. Confidence. Savoir-faire. She typed in only two available times that would "fit my busy schedule." He immediately messaged her back that he could meet next Saturday morning.

She pumped her arm skyward then danced around the room with a startled Hamlet...until reality set in and anxiety walloped her. She dropped the cat, and he glared at her indignantly before slinking behind the couch.

She sank onto the couch in dismay. What if she couldn't get her hair to lay flat? What if she became tongue-tied, and then, in her nervousness, dove into some sickening medical story that left him feeling like he'd eaten rotten oysters? What if he took one look at her and trumped up an excuse to leave five minutes later?

Maybe she could get Roxie to style her hair. After her disastrous date with Caleb last night, Roxie owed her — bigtime!

She texted an S-O-S, and Roxie said she'd be delighted to help. Caleb had apparently already informed her about their ruinous evening, so no doubt Roxie felt obligated to make amends.

"Come by the salon at seven that morning with several outfit options, and I'll pick out the most flattering one when I do your hair and make-up."

Sheri reflexively reached for her phone to call Greg and then stopped herself. What was the point? He was dating Vanessa — and that was a real pity. She and Greg fit together like strawberries and whipped cream but continuing to pine after a man who had surrendered his heart to another woman smacked of emotional masochism. Like it or not, she needed to move on. Greg only liked her as a friend, and with the revolting way she'd looked last night (no love sonnets written about that!), he would never be attracted to her. Nicholas offered an enticing alternative.

Besides, after Vanessa demonstrated such compassion last night, how could Sheri, with a clear conscience, steal her boyfriend? Talk about a low-down thank-you gift. Right up there with Caleb wigging out on the restaurant tab.

Truthfully, Sheri no longer had the stomach for underhanded tactics to swipe Greg away from Vanessa — or to lie to Greg anymore. It was just plain wrong. Immoral, even.

The doorbell rang. When Sheri opened the door, there stood Vanessa with a tureen of homemade chicken noodle soup. "I came by to check on you. You seemed so ill last night I had to see for myself that you were feeling better this morning."

*How nice is that?*

Sheri kicked herself for all the despicable things she'd said and thought about Vanessa in the past. She might be a motormouth, but deep inside her beat a kind heart. Sheri invited her in and gestured toward the kitchen.

Vanessa set the soup tureen and crackers on the kitchen counter. "Have you been drinking enough fluids to stay hydrated?"

Sheri lifted her can of ginger ale. "I'm trying to. I also took the nausea medication you picked up for me last night. Thank you so much."

"It was nothing," Vanessa said with a dismissive hand wave.

Sheri pulled a glass from the cabinet. "Let me get you a drink while we chat in the living room." She loaded the glass with ice cubes and poured the fizzy brew over them. The two women settled onto the living room couch, and Sheri reassured Vanessa that she'd recovered nicely from her food poisoning episode. Embarrassed by last night's events, she also quickly informed her that she would not be seeing Caleb again.

"Good riddance." Vanessa crossed her arms, her lips thin. "He acted more concerned about his stupid car than your health. Greg would *never* treat *me* that way."

No, he wouldn't, Sheri agreed.

Vanessa continued, "At first, I thought Caleb was charming, but he sure showed his true colors when you got sick. You deserve better than that self-centered peacock. And what was with his side-kick, Morgan? I mean, who brings another *guy* on a romantic date?"

*Who indeed?*

"Morgan is his, uh, agent, remember? Caleb wanted me to meet him."

Vanessa chewed her lower lip as though hesitant to speak. "I don't mean to burst your bubble, but Greg and I both got the feeling there was more to those two than a client/agent relationship. Morgan called him 'honey' and wrapped his arm around him. It seemed mighty cozy, to us."

*So much for fooling them.* Sheri sipped on her ginger ale, buying time to come up with a response.

"Oh, you know those theater types. They all call each other 'honey', and they're all a demonstrative bunch." Sheri wasn't sure any of this was true, but it *sounded* good.

Vanessa politely commented, "Maybe so."

Hamlet provided a well-timed distraction when he padded out from behind the couch and meowed.

Vanessa's eyes widened. "Wow! That's one big cat! How'd you get him?"

"An elderly patient of mine died of pancreas cancer, and before she died, she made me promise I'd find Hamlet a loving home. Turns out, I got attached to him before I could find him a home, so he's been with me ever since. He's a Maine coon cat."

"What a handsome kitty you are," Vanessa cooed, stroking him. Hamlet jumped on the couch and settled onto her lap. She indulged the greedy kitty with love pats before confessing, "Greg speaks so highly of you I thought maybe the two of us should become better acquainted. To be honest, I've felt a little threatened by you."

*"Beauty is a doubtful good; a gloss, a glass, a flower. Lost, faded, broken, and dead within the hour."*
~William Shakespeare~

# Chapter 27

Sheri nearly choked on her ginger ale.

*Vanessa feels threatened by me? That's laughable.*

She stared at Vanessa mouth agape. "You don't need to feel threatened by me. Greg is completely smitten with you."

Vanessa tilted her head sideways, as though considering Sheri's assertion. "He may be smitten with my *appearance*, but sometimes..." she paused, and glanced down into her lap. "Sometimes I think I bore him. I know I talk a lot — I always have."

Shame coursed through Sheri. Hadn't *she* thought the same thing about Vanessa? Yet Vanessa had called in nausea medication and prepared and delivered a pot of homemade chicken noodle soup. How nice was that!

Vanessa continued. "I mean, if I were homely or even average looking, would Greg give me the time of day?" She set her glass of ginger ale on a coaster and peered over at Sheri waiting for an answer.

"I, I'm sure he would," Sheri stammered, though his reaction to the mustached geologist made her doubt the truth of her words.

Hamlet whisked his tail across Vanessa's face, and she reflexively grabbed his tail and stroked it. "People seem to think pretty women have it made. But truthfully? We're always wondering if a guy likes us for us, or if he's only attracted to us because of our looks." She scratched under Hamlet's chin, and he banged his head against her hand. "What if I become fat when I'm pregnant, or get wrinkly when I'm old? What if I require a bilateral mastectomy due to breast cancer? Will he still love me?"

Sheri stared at Vanessa in shock.

*A woman as gorgeous as Vanessa is just as insecure as I am! Who'd have thunk?* Apparently, beauty was *not* the one-way ticket to happiness she'd always envisioned. How ironic. Sheri felt insecure because she *wasn't* beautiful, and Vanessa felt insecure because she *was!*

"I mean, I know Greg is *physically* attracted to me, but he genuinely *likes* you—your personality and wit. I'm not sure…" She stroked Hamlet as though lost in thought.

"You're not sure…" Sheri gestured for her to continue.

"I'm not sure Greg actually *likes* me."

"Why do you say that?" Sheri asked, though she already knew the answer. Hadn't Greg confessed he sometimes tuned Vanessa out when she prattled on and on? At the restaurant last night, Sheri could tell by Greg's glazed over eyes that he wasn't listening to half of what Vanessa said.

Hamlet arched his back and purred like a freight train, oblivious to their deep discussion.

"When I ask Greg a question about something I've said, he sometimes squirms and mumbles a response that proves he wasn't paying attention."

*So, take the hint and quit talking so much. You're a nice person, but you wear him out with your chatter.*

No way would she *tell* Vanessa this, however. It would devastate her.

"That doesn't mean Greg doesn't love you." She felt like a fraud, but what else could she say? "A lot of men can't stay focused on drawn-out stories about women's clothes."

Sheri covered her mouth with her hand. *Why did I say that?*

Vanessa's eyes widened, and she stared at Sheri. "*You* think I talk too much too, don't you?"

Her cheeks flushed. *Why did I open my big fat mouth?*

She shouldn't lie, and maybe Vanessa *needed* to hear the truth. She took several swigs of ginger ale to buy time and trump up a tactful response. "Maybe you should ask Greg questions. Seek his opinion about things." Vanessa's eyes met hers then lowered in shame. She stroked Hamlet's tail several times, as though processing Sheri's words. "You know, you're the first person who's ever been honest with me. Is that why I can't keep a boyfriend—because I talk too much?"

"I think you talk about things guys aren't interested in." *There—she'd said it!*

Vanessa's eyes pooled with tears. "I don't know if I can change. I've always been a talker, and I love to shop and decorate."

Sheri put a hand on Vanessa's shoulder. "You're a caring, intelligent, beautiful woman, and somewhere out there is a shy guy who will be delighted to have a wife who carries the conversational load. Just make sure you show interest in *him*, too. Ask him questions and listen to his answers."

Vanessa's eyes widened. "You don't think *Greg* is right for me?"

*Okay! Now you've really dug your grave!*

She cleared her throat. *Proceed with caution.* She grabbed her glass of ginger ale and sipped again. When she could delay no longer, she said, "If you want a guy who will listen to every word you say about shopping and fashion, it isn't Greg."

Vanessa scratched behind Hamlet's ears. "But Greg is the best guy I've ever dated. He's thoughtful and handsome and intelligent and… well, stable."

"He's a keeper all right," Sheri agreed.

Vanessa's eyes widened, and she stared at Sheri with sudden understanding. "You're in love with Greg, aren't you?"

"No!" Sheri responded far too quickly. She hoped her flushed cheeks hadn't given her away. "In fact, I just got asked out by this gorgeous attorney named Nicholas. I can't wait to meet him."

Vanessa seemed unconvinced, so Sheri jumped up, grabbed her laptop from her desk, scrolled to Nicholas's picture, and showed it to her. Vanessa stared at the picture then pointed at the computer screen with her manicured index finger. "I've met that guy before. I'm sure of it. For the life of me, I can't place where, though."

165

"He works for a medical malpractice company."

Vanessa shrugged. "I don't know where, but I'm positive I've met him before." She grinned. "He's gorgeous, isn't he?"

Sheri grinned back, her earlier misgivings rapidly fading. Why brood over Greg when she had a date with a smart hunk like Nicholas? "You got that right, and I'm petrified I won't be able to pull myself together enough to attract him." She pointed at Vanessa. "Even in jeans and a T-shirt, you're drop-dead gorgeous. Luckily, Roxie's promised to help me out."

"Why are you worried then? Greg says Roxie is fabulous. I'll bet with her help, Nicholas will propose by Christmas!"

Sheri laughed. "The only way he'd do that is if *you* went in my place." She paused then commented, "It's ironic, isn't it? You're jealous of my personality, and I'm jealous of your looks!"

"The grass is always greener on the other side," they said in unison, pointing at each other and then laughing.

"Maybe if someone stuck us both in a blender, they'd pour out the perfect woman," Sheri said.

Vanessa glanced at her watch and jumped up. "Holy Moley! I'd love to stay and chat, but I need to get to the bank before it closes at noon."

Sheri walked Vanessa to the door. "Thanks so much for the soup. And I enjoyed getting to know you better."

"Me, too." Vanessa gave her a quick hug. "Good luck with your luscious attorney."

*"There is nothing either good or bad
but thinking makes it so."*
~William Shakespeare~
*Hamlet*

# Chapter 28

When the doorbell rang shortly after her lunchtime bowl of chicken noodle soup, Sheri wasn't surprised to find Greg standing on her doorstep.

"Feeling any better?" He handed her a bouquet of daisies. "I'd have brought you some chicken soup, but Vanessa told me she made you some." He smirked. "Which is a good thing, because I don't know the first thing about cooking. Knowing me, I'd undercook the chicken and give you Salmonella."

She feigned gagging. "Thanks, but no thanks! I've had my fill of food poisoning. Surprisingly, I feel much better today."

His eyes probed her face. "You sure seem chipper for someone who was green around the gills only twelve hours ago."

She grinned and gestured him in. "Come sit down, and I'll tell you why."

After Sheri arranged the daisies into a vase and displayed them on the mantle, they settled onto the couch.

"Okay, out with it," Greg insisted. "What's got you grinning like you just won an Academy Award?"

"Guess who invited me out for coffee and muffins."

He shrugged. "George Clooney?"

She swatted his arm. "Don't be a gooney bird. He's married." She grinned and added, "Besides, it's someone even better than George Clooney."

He shrugged. "I can't imagine. Enlighten me."

With arms spread wide she declared, "Nicholas!"

Greg's eyes bulged. "Nicholas? As in handsome attorney Nicholas and not the fat, chimney-crawling guy in a red suit?"

She clapped her hands in glee. "Can you believe it? He emailed me."

Greg crossed his arms and cocked his head. "What took him so long to respond?"

She filled him in on Nicholas's hectic work and vacation schedule. "He's been touring Europe," she tossed out airily with a wave of her hand.

"I'm sure you told him you couldn't possibly nibble muffins with him on a Saturday morning since you're on a diet, and you normally hike around Radnor Lake with me." Greg winked at her.

"Nope. I blew you off without a moment's hesitation."

Greg sniffed and pretended to wipe tears from his eyes. "You'd turn down a hike with me for some legal scoundrel?"

"In a heartbeat."

He chuckled. "Remind me never to call *you* when my ego needs a boost."

"Duly noted. Roxie offered to fix my hair, clothes, and makeup so I look spectacular."

He frowned. "Isn't getting all dolled up for a thirty-minute mug of coffee overkill? Won't he think you're trying too hard?"

"Au contraire. I only have thirty minutes to convince this guy I'm the missing word in his crossword puzzle. The atrium to his ventricle. The radius to his ulna. The . . ." She jumped up from the couch and paced the living room too excited to stay seated...or come up with another analogy.

"The petunia in his onion patch?" Greg offered.

She impaled him with a glare.

"Perhaps by the end of the date, he'll even quote Shakespeare to you." Greg bent down on one knee and with a fling of his arm, he recited from Romeo and Juliet with a dramatic British accent, "This bud of love by summer's ripening breath, may prove a beauteous flower when next we meet."

She rolled her eyes but couldn't help but smile. "I doubt he'll go that far."

Greg crawled back onto the couch. "Maybe not, but it's still fabulous news. Now you'll have no excuse to gluttonize on ice cream." He wagged a finger at her. "Depression makes you grumpy—and weak."

"Must you wax so eloquently about my flaws?" She crossed her arms. "I much prefer your flattering Shakespearean sonnets that compare me to a summer day."

Greg's eyes locked on hers. "Just because a man knows your weaknesses doesn't make him your enemy. It means he knows how to protect your heart and not push your buttons."

She cocked a brow. "Oh, really? Seems to me it means he knows exactly *how* to push my buttons—like you did last night in front of Caleb, Morgan, and Vanessa."

"Which was unconscionable of me. Hence, the apology daisies." He gestured toward the bouquet on the mantle. "I insist on sitting in the booth next to you in that coffeeshop so I can give you my unbiased opinion of him." He frowned and shook his head. "I sure hope he's a step up from Caleb."

When she glared at him, he raised both hands. "I promise not to say or do anything to give myself away."

She chuckled. "You won't fling a scone at me if I start in on a story about gall bladders?"

"Scout's honor." He formed his hand into a boy scout's pledge. "Unless you get to babbling about bunions and toenail fungus. Then I might be induced to drastic action."

She lasered him with a glare and waved her index finger at him. "You better not embarrass me, or I'll take drastic action on you!"

He ignored her threat. "After your date, we can do our usual morning hike, and I'll tell you what I think of him."

She crossed her arms. "News flash! I can size up a potential boyfriend without your help."

He snorted. "Right! Like you did with Caleb? That guy would have traded you in for another platter of Oysters Rockefeller. Plus, I'll bet my entire 401-k the guy is gay."

*So much for pulling one over on Greg.*

She swatted Greg's arm as though offended and said evasively, "Why would he date me if he were gay?"

"To get desensitized from his medical hang-up." Greg smirked. "I wouldn't quit my day job, if I were you. Your career as a desensitization specialist would be short-lived, I fear."

She lasered him with a glare. "Shut up."

He shrugged unapologetically. "It's clear to me Morgan and Caleb are a couple. Every time Caleb made some flattering comment or gesture to you, Morgan looked ready to wallop him."

"Morgan is his agent. Maybe he was just being protective."

Greg snorted. "They're a couple, Sheri. And if Caleb is gay, it won't bode well for a happy marriage with you."

"Well, it's a moot point now." She flicked her hand dismissively. "After they stiffed us with the bill, I never want to see either one of them ever again."

Greg pursed his lips in thought. "I suppose it's good you got sick last night—it gave you a chance to see his true colors before you got your heart broken. Let's hope Nicholas is a marked improvement over Caleb."

She placed her palms dramatically over her heart and gazed heavenward. "He'll be my perfect Romeo."

"Let's hope not, because that story didn't end well, either."

"Alright. He'll be my Prince Charming, then."

"Well, don't run off to Vegas and elope before I get a chance to check him out. Prince Charming may have issues, too."

Hands on her hips she sputtered, "Give me some credit, Greg! Besides, my mother would kill me if I eloped. She's dying to plan a Christmas wedding."

He suddenly smirked but said nothing. When she threatened him with bodily harm if he didn't tell her why he was grinning, he said, "I will laugh so hard if that picture Nicholas posted online is ten years old, and he's now fat, bald, and endowed with the breath of a bulldog with bad teeth."

She glowered at him. "Don't be a spoilsport. He will be wonderful, and it will be love at first sight for both of us."

"Good luck with that one," Greg mumbled. He stared at the floor shaking his head. "I hope your luck with love at first sight holds up better than mine has. Love at first sight and dread at every phone call."

*Trouble in paradise?*

Hamlet jumped onto Greg's lap, circled three times, and then curled into a ball. Greg scratched Hamlet's neck as though deep in thought.

Two days earlier, she'd have flipped back handsprings to hear things weren't working out with Vanessa, but now that she had gotten to know Vanessa's vulnerabilities, her heart sank. Vanessa would be crushed if Greg broke up with her. Greg hadn't mentioned the problems between them were *that* bad, but judging from the dark circles under his eyes, he hadn't been sleeping well lately.

"Are things with Vanessa not working out?" She did her best to sound nonchalant.

Greg frowned and rubbed his chin. "I know it's tacky to badmouth my girlfriend, but Vanessa's incessant talking wears me out. I bet she even talks in her sleep."

"Have you tried being honest with her?"

He stroked the cat several times before responding. "I've prayed about it, and I just don't feel right criticizing her for something like that. I mean, being talkative isn't a sin. It's just a part of who she is. Who am I to tell her she needs to change? Maybe she's just too talkative for *me*. "

"Hmm. I see your point. Plus, it's not realistic to think she *could* change her whole personality."

He nodded. "Exactly. A long-term relationship won't work if you go into it expecting your partner to change who they are at their core. That's why Jodi and I failed. She wanted to go out with friends every night, and I wanted to stay home and relax — just the two of us — but we both wanted the *other* person to change."

"What are you going to do?" Sheri held her breath as she waited for his response.

Greg lifted open palms. "I don't know what to do. On a purely physical level, Vanessa takes my breath away. And she can be so compassionate. You saw how she took care of you last night. Her patients adore her."

Sheri nodded. "She's definitely a star in a medical crisis."

"I mean, who in his right mind would break up with such a beautiful, intelligent, kind woman?"

His thigh began to thump so hard Hamlet gave him a glare and jumped off his lap. "Plus, she seems crazy about me. She's even dropped hints about what kind of *engagement* ring she wants." Another heavy sigh. "I *should* be elated."

"But you aren't." She tried to ignore her pounding heart.

His lips thinned, and he remained silent, as though pondering his answer. Finally, he blurted, "The thought of spending the rest of my life with her makes me want to run into a giant corn maze and never come out."

Sheri's mouth dropped. Good heavens! She had no idea things were that bad. "That doesn't sound normal for a man in love."

"No, it doesn't." He shook his head. "Instead of my feelings growing with time, I'm starting to make up excuses to avoid her."

Ever since Greg started dating Vanessa, Sheri's conversations with him had seemed stilted, and he had changed the subject every time she asked about his relationship with Vanessa. She felt omitted from his life and assumed he now shared all of his deepest thoughts and feelings with Vanessa instead of her. The rejection had compounded her feelings of loneliness. She hadn't realized his silence actually stemmed from unhappiness. Though she ached for Vanessa, she couldn't help feeling relieved that she had her old Greg back — her best friend who shared everything with her.

"I dread every phone call," Greg confessed. "She calls me at work, sometimes three and four times a day. I told her company policy says no personal phone calls during work hours, so now she calls during my lunch break. If I ignore her calls, she sends incessant text messages until I respond."

"Greg, you have to set boundaries with her. Tell her no contact whatsoever—phone *or* text—during work hours, unless it's an emergency. Then ignore her texts. Sooner or later, she'll get the message."

He released a sigh and dropped his head into his hands. "Except it's not just the frequency of her calls. It's what she talks about—how pretty her friend's dress was, some recipe for crock pot pork chops, or some chick flick she watched." He scowled. "What guy gives a rip about stuff like that? It's all girl talk."

"Why don't you interrupt her and ask a question about something *you're* interested in?"

He responded with a half-hearted shrug. "I guess I could give it a try." His tone suggested he didn't think it would work.

He glanced at his watch and his eyebrows shot skyward. "Yikes! I've got a client in thirty minutes. I need to scram."

"And I've got to start mentally preparing myself for the dreaded annual Claiborne family reunion." She mimed choking herself. "My mother's side of the family is Dysfunction Junction, I'm afraid."

Greg laughed. "That bad?"

"I'd rather attend an execution by hanging. My cousins and Aunt Matilda are snobs, and Grandma Claiborne is meaner than a rattlesnake."

He rose from the couch and stretched. "Well, call me if you get desperate. I'll come rescue you."

She walked him to the door and waved goodbye, torn between delight that she had her best friend back and pity for Vanessa.

*"Hell is empty, and all the devils are here."*
~William Shakespeare~
*The Tempest*

# Chapter 29

Sheri trudged past Aunt Matilda and Uncle Bert's ostentatious cherub fountain, bracing herself for pending disaster. Why had she agreed to subject herself yet again to this annual ritual of abuse by her dysfunctional relatives? She knew why, of course. She'd be even more verbally berated by one particularly dysfunctional relative—her mother—if she *refused* to come. Some choice. Her mother's wrath or a family reunion with relatives befitting a Shakespeare comedy…or tragedy.

The cast of characters?

<u>Uncle Bert:</u> A short, bald plumber who lambasted the evils of Western medicine and put his faith in "miracle herbs." Needless to say, Sheri was the usual victim of his impassioned diatribes and pamphlets on unproven herbs.

<u>Aunt Matilda:</u> Frozen-faced from a boatload of Botox, she generally ignored Sheri, choosing instead to focus on Tess, the "pretty sister," as Sheri once overhead her say to Uncle Bert. Perhaps this year Sheri ought to come equipped with a poster board stating: *Brains Matter, Too.* Unfortunately, vain Aunt Matilda wouldn't be able to *read* the message since she refused to wear glasses in public.

<u>Claire and Clarissa:</u> The evil cousins. They never failed to inquire about Sheri's love life, even though they already *knew* her love life rivaled that of the Pope. Sheri usually resorted to vague replies like, "I'm exploring all my options right now," in an attempt to sound trendy—as though she dated any number of eligible bachelors and simply hadn't made up her mind which man to choose. She fooled no one.

These were merely the lead performers in the evening's dreaded family reunion. Then there was Grandma Claiborne...

Sheri had tried to wiggle out of this year's event, but her mother would hear none of it. Ma had dished up a platter of guilt by reminding Sheri, "Grandma Claiborne might be dead before next year's reunion—she's over ninety, you know. Wouldn't you feel terrible if you missed your last chance to see her alive?"

Hardly. The crotchety old bat would outlive them all—through sheer meanness and spite. Bubble, bubble, toil and trouble...

Sheri begrudgingly shuffled past the gaudy water fountain then down a walkway landscaped with enough begonias and zinnias to support a beehive for a year. She clomped up the giant marble steps and rang a doorbell embedded in a massive wrought iron door befitting a king's palace. She offered up a quick prayer— *Please, God, keep me from slitting my wrists or murdering my cousins.*

Since she'd lost weight and fixed her hair, she hoped the Claiborne clan would no longer view her as a shameful mutation in the family gene pool. Greg insisted they would all rave about her new look, but she knew better than to get her hopes up. Perhaps she could slither in unnoticed and stand near her mother all evening for moral support. Surely, they wouldn't throw barbs in front of her mother...

The front door opened, and Uncle Bert looked her up and down and then turned and hollered behind him, "Hey everybody! Come take a look. Sheri isn't fat and frizzy-headed anymore!" As though suddenly recognizing he'd been terribly rude, he smiled at Sheri then turned back and added, "She looks great!"

Sheri internally groaned. *So much for slipping in inconspicuously.*

The entire brood barreled into the entry hall and stared as though she were a monkey scratching its armpits at the zoo.

Clarissa reached forward and fingered Sheri's hair. "Sheri? Wow! I hardly recognized you. Is that a wig?"

*Love you too, Clarissa.*

Suppressing her urge to snap something ugly—or better yet, Clarissa's neck—she told Clarissa about Foxy Roxie's hair salon. Her cousin responded with a bored shrug. Claire piped in, "How'd you lose all your weight? Did you get gastric by-pass?"

*All that weight?* Claire made her sound like a fat lady in the circus. She'd only lost thirty pounds—hardly a candidate for drastic weight loss surgery.

Not to be outdone by her sister, Clarissa inquired, "Now that you've fixed yourself up, do you finally have a boyfriend?"

*Groan.* Tonight was turning out like last year's fiasco—on steroids—and she hadn't even made it out of the entry hall. Perhaps she could escape by claiming she had to attend to a medical emergency—a mental breakdown. Hers!

Sheri's mother dashed to her side beaming. With a hand on Sheri's back, she said, "Sheri is dating a wealthy CPA now, and they're practically engaged. In fact, I'm hoping for a Christmas wedding."

*What? Was her mother delusional?*

Aunt Matilda offered a tight-lipped smile—as much as her Botox allowed. "Really?"

Sheri speared her mother with a look that could wilt every zinnia in Matilda's yard. Linda ignored her and added fuel to the inferno: "Greg fell in love with my Sheri at first sight. I expect he'll propose any day now."

*Love at first sight? He said I looked like a lunatic in an insane asylum.*

Murmurs erupted across the room. *Sheri has a beau?*

The entire Claiborne clan gawked at her— except Tess, who knew what a pile of rubbish her mother had concocted. Sheri wanted to dive into the pretentious fountain out front and swim away.

*Would Tess spill the beans?*

Sheri shot her sister a pleading look that said, "Please, for once, be a supportive younger sister."

Amazingly, Tess piped in, "Greg's great! He's helping Sheri stay in shape. They exercise together every morning."

Sheri rewarded her sister with a grateful smile. Of course, now she'd be indebted to Tess for the next decade, which would boil down to umpteen nights of free babysitting.

Clarissa crossed her arms and demanded, "If he's so smitten with you, why isn't he here tonight?"

Twenty-five heads all turned and stared at Sheri.

*Inquiring minds want to know. If Greg is so smitten with you, why isn't he here?*

Her mind went blank. She wanted to snap, "Because I told him what a bunch of snobs you are!" She suppressed her uncharitable words, but what *could* she say?

Her mother's eyes widened with panic, and her gaze bore into Sheri. Her stomach sunk to the marble-tiled floor. While livid at her mother for putting her in this predicament, Sheri understood what drove her mother to fib. Aunt Matilda—with her Botoxed face, luxurious mansion, and incessant boasts about her beautiful daughters—could trigger George Washington to lie.

Matilda and Linda had competed since childhood, and now they had forced the rivalry to the next generation.

Sheri tucked a strand of hair behind her ear and cleared her throat.

*Think! Think!*

"Actually, Greg *is* coming. He had to meet with one of his famous country music star clients tonight before they left for their world tour tomorrow."

*That ought to impress the snobbish namedroppers!* Better yet? It was only a partial lie. Roxie had told her once that Greg had several country music singers as clients—all referred by Roxie.

Aunt Matilda's eyes bulged. "Really? Which star? Blake Shelton? Keith Urban?"

"Amy Grant and Vince Gill, maybe?" Uncle Bert suggested.

177

"Greg can't tell me because of client confidentiality," Sheri responded smugly.

Good grief! Had she stooped to Aunt Matilda's level and served up a bowl of bragging? A new low, indeed.

"In fact, why don't I go call Greg and find out when he can join us?" Eager to escape the hyenas, she grabbed at the excuse and bolted for the back door.

Once on the terraced patio, Matilda's poodle, Duchess, greeted her with a wet nose. She bent over to stroke the pooch with Tess following close behind. When they were out of hearing range from the clan, Sheri said, "Thanks for not exposing me, Tess."

Tess placed a hand on her shoulder. "Hey, I know what it's like to have your ego smashed to smithereens by Aunt Matilda. Every year she makes me feel like Prunella next to her precious Clarissa and Claire."

Sheri nearly dropped her phone. "*You* feel ugly? You're prettier than the two of them combined! Plus, *you* have a brain."

Tess snorted. "Not according to Mom. She always threw it in my face how much smarter you were. 'Why can't you study more and make the grades your sister does?'" Tess said, mimicking her mother's nagging tone of voice.

Sheri's jaw dropped. "Ma always told me I needed to study *less* and become more like *you*! 'Spend more time on your hair and less with your nose buried in those books, or you'll never get a boyfriend,'" she said, quoting her mother.

The two sisters laughed, and then Tess dropped her gaze and chewed on her bottom lip. "Listen, I don't want to end up like Mom and Aunt Matilda—always competing and badmouthing each other. Do you?"

Amazed at the unexpected display of vulnerability, she stared at her sister in disbelief. "Of course not! We're family. I've always wished you and I could be closer."

"Good." Tess tucked a strand of hair behind her ear. "Look, I'm sorry about the flack I've given you over the years. From now on, let's have each other's backs. Let's be real sisters to each other."

Sheri pulled her sister in for a hug. "Let's do that."

After the hug, Tess pulled back, her eyes misty. "I'll leave you alone, so you call Greg."

Sheri smirked. "He's actually on a date with Vanessa, but he promised to come rescue me, if things got desperate."

Tess giggled and twisted fingers at her mouth. "My lips are sealed."

Sheri texted Greg, "SOS!!! Come rescue me from a lifetime of wearing the cone of shame."

Greg responded with a text agreeing to come. She texted him the address, and he promised to meet her by the fountain in forty minutes — which, with Greg, would mean exactly forty minutes.

She wasn't exactly tied to the railroad tracks with a villain demanding she pay the rent, but she texted back, "My hero!"

*"But screw your courage to the sticking place,*
*and we'll not fail."*
~William Shakespeare~
*Macbeth*

# Chapter 30

As predicted, Greg arrived exactly forty minutes later. Sheri rushed down the front steps and greeted him in the driveway. "You're a life saver." When she glanced back toward the mansion, she noticed her cousins peeking at them through the front drapes. "You need to act like you're smitten with me."

His eyes widened. "Why?"

Sheri then eyed not only her cousins, but now Uncle Bert and Aunt Matilda staring at them from the window.

Without thinking, Sheri grabbed Greg's suit coat and pulled him toward her and yanked his head forward until their lips met. She held the kiss until, from the corner of her eye, she saw the curtains close. She stepped back. "Okay, they're gone."

She felt her cheeks warm. Had she just forced Greg into a kiss? *What must he think? He's got a girlfriend!*

Many a day she'd dreamed about kissing him, but never in this scenario. What a lousy first kiss—under duress and with Greg completely gobsmacked!

Greg gasped and wiped his mouth with the back of his hand. He pulled back with alarm. "What was that all about?"

She felt her cheeks flush. "My mother told everyone you're smitten with me. She claimed it was love at first sight."

His jaw dropped, and he stared at her with a horrified expression. "What? What gave her that idea?"

"Don't look at me like that."

"Well, *we* shouldn't be kissing when I'm still dating Vanessa. It isn't right."

"It wasn't really a kiss. It was an act of desperation, and desperate times call for desperate measures."

He crossed his arms clearly unconvinced. "I never thought of kissing as a desperate measure."

"Trust me, tonight, it was."

Greg rubbed his chin. "I suppose if I only thought of it as acting a role in a play, it wouldn't really be cheating on Vanessa." He glanced up at her and cracked his knuckles. "You remember I majored in accounting and British literature, not theater, right?"

She smirked. "Shakespeare was a playwright, so you have no excuse."

His eyes darted to the mansion where Aunt Matilda was now in the doorway waving at them to come inside. As they climbed the steps, Greg whispered, "What am I walking into?"

"A brood of vipers."

Matilda opened her arms wide. "Introduce me to your new beau, Sheri. We've waited *years* for this day to happen."

*Love you too, Matilda.*

Sheri held back a biting retort and introduced Greg. Matilda motioned for them to follow her through the foyer toward the din of conversation and laughter emanating from the living room. "I can't wait for you to meet my two beautiful daughters, Clarissa and Claire," Matilda said, bounding ahead.

Sheri lagged behind so she could whisper to Greg, "They're total snobs, and they love rubbing in how pretty and popular they are. I can't stand them."

Matilda turned back around and shouted from the living room, "Hurry up. Everyone is dying to meet Greg."

He released a heavy sigh then mumbled to Sheri, "Why did I agree to this?"

"Because you're my best friend, and this is what best friends do for each other."

He wagged his index finger at her. "You owe me big time."

She kissed his cheek and ushered him toward the formal living room where everyone was congregated. "Time to put on your suit-of-armor and rescue a maiden in distress," she whispered. "And don't forget—you're crazy about me!"

"Or just plain crazy," he sputtered through clenched teeth.

Sheri linked her arm through his as they entered the massive, vaulted-ceiling living room. Aunt Matilda outstretched her arm toward the clan. "Welcome to the family, Greg."

Greg swallowed a lump the size of Rhode Island.

*Welcome to the family?*

Had someone now spread the rumor they were *engaged?* What had he gotten himself into?

"Nice to meet you, Matilda." He hoped his silly grin would belie his total shock. "Sheri has told me so much about you."

*All bad, and I dread every second in your presence.*

Matilda gripped his hand and squeezed. She leaned in conspiratorially. "I, for one, always *knew* there was a swan underneath Sheri's ugly duckling exterior. After all, she does have Claiborne genes."

Greg wrapped a protective arm around Sheri's shoulders. "She's the most beautiful swan in the pond."

*Oh brother! That was lame, really lame.*

Matilda's lips tightened. "You say that because you haven't met *my* lovely daughters yet."

Greg noticed Sheri and Tess exchanging looks that could ignite World War III. Aunt Matilda *was* despicable. No way would he let this Botoxed ogress demean his best friend. Sheri had worked too hard these last few months to tolerate such abuse.

He turned to Sheri and caressed her cheek, gazing at her as though he adored her. "I'm sure your daughters are quite lovely,

Matilda, but no one will ever hold a candle to my darling Sheri. I've loved her since the first time I glimpsed these auburn curls."

He reached for a strand of her hair, fingered it, and then kissed it. "So beautiful."

He noticed Sheri chomping on the inside of her cheeks to keep from laughing.

Matilda harrumphed and couldn't suppress a scowl. Before she could rope him inside to meet her daughters, a bald man who was short enough for Greg to use as an armrest wandered over and slapped Greg on the back. "So, you're the guy who's stolen our Sheri's heart."

*Actually, Nicholas has that honor, but somehow, I'm the one who got roped into this family brouhaha.*

"Sheri and I have been seeing a lot of each other lately." he replied evasively.

*Sweating on hiking trails, trading insults, and getting our eyebrows plucked.*

"Do I hear wedding bells?" Bert asked, a huge grin plastered across his face.

Greg noticed Sheri's cheeks flamed with embarrassment. She piped in, "Not wedding bells, Uncle Bert. I think your hearing aid has malfunctioned again. Maybe you need to replace the batteries."

"Pretty soon, I won't need my hearing aid no more. I discovered this miracle herb that completely restores hearing. You really ought to look into it, Sheri." He pulled a folded brochure from his back pocket and handed it to her. "This herb is way cheaper for your patients than hearing aids. I kept this to give to you."

She didn't argue with him, politely took the pamphlet, and mumbled something about checking it out. She then grabbed Greg's arm and hurried him away from Bert to join her sister and mother. Sheri's mother gripped his hand and thanked him profusely for coming. Tess also offered a friendly greeting. Thank goodness at least two of Sheri's relatives were non-venomous.

He noticed two attractive women with haughty expressions eyeing him from the adjoining room. They must be the stuck-up cousins Sheri had warned him about — the two who had spied on them from the window.

He decided his best strategy was to disarm them with flattery. He forced himself to paste on a huge smile then strode over to the uppity duo. "You must be the lovely Claire and Clarissa. Sheri told me I'd be privileged to meet her beautiful cousins tonight."

The mouths of both women dropped. They clearly hadn't expected Sheri to say anything positive about them.

Greg continued. "Sheri says you went to high school together."

"We went to the same school, but we hung out in completely different circles," Claire quickly pointed out. "Clarissa and I were varsity cheerleaders. Sheri hung out with the nerds and musicians."

"Smart *and* talented, isn't she?" he countered, wrapping a protective arm around Sheri's shoulders. "Hanging out with the world's future movers and shakers really paid off for her, didn't it? A Johns Hopkins medical degree. You can't beat that."

The two women stared at him as though it never dawned on them that associating with nerds and geeks might trump hanging out with the popular crowd.

To avoid insulting them, Greg said, "I'll bet you have lots of riveting stories about your years as varsity cheerleaders. I'm dying to hear them."

Greg forced himself to listen as the two sisters gloated about their glory years in high school.

When he had listened for as long as he could stand, Greg offered to grab them both a drink — anything to escape the banal chatter.

How had he, a man with the social skills of a waltzing baboon, been lopped into the role of Sheri's charming suitor? It was laughable, but so far, he'd done surprisingly well, he thought.

He and Sheri wandered toward the kitchen hoping he could limp through the rest of the evening without nervously plunging into financial planning lectures.

As they poured two goblets of wine for Sheri's snobby cousins, an old woman whose stooped posture and sour expression rivaled the witch from Hansel and Gretel, hobbled over and inspected Greg with the precision of a military lieutenant. She tapped her cane on the floor. "Are you pursuing our Sheri for her money?"

Taken aback, Greg blurted, "I-I beg your pardon?"

"You heard me, young man." She crossed her arms and glared up at him. "I want to know your intentions concerning my granddaughter."

Before he could answer, Sheri chimed in, "Grandma! Greg and I only started dating a few months ago. These questions are totally inappropriate."

She turned to Sheri and demanded, "How do you know he isn't a shyster just after your money?"

Sheri raised her hands. "Money? What money? I'm still paying off medical school loans."

Ignoring her, the old bat poked a gnarled finger in Greg's chest. "I won't tolerate a gold digger."

Greg swallowed and forced himself to remain civil. "Mrs. Claiborne, I assure you, I am gainfully employed, and my accounting practice is financially prosperous. I promise you, I don't need Sheri's money." He smiled at Sheri and added, "Or lack thereof."

"In that case, it's nice to meet you." The old lady harrumphed and offered up a hint of a smile before tottering away.

Sheri touched his arm with a stricken look. "Greg, I am so sorry. I had no idea she would accost you like that."

"Well, she's a charmer, isn't she!" He shook his head still in shock. "I hope you age with more grace than your grandmother."

"You got that right. It's a miracle my mother didn't wind up in a mental institution with that woman as a mother."

They brought Clarissa and Claire their goblets of wine and spoke pleasantries for several more minutes before excusing themselves.

At Matilda's insistence, they took a tour of the house. Greg noted a massive crystal chandelier in the dining room that no doubt trumped the cost of his MINI Cooper. He whispered to Sheri, "How did Bert and Matilda get so wealthy?"

Sheri chuckled. "A toilet flapper."

Seeing his shocked expression, Sheri explained. "Bert is a plumber. Years ago, he designed and patented a toilet flapper that became an industry standard."

They entered the solarium which displayed Greek statues, and a Steinway grand piano. "Nobody in the family even plays the piano," Sheri whispered. "Matilda bought it just for show and the occasional party."

They wound their way up a circular marble staircase with a decorative wrought iron stair railing. In awe, Greg said, "He really got this rich from a toilet flapper?"

"Yup. And he didn't even go to college. He came up with an invention that took off, and voilà." She gestured around the mansion.

He shook his head. "Boy, did we choose the wrong fields."

"Speaking of poor choices, you've made your token appearance for the night. Let's get out of here before you have to meet any more of my odious relatives."

His heart stopped for a second. "There's *more*?" When she nodded, he said, "You really do come from Dysfunction Junction. Let's get out of here before I get accosted by your grandmother again. She's scary."

Sheri grinned. "Hey, she didn't whack you with her cane—that means she likes you."

As they escaped toward Greg's car, she said, "You deserve an Academy Award for convincing them you're gaga for me, and kudos to you that you didn't resort to retirement planning lectures."

His chest swelled with pride. "Glad to be of service, Ma' lady. You've worked too hard to be put down by them. Besides, they should love you no matter how you look — they're family. You'd think they'd be proud of you for making it through medical school."

She smiled up at him. "That's sweet. I appreciate the loyalty."

When they reached his car, he bowed at the waist. "Parting is such sweet sorrow that I shall say goodnight till it be morrow."

"Your stage debut is over, Romeo, so you should save quotes like that for your real Juliet: Vanessa."

He chuckled and crawled into his car then lowered the driver's window to say goodnight. Suddenly, Sheri stuck her head through the open window and grabbed his lapel. "Quick! Kiss me! Clarissa and Claire are spying on us again."

He clasped his hands behind her head and obediently pulled her closer until their mouths touched. He was surprised by how soft and tender and inviting her lips felt against his. He tugged her nearer — the cousins were still watching, right? When she parted her lips and began kissing him back, an unexpected desire for this moment to never end coursed through him.

He raked his fingers through her hair and kissed her with abandon, telling himself duty demanded he do so. As he nibbled and tasted and explored her luscious mouth, he tried to block out that he was enjoying this too much. Way too much!

Suddenly, she pulled away. "They're gone now. Your duty is over."

Heart still pounding, he blurted out, "Duty? I'd hardly call what just happened between us a duty."

She tucked a strand of hair behind her ear, her hands tremulous. She stared down at her feet and said nothing, as though deliberating her words. Finally, she said, "Greg, you're dating Vanessa. We only kissed tonight to fool my cousins, remember?

187

Desperate times call for desperate measures, and all that." She met his gaze. "That kiss doesn't mean anything—it can't."

Conviction splashed over him like a bucket of ice water. Vanessa! How could he have kissed Sheri so passionately while still dating Vanessa? Was he some low-class, dirty rotten two-timer? Even worse? He had *enjoyed* every second of his low-class, dirty rotten two-timing! In fact, he craved a repeat performance.

How had good old Sheri—his best friend—become a woman he now wanted to lavish with kisses? Unthinkable! He had pledged to just be her accountability partner. He dropped his head in shame as Sheri's words reverberated in his brain. "That kiss doesn't mean anything—it can't."

*But it did mean something. They meant everything.*

He stuffed his disappointment and reminded himself Sheri had her heart set on Nicholas. Hadn't she been pining after the guy for weeks now? Tonight's kiss had been nothing more than a ruse to deceive her odious relatives. A stage act and nothing more.

Even though he had planned to break up with Vanessa when he drummed up the courage to do so, it was still wrong to give in to his physical desire for Sheri until the breakup had materialized.

Besides, Sheri was probably telling him to stick with Vanessa because she didn't want him—not in the way he wanted her.

*She wants Nicholas, and don't forget it.*

He made himself look at Sheri with a forced smile. "Of course, it didn't mean anything—it was all for show."

Sheri immediately turned her face, but not before he caught what looked like a hurt expression. Or was it?

He tapped his fingers on the steering wheel debating whether to share his true feelings for her or not. His inner pessimist won the debate, and he decided not to risk it. He forced himself to say, "You need to turn in early, so you'll be ready for your date with Nicholas tomorrow."

"Nicholas?" Her brain must still be in a fog.

*Hello!* Had she forgotten about her date with Prince Charming in the morning?

She laughed nervously. "Oh, right. Nicholas." She averted her eyes and added, "Wish me luck with him tomorrow."

He nodded and raised his car window. She waved goodbye.

*No way will I wish her luck. I hope the guy has toilet paper on his shoe.*

Sheri was *his* soulmate. He knew that now to the bottom of his heart. If only *she* didn't have *her* heart set on Nicholas.

He needed to end things with Vanessa—and he would—if only he could screw his courage to the sticking place and just *do* it.

Truth be told, he'd rather stick a fondue fork in his eye than hurt Vanessa. She was a kind and compassionate woman. How could he make her cry? How could he do to her what Jodi had done to him?

He also dreaded the long, drawn-out ordeal of trying to explain *why* he didn't want a future with her. How do you tell a woman her personality drives you crazy? That she talks too much. That she bores you. Cruel, cruel, cruel.

He could picture it now—Vanessa would cry, and talk, and cry, and talk, and cry and talk some more. Then she would text, and call, and text and call, and rehash and cry and text and call some more. The thought of it exhausted him.

Hmm...maybe he could procrastinate the break up and its undesirable consequences until he saw how things with Sheri and Nicholas progressed.

*Why go through torture for nothing?*

*"All things that are,*
*Are with more spirit chased than enjoyed."*
~William Shakespeare~
*The Merchant of Venice*

# Chapter 31

Sheri arrived at Roxie's salon Saturday morning with eight different outfits and an equal number of contradictory emotions. After weeks of biting her nails waiting to hear from Nicholas, finally, he had asked her out. How flattering! How exciting! She *should* be thrilled...except after last night's spectacular kiss with Greg, how could she possibly pursue a relationship with Nicholas? Her heart now longed for Greg, not Nicholas.

Except Greg clearly didn't return her feelings, or he would have spoken up and professed his love for her last night. But he hadn't — even when she'd claimed the kiss couldn't mean anything because he was involved with Vanessa.

If he had feelings for Sheri, why hadn't he promised to break up with Vanessa? Instead, he'd stuck to his role as her *pretend* boyfriend...except for that one nanosecond when she could have *sworn* he felt something for her. She'd seen passion in his eyes...hadn't she? Or, was it just wishful thinking on her part? If so, she needed to quit torturing herself by longing for Greg. She should start pursuing Nicholas. Except last night...

*Okay, I've officially talked myself into an endless loop.*

Move on, she told herself, as she awkwardly tried to open the doors to Roxie's salon while simultaneously holding an armload of clothes on hangers.

Seeing her plight, Roxie rushed to her rescue. "Here, let me help you."

*Here's hoping Roxie can help me wow Nicholas...or Greg.*

She felt like an ice skater about to launch into a challenging triple axel that would either win her Olympic gold or a humiliating tumble onto her derrière.

"How does Greg feel about your date with Nicholas?" Roxie asked, as Sheri draped her armload of outfits over a chair.

"I think he's excited for me." She averted her eyes.

What else *could* she say? No way would she divulge she'd enjoyed a passionate kiss with Greg last night, especially when he was still dating Vanessa. She felt guilty enough as it was.

"He wasn't too happy about Caleb."

"That's because Caleb was more worried about his car than my health."

As Roxie ushered Sheri to the nail polish station, she shook her head in disgust. "It certainly wasn't Caleb's finest hour, was it?" While Sheri seated herself, Roxie examined all the choices for nail polish then decided on a raspberry sorbet. She pulled the bottle from the rack and shook it.

"Speaking of Caleb, do you know how his audition went? Did he get the leading role?" While still hacked off at him for his egregious behavior in the restaurant, Sheri had invested too many hours tutoring him to want to see him fail.

Roxie brightened as she screwed off the cover of the polish and blotted the brush on the side of the bottle. "He made it to the second-round audition, but in the end, they chose someone else."

"That's too bad." Sheri was surprised by how much she actually meant it. Caleb had worked so hard for the role.

"He *did* land the role of understudy though, so that will provide fabulous exposure to celebrities." Roxie stroked polish onto Sheri's thumbnail.

"Who knows? Maybe the lead will get sick or have a car wreck."

"Stranger things have happened," Roxie agreed, polishing Sheri's index finger.

Sheri smirked. "Maybe he should offer the leading man a platter of oysters."

"Wicked girl!" Roxie pointed at her with the polish brush. "I'll have to pass that suggestion along to Caleb."

"Don't you dare! I wouldn't wish that illness on my worst enemy."

Roxie finished polishing the other three nails then grabbed Sheri's other hand. "I'm still convinced one of these days you and Greg will wind up together."

*In my dreams.*

She forced herself to maintain a casual tone. "Afraid not. We're just chums. Besides, I can't compete with a woman as gorgeous as Vanessa."

Roxie shook her head. "Why does Greg have to be like every other bone-headed, testosterone-driven male who only thinks from the waist down?"

Sheri giggled at Roxie's scathing assessment of the male gender.

Roxie softened her insult by adding, "Luckily, Greg's not the impulsive type when it comes to decisions as important as marriage. He'll smarten up eventually—I hope." She stroked on a second coat of polish and placed Sheri's fingers under the heat lamp. "Before long, you two will walk down the aisle—mark my words."

"Uh-huh. Just like your prediction that Caleb would make Greg jealous?"

Roxie shrugged. "Okay, maybe I missed the mark on that one, but I still say you and Greg belong together."

"I have to admit, once I got to know him, my feelings for him deepened—a lot." She sighed wistfully. "Greg's a great guy."

They chatted about one of Roxie's challenging clients, and then Roxie pulled Sheri's hands out from under the heat lamp and applied a third coat of polish. "Competition from Nicholas will be just the thing he needs to wake up and appreciate the new you."

"Because competition from Caleb worked so well?"

"Caleb turned out to be a selfish twit. Greg saw right through him."

"Unfortunately, Greg has also seen me at my worst — bawling my eyes out, binging on ice cream, barfing up oysters, and dripping with sweat in the heat of summer. Hardly fodder for male fantasies. All it takes is one look at beautiful Vanessa batting her eyelashes, and he's hypnotized again." Sheri shook her head in disgust. "Testosterone is such an annoying hormone."

Roxie raised a pair of sharp scissors and snapped them open and closed. "I could take care of that."

"Roxie!" Sheri giggled.

"Hey, it would take care of that pesky testosterone problem. And unlike you paranoid doctors, I don't need a signed consent to use sharp scissors."

Sheri snickered. "Remember how Greg whimpered about his eyebrow waxing? Wouldn't he turn green if he could hear us now?"

"He'd run for the exit — with track sneakers."

Roxie placed Sheri's fingers under the heat lamp for their final drying. While waiting for the polish to dry, she applied foundation, blush, mascara, and eyeliner. "All you need now is lip liner and lipstick." She pulled a lip liner pencil from her makeup caddy. "Hold still."

Roxie carefully etched a line around Sheri's lips then filled it in with lipstick. She blotted with a tissue and added a light coat of clear gloss. "You want your lips to look succulent and full." Roxie demonstrated how to pout with full, seductive lips. "If there's a lull in the conversation, look him in the eyes and smile with a pouty-lipped pose. It drives men crazy, and they don't even know why." Roxie grinned. "That's how I snagged up my husband."

"It seems so manipulative," Sheri said with a frown.

Roxie pulled back and crossed her arms. "Hey, don't argue with success!"

"Where'd you learn all these tricks?"

Roxie grinned. "My clients. Most of them are singers and actors. They've got seduction down to a science."

"It seems wrong—like trickery."

Roxie shrugged. "Wasn't it Shakespeare who said, 'All's fair in love and war?'"

"Afraid not. John Lyly."

Roxie pulled back in awe. "How do you and Greg know all that stuff?"

"While you were learning how to straighten hair and seduce men, nerds like Greg and me studied literature. Now, twenty years later, you're happily married, and I'm still reciting love sonnets to my cat." She crossed her arms in disgust. "You tell me who has the more useful knowledge."

Roxie waved a dismissive hand. "Don't worry. When I'm through with you, you'll have Nicholas as mesmerized as Hamlet near the fishbowl."

Sheri laughed. "And you said I was a wicked girl?"

"Guilty as charged." Roxie raised both arms overhead as though surrendering to the police.

Roxie transferred Sheri to the hairstylist chair and shaped her hair into a chic stacked bob. She pulled back to inspect her work. "Perfect!" She spritzed on a thin coat of hairspray to set the style.

Sheri appraised the finished results with a hand mirror. "Looks great, Roxie. Thanks."

Roxie yanked off the plastic cape and shook the loose hair onto the floor. "I'll sweep it up later. Let's check out the outfits you brought."

After perusing all the possibilities, Roxie settled on an apricot top, a flirty white pencil skirt, and a coordinating scarf.

"I got you something." Roxie retrieved a plastic bag from her drawer at her hair station. She pulled out a girdle-like thing that went clear from the mid-thighs to the shoulders.

"It's a new type of body shaper. All my clients are wearing them," Roxie enthused. "It tightens the gut, raises the bust, and shapes the buns. Trust me—you'll love what it does to your figure."

Sheri held up the garment and eyed it suspiciously. "Thanks —
I think. Since I've gained back five of the pounds I'd lost, I can use
all the help I can get."

Roxie held an index finger to her lips. "This is our little secret.
What Nicholas and Greg don't know won't hurt 'em."

Sheri rushed into Roxie's bathroom and tugged on the body
shaper, then stepped into the designated outfit. She twirled in
front of the mirror and grinned, excited at how slim and attractive
she felt.

As Sheri strolled out, Roxie extended her arms and gushed,
"Girlfriend, he's as good as yours."

Sheri glanced at her watch and jolted. She only had ten minutes
to reach the restaurant. "Not if I'm late. He might not wait for me."
She grabbed her armful of alternate outfits and dashed out the
door, calling over her shoulder, "Thanks, Roxie."

She sped through four yellow lights and turned into the parking
lot at eight o'clock on the nose. Not surprisingly, she could see
Greg's car already parked out front.

Her stomach clenched. Would it be awkward seeing him after
last night? Should she pretend the whole kissing episode never
happened?

*"A high hope for a low heaven: God, grant us patience!"*
~William Shakespeare~
*Love's Labor's Lost*

# Chapter 32

Sheri dashed into the coffee shop and glanced around to see if Nicholas had arrived. No sign of him. Mr. Punctuality, however, sat with *The Tennessean* and a large coffee. He glanced up and then took a second appreciative look. "Sheri? Wow! You look sensational."

Her cheeks warmed at the compliment.

"Turn around and let me look at you." He rotated his index finger in a circle.

She twirled around noticing several other diners staring at her.

*Swell! Must I make a spectacle of myself every time I step into a restaurant?*

She quickly strolled back to Greg with opened palms. "Well? What's the verdict?"

"Nicholas will be bowled over." He glanced toward the entrance. "If he bothers to show up, that is."

He patted the table behind his. "I saved this spot in hopes you'd get here before Nicholas." He gestured for Sheri to sit down. "I'll be as quiet as a dust bunny under the bed, I promise."

"You promise not to whack me in the forehead with a scone if I lapse into a gross medical story."

He lifted his right hand in a pledge. "Scout's honor."

She eyed him suspiciously. "Were you ever a boy scout?"

He squirmed in his chair and avoided eye contact. "Well, no."

"So, your promise is meaningless, and I'll probably be clobbered with a flying disc of dough?"

"Only if you wax eloquent on disgusting medical topics. Remember—nothing that oozes or smells bad."

She eviscerated him with a glare then glanced at her watch. Five minutes after eight. Unlike Greg, Nicholas apparently wasn't neurotic about punctuality. Should she order herself a coffee or wait for him to arrive? She decided to wait. She drummed her nails on the table and tried to ignore her churning stomach.

Engrossed with his crossword puzzle, Greg asked, "What's the capital of Estonia? Seven-letter word. Begins with a T."

She pursed her lips and pictured a map of Europe. "Tallinn."

He nodded and wrote the word onto his crossword puzzle. He twirled his pencil in his fingers and asked, "What's a part of the brain that begins with the letter P?"

"Pituitary? Parietal lobe? Pia mater?"

His lips pursed in concentration. "No, it begins with a P-u."

"P-u? Hmm." She visualized the anatomical map of the brain. "Putamen."

"Putamen?" He raised his pencil and pointed at her. "I didn't know I had one. Is that the part of the brain that makes a person show up on time?" He glanced at his watch. "If so, your precious Nicholas doesn't have one. Neither does Vanessa," he added with a scowl. He wrote the anatomical term into his puzzle, and then commented, "Can you believe how far we've come since we first met?"

*If I look so good, how come you don't want me?*

The unbridled thought stabbed her with sadness. Clearly, Greg would never see her as anything more than the ugly duckling he'd helped get in touch with her swan potential. She was the sister he'd never had. A hiking buddy and Shakespeare enthusiast. Someone to tease about her gross medical stories. He shared everything with her because she was his best friend— like an old pair of shoes— comfy and familiar. No wonder Greg couldn't see himself as her husband and lover. He'd seen her fat, depressed, and frizzy-headed. He'd seen her in grungy sweats ready to shovel in a giant bowl of ice cream. She lacked pizzazz. Mystery. Enchantment.

Although… he *had* seemed enchanted last night when they'd kissed. But perhaps his response was purely visceral. Hormones, pheromones, synapses firing in the amygdala of his brain—these provided the perfect biological explanation for his response. Didn't Tina Turner sing "What's Love Got to Do with it?" Their kiss probably meant nothing special to him, or he would have said something. Bottom line? Greg didn't want her, or at least not enough to break things off with Vanessa.

With renewed purpose, she resolved she *would* make Nicholas fall in love with her. Greg was a lost cause, so she mustn't waste any more energy pining for him. Time to enchant Nicholas. Except… Nicholas might have stood her up. She looked at her watch and sighed.

As though reading her mind, Greg said, "Relax, he's probably just running late." He shook his head scowling. "Welcome to my world. I now tell Vanessa to be ready a full thirty minutes before I plan to arrive at her condo. Even then, I still twiddle my thumbs for fifteen minutes while she fusses with her hair."

Sheri shrugged unsympathetically. "That's the price you pay for dating a beautiful woman."

"*You're* beautiful, and you're on time," Greg countered.

*Beautiful? Since when did Greg see me as beautiful?* And she was punctual—that ought to win brownie points.

Just then, Nicholas pushed open the front door and scanned around until he spotted Sheri. He smiled and waved. As he strode toward her, she rose, sucked in her gut and straightened her spine the way Roxie had taught her.

Wow! Nicholas was even better looking in real life than in his picture. His wide shoulders and muscular arms suggested he lifted weights. His tailored jeans hinted of casual grace, and his smile could hang in a dentist's office as the "after" shot. She turned to Greg and smirked.

*Nicholas is definitely not fat, bald, or endowed with the breath of a bulldog with bad teeth. So there, Greg Palmer.*

*"When sorrows come, they come not as single spies,*
*but in battalions."*
~William Shakespeare~
*Hamlet*

# Chapter 33

Nicholas held out a hand and shook Sheri's with a firm handshake. "Nice to meet you."

Her brain turned to oatmeal. "Ah, nice to meet me too." Her cheeks warmed in embarrassment at her faux pas. "I mean, nice to meet *you,* too."

*Swell. Off to an impressive start.*

He smiled warmly. "Don't worry, I'm nervous, too."

Her knees turned to jelly in the presence of this charmer.

As the waitress took their order, Sheri noticed Greg glancing up from his crossword puzzle and appraising Nicholas. His mouth remained in a perpetual scowl, and he flicked his newspaper far too often.

"How long have you been online dating?" Sheri asked, as the waitress poured their coffee.

He swallowed a sip of coffee before answering. "Actually, you're the first woman I've attempted to date since my wife died three years ago."

Poor man. He's been grieving for three years. "I'm sure it's been a difficult three years."

He shrugged. "Sometimes tragic things happen, and I'm not sure we ever really know why." He stirred more creamer and sugar into his coffee. "I don't think I'll ever get over losing the love of my life, but I've come to accept that I need to move forward. I have to *make* myself start dating, whether I want to or not."

*Gee, thanks! He makes a date with me sound as enticing as cleaning leaves out of the gutters.*

Sheri ripped open two packages of Splenda and dumped them into her coffee, not sure how to respond to his lackluster excuse for asking her to join him for coffee.

The waitress arrived with warm blueberry muffins the size of beach huts. Yum! She nibbled the sugary treat hoping their conversation wouldn't be stilted.

After an awkward silence, Nicholas confessed, "To be honest, I don't know if I'm even ready to date yet. I chose you as my first choice because you're a doctor. I figured a doctor would understand everything I've been through and that I'm still grieving for my wife."

"Certainly," she said, trying to hide her disappointment that he hadn't selected her because he'd been blown away by her beauty. Still—if she became a sympathetic ear, he might eventually fall in love with her.

Between bites of muffin and sips of coffee, Nicholas shared the painful ordeal of his wife's five-year battle with ovarian cancer before she died three years ago.

"Monique was such an amazing woman—caring, beautiful, funny. She was a killer tennis player, a fabulous cook, and such a loving mother to our Maddie."

Sheri's eyes welled as he described Maddie's devastated reaction to her mother's death. He had endured so much pain she could now understand how it might take years for him to heal. Sheri reached for his hand when he shared Monique's last lucid words to him. She had told him she loved him and wanted him to remarry when he felt emotionally ready. She wanted him to find happiness again. He had cried and begged God not to let her die and leave Maddie without a mother.

Their coffee date stretched into two hours as Nicholas elaborated on the side effects of Monique's chemotherapy, and her slow, painful demise. She had died gaunt, bald, and desperately praying for a miracle.

200

Nicholas suddenly glanced at his watch and jolted. "Good heavens! I had no idea I droned on so long. I lost track of time."

"It's fine." Sheri patted his hand. "I appreciate you sharing your story with me."

After he paid for their breakfast, Nicholas walked her to her car. "I wanted you to know my story, so you'd know I come with baggage." He smiled sadly. "I'll always love Monique, but I know it's time I try to find a woman to replace her."

"I'm sure it will take time." Sheri noticed Greg eyeing them through the glass window of the restaurant.

"Thanks for being such a good listener. I enjoyed our time together." He promised to call, then bent forward and planted a chaste kiss on her cheek. Her spirits lifted.

*He must not find me completely repulsive.*

Surprisingly, she wasn't sure how she felt about that. While Nicholas was, without a doubt, the most handsome man she had ever dated, after two hours of excruciating details about his wife's ovarian cancer and death, she felt like a wilted tulip — droopy and drained. Their time together seemed more like an intensive grief counseling session than a date.

Truthfully, after a fifty-plus-hour workweek, the last thing she wanted to do on a beautiful Saturday morning was listen to stories about failed chemotherapy, excruciating pain, and death.

Yes, her attitude stunk. No doubt she'd lose her medical license if anyone on the state board knew the heartless thoughts that occasionally ran through her head during the last two hours. At one point she'd wanted to snap, "It's been three years. Get a grip and move on!"

As if it were that easy! Like Nicholas could just make up his mind one day to be done grieving.

As she drove home, guilt pierced her conscience. She claimed to be a compassionate doctor and a Christian, but today, her compassion matched that of a black widow spider as it bit off the head of its mate. Nicholas had suffered unspeakable anguish. He *needed* to vent and get it out of his system, and like he said, who better to vent to than a doctor?

Maybe now that he had unloaded his tale of woe, he'd be ready to form a new relationship—with her. Maybe she could *help* him move forward with his life. He'd been a kind and devoted husband to Monique, and if he ever loved Sheri as much as he had loved her, she'd be a lucky woman indeed.

She pulled into her driveway, her spirits buoyed. Since Greg didn't want her—and probably never would—she, like Nicholas, needed to move on with her life. She bound up her front stairs determined to make things work with Nicholas.

*"Love is as a fever, feeding on that which doth preserve the ill."*
~William Shakespeare~
*Sonnet 147*

# Chapter 34

As she unlocked her front door, Greg's MINI Cooper pulled into the driveway. Eager for his feedback, she dashed to his car. "What'd you think?" She hoped Greg would say, "He spent two hours with you, so he must really like you."

He crawled out of his car and locked it before informing her, "He's still in love with his dead wife. In his mind, Monique was Betty Crocker, Christie Brinkley, Serena Williams, and Mother Teresa all rolled up into one." He shook his head. "She'd be a tough act to follow."

Sheri's spirits nose-dived. Greg had verbalized her worst fear. If competing with Vanessa wasn't challenging enough—try competing with a *dead* woman who, apparently, was a paragon of perfection. "I'm hoping if I show him how compassionate and caring I am, he'll eventually fall in love with me."

"I suppose it's *possible*." Greg's tone of voice was the same one you'd use to suggest the Second Coming of Christ might occur tomorrow at noon—theoretically possible, but highly unlikely.

Greg followed her into the living room. "Nicholas even said he picked you because you're a physician. If you ask me, he's looking for a grief counselor, not a girlfriend."

They sank onto the couch. "The guy could have just purchased a parrot and taught it to say, 'How did that make you feel?' or, 'Tell me more'." His voice mimicked the squawk of a parrot.

She swatted his arm. "That's not true!"

"He didn't ask about *your* life." He raised upturned palms. "Just saying…"

A wave of despair washed over her. Would Nicholas ever fall in love with her if Mrs. Bluebeard's Ghost still lived in his heart and soul? Would he ever see her as anything more than a listening ear and walking encyclopedia on chemotherapy?

More disconcerting? Did she even *want* him to fall in love with her when she knew in her heart she loved Greg? Greg was her soulmate, whether *he* knew it or not. If only Vanessa wasn't so breathtakingly gorgeous and kind.

Greg's pessimism, however, triggered her to defend Nicholas. "He *did* kiss me goodbye. That shows promise."

Greg snorted. "Pul-lease! You call that namby-pamby peck on the cheek a kiss? That's the kind of kiss I give my Grandma Palmer."

"It was still a kiss," she retorted, arms crossed.

"Pffft. That was so *not* a kiss." He scooted closer to her on the couch and pulled her into his arms. "In case you've forgotten last night, let me teach you what a real kiss feels like," he murmured.

Before she could protest, he crushed his lips against hers—warm and insistent. His hands dove into her hair, and his firm lips parted hers and explored eagerly. He tugged her closer. Before she could stop herself, she responded with an intensity that made her breath jagged. Her heart hammered, and she drank in his touch as adrenaline coursed through her like waves at high tide. She wrapped her arms around his neck wanting to satiate the pent-up desire he stirred inside her. He deepened the kiss and then abruptly pulled away. Gazing into her eyes, he whispered, "*That was a kiss. See the difference?*"

*What??*

Embarrassment washed over her like a bucket of cold, dirty pond water.

*Was that magnificent moment between them nothing more than a pedantic kissing lesson to him?*

She wanted to clobber him with her couch pillow. Or better yet, the fireplace andiron.

Her cheeks burned with humiliation. What must he think of her wanton response to his kiss? She'd been so entangled in a web of desire she'd acted as though they were romantically involved — which they weren't. And what about Vanessa? Her new friend?

*The one who made you chicken soup when you were sick.*

Kind, sweet Vanessa, who deserved better than this from *both* of them. Shame and guilt coursed through her in equal measures. She needed to play along that this had merely been a didactic exercise — for Vanessa's sake — and her pride.

She cleared her throat and straightened her hair, too mortified to look Greg in the eyes. "Yes, I do see the difference. But this was my first date with Nicholas. He could hardly kiss me like that right in front of a restaurant's large picture window. Everyone would see us."

Greg turned her face gently with his fingers until their eyes locked. "Sheri, when you find your true love, he will kiss you like I did, even if people *are* watching." He gripped her shoulders, his gaze boring into her. "He won't be able to stop himself." When she stared down at her feet and didn't respond, he added, "He'll be so in love with you, he'll follow his heart and won't be controlled by what other people think."

When she glanced up, his gaze pierced so deeply into her soul her breath caught. She wished Greg would confess *he* loved her like that. But once again, he said nothing. Absolutely nothing. Which meant...

An inner voice mocked her: *No one will ever love you that way. Certainly not Greg!*

Her eyes filled, and she looked down at her contorted hands in her lap.

*Nicholas is still enmeshed with his dead wife, and Greg thinks I'm nothing more than a pathetic nerd in need of a love tutor.*

As though he sensed her disparaging thoughts, Greg gently tipped up her chin and forced her to look at him. He caressed her cheek tenderly. "You deserve to be loved like that, Sheri. Don't settle for anything less."

"I've lost hope that a love like that exists — at least for me."

He brushed a tear from her cheek with his thumb. "Nicholas may be handsome, but unless he loves you as much as he loved his first wife, you'll be miserable. You'll feel like the runner-up in a beauty pageant—always his second choice."

*That's exactly how I'd feel.*

He reached for her hand and squeezed. "There's somebody special out there for you. I'm sure of it."

She smiled weakly. "For small creatures such as we, the vastness is bearable only through love."

His lips pursed in thought. "Robert Browning?"

She shook her head. "Carl Sagan."

He touched her arm and whispered, "Someday *our* vastness will disappear because of love."

To lighten the mood she added, "And if not, we'll return to our workaholic ways and pretend it doesn't bother us in the slightest."

He chuckled. "And when that fails, there's always French Silk ice cream, right?"

She groaned. "Speaking delicious high-calorie treats, I suppose I need to burn off that huge blueberry muffin I just consumed. How many calories do you suppose that thing had?"

"Four hundred and ninety."

"What?" Her mouth dropped in disbelief. "No way."

"Way. I researched it while Nicholas droned on about his dead wife."

"Four hundred and ninety calories for one lousy muffin?" Her shoulders sagged.

"It *was* a humungous muffin—and you ate every single bit of it, I might add."

She popped his arm. "Oh, shut up, spoilsport." She released a frustrated sigh. "Now I'll have to walk *five miles* to burn the thing off."

He touched her nose and grinned. "Afraid so, my little glutton. Chop, chop. Time to get a move on."

She headed toward her bedroom to change. "Let me peel off this body shaper thingy and throw on some shorts."

His brow cocked. "Body shaper thingy? Dare I ask?"

"It's the newest in girdles. They're supposed to deceive men into thinking we're ten pounds lighter and far less saggy than we actually are."

"They should be outlawed!" he bellowed, as she closed her bedroom door.

"Why?" she hollered through the door, peeling off her clothes.

"You date a girl and she's all curvy and slim and sexy. Then you marry her, she peels off her girdle, and you find out she's a fat, saggy blob."

She would have lashed him a thousand times with her girdle-thingy if she'd been dressed in more than her underwear. She pulled on some shorts and a T-shirt and sucked in her first deep breath since tugging off the confining corset.

*Ah, to breathe. Happy day!*

"I'll bet Vanessa wears one," she tossed out saucily, as she entered the living room carrying her socks and sneakers.

"No way!"

"Way," she insisted, as she pulled on her socks. "Roxie says everybody is wearing them these days."

"Well, I'm sure your Greek god appreciated how you looked in your body shaper thingy — even if it is a garment of treachery and lies."

She glanced up and grinned. "Greek god, huh? Jealous, are we?"

Greg scowled. "You have to admit the guy has the looks to make any man feel inferior."

"He *is* a fox, isn't he?" she said, purposely baiting him. "Can you believe he said he'd call me again?"

*Was that a frown on Greg's face?*

He jumped up from the couch and bee-lined for the door. "Let's get going — before it gets too hot to hike."

*Is Greg jealous?*

He *had* kissed her passionately both last night and today. Was his line about the kiss being merely a kissing lesson all a cover-up? Had Vanessa's spell over him finally lessened? If so, why hadn't he broken up with her? Why hadn't he confessed his true feelings for Sheri? Maddening, infuriating, exasperating man!

Deep in her heart, she knew Vanessa was all wrong for Greg. She would never be his soulmate.

*Because I'm his soulmate, if only the stupid lunkhead would figure it out.*

Guilt flooded Greg like an overflowing toilet in need of one of Bert's patented flappers. He had no business kissing Sheri when he hadn't yet broken up with Vanessa. He had degenerated into a two-timing scoundrel. He needed to call things off with Vanessa, and the sooner the better—except Vanessa had flown to Atlanta for a week-long nursing conference, and then she'd booked a two-week vacation in Jacksonville to visit her parents. She was a nice person and deserved better than a tacky telephone breakup, especially since they had dated for months now. He should have broken things off a month...but he hadn't.

In three weeks, when she returned from Florida and the timing was right, he'd call things off. Then he could finally tell Sheri how he felt about her. He could only hope Sheri and Nicholas weren't a bona fide couple by then, as it would be hard to compete with Adonis with a law degree.

*"Death lies on her like an untimely frost,*
*upon the sweetest flower of all the field."*
~William Shakespeare~
*Romeo and Juliet*

# Chapter 35

After her third date with Nicholas, Sheri wanted to nominate his dead wife for sainthood. Monique bore her pain without complaint. Monique made the flakiest piecrust. Monique could write a book on perfect parenting. Monique this, Monique that. Blah, blah, blah.

She had hoped after Nicholas vented about his dead wife for two solid hours on their first, second, and third dates that he'd be ready to move on. But as she slumped on the couch in his living room and stared at the eight by ten wedding photo of Monique and her adoring groom prominently displayed on the fireplace mantle, she wondered if Nick was a lost cause.

"You ready for the big surprise I promised you earlier this week?" Nicholas asked, grinning.

Sheri's breath caught. It seemed too early for an engagement ring, but you never knew. Maybe he was lonely and missed being married. Maybe her hours of listening had finally paid off.

Nicholas reached into the cabinet and pulled out a box, except... it wasn't a jewelry box. It was a DVD box. Looking ever so pleased with himself, he popped the DVD into the player and explained, "I thought I had lost this particular DVD, but I found it this week."

Okay, definitely *not* an engagement ring. Her mother would be so disappointed.

Sheri, in her ongoing effort to stop her mother's badgering, had told her mother earlier in the week Nicholas had promised her a "big surprise" tonight.

Linda immediately conjured up an engagement ring as the big surprise. "After the fourth date with your father, I *knew* he was the one, and last week, you told me things with Nicholas were getting serious."

Okay, Sheri *had* grossly exaggerated the seriousness of her relationship with Nicholas in a futile attempt to prevent the dreaded daily phone call from her mother asking, "How's the husband hunt going?"

Her relationship with Nicholas was serious alright—seriously boring! But her mother didn't need to know that.

"You wait and see," Linda insisted. "He's tired of being alone." She'd patted Sheri's cheek with a confident smile. "We're going to get our Christmas wedding, after all."

Sheri *should* have told her mother right then and there that the relationship with Nicholas was going nowhere fast because he was still obsessed with his dead wife. But she hadn't. Why? As long as Ma thought things were moving forward with Nicholas, she left Sheri alone. No dreaded daily phone call. No interrogation. A little white lie was a small price to pay for one's mental health, right?

Pulling her thoughts away from her conversation with her mother, Sheri asked Nicholas, "What's the big surprise? Are we watching a movie tonight?"

*Please God, not War and Peace.*

Greg turned up the volume slightly. "Even better. It's a DVD from a Disneyworld vacation I took twelve years ago with Maddie and Monique. Now you'll get to see Monique and Maddie in real life before she got cancer. I knew you'd want to see this."

*Lucky me!* Was it not enough to weather hours of him droning on about his adored dead wife? Now she had to endure video footage of his paragon of perfection? What next? A date with a Ouija board and psychic to conjure up Monique from the dead?

Sheri could not even make herself feign enthusiasm for the video footage. She did manage to stifle a curse.

Clueless to her sour mood, Nicholas enthused, "Maddie's expression when she meets Mickey and Minnie is priceless. You've got to see it."

*Shoot me now. I do not want to spend my Saturday night watching somebody else's kid posing with imaginary mice.*

She shifted her weight on the couch and hoped her snarky attitude didn't come through in her tone of voice when she'd informed him, "I can hardly wait."

She forced herself to stay awake as little Maddie obtained signatures in her autograph book from Mickey and Minnie. Then Donald Duck. Now Snow White and Rapunzel. Yawn and double yawn.

An hour later, she couldn't keep her eyes open — short of prying them apart with toothpicks. She straightened her back and wiggled her toes — anything to stay awake. When fidgeting failed to arouse her, she excused herself to the bathroom and splashed cold water on her face.

*Stay awake! If you pay your dues and watch his dullsville DVDs, maybe he'll eventually fall in love with you.*

Resolve renewed, she shuffled back to the couch, stifled a yawn, and plunked down next to him. Maybe he needed a hint there was a woman in the room — a *living* woman.

Unfortunately, the only women Nicholas seemed to have eyes for were dead or imaginary. Perhaps Sheri should wear glass slippers and chimney ashes for their next date. At this rate, she'd still be plopped on Nick's couch at midnight watching Maddie obtaining Belle's signature. How many Disney princesses were there?

Should she feign food poisoning? That would provide an excuse to go home. Except… Sheri had made the chili they'd eaten for supper. Food poisoning wouldn't bode well for her cooking skills, especially when earlier that evening Nicholas declared, "Monique made the tastiest chili. I should give you her recipe."

Sheri had been tempted to dunk his head in her crockpot full of apparently inferior chili.

*Why couldn't Monique burn her roast and scald her chowder like normal women?*

"I'm making sure the smoke detector batteries still work," Sheri joked, every time she set off the alarm after burning toast.

Her conscience goaded her. She should take more of an interest in Nick's life. Monique's death had devastated him, and Maddie *was* an adorable child. But a three-hour stroll through Disneyworld had atrophied Sheri's brain into a blob of porridge—lumpy and burnt—and probably nowhere near as tasty as Monique's porridge.

She jumped up from the couch. "Why don't I fix us some popcorn?"

Perhaps while sharing a bowl of popcorn their fingers would touch, and he'd realize a live woman trumped a dead one any day. She located the microwave popcorn and cooked up a batch. The delicious aroma wafted from the kitchen into the living room and her mouth watered. Yum! She yanked off a couple of paper towels, grabbed two cans of Diet Coke, and wandered back to the couch with the inviting bowl.

*This'll do the trick!*

When Nick didn't even notice her return, she wanted to heave the soda cans at the television screen. He pointed at the screen. "Look! Monique is pushing Maddie on the swing."

Sheri stifled a groan—and the urge to dump the entire bowl of popcorn on his head.

Okay, subtly was a waste of time with this guy. Time for drastic action.

"Nicholas? How about we turn off the television and *talk* while we eat our popcorn? I'd like a break from watching videos."

"Sure," he said, though his eyes were still glued to Maddie and Monique and that blasted swing. He reached for the remote, still enthralled by his daughter's giggle and the back and forth of the swing.

*Why had he bothered to invite me over?*

212

Did he seriously think she wanted to watch his dead wife and six-year-old for three-hours straight? Maddie was now a college freshman!

He turned off the television and grabbed a handful of popcorn. "Thanks for making this." He actually looked at her and smiled — a bona fide miracle. "And thanks for watching all these DVDs with me. I'm sure they bore you to tears, but it helps me heal to watch them *with* someone. In the past, I've watched them alone and cried myself to sleep."

A two-ton truckload of guilt clobbered her.

*You are a terrible, horrible, no-good person, Sheri Morris.*

Convicted, she said, "I'm happy to watch them with you, Nick."

She should be flattered he felt safe enough emotionally with her to share his painful memories.

After their bowl of popcorn, Nick plopped in another thriller — their summer vacation to Kentucky Kingdom where Monique and Maddie enjoyed the water slide.

Sheri didn't mean to fall asleep, really, she didn't, and she certainly didn't intend to snore like a lumberjack or drool on Nick's shoulder. No doubt his precious Monique neither drooled nor snored.

*"False face must hide what false heart doth know."*
*~William Shakespeare~*
*Macbeth*

# Chapter 36

When Sheri pulled into her mother's driveway, she couldn't help but notice the fluorescent pink van embossed with golden wedding rings and the words, "Cyndi's Wedding Designs" plastered on the side. A sinking feeling settled in the pit of her stomach.

*What was her mother up to?*

Linda had insisted she had a "wonderful surprise" for Sheri tonight, but never in a million years had Sheri expected this. When she'd besieged her mother to tell her what the surprise was, Linda twisted her fingers near her mouth and offered an infuriating, "My lips are sealed."

No amount of requesting, begging, badgering, or threats to no-show wore her mother down. She couldn't motivate herself to resort to waterboarding to extract it out of her, as that dratted commandment, "Honor thy father and thy mother that it might go well with you", had been drummed into her since birth.

Linda had grinned and insisted, "Be at my house Friday at five o'clock sharp. You'll be thrilled, I promise."

After eyeing the gaudy Pepto Bismol pink van in the driveway, Sheri was definitely not thrilled. She could think of no acceptable explanation for the tacky van since she wasn't engaged nor likely to become engaged in the next millennium.

She trudged up the steps and let herself in, already dreading her not-so-wonderful surprise.

Linda Morris hurried into the entry hall beaming. She offered Sheri a warm hug and pulled her toward the living room. "Come, and I'll show you my wonderful surprise."

Sheri lagged behind fearing the worst. As she rounded the corner and gazed into the living room, she froze.

*What on earth?*

There, on a half-dozen portable clothes racks, hung a dozen or more wedding gowns. Across the room hung bridesmaid dresses in cranberry, black, emerald green, and royal blue—dozens of them. Next to the dresses stood poster boards with invitations, and bulletin boards loaded with pictures of catered reception dinner ideas. Next to the umpteen racks of wedding apparel stood a woman elegantly attired in heels and a tailored navy business suit. Sheri stared at the wedding-shop-come-to-roost too shocked to utter a sound.

Surprise!" her mother shouted, raising her hands as though hosting a surprise birthday party. Linda's face glowed brighter than a room full of fireflies. Right now, Sheri would *prefer* a room full of fireflies to a room full of wedding paraphernalia.

"Isn't it thrilling?" her mother gushed, opening her arms and hugging a still stunned Sheri.

*Try humiliating — I'm not even engaged.*

Talk about awkward—this poor woman must have spent a good hour dragging in dresses and poster boards and bulletin boards from her van and then setting them up into a tasteful display. How could Sheri now tell her there would be no wedding, because there was no bridegroom? Perhaps she could tell the woman her mother was delusional and in need of serious psychiatric help. That would work.

Oblivious to Sheri's inner ranting, Linda prattled on. "Since you're so busy with work, and exercise, and dating Nicholas these days, I've hired Cyndi to help us with our wedding plans. Look— she's brought everything right to you. Isn't it wonderful?"

Linda extended her arm toward all the racks of wedding gowns as though she were Vanna White on *The Wheel of Fortune*. Perhaps Sheri should get her mother a job as a game show hostess—maybe then she'd be too busy to meddle in Sheri's life.

"Sheri, meet Cyndi Taylor, of Cyndi Taylor Wedding Designs. She's a wedding planner for busy professionals like you. She's already done all the research based on what I've told her, and she's brought over some lovely gowns in your exact size to try on."

Not wanting to be rude, Sheri forced herself to greet the wedding planner with a polite nod and a friendly smile. "Would you excuse us for a minute please, Cyndi? I have an urgent matter to discuss with my mother before we get started with the dresses."

"By all means." Cyndi offered a friendly nod.

She yanked on her mother's arm with the force of Hurricane Katrina until they were safely secluded in the kitchen. Sheri made sure the door was shut before she lit into her mother. Arms crossed she snapped, "Mother, have you lost your mind? A wedding planner?"

Linda's eyes widened with shock. "Cyndi comes highly recommended. I thought you'd be thrilled."

"Thrilled? I'm not even engaged, so why are you wasting this poor woman's time?"

Her mother looked dumbfounded. "After you told me Nicholas had a big surprise for you, I thought we needed to get going with our wedding plans. Christmas is only two months away, so we can't dawdle, or your wedding will be an embarrassing, half-baked affair."

Sheri raised hands of exasperation. "What wedding? We have no groom, and you kind of need a groom to have a wedding." Try as she might, she couldn't suppress the sarcasm in her tone.

Linda's lips thinned, and her eyes narrowed. "Don't get smart with me, young lady! You told me yourself things were progressing splendidly with Nicholas." She jabbed an accusing finger in Sheri's direction. "Those were the exact words you used."

Drat! She *had* used those exact words—but only to get her mother off her back.

"Naturally, I assumed when he told you he had a big surprise for you that a wedding proposal was forthcoming." Her mother's shoulders sagged. "You mean he didn't propose?"

Sheri hung her head. "No, Ma, he didn't. And he's not going to."

Linda stared at her in bewilderment. "I-I don't understand. Last week you said—"

"I know what I said," Sheri interrupted, struggling to keep her voice calm. "Things aren't going to work out with Nicholas, after all."

Guilt coursed through her. Last week she *had* told her mother things looked "promising" and "were becoming serious." Her goal for the little white lies? Mental health—otherwise known as an end to her mother's inquisitions about her love life.

Only now, her little white lies had come back to bite her in the butt with the fangs of a saber-toothed tiger.

She'd planned to tell her mother that her relationship with Nicholas hadn't worked out—really, she had—once she dug up the courage to break things off with Nicholas. But in the meantime, dating Nicholas had provided a convenient way to keep her mother from driving her crazy—until now.

She should have given it more thought before exaggerating the seriousness of her relationship with Nicholas. She definitely shouldn't have told her mother Nicholas had promised her "a big surprise." After all, if you gave Linda Morris an inch, she'd take it and run... straight into the office of a wedding planner.

Linda and Sheri simultaneously flopped into kitchen chairs. "What happened with you and Nicholas?" Linda asked glumly.

"Turns out, Nicholas is still in love with his dead wife, and I'm tired of competing with a ghost."

Linda crossed her arms and glared at Sheri. "You could have told me, you know."

*Yes, I am partially responsible for this fiasco.*

217

"I should have," Sheri admitted, feeling like pond scum. She chewed her bottom lip and stared down at her hands. "I didn't want to let you down again. I know you're dying to plan a Christmas wedding, but it's not going to happen." She reached for her mother's hand and squeezed. "Ma, I'm sorry I wasn't honest with you, and I'm sorry I'm not going to be a Christmas bride."

Linda released a loud sigh. "And I'm sorry I jumped the gun and called a wedding planner." She glanced toward the living room. "This is so embarrassing. What are we going to tell Cyndi?"

The two women stared at each other.

*How about, "You got any smart, good-looking grooms who love Shakespeare in those wedding books of yours?"*

Linda leaned her elbows on the kitchen table and dropped her head into her hands. "What are we going to do? Cyndi came all this way, and she's worked so hard to set up her displays for us. I don't think I can face her." She looked across the table at Sheri with such a sad, defeated expression, Sheri now felt worse than pond scum. She felt like the putrid pus of a draining abscess.

"Let's tell her my engagement fell through today, and there isn't going to be a wedding, after all."

Linda's eyes suddenly widened, and she banged her forehead. "Oh, no! I told Matilda you and I were meeting with the wedding planner today."

*"You what?"*

Just then, the doorbell rang, and the front door opened. Both women heard the unmistakable voice of Aunt Matilda. "Hello, everyone. I'm here," she trilled from the entryway.

"What's Matilda doing here?" Sheri hissed.

Linda's eyes widened with alarm. "She invited herself to join us today, and I didn't know how to say no."

*"Oh great!"* Sheri stared at her mother in horror.

Linda stared down at her hands guiltily. "Matilda was the one who recommended Cyndi. She used her for Clarissa's wedding."

*Bad, bad, and getting worse.*

They could hear the muffled voices of Matilda and Cyndi chatting in the living room.

"But Matilda thinks Greg is the bridegroom, not Nicholas. I was about to correct her, but she had to take another call before I had the chance."

"After the family reunion, I can see why she'd jump to that conclusion."

Linda stood up and began to pace. "How am I going to face Matilda after this?"

*Ma and her childish feud!* Sometimes Sheri wanted to snap, "Grow up, both of you!"

Linda crossed her arms and sputtered, "She'll rub it in, you know she will. I'll never hear the end of it."

Her pacing reached a frenetic speed. Any more agitated, and she'd be wringing and washing her hands like Lady Macbeth.

"What am I going to tell Matilda?" Linda whined. "I can hear her now." With hands on her hips, Linda whispered in Matilda's condescending voice. "Can't your Sheri hang on to a man?"

*Apparently not, or at least not a man I'd want to hang on to.*

"Linda? Where are you?" came the voice of Matilda from the living room.

"That woman loves to rub it in my face that you aren't married." Linda reached the end of the kitchen and circled back around. "I'm sick of her putting me and my family down. She smiles to my face and then stabs me in the back with insults."

*A regular Botoxed Brutus.*

"Linda? Let's get started. I haven't got all day," Matilda hollered from the living room.

How Sheri dreaded having to confess to Matilda and Cyndi that she wasn't engaged and wasn't likely to become engaged in the next century. She nibbled on her thumbnail trying to come up with a plan, a scheme—anything—that would get her out of this pickle while still saving face. Coming up with nothing, it dawned on her.

*This isn't my problem. Ma called the wedding planner, not me. Let her face the consequences of her impulsiveness.*

Not wanting to face the guilt already growing in her chest for abandoning her mother, Sheri grabbed her purse and headed toward the back door of the kitchen that led outside. "I'm leaving. Just tell Matilda and Cyndi I called off the engagement today."

With that, Sheri bolted out the back door, down the back steps, and headed toward the driveway.

Linda charged after her. "You can't leave me in there to face those two alone. This is your fault as much as mine. You lied to me."

"I never asked a wedding planner to come. You dug yourself into this hole, so you can dig your way out."

Linda grabbed Sheri's arm. "How dare you abandon me. Is that any way to treat your mother?"

*It is when she calls a wedding planner when I'm not even engaged!*

Sheri yanked her arm free, but in the process, Linda lost her footing and landed straight into the holly bushes surrounding the house. Attempting to free herself, she managed to get her knit sweater tangled in the prickly bush.

They could hear Matilda hollering in the kitchen, "Linda? Sheri? Where are you?"

*"Lord, what fools these mortals be!"*
~William Shakespeare~
*A Midsummer Night's Dream*

# Chapter 37

Guilt coursed through Sheri like a dram of poison.

*What possessed me to run away like this? I need to woman up, go in there, and tell them the truth.*

Meanwhile, Linda, caught in the holly bush, tugged and pulled trying to extract her knitted sweater from the brambles. The more she pulled, the more entangled she became. "Help me, Sheri."

Suppressing a groan, Sheri attempted to pull back a branch, but the sweater was thoroughly entwined with the branches and prickles. Sheri tried to snap off the branch, but it was too large. Could she somehow pull her mother out?

She grabbed her mother around the waist and using all her might, pulled away from the holly bush. In the process, she lost her balance and fell straight into a thicket of poison ivy traversing up the side of the house and twining its way around a holly bush that clearly hadn't been pruned since her father's death.

Despite her sore bottom, Sheri instinctively pulled back in a desperate attempt to get away from the diabolical plant.

*Won't I look pretty with blisters all over my face tomorrow?*

She was already dreading the intense, "I-could-claw-myself-to-death" itching. She and poison ivy had become sworn enemies decades ago, but she managed to come in contact with her nemesis on a maddeningly regular basis. Yes, she knew the sing-song rhyme, "Leaves of five, let them thrive. Leaves of three, let them be," but she still somehow encountered the shiny three-leaved devil nearly every year.

How she wished she could run inside and wash the toxic ivy oil from her face and hands before she ended up looking like a World War I mustard gas victim. But her mother was now in panic mode.

"Help me," Linda whined. "My hair and sweater are all tangled up. I can't move forward because they're caught in a branch, and if move backward, it pulls my sweater completely off." She squirmed frantically—like a trout flapping in a fisherman's net.

Sheri jumped up and surveyed their predicament.

"Do something," her mother whimpered.

"What do you expect me to do? Buy a chain saw and cut the holly bush down?"

*If looks could kill.*

"You don't have to get snippy with me, Sheri Marie Morris."

Sheri released a sigh. "You're right, Ma. I'm sorry—I didn't mean to take out my frustration on you."

Linda scanned the ground with fearful eyes. "There's bound to be spiders everywhere just waiting to gnash their horrid little fangs into me."

Sheri surveyed the ground praying there *weren't* any spiders around, as her mother had an irrational fear of spiders. Not a mild fear of spiders, mind you, but total arachnophobia. Even a harmless daddy long-legs left her shrieking and shaking as if it were a Tyrannosaurus rex. Sheri's father had always had to disposed of all spiders before Linda would consider reentering a room. Then her mother would call the exterminator and demand an emergency spraying.

No amount of biology lectures on Sheri's part— "Spiders are good, Mom. They eat flies and mosquitos," made a bit of difference. Linda heard none of it. "I don't want those creepy-crawly critters anywhere near me."

*Let's hope the nearest spider is a mile away.*

Linda made a last desperate attempt to escape her holly bush prison, but she was as stuck as a fly… in a spider's web.

"If you don't get me out of here, I'm gonna scream bloody murder until someone comes and rescues me."

Meanwhile, they could hear Matilda and Cyndi calling their names as they wandered around the house. "Sheri? Linda? Where are you?"

Sheri squatted down to explore their options. If she could get her mother out of the bulky knit sweater ensnared in the branches, she could then back out of the brambles.

"Ma, I'm going to help you out of your sweater since it is keeping you tethered to the bush."

Linda's head jerked up, and her eyes enlarged to the size of moon pies. "But then I'll be out here in just my bra. What if the neighbors see me? Or even worse, the mailman?"

Sheri crossed her arms. "You got a better idea?"

Linda harrumphed. "Fine."

With Sheri's help, Linda managed to pull off her heavy sweater and extract herself from the prickly bush.

Once Linda was no longer ensnared, Sheri worked on disengaging the sweater from the brambles.

Linda glanced down at her scantily clad chest. "Hurry up! I look like a trollop standing out here in my bra." She crisscrossed her arms over her chest to cover herself. "The last thing I need is nosey Gertrude Danbury seeing me out here like this. Knowing her, she'll call the police and report me for indecent exposure."

Sheri tugged and pulled until the sweater—now filthy, snagged, and stretched out—lay in her hands. But at least Linda didn't have to walk into the living room dressed like a "trollop."

She handed the sweater to Linda, and as Linda was about to pull it over her head, Sheri saw her mother's worst nightmare. There—directly above Linda's head—sat a gigantic spider the size of a toddler's hand. He was spinning a web with intricate zig zag lines. Down he dropped, weaving a delicate web.

This was not any old spider. No, this had to be one of those massive yellow and black garden spiders with a huge splotchy bright yellow thorax, creepy black legs, and intimidating pedipalps. Truthfully, this arachnid even gave Sheri the heebie-jeebies

*Argiope aurantia.*

Why Sheri could remember such useless facts as the genus and species of a garden spider was beyond her. The joys of being a biology major with a photographic memory. All she knew was that said Argiope aurantia was directly over her mother's head spinning his web industriously. Up and down he dropped and rose, creating magic with the tiny threads of silk that he extruded from his spinneret. Perhaps the eight-legged opportunist had concluded Linda would make a tasty snack. If luck was on his side, he would have enough food for a lifetime.

*Should I warn Ma there's a giant spider overhead, or should I hope she gets her sweater on, and we get out of Dodge without her noticing it?*

Sheri remembered the last time her mother had come in contact with the teeny-tiniest of brown spiders. Talk about hysterics.

"How do you know he's not a brown recluse?" she shrieked in a tremulous voice, refusing to reenter the room until Sheri had squashed it. "People lose limbs from brown recluse spiders."

When Sheri suggested her mother check out the thorax of the spider to look for the tell-tale violin shape of a brown recluse, Linda recoiled. "I wouldn't get close enough to that vile beast to see if he had an entire orchestra on his back. Get rid of it!" she demanded, pointing with a shaky finger in the direction of the spider.

*Vile beast?* If she flipped out about the tiniest of brown spiders, she'd probably go into cardiac arrest if Sheri pointed out the ginormous yellow spider one foot above her head.

*Maybe I should just pretend I never saw it.*

Suddenly, before Sheri could utter a warning, her mother stretched her arm overhead about to put on her sweater and landed her hand straight into the spider web — actually touching the spider.

224

She jerked back after eyeing the yellow "beast" and let out a blood-curdling scream. She dropped her sweater, dashed out from the bushes, tripped over a hedge, then sprinted around the corner of the house toward the front door as though being pursued by a rabid dog.

*So much for not alerting the neighbors!*

In a tremulous voice, Linda hollered back, "D-did you see that thing?"

"Garden spiders are harmless, Ma," Sheri shouted, as she went in hot pursuit of her mother. "They just look intimidating."

Before Sheri could reach her, they heard the voices of Matilda and Cyndi from the front porch.

Sheri groaned. Right now, she wished the spider had pulled her up into its web and swallowed her whole—anything to avoid this humiliating encounter.

"Are you okay?" Cyndi yelled, trotting down the front steps toward Linda. "I heard the most terrible shriek. I thought somebody was being murdered." Eyeing Linda—clad only in her bra from the waist up and with her hair all mussed up—Cyndi covered her mouth, her eyes wide. "Were you assaulted?"

Linda dashed across the front lawn to meet up with Cyndi. "Yes. By a vicious spider."

"Really?" Cyndi said, her forehead etched with concern.

"Really?" Matilda said, in a tone suggesting skepticism. Since Ma's spider aversion went way back, Matilda had no doubt witnessed her theatrics before.

"How dreadful. Let's get you inside," Cyndi soothed, draping a comforting arm around Linda's shoulders. Sheri trailed behind them.

A shrill voice echoed from the yard next door. "Yoo-hoo. Linda? Are you alright?"

Linda turned toward the voice, groaned, and mumbled to Sheri, "Gertrude Danbury! I knew that busybody would stick her nose in our business."

A crotchety older woman with a cane tottered across the yard and up the walkway toward the porch. "I heard a terrible scream. Are you okay, Linda?"

"I'm fine, Gertrude," her mother said through clenched teeth.

Gertrude eyed her like a news reporter then demanded, "Why are you out here topless? The mailman might see you and report you for indecent exposure."

Sheri handed her mother the stretched out and now tattered sweater, and Linda quickly pulled it on, refusing to answer.

"What were you doing crawling around in the bushes?" Gertrude added.

So, she *had* been spying on them!

Before Linda could answer, Gertrude pointed toward the pink van. "And what's up with that wedding planner van? Sheri's not engaged."

Linda speared Gertrude with a "shut-up-this-second-or-I'm-going-to-murder-you-with- spider-poison" glare. She ignored the question and instead shared her harrowing spider story complete with theatrical hand gestures.

"You always were a scaredy-cat around spiders," Matilda muttered unsympathetically.

Cyndi then asked the dreaded question: "What were you two doing out here, anyway?"

Yes, what *were* they doing out here?

Linda and Sheri turned and stared at one another. Linda's cheeks flamed, but she didn't say a word. Sheri's brain turned to oatmeal.

*Busted!*

*"A wicked conscience moldeth goblins*
*swift as frenzy thoughts."*
~William Shakespeare~
*Troilus and Cressida*

# Chapter 38

Sheri wished the Rapture would occur right now. *Beam me up, Jesus, so I don't have to embarrass myself in front of these women.*

She sucked in a deep breath bracing herself for total humiliation. She had dug her grave. Time to jump in the coffin and slam the lid.

Before Sheri could 'fess up, however, Linda blurted out, "We were looking for Sheri's engagement ring."

Sheri had to force her eyeballs to stay in their sockets.

*What engagement ring??*

"Sheri's engagement ring was so pretty, I wanted you to see it before we started looking at wedding dresses. Plus, we needed the ring to select her wedding gown."

Gertrude scowled at the lame explanation, and Cyndi scratched her brow.

"Why would you need the ring to look at wedding dresses?" Gertrude demanded.

"We wouldn't want her ring to clash with her gown, now would we, Gertrude?" Linda snapped.

All eyes stared at Linda skeptically. Cyndi politely said, "Of course not."

Matilda piped in, "Why would you leave a valuable diamond ring out in the shrubs?"

"That wasn't very smart," Gertrude agreed.

Sheri turned to her mother. *What excuse would she trump up now?*

Linda fried Gertrude with a glare. "We didn't leave it out there on purpose. Sheri lost it."

"A likely story," the wizened neighbor mumbled.

"I'm perfectly fine now, so you can go home, Gertrude," Linda said with a dismissive flick of her wrist.

Unwilling to be dismissed without having the final word, Gertrude sputtered, "Sheri's not engaged, or you would have been bragging about it to everyone in the neighborhood. And that ring-in-the-bushes story sounds like a pile of rubbish to me."

"Goodbye, Gertrude." Linda practically pushed her neighbor off her yard."

As the four remaining women ambled up the steps toward the front door, Matilda asked, "How did Sheri's engagement ring wind up in the bushes?"

Linda's cheeks turned pink, and she paused, as though trying to conjure up an answer. Finally, she blurted, "Sheri was trimming the hedges today, and when she came inside to shower, she noticed her ring was missing."

Cyndi and Matilda glanced at the shrubs and the two women made eye contact. And who could blame them? The hedges had shoots sticking up like the prongs of a fork because they hadn't been trimmed in months.

Matilda's eyes narrowed. "I thought Sheri had to work all day, and that's why we couldn't meet until after five."

*You're a lousy liar, Ma.*

Since Sheri felt at least partly responsible for their present fiasco, she decided to come to her mother's rescue. "I came at the crack of dawn. Before work."

"Your neighbors don't mind you using a noisy hedge trimmer that early in the morning?" Matilda asked.

"They're all early birds," Linda insisted.

"By the time I came in to shower, I discovered my ring was missing, but I didn't have time to go look for it, or I'd be late for work."

"Were you able to find it?" Cyndi asked, playing along with their charade.

Sheri feigned a shoulder slump. "Unfortunately, no. But we've wasted far too much of your valuable time already. I'll search for it once we're done checking out all your lovely gowns and dresses."

Linda nodded, clearly delighted to have the focus switched away from why they had left the house in the first place. "Yes, let's get started."

Cyndi brightened at the mention of her dresses. No doubt she was thinking, "Maybe I'll get a sale out of this weird family, after all."

Except weird family had no wedding to plan.

Sheri knew she should just tell the truth, but after all the talk about a missing wedding ring, she couldn't make herself throw her mother under the bus. Her mother would be so humiliated — especially with Matilda standing there. Thus, she would play along with a pretend wedding, and then, in a few days, she would call Cyndi and tearfully confess the wedding was off because her fiancé had fallen in love with someone else. Cyndi would then be obliged to offer her deepest condolences. She couldn't very well yell at Sheri for wasting her time and wigging out on the wedding plans if Sheri was jilted. Sheri would offer to pay Cyndi fairly for any time she'd already invested.

As they gathered around the racks of dresses, Cyndi asked, "When's the big day?"

*Try forty years from now, when I'm in a nursing home and some demented octogenarian proposes to me.*

"December twentieth," Linda blurted out at the exact same time Sheri said, "December twenty-seventh."

They looked at each other wide-eyed.

*How do we bluster our way out of this one — we don't even know the date of the wedding?*

"Actually, we haven't totally nailed down the date yet, but with Sheri's hectic work schedule, we figured it was best to get started early. We want everything perfect—not some slipshod affair."

Linda looked down at her nails and added evasively, "Turns out, it might not be until *next* Christmas."

Cyndi's head jerked up. "As in next *year?* Why did I have it in my head that we needed to get things rolling immediately?"

*Why indeed.*

Sheri turned toward her mother, bracing herself for the next lie. *The Titanic* had hit an iceberg, and now it was filling with water.

Linda's cheeks turned a vibrant shade of fire engine red.

"We *do* want a Christmas wedding," Linda insisted, raising a pacifying hand, but it may not be until *next* Christmas. They're still debating whether to marry now or wait until next year."

Cyndi stared at them as though they had a screw loose. Several screws, actually. Managing lunatics must not be part of the wedding planner training course. She inhaled a deep breath, as though bracing herself for what came next and then plastered on a forced smile. "Well then. Shall we get started?"

Linda, Sheri, and Matilda strode toward the gowns. "Come look, Sheri. They're all so lovely," Linda said.

Sheri examined each of the wedding gowns—from simple satin, to fancy lace and frills, but in the end, she favored one in white velvet that flowed becomingly and was beaded around the neckline and sleeves. Simple but elegant. Regal, even.

"Try it on," the wedding planner insisted. "I'll bet with your height and auburn hair it will look spectacular."

"It *is* an elegant gown," Matilda agreed.

"Let me wash up first," Sheri insisted. "I wouldn't want to get it dirty."

"Good thinking," Cyndi agreed, her eyes widening in alarm at the thought of grunge all over her expensive gowns.

"I should probably scrub up, too," Linda said, holding out her grimy hands. "We'll be back in a minute."

Sheri and her mother hightailed it to the bathroom. Once inside, Sheri shut the door and locked it, so they could talk.

"I thought you were going to tell her you weren't engaged," Linda hissed, turning on the faucet.

"How was I supposed to say that after you told her we were looking outside for my *engagement* ring?"

"You could have told her we needed to find the ring, so you could return it to the groom, since you were no longer engaged."

Sheri ran her hands under the warm water then pumped on liquid soap and began to methodically rub each finger. "Ma, that makes no sense. If the wedding had been called off, you would have told Cyndi she didn't need to come at all today, nor would we have blurted out a wedding date."

Linda pumped soap into her hands. "When she asked what we were doing out there in the bushes, I couldn't think of a thing to say, so I blurted out the first thing that came to mind."

"Which is why I couldn't very well tell her I *wasn't* engaged. It would make you look like a liar — which, of course, you are."

Linda scowled. "Well, so are you! You told her you were trimming hedges this morning. They look so shaggy nobody believed you." She rinsed the soap off her hands and reached for the hand towel from the rack. Her shoulders sagged. "What are we going to do?"

Sheri rinsed the soap off her hands and turned off the faucet. She grabbed the towel from her mother and began to wipe. "We're going to go out there and feign excitement about Cyndi's dresses. We'll pick out a gown, bridesmaid dresses, invitations and what all. We'll let her write it all down, but we'll tell her not to order anything until we pick an actual wedding date. Then, in a week, I'll call and tell her Nicholas broke off our engagement."

Linda chewed her bottom lip considering the idea.

Sheri continued. "I'll act inconsolable and tell her I'm very sorry, but I won't be needing her wedding planning services, after all."

"That might work." Her eyes widened in alarm. "No. Wait — Matilda thinks you're engaged to Greg, not Nicholas."

231

"Ma, what different does it make *who* Matilda thinks I'm engaged to, if I'm not even engaged— especially if I'm calling off my fake engagement next week."

"What if she runs into Greg?" Linda countered. "She would be sure to mention how excited she is about the upcoming wedding, and then Greg will be broad-sided, and he'll tell Matilda he doesn't know what she's talking about."

Sheri glanced at herself in the mirror and was aghast to see her hair so full of holly bramble and twigs she looked like a porcupine. She plucked out as many as she could.

"I'll talk to Greg. He's met Matilda and Grandma, so he knows what we're up against. Besides, he's already faked being my boyfriend. Perhaps we should take our relationship to the next level and have him fake being my fiancé."

Linda gripped her arm. "You'd do that for me—ask Greg to be your pretend fiancé?"

Sheri shrugged. "Sure—as long as you promise to quit meddling in my life."

"Promise!" Linda made the sign of the cross on her chest. "Cross my heart and hope to die."

Sheri wagged a scolding finger at her. "You remember that the next time you're tempted to meddle. I mean it, Ma."

Once they emerged from the bathroom, Sheri brought the velvet gown with pearl trim into the bedroom to try on. Her mother helped her adjust the folds and pull up the zipper. Sheri twirled in front of the full-length mirror and couldn't help but grin.

*Not bad—not bad at all!* "I love it!"

Linda Morris clapped her hands into a prayer pose. "Oh, Sheri, you look positively stunning! This is the dress. I'll lend you my pearls as your something borrowed. They will look wonderful with this pearl beading."

"Let's go see what Cyndi and Matilda think."

They returned to the living room and modeled the gown for Cyndi and Matilda.

Shockingly, even Matilda offered a rare compliment and said that the gown looked lovely on her.

*How nice – I've found the perfect dress for my non-existent wedding.*

While Sheri changed out of the gown and carefully hung it back in its plastic bag, Matilda bid them adieu, claiming she had a bridge club to prepare for.

Cyndi next wanted them to select bridesmaid dresses. Sheri settled on cranberry for the Matron of Honor (Tess) and forest green for the bridesmaids.

"Cranberry and forest green will look festive at Christmastime, and Claire and Clarissa's hair will contrast nicely with the green," Sheri said.

Linda's eyes widened in horror. "Claire and Clarissa? You're not inviting those glory hogs to be your bridesmaids." She crossed her arms in protest. "I forbid it!"

"Ma, they're my only cousins, and they asked me to be in their weddings."

"Only because they knew you wouldn't upstage them. Face it, Sheri. When they got married, you were plump and frumpy, so they had nothing to worry about."

*Gee, thanks, Ma.*

"Don't you have any dowdy, old maid girlfriends you could ask? Preferably ones with bucked teeth and an extra fifty pounds?"

"Mother!" Sheri hissed, mortified the wedding planner was hearing such talk. Plus, Cyndi had planned Clarissa's wedding! Would it get back to Matilda that Linda called her a glory hog?

She glanced over to see Cyndi's reaction, but thankfully, she had wisely taken a sudden obsession with straightening her gowns. She avoided eye contact at all costs.

"A wedding is not a Miss America pageant," Sheri pointed out. "Besides, Tess and I are committed to developing a better relationship with Claire and Clarissa. This feud between you and Matilda has got to stop, and not inviting her daughters to be my bridesmaids will only antagonize things between you. I refuse to fan the flames of your hostility."

Linda refused to back down. "I still say you don't want the bridesmaids sucking the attention away from the bride. If you insist on keeping those show-offs in your wedding party, dress them in something hideous." She turned to Cyndi. "Do you have any gowns that are baggy and unfitted? A muumuu, perhaps? And we'll need a garish color." She tapped her lip with her index finger. "Hot orange or puce, perhaps?"

*Hot orange muumuus — for a bridesmaid gown?*

Cyndi's eyes widened in alarm. "I'm afraid there's no demand for dresses of that description, Ma'am," she said with a frosty voice. It must horrify her to have a wedding with her name as the wedding planner if the bridesmaids were attired in hot orange muumuus.

"Mother — remember, you promised not to meddle. Now, I insist on having Clarissa and Claire as bridesmaids, and they will wear attractive cocktail dresses in a tasteful forest green."

"What about fluorescent chartreuse?" Linda piped in, refusing to expel her phobia of Sheri being upstaged by her cousins.

*Why were they arguing about bridesmaid's dresses for a non-existent wedding, anyhow?*

Sheri gripped her mother's shoulders and forced her to look her in the eyes. "Mother, listen to me. I have been upstaged by Claire, Clarissa, and Tess my whole life. I learned a long time ago not to base my self-esteem on my looks. There will always be women who are prettier than me, and I've learned to be okay with that. Besides, if I dress the bridesmaids becomingly, it's a reflection of *our* good tastes."

Linda's lips pursed in thought.

Sheri continued. "If we dress them in something ugly, people will whisper, 'Aren't those bridesmaid dresses hideous? Sheri and Linda Morris have no fashion sense at all.'"

"You're right. I didn't look at it that way."

"An excellent way to look at it," Cyndi interjected quickly. "Tasteful and becoming is always best, so cranberry and forest green cocktail dresses it is."

She hastily scribbled the selection into her notebook and then announced, "I think we've accomplished quite enough for one day." She began to pack up her things. "Once you select an actual wedding date, give me a call."

Sheri heard Cyndi mumble under her breath. *"Or not."*

They helped Cyndi transport all the gowns and dresses and wedding paraphernalia back into her van. Sheri had the distinct impression from Cyndi's chilly demeanor that she had been on to their charade the entire time. She would bet money Cyndi had figured out the gown fitting was a sham...for a sham wedding. Why waste any more time looking at invitations, flowers, or reception plans for a sham wedding?

As the pink van squealed out of the driveway, Sheri hoped she never had to face the woman again.

The second the van sped out of sight, Sheri turned on her mother. "That was the most embarrassing thing that has ever happened to me."

Conjuring up her disastrous dinner date with Caleb and Morgan, she amended her statement. "Second most embarrassing." The disastrous date where she'd flung a dinner roll at Greg and where Theresa declared them both certifiably crazy came to mind. "Okay, third most embarrassing." Her coffee shop encounter with Jeremy the Jerk, where the patrons were snickering and elbowing each other, also popped into her head. "No, the fourth most embarrassing thing. But still! I am mortified."

Her mother smiled as though unconcerned. "Our time wasn't a complete waste—we picked out a lovely wedding gown and beautiful Christmas bridesmaid dresses."

"For a *pretend* wedding, with a *pretend* groom, who gave me a *pretend* engagement ring."

Linda shrugged, offering no apology.

"Do me a favor. The next time you want to surprise me, buy me some earrings—or a fat-free, sugar-free hazelnut latte."

Her mother's eyes suddenly pooled with tears. "I don't mean to meddle. It's just that since your father died, I feel so useless and unneeded. You girls are so busy with your careers, and I can't make a life out of just attending Jacob's T-ball games."

Sheri pulled her mother in for a hug. "I know you're lonely since Dad died, but it's been over a year now. What do you say we look on the Senior Singles website?" Sheri elbowed her mother. "Maybe we'll be planning *your* December wedding, instead of mine."

Linda waved a dismissive hand. "Oh, stop—I'll bet there aren't any decent men my age."

"I don't know about that. There were plenty of sixty-four-year-old men online when I looked." Sheri left out the minor detail that said sixty-four-year-old men were looking for forty-year-old women.

"I suppose there's no harm looking." Her mother grinned. "Who knows? I might find me a hottie."

"Let's sign you up. We'll call it my early Christmas gift to you."

*"I would challenge you to a battle of wits,*
*but I see you are unarmed."*
~William Shakespeare~
*Much Ado about Nothing* (Paraphrased)

# Chapter 39

"Wait—your Aunt Matilda invited us to *our* engagement party?" Greg stopped dead in his tracks on the hiking trail and stared at her. "Did I miss something—like maybe a marriage proposal?"

Sheri popped him on the arm. "Don't be a dunderhead. Of course, you haven't missed a marriage proposal. It's my mother—she's up to her old tricks again."

As they continued their trek around Radnor Lake, Sheri recanted her misadventure with prickly holly bushes, poison ivy, garden spiders, snoopy neighbors, and an unsuspecting wedding planner.

Okay, it *was* pretty funny. He could picture Sheri's mother shrieking about a garden spider while clad only in her bra, all the while with a nosy neighbor and Matilda interrogating her. But still...a fake engagement party?

"Can't you just tell Matilda that your mother was mistaken about us being engaged?"

She rewarded him with a "you moron" glare. *O-kay! Apparently, not.*

"I planned on telling Matilda and Cyndi exactly that, but Ma freaked out and said Matilda would never let her live it down. She insists Matilda will make snide remarks about me never being able to snag up a man."

Greg rolled his eyes. "Do we live in Peyton Place?"

"You've met my Aunt Matilda. I swear, the woman eats eye of newt and wing of bat for breakfast."

"She did seem to flaunt her house and furnishings at the reunion."

"Let alone her precious Claire and Clarissa." Sheri crossed her arms in disgust. "To listen to Matilda, *her* daughters hit the genetic jackpot and I'm an embarrassing mutant."

He smirked. "Bitter, are we?"

"Not a bit," she insisted, though her pace picked up, and he had to jog to catch up with her.

"The lady doth protest too much, me thinks."

Her eyes narrowed. "The lady doth protest that her mother put her in a predicament of being shamed for life by Matilda, or of faking an engagement with you. It's a lose-lose proposition, no matter how I look at it."

*A lose-lose proposition? Way to boost a guy's ego.*

"Gee, thanks! Guess I'm a real loser compared to your precious Nicholas, huh?" He formed the letter L with his fingers on his forehead.

She reached for his arm apologetically. "No, I didn't mean it like that. I just don't like being forced to fake an engagement. I still say I should just tell Matilda we called off our engagement and be done with it, but Ma won't hear of it. 'Then she'll really have fodder to say you can't hold onto a man,' Ma insists."

He picked up a small tree limb that had fallen into their path and flung it into the woods.

*Would a real engagement to me be so terrible?*

They trudged in silence until Greg asked, "So, when is this illustrious engagement party of ours supposed to take place?"

"Matilda told me to check your schedule so we can pick a date."

Greg whacked his forehead with the palm of his hand. "That's right! Since I'm supposedly the accountant for a barnyard of famous country musicians, she no doubt thinks my social calendar is slammed."

She chuckled. "You mean you don't have appointments with Taylor Swift and Keith Urban this week?"

He snorted. "My new client, Jason Bodine, is a country musician alright—or so he claims. He played me a song he wrote from his self-recorded CD, and I had to chomp on the inside of my cheeks to keep from laughing."

"That bad?" Sheri stepped around a patch of mud in their path.

"The word caterwauling came to mind. The guy moved here from Texas hoping for a lucky break, but I'd sooner hear a moose in heat than that guy in concert."

She elbowed him. "Perhaps you should invite him to our engagement party as the featured entertainment."

Greg laughed. "Can you imagine Matilda's reaction the second he opened his mouth."

"It *would* be entertaining, though not in a way *she* might prefer."

She grabbed his arm with both of hers, her eyes twinkling with a devilish gleam.

He did a double take, and a sinking feeling settled in his chest.

*She's up to something. She's positively smirking.*

"What's going on in the scheming mind of yours?" he demanded.

Sheri rubbed her hands together in glee and broke into an evil laugh. "Let's tell Matilda one of your clients can provide entertainment at the party. It'll serve Matilda right for all the years she's bullied and demeaned my mother and me."

Greg crossed his arms like a railroad crossing sign. "No way! I want no part of this." He marched ahead as though trying to escape. The devil doesn't wear Prada, the devil is in gym shorts and Nikes.

She ran to catch up to him then grabbed his arm and pulled him to a stop. "Come on, Greg! It'll be fun. A week or two after the party, I'll tell Matilda you and I decided to call off the wedding because we are better suited as friends than spouses. I promise." She raised both hands. "What could possibly go wrong?"

"If you and I are involved, everything."

She clutched his arm and gazed up at him imploringly. "Please? For me?"

Pleading puppy dog eyes that were hard to resist gazed back at him. "Pretty please? Matilda *needs* to be humbled, and Jason Bodine's singing will be just the ticket to pull her down a notch."

He released a heavy sigh and scratched the back of his neck.

*This is a bad idea. I should say no.*

He relented slightly. "Tell you what—I'll give you the guy's name and phone number, but what you tell your Aunt Matilda is between you and her. Keep me out of it."

"So, you'll come to the party and pretend you're my fiancé?"

"I guess," he said, with an unenthusiastic shrug.

"Yes!" She pumped her arm in victory then rose up on tip-toes and kissed his cheek.

Greg couldn't help but smile. "I *do* have a suggestion, if you want Jason to sound his worst."

Her face lit up. "Tell me."

"Ask him to play his original tunes. Trust me, he's an even poorer songwriter than he is a singer. The song he played for me went on and on about a leaky roof. It was supposed to be an analogy for his leaky heart after his girlfriend ditched him. The lyrics used the words roof, goof, poof, and beer all in one verse."

"Beer? That doesn't rhyme with roof and goof."

He forced himself to keep his face deadpan. "And your point?"

They burst into laughter.

"This is going to be fun!" Sheri insisted, rubbing her hands together. "I can't wait to see Matilda's face when he howls like a hyena."

"How many people is she inviting, do you suppose?"

"If I know Matilda, she'll invite everyone she knows—for bragging rights."

"With any luck, Jason's singing will trigger so much conversation, the guests will forget it was supposed to be an engagement party for us."

Sheri grinned. "Perfect."

"See if Matilda and Jason are up for next Saturday night. With his voice, I can't imagine he books more than one concert a year."

"And definitely no repeat business," Sheri added with a wink.

"On a positive note, if Matilda Moneybags pays him for the concert, the guy might actually pay me some of the two thousand bucks he owes me for doing his taxes."

Her eyes widened. "Two thousand dollars? Just to file a tax return? That's robbery, Greg."

"Actually, *he* may be the robber. He got audited by the IRS for 'creative accounting practices', shall we call them." Greg etched the words with his fingers. "He came to me to help him dig through his accounts and respond to the IRS."

"Too bad he isn't as talented at songwriting as he is at fudging his finances."

"You got that right. He owes the IRS five grand in back taxes and penalties for trying to deduct his car loan payments *and* mileage."

Sheri did her best to maintain a poker face. "You mean I'm not supposed to do that?"

His face must have registered shock because she cackled and pointed at him. "Got you!"

He made a hand gesture of wringing her neck.

When they reached the end of the hiking trail, Greg promised to provide her with Jason's phone number.

*Hey, I'm just trying to help a struggling musician get out of dire straits with the IRS, right?*

*"The man that hath no music is fit for*
*treason, stratagems, and spoils."*
~William Shakespeare~
*The Merchant of Venice*

# Chapter 40

As Sheri and Greg tromped up the marble steps to Aunt Matilda and Uncle Max's mansion, a truckload of guilt pummeled Sheri's chest.

*I'm not normally a mean and spiteful person. Why am I doing this?*

Yes, Matilda could be insulting, but was that any reason for Sheri to lower herself to Matilda's level? It was wrong. Unchristian. And a stupid idea on every level.

Greg told her he also had serious misgivings about what she'd planned, but thankfully, he still agreed to show up and play the role of her adoring fiancé.

Sheri would tell Matilda in a couple of weeks that the wedding was off, but for tonight, they would feign being deeply in love. Correction—*Greg* would feign being deeply in love, because Sheri already *was* deeply in love with Greg.

She mashed her index finger on the doorbell and whispered to Greg, "I wish I hadn't arranged for Jason to come tonight. I regret it already."

"As well you should, but as Shakespeare said, 'What's done, is done.' We'll just have to smooth things out as best we can."

She heard footsteps approaching, and Matilda opened the door and greeted them with a stiff peck on the cheek. "Come in." She flagged them inside with her hand. "Everyone is here. I've had a great turnout for the party."

*I feel like a traitor. Et tu, Brutus?*

Matilda ushered them toward her large solarium where Jason was already set up and chatting with Uncle Max and Clarissa.

Jason at least *looked* the part of a successful country musician with his T-shirt, tight jeans, cowboy hat and boots, and obligatory acoustic guitar. He hadn't shown up drunk, and he was handsome, in that rugged, scruffy-faced, Texan cowboy way. Plus, he seemed to interact with his benefactors nicely.

*So far, so good, but what will people think, if he sings as badly as Greg says he does?*

She scanned the room — at least fifty people — most of whom she recognized as distant relatives. Before she could stew any further about the upcoming entertainment, her mother strolled over, her face aglow. She held the hand of a tall, older gentleman.

*Who is he?*

Linda introduced her new boyfriend, Richard, to Sheri and Greg.

*Mom has a boyfriend? When did that happen?*

Linda pulled Sheri close and whispered, "I met Richard through that Senior Singles website you signed me up for. He's wonderful. He lost his wife to cancer last year, and he treats me like a queen." Her face lit up, and she giggled like a high school sophomore describing her first school crush.

Sheri tried to quell her worst suspicions. Was this some shyster after her mother's...her mother's *what?* Ma wasn't rich or beautiful, so what was his agenda? Was Richard even his real name?

Eyeing the guy, she saw nothing immediately off-putting, but her mother was clearly smitten, and that would blind her to any glaring character flaws. Plus, Ma was lonely, which made her easy prey for con artists and psychopaths.

*Yeesh! I sound like Greg checking out my online prospective boyfriends.*

Greg must have sensed her unease because after he shook hands with Richard, he draped a reassuring arm around her shoulders and whispered, "Give him a chance. He might be perfect for your mother."

They chatted a few minutes—if you call Sheri giving Richard the third-degree chatting.

*Where can I rent a lie detector test...*

Richard was a lawyer. Sheri would try not to hold that against him since he didn't sue doctors or advertise on TV. He specialized in corporate law.

The four of them wandered over to the refreshment table, and Sheri filled her plate with veggies, dip, cheese, and crackers. She introduced Greg to a few distant relatives and then forced herself into an obligatory interaction with Grandma Claiborne while Greg was in the bathroom.

"I see you finally got someone to propose to you," Grandma said. "He seems like a decent enough fellow." She eyeballed Sheri up and down before adding, "He's probably the best you'll be able to snag up at your age, so I wouldn't dawdle on the wedding date."

*Always the charmer, Grandma. No wonder Matilda turned out mean — the apple doesn't fall far from the tree.*

Sheri excused herself post-haste before her deflated ego drove her back to the refreshment table to fill up on chocolate chunk frosted brownies. And fudge.

Grandma tottered away, no doubt seeking out another relative to demoralize.

After Greg wandered back from the bathroom, Aunt Matilda tapped a wine glass with a knife to get everyone's attention. She introduced Greg to everyone with the snide remark, "Let's all give Greg a hearty and grateful round of applause, since some of us never thought this day would come." Everyone tittered at the dig.

*Thanks a lot! I no longer feel bad about lining up Jason.*

Matilda smiled and added, "In all seriousness, he's a charming fellow, and we're thrilled to have him join the family. Greg— welcome!" She began to clap, and everyone joined in.

Sheri's eyes unexpectedly pooled with tears.

If only Greg *were* joining the family.

She forced herself to paste on a smile as Greg wrapped his arm around her back in a feigned show of affection, as he waved an acknowledgement to Matilda's greeting.

*Will I be able to keep up this painful charade all night?*

*If only Greg hadn't met Vanessa.*

While Sheri knew Vanessa no longer held the control over his heart that she once did, he still hadn't broken up with her or made any mention of a future with Sheri.

On a positive note, he hadn't mentioned a future with Vanessa, either.

Her gut told her Greg would eventually figure out Vanessa was all wrong for him, but yeesh, would it be in this century? And when he did, would he see Sheri as anything more than his exercise chum?

Before she could ponder these questions further, Matilda introduced Jason as "country music's future superstar."

Jason tipped his cowboy hat and greeted the audience standing in Matilda's solarium with a warm smile. "I wrote this first song when the love of my life dumped me, leaving my heart as leaky as a worn-out roof. I'm hoping it will be my first number one hit."

A hush fell over the room as the audience waited with eager anticipation.

Sheri made eye contact with Greg and felt her stomach tighten.

*If he's as terrible as Greg claimed, Matilda is going to kill me.*

Jason strummed a few opening measures and then launched into his "future hit". As he croaked out the opening line in a pitchy Southern twang, Sheri forced herself not to look at Greg, or they'd both break into hysterical laughter — or tears.

She glanced around the room to gauge the reaction of the other guests. Her mother and Richard stared at Jason with mouths agape. Most of the other guests looked shell-shocked. Grandma Claiborne made no effort to be polite. She clamped her hands over both ears, her mouth in a lemon-sucking scowl.

Then disaster struck. When Jason attempted to hit a particularly high note on the word "roof", Matilda's poodle, Duchess, began to howl. Not quietly, but with her snout skyward, her lips pursed, and with a tremulous tone that almost matched Jason's. Correction—Duchess did a better job staying on pitch.

All around her, the guests started snickering at the howling pooch, and soon, Sheri noticed the shoulders of nearly everyone in the room shaking with unabashed laughter. Most had resorted to covering their mouths in a futile attempt at politeness. Jason carried on as though oblivious to the yowling dog.

How would Aunt Matilda react to such a ghastly performer in her home—especially one she bragged would someday be a country music superstar?

Sheri forced herself to peek over at Matilda, and her heart jolted. Matilda's jaw was clenched, and rage that matched Cruella de Vil's, when she discovered the 101 Dalmatian puppies had all escaped, came to mind. Sheri could almost see the steam shooting straight from the top of her head.

*Inviting Jason to sing had been a bad idea—a very bad idea.*

Never one to tolerate public humiliation, once Jason finished his song, Matilda clapped politely and said, "Thank you for sharing your heartfelt selection with us, Jason. We were all so..." she hesitated, as though struggling to come up with an appropriate word. She cleared her throat and finally settled on, "taken by your singing."

*Taken with wanting to stuff our ear with cotton balls.*

The guests clapped anemically—except for Uncle Max, who everyone knew was both deaf *and* tone-deaf. He shouted enthusiastically, "Sing us another, Jason."

One guest glared at Max like he wanted to kick him in the shins.

Sheri overheard her mother whisper to Richard, "Where on earth did Matilda find this guy?"

Richard whispered back, "America Ain't Got Talent."

246

"The dog had a better singing voice," Linda whispered back, and the two of them shared a private chuckle.

Greg whispered in Sheri's ear, "If I ever get tired of spreadsheets, I may take up singing. I couldn't be any worse."

To his credit, Jason handled the howling dog like a star. He stroked Duchess on the head and thanked her for providing back-up vocals. He then complemented Matilda for promoting the arts in the canine population. His gracious response broke the ice, and everyone warmed up to him. "Duchess here reminds me of another song I wrote called, 'It's a Doggone Shame She's Gone.'"

Thankfully, this song didn't set Duchess on a howling frenzy. Unfortunately, his third song, "She Done Me Wrong," triggered Duchess to vocalize every time Jason hit one particularly high note in the chorus.

Matilda grabbed Duchess's collar and forcefully dragged the poor pooch from the room. Even clear across the house, you could make out faint dog howls with every strained note.

Matilda returned from escorting Duchess out of the solarium and stood next to Sheri. Staring straight ahead, she hissed, "It's payback time."

A shiver of dread coursed down Sheri's spine.

*What did she mean by that?*

When Jason finished his third song, Matilda clapped her hands, and with a smug smile announced, "I'm sure you all remember Sheri sang with the show choir when she was in high school. I think to honor her engagement tonight, she and Jason should sing a duet, don't you?"

Sheri froze.

*Sing a duet – with Jason? No way!*

Even Barbara Streisand would sound dreadful if forced to sing with the man.

Matilda mumbled, "You so deserve this," and pulled on her arm, trying to force her onto the makeshift stage. "We're all dying to hear Sheri sing with Jason, aren't we?" She clapped and egged on the audience.

Sheri's heart hammered at the humiliating prospect. She had to find a graceful way to bow out. "I-I haven't sung publicly in twenty years. I'll pass, thank you."

Matilda would hear none of it. She gestured with her hand for the crowd to cheer her on. Soon Matilda had everyone chanting, "Sheri! Sheri! Sheri!"

Matilda gripped her arm with the strength of a vice grip and forcefully "encouraged" her onto the stage. With a deceptive smile, Matilda said in a volume only Sheri could hear, "You think you can make a fool out of me? Think again, Missy!"

"I-I don't know what you're talking about," Sheri said, trying her best to sound convincing. "I'd never heard him sing before."

Clearly unconvinced, Matilda whispered back, "If you think that howling hyena is good enough to perform in my home, then he's good enough to sing a duet with you." With her back now fully turned to her guests, Matilda snapped, "What goes around, comes around."

Convicted by her aunt's scathing retort and pressured by the audience's cheers, Sheri could see no way out. She gazed down at Greg with a pleading look, but he only shrugged and raised his hands as if to say, "What can I do?"

Tess hollered, "You can do it, Sheri. You have a fabulous voice."

"You can do it!" Greg added.

Sheri shrugged in surrender. "All right, I'll give it a whirl, but don't expect much."

They all applauded and whistled.

She thumbed through the book of country songs and lyrics that Jason had brought with him, and they settled on "I Will Always Love You." Sheri would sing the verses and Jason would harmonize on the chorus.

*I deserve this. I need to suck it up, make a fool of myself, and then dig a hole to hide in.*

Thankfully, Jason was a skilled guitarist, so as she sang her first verse, it didn't sound half bad. The chorus? Well, if you can't say something nice...

She made it through the second verse sounding even better than she had on the first, as her voice no longer shook. After they finished the final chorus, Sheri was ready to dive off the make-shift stage and sprint toward the front door. Instead, everyone demanded an encore.

Greg gazed at her with such pride, she couldn't help but smile. He clapped and whistled and yelled, "Encore!" louder than everyone else.

Jason politely suggested Sheri do a solo this time since she was the guest of honor. The audience whooped and shouted in agreement.

Sheri wasn't sure they wanted to hear *her* sing, as much as they *didn't* want to hear Jason sing.

"What's your favorite song?" he asked.

Without deliberation, she named "I Can't Make You Love Me." She'd always loved Bonnie Raitt's rendition.

Since Matilda's spacious solarium held a gorgeous Steinway grand, Sheri said she'd accompany herself on the piano.

*Here's hoping I don't get Duchess howling, though it would serve me right.*

She launched into the familiar tune and lyrics. Without intending to, she found herself singing the words straight to Greg, as they seemed apropos:

**I can't make you love me, if you don't.**
**I can't make your heart feel something it won't.**

Her eyes pooled as she sang the sad refrain about unrequited love. By the song's conclusion, she felt as though only she and Greg were in the room. His eyes bore into hers, and she was convinced he understood what she was feeling. But would it change anything? If he didn't love her by now, he never would.

A tidal wave of despair washed over her. The irony of this night—attending a phony engagement party with a man she loved desperately, while singing a song about how she couldn't make him love her—became too painful to bear. After bowing and acknowledging everyone's claps and whoops of praise, she quickly excused herself before she burst into tears in front of everyone.

She bolted for the bathroom with Tess following close behind. Tess locked the bathroom door behind them and gave her a hug. When Sheri burst into tears, Tess said, "You're in love with Greg, aren't you?"

Sheri nodded. "With my whole heart. But like the song says, I can't make him love me back."

As she released the roller coaster of emotions the evening had stirred up—her shoulders heaved, and she sobbed onto her sister's shoulder.

She snatched up a wad of toilet paper and wiped her eyes, careful to avoid smudging her mascara.

Tess wrapped an arm around her shoulders. "It's obvious to me and everybody else that Greg is head over heels in love with you, too. Why do you think everyone believed this bogus engagement party was for real?"

Sheri shrugged, too miserable to utter a word. She wiped her eyes again. "But if he loves me, why doesn't he say so? And why hasn't he broken it off with Vanessa?"

Tess rubbed soothing circles across Sheri's back. "Have you asked him that?"

"Of course not," she snapped. She twisted the damp toilet paper with shaky fingers. "I'm afraid to. What if he tells me he's not attracted to me in that way? It would make things so awkward, and it would probably destroy our friendship."

"Do you really believe that?"

She raised exasperated hands. "Yes. No. I don't know! Sometimes I'm convinced he's attracted to me, but he told me once Vanessa is so beautiful she takes his breath away. How can I compete with that?"

Tess squeezed her shoulders. "You don't compete. Be yourself, and if you two are meant to be together, it will all work out. You need to give him more time."

Sheri snorted and tossed her crumpled toilet paper into the wastebasket. "Time. Because time has worked so well for me so far? I'm forty-years-old and still single because time is *not* my friend." She unrolled more toilet paper and blew her nose. "Greg knows me so well. Too well. If he doesn't love me by now, he's never going to, and more time won't change a thing."

"I disagree. Greg may have been smitten with Vanessa, but he's grown tired of her. Beauty alone won't keep him long-term—not if there isn't a deep connection like what he shares with you."

"You really think so? Vanessa is drop-dead gorgeous, and other than talking too much, she's actually a nice person."

Tess gripped her shoulders. "Listen to me. Far better to be the one he loves *last* than the one he loved *first*."

She gazed into her sister's eyes. "You really think there's hope?"

"I know so. Greg is the analytical type. He won't make a permanent life decision impulsively. Give him a little more time to figure out that you're the one he wants to spend his life with. He'll come around, I promise."

Was Tess only saying what she thought Sheri wanted to hear, or did she mean it? She *seemed* sincere...

Sheri blew her nose, tossed the dirty tissue into the trash, and washed her hands. "Well, we can't stay in here all night. Time to paste on my happy face and go mingle again." Her shoulders slumped. "I'd sooner operate on a gangrenous bowel than have to face Greg right now."

Tess winced. "You and your gross medical talk! Honestly, you need to quit that, if you want to win Greg over." She pulled Sheri in for a warm hug. "I'm here for you, Sis."

Sheri hugged her sister back. "Thanks, Tess."

She pushed open the bathroom door and there, standing right in front of them, was Aunt Matilda.

Her livid expression confirmed she'd overheard their conversation.

Tess and Sheri's eyes met in horror, and they froze.

*Busted!*

*"The whirligig of time brings in his revenges."*
*~William Shakespeare~*
*Twelfth Night*

# Chapter 41

"H-how much did you hear?" Sheri asked, already knowing the answer.

Matilda's brow rose, and a condescending sneer crossed her face. "Enough to know this whole evening was nothing but a charade. What kind of a stunt were you and Linda pulling?"

"No stunt," Sheri managed to eke out.

Matilda crossed her arms. "I forked out a bundle of money to honor you and Greg with this party because I knew Linda couldn't afford it. Now I find out you're not even engaged?" Her lips thinned, and her eyes burned with rage. "I demand an explanation."

Right now, like Hamlet, Sheri wanted to melt, thaw, and resolve herself into a dew. Anything to escape Aunt Matilda's wrath.

She could feel her cheeks burning. Tess was in even worse shape—she stood in stupefied shock, her body shaking.

Sheri would have to suck it up and grovel. She fixed her eyes on the floor. "I am so sorry, Aunt Matilda. Please don't blame Mom. This whole misunderstanding is my fault."

"Misunderstanding? Don't patronize me, young lady."

Sheri explained how she'd felt pressured to find a husband in time for a Christmas wedding, and to get her mother off her back, she'd exaggerated the seriousness of her relationship. She didn't bother to mention Nicholas rather than Greg, as that would only complicate things. "When Mom surprised me with a wedding planner and then told me she had mentioned it to you, she was too embarrassed to tell you there *was* no engagement. When you offered to host this party, I cooked up the idea of pretending Greg and I were engaged and going through with the party. I planned to call off the engagement in a couple of weeks"

Matilda's eyes narrowed. "Greg was willing to go along with your shenanigans?"

"He didn't want to because he thought it was dishonest. But he's my best friend, so I talked him into it."

Matilda eyed Sheri. "Any man who would do that for you is far more than a best friend. It's obvious to everyone but you that he's in love with you. That's why I believed it when Linda told me you two were engaged." She offered Sheri the slightest hint of a smile. "Perhaps there *will* be a wedding in your future, after all. My party may have just come a little early."

Sheri ventured a quick glance in Matilda's eyes. She seemed to be softening. As Matilda turned to walk away, Sheri reached for her arm. "Matilda? Please don't mention this to Mom. She's always felt intimidated and inferior to you. It would kill her if she found out you knew the truth."

Matilda pursed her lips. "Well, I suppose I could keep this unfortunate event as our little secret."

Sheri forced herself to meet Matilda's gaze head-on. "Mom *wants* to have a better relationship with you, but she doesn't know how to fix things after all these years of feuding."

As though mulling over Sheri's earlier statement, Matilda said, "I don't know why Linda would feel inferior. She's raised two highly accomplished daughters, and now that you've put some effort into your appearance, you've become quite attractive." She turned to Tess. "You, of course, have always been beautiful."

"Thank you," Tess mumbled. "Like Sheri, I wish our families could become closer. I'd love for Claire and Clarissa to become like sisters to me."

Matilda stiffened. "Well, you'll have to discuss *that* with them. They do have very busy social lives and won't have time for idle chit chat."

*O-kay, the old Matilda is back bearing her claws.*

254

"We probably need to get back to the party," Sheri said. "I'm sure Greg is wondering where I've run off to."

Taking the hint, Tess added, "Colton and I should probably get home and relieve the babysitter."

Matilda promised to say nothing to Linda, though Sheri bet Matilda would be hard-pressed to ignore such a golden opportunity to one-up her sister. She now had powerful ammunition.

Sheri hightailed it to the living room more than ready for this disastrous evening to be over. How she dreaded facing Greg.

*Remember, act cool and collected – like nothing happened.*

Perhaps with Greg's lackluster ability to read women, he might not have noticed her meltdown. Maybe he concluded she was talented at emoting when she sang. She could only hope…

*"Cowards die many times before their deaths;*
*the valiant taste of death but once."*
~William Shakespeare~
*Julius Caesar*

# Chapter 42

Sheri seemed so sad and vulnerable when she sang that Greg would have sworn she'd been singing the words straight to him. They could not go on as they had. He was in love with Sheri, and after tonight's performance, he was convinced—no, suspicious—she loved him, too. But meanwhile, he was still dating Vanessa because he'd been too much of a coward to fling himself into the emotionally-draining angst of a break-up. Vanessa was a kind person, and he didn't relish hurting her the way Jodi had devastated him. If only he didn't want to stuff a sock in her mouth every time she opened it...

Even if he *did* break things off with Vanessa, what about Nicholas? If Sheri was in love with Greg, why was she still dating Nicholas? It made no sense. Granted, the guy was charming, far better looking, richer, and better educated than Greg—okay, maybe *that* was why she was still dating Nicholas! Maybe Greg was delusional that Sheri loved him, when she had a catch like Nicholas on her arm.

Perhaps the whole *I can't make you love me, if you don't* performance was just that—a performance. Sheri was a talented singer. For all he knew, every guy in the room thought she was singing the song only to him. She had sung solos in her high school show choir. Maybe she had a knack for emoting and drawing in her listeners.

Talk about frustrating. Did Sheri love him, or had she given her heart to Mr. Nicholas Perfect, Esquire?

He needed to meet this Nicholas firsthand and witness Sheri around him. She might be a talented singer, but she was a lousy actress. If she was in love with Nicholas, Greg would see it and feel it, and all would be lost. If she wasn't in love with Nicholas, Greg would break things off with Vanessa — as kindly as he could — and profess his love to Sheri.

Time for a double date with Sheri and Nicholas. Time to read the tea leaves and uncover his fate.

To be, or not to be…

*"Heat not a furnace for your foes so hot*
*that it do singe yourself."*
~William Shakespeare~
*Henry VI*

# Chapter 43

"Why don't we do a double date," Greg suggested, as they trudged their final quarter mile around Radnor Lake.

"No way. After our disastrous double date with Caleb, I don't have the stomach for it."

Greg wiped his brow with his T-shirt. "Don't you think it's time I check out this Prince Charming of yours?"

"What if you don't like him?" Sheri pushed a tree branch out of the way to avoid getting whacked in the face.

"You'll ditch him." He pointed an index finger at her. "You know you can't stick with anyone I don't approve of—that was in our original Operation Soulmate agreement."

"Oh brother!" She rolled her eyes. "You sound exactly the way I suspect my father *would* have sounded if I'd ever managed to snag up a date in high school."

"Not at all," Greg insisted, kicking a rotten branch off the trail. "But you're so smitten with this hotshot lawyer, it has clouded your judgment. You need my objectivity, so you won't be hoodwinked by Mr. Wonderful."

*Try Mr. Boring.*

She needed to break things off with Nicholas, as he hadn't triggered Greg's green-eyed monster any more than Caleb had. Sure, Greg sounded protective and patronizing, but not jealous.

"What do you say?" Greg persisted. "All four of us could go out to dinner and get to know each other."

What harm could come from it? At least Nicholas was straight, and they *were* actually dating. Plus, maybe Nicholas wouldn't drone on ad nauseum about his dead wife around Greg and Vanessa.

"I guess we could give it a try."

"This Friday, Kobe Steakhouse, seven o'clock. See if Nicholas is up for it, and I'll check with Vanessa."

"Didn't she just get back from her nursing conference and two-week vacation?" Sheri stepped around a pile of mud. "She'll want you all to herself, if she's been gone for three weeks."

Greg shrugged. "I'd rather go out on a double date. I'm dying to meet Nicholas."

"But won't Vanessa mind?"

He shrugged again, avoiding her question.

*That's weird. Does he not want to be alone with Vanessa?*

Before she could ask him, he inquired, "Is there some reason you don't *want* me to meet this Nicholas of yours?"

"No!" she insisted. I'm sure we'll have a fabulous time."

*Couldn't be any worse than our date with Caleb and Morgan.*

"Monique loved Japanese food," Nicholas said, as he and Sheri strolled into Kobe Steak House for their double date with Greg and Vanessa. "She always ordered fried rice with shrimp."

"Really?" Sheri attempted to force herself to sound interested.

"She even liked that awful Chinese mustard."

How about asking if I like Chinese mustard, Sheri fumed.

Even after more than a month of dating, he still made his dead wife the topic of almost every conversation. Sheri felt like a creep, but she now resented the poor woman. Like she could help dying! Talk about irrational.

Sheri was more than ready to call it quits with Nicholas, but she feared what it would do to his psyche to be ditched by his first post-Monique girlfriend. After he'd spilled his soul to her, how could she bail from the relationship without seeming heartless? Would he regress back to sobbing over his Disney DVDs?

Nicholas escorted her into the restaurant, and the hostess guided them to their reserved table. Greg and Vanessa hadn't made it yet—no surprise there. No doubt they would wander in a half hour late, which would drive Greg crazy. She remembered him fuming several months ago about Vanessa's chronic tardiness. "We arrived a half-hour late to our last movie date because Vanessa had to fuss with her hair for twenty minutes after I arrived." He shook his head in disgust. "If I'm going to fork out twenty-five bucks for movie tickets, I don't want to miss the first third of the film."

Sheri had to smile—Mr. Punctuality and Miss Never-on-time as a couple? It rivaled a hippo mated with a giraffe. Despite the mismatch, Greg still hadn't drummed up the courage to break up with her.

Not that Sheri was anyone to point fingers. She hadn't screwed her courage to the sticking place to break up with Nicholas, either. She needed to do it and get it over with, as she couldn't imagine spending the rest of her life in the shadow of a perfect woman. Plus, the longer she waited, the harder it would be.

They ordered a pot of tea, and as Sheri poured tea into her delicate teacup, Nicholas said, "Monique loved lemon zest tea. She drank it every day." Sheri covered a yawn with her hand.

After finishing up a pot of tea, Sheri glanced at her watch. They'd been waiting for thirty minutes. "I'm sorry they're late. Unfortunately, Vanessa is never ready when Greg comes to pick her up, and it drives him crazy. He hates being late."

Nicholas smiled. "Monique was always late, too. I don't think she put on her dress until I told her we were already ten minutes late."

*What? Monique had a dent in her armor?*

"Didn't it drive you nuts? It makes Greg furious when Vanessa keeps him waiting."

He shrugged. "I guess after a couple years of marriage, I just resigned myself to always being late. Monique had so many wonderful qualities, I accepted her tardiness as her one and only vice."

Wow! Here was the perfect man for Vanessa!

Forty minutes and two pots of tea later, Greg rushed into the restaurant looking frazzled. Vanessa, dressed in four-inch heels and a red knit dress that clung to her curves seductively, strolled in smiling and unruffled.

Greg shook Nicholas's hand. "I'm sorry we're so late. Vanessa was still in the shower when I arrived to pick her up."

Vanessa grinned impishly and raised upturned hands. "What can I say? Time got away from me."

When Sheri turned to introduce Nicholas to Vanessa, she noticed his eyes already transfixed on her. He stood with his mouth ajar, as though bewitched by her beauty. He reached for her hand and cupped it between his. "It's nice to meet you, Vanessa." His eyes remained locked on hers.

"You too."

He seemed to hold onto Vanessa's hand far longer than necessary for a casual introduction.

Vanessa cocked her head as though appraising Nicholas. "I know you from somewhere."

His face lit up. "I thought you looked familiar, too. We've met before—I'm sure of it— but for the life of me, I can't place where."

After several minutes of discussion, they figured out Vanessa was the charge nurse on the oncology ward where Monique received her chemotherapy and transfusions.

"Of course! You're Monique's husband! Oh, my goodness!" Vanessa cupped her face with her hands. "I can't believe I'm seeing you again after all this time."

"Monique bragged about you every day—how you could cheer her up, even at the very end when things became hopeless." He

261

pulled Vanessa in for an impulsive hug. "It's so good to be with someone who knew my Monique!"

Sheri clenched her teeth.

*Had that hug lasted way longer than necessary?*

True, she was ready to call it quits with Nicholas, but must he replace her with so little thought?

He cupped Vanessa's hand between his. "I never adequately thanked you for all you did for her."

"It was nothing. Besides, Monique said you were the best husband in the world, so I wanted to do everything I could to ease your suffering. And hers."

*She's making me look worse and worse. I wanted to douse him with a pot of chili when he droned on about Monique.*

Nicholas waved a dismissive hand as though embarrassed by the flattery. "I don't know about that, but I tried my best to support her."

Staring up at him, Vanessa said, "I always wondered how you and little Maddie made out. Do you have any pictures of her?"

Nicholas pulled out his wallet, and the two sat down next to each other at the restaurant table. Vanessa leaned close with her head mere inches from Nicholas's as she inspected a picture of Maddie. "She's around sixteen now?"

Nicholas chuckled. "Try eighteen. She's a freshman at Stanford."

Vanessa covered her mouth with her hand. "What? Oh, my goodness! Time sure flies."

Nicholas pulled out more photos of Maddie in her senior prom dress and her high school graduation cap and gown.

"Such a beautiful girl." Vanessa stared at the photo and then looked up. "Stanford—you must be proud of her."

"I am."

*Hello? Have you forgotten about Greg and me?*

Sheri was tempted to wave a hand in front of Nicholas. "Remember us?" Instead, she sank into her chair and made eye contact with Greg. As though shocked himself at the turn of events, Greg crossed his arms but said nothing.

"Maddie looks just like Monique," Vanessa insisted. She suddenly gripped Greg's forearm and gazed up at him. "How has she handled losing her Mama? That must have been so hard." Concern radiated from her eyes.

He offered a sheepish smile. "Far better than her old man, I'm afraid. I've been a basket case since the day Monique died. In fact, I've only recently started forcing myself to date Sheri."

*Forcing himself to date Sheri? Gee, thanks! Way to make a girl feel one step above emptying the mouse trap.*

Vanessa gripped his forearm, her tear-filled blue eyes boring into his. "If you need to talk, you can call me anytime. Grieving is a long, complex process, and sharing your feelings is the only way to push forward. You mustn't bottle it in."

A wave of pain crossed his face, and he stared down at his hands. "That's what I've done for three years now—bottle it in." His eyes misted, and he turned his head. "I miss her every day."

"Of course, you do," Vanessa soothed. "Monique was a wonderful woman. One of my all-time favorite patients." Her eyes welled up, and she brushed a tear from her cheek with her perfectly manicured finger. "I cried like a baby at her funeral."

"It meant so much to me that you came. With all the patients on the oncology floor, you put forth the effort to come to her funeral." Their eyes met, and Nicholas gripped her hand and squeezed.

"Wild horses couldn't have kept me from that funeral." Vanessa brushed another tear from her cheek. "It was the least I could do."

*Yeah, yeah, enough with the Monique fan club!*

Greg and Sheri made eye contact again. The message was clear: she and Greg could go on a four-mile hike around Radnor Lake, and neither Vanessa nor Nicholas would even notice they'd left.

After Vanessa dabbed her eyes, she asked Nicholas, "So what have you been up to these last three years?"

The two launched into a discussion about Nicholas's job and his recent trip to Europe. He regaled her with interesting travel stories about Prague and Budapest. Amazingly, Vanessa could get Nicholas to open up about his *current* life and not dwell on the ghost of Christmas past. Through Vanessa, Sheri learned Nicholas ran half-marathons and hoped to compete in the next Country Music Marathon. He loved pizza topped with pineapple and ham, and his father worked as an architect. His mother's career as a legal secretary ignited his spark for the legal profession.

*How come I could never drag any of this out of him?*

Nicholas then asked Vanessa to fill him in on everything that had happened in *her* life since Monique's funeral. He confessed with a grin, "I didn't recognize you at first because you weren't a blond when Monique was alive."

Vanessa gestured toward her hair and giggled. "Someone once told me blonds have more fun, so I decided to give it a try, and I've never looked back."

"It suits your spunky personality," Nicholas insisted. "It looks fabulous on you."

*How come Nicholas never commented on my hair or personality?*

Every now and then, Vanessa and Nicholas pulled their eyes away from one another and attempted to engage in conversation with Greg and Sheri, but the conversation was stilted. "Yes, Nicholas, I *did* have a good week at work. And you?" or, "My wanton soup is delicious. Thank you for asking, Vanessa."

After they ordered their entrees, Vanessa and Nicholas chatted and laughed and smiled so much, it could only mean one thing — they would soon be a couple, and she and Greg quickly forgotten.

Somehow Vanessa could pull Nicholas out of his brooding. He mentioned a new Ethiopian restaurant he wanted to try and his plans to remodel his kitchen.

Vanessa's face lit up. "I love remodeling and decorating. I've learned so much from watching the Home and Garden channel — the one where they flip old houses."

Their Japanese chef appeared with bowls of raw veggies, shrimp, chicken, and rice. After he warmed the hibachi, they oohed and aahed as he chopped vegetables at lightning speed, flipped knives, and tossed the eggshells into his white chef's hat. He formed a flaming volcano out of onion rings and then served them generous portions of everything. They dug into their entrees with chopsticks.

"I'd love for you to see Maddie again," Nicholas said. "And I know she'd love to see you, too."

"I can't wait to see her again."

"How about I call you when she's home for fall break? We could invite you over for dinner." His face beamed. "In fact, maybe you could give me some pointers with my kitchen renovation. Like you, I've started watching the Home and Garden channel, and I suspect they make it look way too easy."

*How come he never asked me for help with his kitchen reno? And why couldn't we have watched the Home and Garden channel instead of his endless DVDs of Maddie on a swing?*

Aware of her own green-eyed monster, Sheri glanced over to see how Greg was handling Nicholas encroaching on his girlfriend.

Greg's jaw was clamped shut like a polar bear's mouth on a seal pup. *Hmm. Not good.*

So, Greg had picked up on the obvious chemistry between Nicholas and Vanessa, as well. Vanessa and Nicholas had fallen for each other hook, line, and sinker, and Greg and Sheri could do nothing but watch it unfold right before their eyes.

She *should* be glad, of course. She and Nicholas weren't a good fit. She had procrastinated ending things because of her guilt at how it would affect him. She gritted her teeth every time he mentioned Monique. Around Vanessa, however, he radiated happiness, and he focused on the future instead of the past. Maybe because Vanessa had *known* Monique and had nursed her through

265

chemotherapy and death, Nicholas didn't feel the need to dwell on the past since Vanessa already knew it.

Sheri *should* be elated for Nicholas. He *deserved* happiness after all he'd been through. But somehow, she felt like a pile of junk mail tossed into the recycling bin without a moment's hesitation.

At least she had only invested one month on Nicholas. Poor Greg had invested four months on Vanessa, yet in one hour flat, Nicholas had swiped his girl.

As though not wanting to prolong their misery, Greg suggested to Nicholas, "Why don't I drive Sheri home, and you can take Vanessa. That way, you two will have more time to catch up. Plus, you can show her your kitchen."

"You wouldn't mind?" Nicholas asked, his face already glowing at the prospect of more time with Vanessa. "I wouldn't want to intrude," he said unconvincingly.

Vanessa grabbed Nicholas's arm. "I'd love to see more pictures of Maddie. Plus, we can brainstorm how to turn your kitchen into a showstopper." She clapped her hands in glee. "This will be so much fun! We can pick out paint colors, and cabinets, and back splashes, and a stainless-steel gas stove. I'll help you pick out curtains and decorations to match."

The two men settled the bill, and then Nicholas and Vanessa offered Sheri and Greg hasty goodbyes. Nicholas wrapped his arm around Vanessa's elbow and escorted her out of the restaurant without looking back. Greg and Sheri stared at one another too stunned for words. Finally, Greg mumbled, "Let's go."

*"How weary, stale, flat, and unprofitable*
*Seem to me all the uses of this world."*
~William Shakespeare~
*Hamlet*

# Chapter 44

A deluge of rain pummeled the windshield of Greg's MINI Cooper as it sloshed through puddles on the drive to Sheri's house. Even with the wipers on full throttle, Greg sputtered, "I can barely see ten feet in front of me."

Cannonballs of thunder boomed, and bolts of lightning sizzled against the ebony sky. Spine rigid and jaw clenched, Greg white-knuckled the steering wheel.

As they neared Sheri's neighborhood, he unexplainably jerked the car into a grocery store parking lot.

"Why are we stopping here?"

"Ice cream," Greg growled, pulling into a parking space. "The more chunks of chocolate the better."

Sheri would have attempted a smile, but she felt too glum.

*Why not binge on ice cream?*

She'd fussed with her hair, coordinated the perfect outfit, and even worn an uncomfortably tight Spanx for tonight's date, and where had it landed her? In a dreary grocery store parking lot about to binge on ice cream with someone who had also been jilted. If misery loves company...

She stared out her passenger window morosely.

*At this rate, I'll wear adult diapers before I wear a wedding gown.*

Greg turned off the ignition and slumped against the driver's door to wait out the storm.

To fill in the silence, Sheri commented, "J.M. Barrie once wrote, 'Even love unreturned has its rainbow.' Right now, I'd like to see a whole lot less rain and a whole lot more rainbow."

Greg snorted. "You got that right. Our love lives match Noah floating around in a smelly ark for months on end with a bunch of noisy animals." He gestured toward the bleary sky. "No rainbow in sight for either of us."

They slouched against their respective car doors and sulked. Five minutes later, the rain weakened to a drizzle.

"Here goes." Greg opened his car door and dashed into the store. He emerged from the store five minutes later and raised the ice cream carton like a Heisman trophy. After backing his MINI Cooper out of the parking place, he headed for Sheri's house. When they reached her driveway, another torrent of rain slammed against the windshield.

Greg raised exasperated hands. "Not again!"

She eyed the sky. "Doesn't look like it's going to let up anytime soon. She eyed the carton of ice cream. "If we dawdle, our ice cream will melt. I say, let's make a run for it."

"Forget it!" Greg gestured toward his suit coat. "This thing cost me a fortune, and I don't want to ruin it. Roxie made me buy it because she said it would attract females." He released a cynical snort. "Ha! The only females this overpriced piece of wool will attract are ewes."

Sheri placed a comforting hand on his arm. "Well, I thought you looked handsome and debonair in your fancy duds tonight." She fingered the high-quality fabric. "It *is* an exquisite suit coat."

"What difference did it make? Definitely not worth the investment."

*Ouch!*

Daggers of pain pierced her heart. Apparently, it didn't matter if *Sheri* thought he looked handsome and debonair, because what *she* thought about him didn't matter. She quickly turned her head, so Greg couldn't see the tears in her eyes. He obviously didn't care a whit that she found him attractive and had feelings for him.

*He probably never will.*

Tess and Aunt Matilda were wrong about Greg being in love with her. She sniffed back tears. She needed to accept that she and Greg would never be more than friends.

He must have heard her sniffle because he touched her shoulder. "I didn't mean that the way it sounded."

"What *did* you mean then?" she eked out, unable to hide her hurt.

"I meant, I don't *have* to try to impress you—I can totally be myself. I don't *have* to wear expensive suit coats for you. You've seen me overweight, nerdy, bungling up dates, and dripping with sweat, and you still like and accept me exactly the way I am."

"Okay. I get it now." She brushed tears off her cheek. That *did* sound better.

He reached for her hand. "No, I don't think you do." He cupped her hand in both of his. "Sheri, look at me."

She forced herself to turn her head and peer into his eyes.

"You mean the world to me. I've never known anyone I can be so authentic with. I don't have to hide my inner Shakespeare muse or my tendency to blather on about financial planning. I can be totally myself with you."

"We do know each other well, warts and all,"

"Because of you, I'm a better man—a healthier man."

The obvious question remained: *If you think we're so well-suited, why don't you want me as your girlfriend? Is it because I'm not pretty enough?*

Too despondent to ponder it any more, she unbuckled her seatbelt, yanked her house keys from her purse, and bolted up the stairs toward the front door.

Greg followed close behind carting the ice cream. Once inside, he brushed the rain off his suit coat and hung it in the closet. "After all the bucks I forked out for this thing, it better not shrink."

Sheri brewed a pot of decaf and spooned up two bowls of French Silk ice cream. They settled onto the couch, and Hamlet kneaded his paws into Sheri's thigh as he waited impatiently to lap their empty bowls.

They savored several spoonfuls before Greg confessed, "Truthfully, I *should* be relieved Vanessa took a shine for Nicholas. It saved me the trouble of breaking up with her tonight."

Her hand froze midair. *He planned to break up with Vanessa tonight?*

Greg spooned in another bite of ice cream. "We had a huge fight on the way to the restaurant tonight, and frankly, I would have ended it then and there, except we had our double date already arranged with you and Nicholas."

"What did you argue about?"

He scowled. "What else? Her incessant lateness. I jumped all over her for making you and Nicholas wait forty minutes because she couldn't plan her time better." He rubbed his chin. "I suspect with time, I would have grown to despise her—and she, me."

Sheri sipped her coffee and offered up her own confession. "I was so sick of hearing about Nicholas's dead wife. All he ever talked about was how perfect Monique was. There was no future with him."

Greg's eyes widened. "Wait, I thought you were crazy about him."

She averted her eyes. She hadn't shared her true feelings about Nicholas with Greg because she'd hoped to make him jealous. She couldn't tell *him* that, however, so she said, "I was flattered, but he definitely wasn't my soulmate." She swallowed another sip before adding, "I'm glad Vanessa wooed him away. It saved me the guilt of breaking up with him. It did hurt my pride to be so easily discarded, though."

"So, you aren't in love with Nicholas?" Greg asked, as though still not convinced.

She scratched Hamlet behind the ears contemplating how best to answer. "I was in love with the *idea* of Nicholas—a handsome, intelligent guy interested in me, but I definitely wasn't in love with Nicholas. He bored me to tears."

Greg broke into a huge grin. "Let me get this straight. You and I are stuffing our faces with ice cream because two people who weren't right for us in the first place found somebody else?" He burst into laughter. "How pathetic is that?"

Sheri dropped her head in her hands. "What is wrong with us?"

"Bruised egos?" Greg suggested.

"Masochism?" she countered.

Greg raised a finger. "I know! A hankering for French Silk ice cream, and we needed the guise of a broken heart to justify it when we're supposed to be on a diet."

"Bingo!" she said pointing at him. She reached for her spoon and savored another delicious mouthful before moaning with pleasure. "If I only had one day left to live, I'd spend the whole day eating French Silk ice cream."

"You and me both," Greg agreed, licking his lips.

After they surrendered their empty bowls to Hamlet, Sheri commented, "I guess it's back to the drawing board for each of us. At least we're experienced daters now."

"I suppose our dates couldn't go any worse than mine with Theresa or yours with Caleb."

She scowled at him. "Thanks for reminding me."

"Any time," he said with a wink.

She jumped from her chair and headed toward her study. "Maybe the perfect person for each of us has joined the website while we were gluttonizing on ice cream. Let's take a look."

"No!" Greg wailed. "No more geologists with mustaches."

"Oh, ye of little faith." She circled back, grabbed his hand, and pulled him off the couch. "Come on—no harm looking."

They wandered into the study and logged onto the dating site.

As soon as Sheri opened the profiles of available men her age, a face befitting a serial killer stared back at her—ominous and brooding. Perhaps his mother had signed him up for the site against his will, so he was purposely trying to repel women.

Greg grinned and pointed at the screen. "How about this guy?"

She whacked him in the belly. "Only if you want me in a coffin."

Greg skimmed the man's profile. "You might be right. Says here his favorite hobbies are target practice and hunting."

"Suppose he murdered his last three girlfriends?"

She scrolled through several more candidates, but they were — as usual — too old, too weird, or too likely to mooch like Jeremy the Jerk. When she scrolled to the new listings, she did a double take. While nowhere near as handsome as Nicholas or Greg, a guy named Michael Abington stared back at her with warm brown eyes. He wasn't covered in tattoos, nor was he dragging a deer carcass across his shoulders. Even better? He worked for the state of Tennessee as a civil engineer — smart and stable, right?

"This one looks promising." A glimmer of hope igniting like a pilot light. While she felt none of the visceral reaction she'd experienced when she first glimpsed Nicholas, this Michael Abington wasn't *un*appealing, and he must be smart if he made it through engineering school.

Greg skimmed the man's profile and shrugged. "No obvious red flags he'll slit your throat and toss you in a dumpster."

She waved a scolding finger in his face. "Behave yourself."

"Go ahead — email him. What have you got to lose? — except maybe your liver."

She lasered him with a look that could curdle honey then shot off a quick email.

Once she'd sent her note, she suggested they check out women for Greg. Surprisingly, he showed no interest. None. Nada.

"Still roiling from your break-up with Vanessa?" she asked, trying to sort out his morose mood.

"No, it's not that…" He shrugged but offered no explanation.

*What was up with Greg?* She stared at his brooding face, clueless why he seemed so glum. He said Vanessa's incessant chatter and tardiness drove him crazy, so it couldn't be that.

Greg unexplainably stood, stretched, and claimed he was ready to call it a night. "I'm bushed." He retrieved his coat and then trudged toward the front door refusing to expound on his mopey demeanor.

She glanced at her watch — not even nine-thirty.

*What's the deal? And they accuse women of being moody?*

*"Love looks not with the eyes, but with the mind, and therefore is winged Cupid painted blind."*
~William Shakespeare~
*A Midsummer Night's Dream*

# *Chapter 45*

Greg backed out of Sheri's driveway and pounded the dashboard.

*Why couldn't she see they belonged together?*

He, Greg Palmer, was her soulmate, not some civil engineer floating around in cyberspace. He'd tried to tell her that tonight on their drive home, but she didn't seem to get the message. Or didn't *want* to get the message. Maybe she still viewed Greg as a chum. She was obviously still looking for *her* Mr. Right or she wouldn't be on the dating site tonight.

Sheri was *his* Mrs. Right. Whether she was beautiful or fat and frizzy-headed, he loved her. He loved her for who she was—on the inside. Her humor. Her brains. While her improved looks definitely frosted the cake, he'd found his soulmate in Sheri—no matter how she looked.

When she had seemed smitten with Nicholas, he couldn't very well confess his feelings, especially since he hadn't yet broken things off with Vanessa. But once Vanessa and Nicholas paired off tonight, Greg assumed Sheri would see the obvious—they belonged together. Instead, she drooled over some engineer and even sent the guy an email! He gripped the steering wheel so hard his knuckles ached.

Why was she checking out complete strangers when Greg adored her? He wanted to wave his hands in front of her face and shout, "Remember me? The guy you kissed passionately? The guy you said looked handsome and debonair in his expensive suit coat? The guy who loves you exactly the way you are?"

*You have to tell her how you feel.*

He made a left turn and merged onto the interstate mulling over the possible repercussions of total honesty. What if she didn't feel the same way? Would she end their friendship because it would make things too awkward? He couldn't bear to lose her. Sheri as a best friend beat no Sheri at all. He savored their time together — talking, hiking, laughing, nibbling ice cream, quoting Shakespeare, tackling difficult crossword puzzles, teasing each other, and most of all, kissing.

Annoyed by the slowpoke Cadillac in front of him, Greg pulled into the pass lane and mashed on the accelerator.

*Get a move on, buster!*

No, he couldn't risk honesty — not yet. He'd have to be patient and wait for the glorious day when Sheri discovered she loved him as much as he loved her. In the meantime, he'd have to let her flounder with another guy. With any luck, this Michael Abington would be another dud like Jeremy the Jerk and Caleb. Maybe he'd drone on with laborious details about building bridges. Greg would look great in comparison.

He veered back into the right-hand lane ahead of the dawdler in the Cadillac and offered up a heartfelt prayer.

*God, if Sheri and I are meant to be together, make it happen. Open Sheri's eyes to what we have.*

*"Mischief, thou art afoot. Take thou what course thou wilt."*
~William Shakespeare~
*Julius Caesar*

# Chapter 46

Sheri squirmed in her chair at Panera Bread and sipped on her second glass of ice water. She pulled out the compact mirror from her purse and double-checked her hair and lipstick. No disasters there. She glanced at her watch, and her stomach tightened. Michael was late. Would he be another Vanessa—always making people wait thirty minutes while she got ready? How rude! That was one thing she and Greg had in common—punctuality.

She released a frustrated sigh. If only Greg cared for her the way she cared for him, she wouldn't be stuck in a restaurant waiting for some total stranger to show up—a stranger who apparently didn't know how to tell time.

She drummed her fingers on the table, annoyed her date had wasted fifteen minutes of her time already—*if* he bothered to show up at all. With her abysmal track record with men, she wasn't sure she even *wanted* him to show up.

The man she *wanted* was Greg, but he viewed her like a bowl of oatmeal—good for his health but not very exciting. She mulled over his words: "You've made me a healthier man."

*Seriously? He could trade me in for a treadmill and salmon patty.*

He acted so mopey and depressed the night his relationship with Vanessa ended that she knew Vanessa must still hold his heart—whether he admitted it or not. Even though Vanessa grated on his nerves, he probably still loved her. Why else would he not be willing to look for a new girlfriend online?

She glanced at her watch and scowled. Twenty minutes late. She pulled out her smartphone to check her emails— might as well make the best use of her idle time.

Five minutes later, the front door of the restaurant opened, and in walked Greg.

"Greg? What are you doing here?" She noticed how handsome he looked in his expensive wool suit coat. Why had he dressed up?

He grinned. "Making sure this Michael Abington isn't a creep."

She frowned. "At this point, I wouldn't know. He hasn't bothered to show up, nor has he called to apologize for being late."

Greg shook his head. "Don't you hate that? Like you have nothing better to do on a Saturday morning than sit around waiting for him. It's so rude." He sank into a chair at the table next to Sheri's. He pulled out his iPad and waved it at her. "I brought this, so I can eavesdrop without raising suspicion."

"I don't need a bodyguard, Greg." She rattled the ice cubes in her tea glass as a show of irritation.

Greg raised an eyebrow as if to say, "I beg to differ." He stepped away to order some coffee then returned to the table.

Just then, an average height man dashed through the door. "Sheri?" he said breathlessly. "I'm so sorry I'm late. There was a huge pile-up on I-40. A tractor-trailer overturned. I left the house an hour ago because I wanted to be here early."

Sheri's annoyance melted like her ice cubes. At least he acknowledged he was late and apologized. How could she hold a grudge when it wasn't *his* fault I-40 had a wreck?

After perusing their menu choices, they stood in line to order panini sandwiches and tomato basil soup.

Greg strolled to the coffee counter under the guise of refilling his coffee cup. He took his time with the skim milk and Splenda, so he could eavesdrop on Sheri and Michael's conversation.

Unfortunately, so far, the guy seemed half decent. Downright engaging, in fact.

As he heard Sheri giggling at Michael's imitation of his overbearing boss, his stomach clenched. Michael continued his story using exaggerated arm gestures and a booming voice. Now Sheri was laughing.

She responded with a story of her own about an odd patient she recently doctored. Michael rewarded her with a hearty belly laugh.

*How come she never told me about that weird patient?*

Greg tried to ignore the terror—and jealousy—gripping his heart. Easy conversation, happy smiles, engaging nods, and hearty laughter flowed naturally between Sheri and this engineer.

*This guy is serious competition — he's really likeable.*

Why couldn't the guy pick his nose, or belch, or do something equally repulsive? Why hadn't he asked Sheri to buy his meal since she was a rich doctor? Or start sobbing about an ex that broke his heart and left it like a leaky roof? Instead, he entertained her with hilarious stories and impressive imitations of his boss.

*What are you going to do about it?*

His inner worrywart bit its nails to the quick. If he didn't do something quick, this snake charmer would swipe his Sheri away like Nicholas had swiped Vanessa.

*What can I do?* Greg hurled at his inner critic. *I can't challenge the guy to a duel.*

"Hey, watch what you're doing," a lady next to Greg at the coffee counter scolded. "You're making a mess." Greg glanced down to see his coffee cup not only full but overflowing all over the counter. He'd been so distracted with his eavesdropping he'd forgotten all about the pitcher of milk in his hand, and he'd poured milk all over the counter.

Greg tipped up the pitcher and frantically grabbed for paper napkins to sop up his spill. In the process, he knocked over his coffee cup—straight into the crotch of the woman standing next to him at the counter.

She jerked back and glared. "What is wrong with you? Are you on drugs?"

"I — I'm sorry," Greg stammered, his cheeks no doubt the color of Sheri's tomato soup.

"Clumsy oaf!" she hissed before stomping off to the lady's room. Thank God the woman had on ratty jeans and a sweatshirt, not an expensive pair of white trousers because she looked angry enough to sue.

After cleaning up his mess, Greg picked up his now empty coffee cup and filled it again. He glanced up and noticed Sheri watching him. She smirked and shook her head with a "I-can't-believe-you-just-did-that" expression.

*Swell! Way to impress the ladies.*

Thankfully, she didn't comment on the minor mishap to Michael, as he hated to look like a bungling doofus next to Mr. Personality.

He trudged back to his table and did his best not to acknowledge Sheri in any way.

Michael regaled her with stories about his recent camping trip out West where bears invaded his food stash in the middle of the night. He described the thrill of seeing Old Faithful shoot out of the ground. If the guy wasn't capturing the heart of the woman he loved, Greg would *like* this guy.

Sheri recounted stories of a past trip she'd taken to Yosemite and Sequoia National Park. She described her awe at seeing the thousand-year-old trees and colorful Western bluebirds and tanagers.

*Drat! They both liked to travel and explore National Parks. Bad, bad, and getting worse.*

Panic soured the coffee in Greg's stomach. If he didn't do something, this engineer would march off into the sunset — no doubt to the Grand Canyon — with Sheri by his side. Greg had to do something — *but what?*

Just then, Sheri excused herself to go to the restroom. Now was his chance — except he had no idea what to do. Somehow, he had to convince this Michael Abington that Sheri was not the right woman for him. But how?

Plan A: Be totally honest. Confess to Michael that he is in love with Sheri. Tell him Sheri is his soulmate.

Greg drummed his fingers on the table considering this option. No, it wouldn't work. The guy would respond, "If Sheri is your soulmate, why is she checking out other men on dating websites? And why would she agree to meet up with *me* today?" He'd then offer Greg a pitying look and say, "Sorry, dude, it doesn't sound like she's that into you."

He would then get an alarmed expression and pull away. "Why are you spying on her date with me?" He'd eye Greg like he was a crazed stalker. He might even offer to help Sheri take out a restraining order against him. Plan A? Definitely a bad idea!

Plan B: Tell Michael that Sheri used to be fat, frizzy-headed, and frumpy, and would likely let herself go once she snagged up a husband. Plus, she worked ridiculously long hours.

Hmm. That made Greg sound mean and petty. Cruel, even. Besides, as an engineer, Michael no doubt worked long hours himself. And who was Greg to talk about a history of frumpy! At least Sheri never sported a unibrow. Plan B? No way.

Plan C: ...

Plan C: ... ...

Plan C: ... ... ...

He *had* no Plan C!

Desperation welled up inside him like a Yellowstone geyser. Sheri would return any second, and if he didn't do something quick, he'd lose her forever.

Greg jumped to his feet and approached Michael's table doing his best to ignore the rational inner voice inside him screaming, *"Sit down and shut up!"*

He cleared his throat to get Michael's attention then plunged ahead before he lost his nerve. "Hey, listen, buddy. I used to date Sheri Morris, and I thought I ought to warn you about her."

Michael's brows rose. "Warn me? Why? Sheri seems like a great gal. Is there something wrong with her?"

Greg had to think fast. He had no idea what to say that would make Michael run for the hills. Is something wrong with Sheri? His mind went blank.

*There's nothing wrong with Sheri – she's perfect – at least for me.*

Before he could stop himself, he blurted, "Bedbugs."

Michael jerked back, as though merely *talking* about bedbugs would somehow infest him. *"What?"*

"Yes," Greg continued, squashing his conscience. "Everywhere. They infested her clothes, car, and house, but she was too cheap to hire an exterminator. I only went out on a few dates with her, but I got so infested with the nasty little buggers, I had to spend a small fortune to get rid of them."

Michael's eyes darted to his sleeves, and he brushed them vigorously with his hand, as though fearful the pests might have already jumped on him.

"You think she still has them?" His eyes widened in alarm.

Greg shrugged. "Who knows? But if I were you, I wouldn't risk it." He raised a hand. "Don't get me wrong—Sheri is a great gal, but if I had my life to live over, I would *never* have dated her." He then added in a confiding voice, "And between you and me? Her mother is a piece of work. Total nut job." Greg spun an index finger at his temple. "I sure hope for Sheri's sake it isn't genetic because her mother is certifiably crazy."

Michael leaped from his chair and dashed toward the door. He called over his shoulder, "Thanks for the warning, buddy. I'm out of here!"

Once Michael left, crushing guilt pummeled Greg's chest. *You had no business scaring him off like that. How could you do that to Sheri?*

His heart responded, *because I'm in love with her, and I can't stand the thought of losing her.*

The imaginary angel on his shoulder wagged its finger and hissed, "That's no excuse! You lied, and Sheri will be devastated.

You can't go around controlling people like that. Shame on you, Greg Palmer! Shame! Shame!"

Greg didn't need an imaginary angel bawling him out—he already knew what he'd done was despicable. Low-down. Reprehensible. Unconscionable. What had he been thinking?

He had to tell Sheri the truth. Perhaps he could undo his damage by emailing Michael and 'fessing up. Maybe it wasn't too late to fix his treachery. He would do it the minute he got home.

*"The fault, dear Brutus, is not in the stars, but in ourselves."*
~William Shakespeare~
*Julius Caesar*

# Chapter 47

Sheri wandered back from the bathroom and not seeing her date, she inquired of Greg, "Where's Michael? Did he go to the restroom?"

"No, he just up and left." Greg shrugged and attempted to sound casual. No way would he tell Sheri what he'd done here in the restaurant—she might fling her tomato basil soup at him, and this suitcoat cost way too much to risk it.

"Left?" She glanced toward the door. "Why?"

Greg did his best to look innocent.

Hurt crossed her face. "I don't understand. Did I say something wrong?"

"No. You were fine."

"Do I look bad?" She gestured toward her outfit.

"You look great."

"I thought we were getting along great. I don't remember saying anything disgusting."

"You didn't."

"Then why did he up and walk out on me without so much as a goodbye?" She sounded on the verge of tears.

Greg felt like a bully who kicked puppies. And bunnies.

He was about to confess when Sheri blurted, "It's because I'm not pretty enough, isn't it? It doesn't matter how smart, or funny, or engaging I am. It'll never be enough." She crumpled her napkin and pounded the table. "That's it! I give up."

She jumped to her feet, grabbed her tray, and flung her half-eaten sandwich and soup into the trash. She tossed her utensils into the appropriate compartment and slammed her tray on top of the trash bin. "I'm through with men." Tears poured down her cheeks as she stormed out the door and stomped toward her car.

Greg tore after her. "Sheri, wait!"

"Why?" She brushed tears from her cheek. "So you can watch me lose another guy? Do you know how humiliating that is?" She yanked her car fob out of her purse and mashed on the button to unlock her door.

"Sheri, hold up," he said, grabbing her arm.

Crushing hurt radiated across her face, and Greg wanted to drink a dram of poison like Romeo.

"Face it, Greg. When it comes to men, I'm a total loser. If a girl isn't pretty like Vanessa and Tess, she's toast."

"You're not toast!" He gripped both her shoulders gently.

"Yes, I am." Her hands balled into fists. "You want to know how much of a loser I am? I'm such a loser I faked dating Caleb for three weeks just to try and make you jealous. Is that desperate or what?"

*Sheri used Caleb as a decoy to make me jealous? How deceiving! How manipulative! Well, okay, who am I to point fingers right now?*

She continued her rant. "What kind of person deceives her best friend like that? It's pathetic and immoral and downright wrong." She brushed tears from her cheek. "I've felt guilty about it ever since."

Thinking of his own treachery, he squeezed her shoulders. "Actually, it's not that pathetic. Trust me, I completely understand why you did it."

*Boy, do I understand.* "It's okay, Sheri. I forgive you."

She jerked his hands off her shoulders and flung them away. Crossing her arms petulantly she snapped, "It's *not* okay. Did you not hear what I said? I *lied* to you." She glared up at him accusingly. "You should be furious with me."

"I'm not angry because—"

She raised a hand and interrupted him again. "It gets worse. Nicholas bored me to tears, but I *pretended* I liked him to try and

284

make you jealous. So, I've deceived you, not once, but twice! I'm telling you, I'm a despicable, horrible, ungodly human being."

He scratched his head processing everything she'd said.

*If she went to all that trouble to make me jealous, it means she cares — doesn't it?*

His heart lifted like an eagle in an updraft. He couldn't help but grin in delight.

She whacked him in the belly. "Quit smiling! Do you get some perverse pleasure from my misery?"

"I'm smiling because if you went to all that trouble to make me jealous, it means you care about me."

Hands on her hips, she snapped, "Of course, I care about you. That's what I've been trying to tell you. But to you, I'm nothing more than a hiking buddy."

He cupped her face with both his hands, his eyes beseeching hers. "Sheri, you're not just a hiking buddy. You mean the world to me. I love you."

She pulled back and crossed her arms. "You're only saying that so I won't fling myself in front of a moving train—like Anna Karenina."

Greg chuckled. "I love you, Sheri Morris. Passionately. With my whole being."

He then confessed why Michael had bolted from the restaurant while she'd been in the bathroom.

She stared up at him in horror—a mixture of humor and rage stirred into one. "You told him I had bedbugs?"

*Guess I better not tell her what I said about her mother!*

Hands on her hips she demanded, "What if he posts online that I'm infested with bedbugs?"

Greg shrugged. "Who cares? You don't need that dating website anymore. Just take down your listing."

She frowned. "Couldn't you come up with something better than bedbugs?"

He raised hands of surrender. "Not in the time it takes you to go to the bathroom."

She shook her head scowling, as though not yet ready to let him off the hook for his treachery. She then jabbed his chest with her finger. "You are so emailing Michael and telling him I was never infested with bedbugs." She glared at him and added, "I should be furious with you."

He pulled her into his arms and whispered, "But you're not, because you know it was the desperate act of a man in love."

A slow grin spread across her face as his words sunk in. "You really love me, Greg?"

He reached for her hands and tugged her close. "How do I love thee? Let me count the ways."

He kissed her softly. "One." He kissed her again. "Two." He kissed her again, this time, more passionately. "Three." By the fourth kiss, he couldn't remember how to count.

She giggled. "You only love me three ways?"

He caressed her cheek and whispered, "I love thee to the depth and breadth and height my soul can reach."

As though in synch with him, she added, "When feeling out of sight for the ends of being and ideal grace."

They continued the sonnet together, ignoring the stares of Panera Bread patrons who no doubt wondered why two forty-year-olds were smooching in a public parking lot right in front of a large picture window. Greg didn't care—he'd finally captured the heart of the woman he loved more than life itself—his soulmate.

He whispered in her ear, "I love thee to the level of every day's most quiet need, by sun and candlelight."

They interrupted the sonnet to kiss. And kiss again. Greg gazed down at his beloved—delighted to see happiness gazing back at him.

*She loves me!*

He could scarcely believe his good fortune. He'd found a woman so perfect for him that she even shared his love of Shakespeare—and wristwatches.

Between kisses, they added another line of their favorite sonnet until they ended with the last two lines: "I love thee with the breath, smiles, and tears of all my life. And if God choose, I shall but love thee better after death."

He touched his forehead to hers wanting to savor this moment of unsurpassable happiness. He cupped her face tenderly and whispered, "Sheri, will you marry me?"

He had to ask before he lost his nerve—or before she found out what he'd said about her mother.

She grinned impishly. "Do you promise never to let your unibrow grow back?"

"Scout's honor." He pulled her in for a kiss, with all talk of unibrows banished forever.

*"Love is an ever-fixed mark that looks on tempests and is never shaken. Love alters not with his brief hours and weeks, but bears it out, even to the edge of doom."*
~William Shakespeare~
*Sonnet 116*

# EPILOGUE

The church had never looked prettier. Boughs of fragrant pine dotted with holly berries adorned every windowsill, and white candles cast a soft glow over the sanctuary. Dozens of red poinsettias graced the front of the church, and a giant pine decorated with sparkly white ornamental balls, angels, and clear white lights added an elegant touch. Wreaths with giant red bows decorated the side of each pew. After inspecting the church decor one last time, the wedding planner, Cyndi, herded the wedding party to a side room off the vestibule. "We don't want the guests to see you before the processional."

Roxie spritzed a finishing mist of hairspray to Sheri's hair with a satisfied sigh. "I do declare you look as pretty as a magnolia in the moonlight. Greg will be completely gobsmacked. You mark my words."

Sheri gazed into the hand mirror Roxie provided and offered a grateful smile. The intricate design of soft curls and baby's breath looked—dare she say it—pretty. "Roxie, you truly are a miracle worker. This looks fabulous."

"It does," Tess agreed, as she smoothed the skirt of her cranberry matron-of-honor dress. "You look gorgeous, Sis."

"Hard to believe, but she actually does," Sheri overhead Clarissa mumble to Claire. Apparently, the evil twins had expected Sheri to look no better than a troll under a bridge.

Sheri ignored the barb, determined she would not allow anyone or anything to ruin her special day.

*As long as Greg finds me attractive, who cares what Claire and Clarissa think?*

Speaking of Greg, how was he holding up? Was he nervous? Excited? Ready to bolt?

*Don't be ridiculous. He's as pumped about this as you are.*

The wedding planner clapped her hands to get their attention. "The processional begins in thirty minutes. Now remember what we practiced last night—short, gliding, graceful steps." Cyndi demonstrated the proper way to walk with flowing movements.

Clarissa rolled her eyes, as though insulted anyone would think she didn't know how to make a grand entrance.

Linda Morris strolled over and squeezed Sheri's shoulder, her face beaming. Either that, or she'd applied too much blusher. "Can you believe it? We got our December wedding, after all. It's an honest-to-goodness Christmas miracle."

This hardly met Sheri's definition of a bona fide miracle, but then again, considering all the bumps in the road since the start of her unlikely romance with Greg, maybe it was a miracle!

"It *is* a miracle," Claire said, her sweet tone a cover-up for the insinuation that Sheri couldn't get a man to marry her short of a miracle.

Sheri sucked in a cleansing breath.

*Let it go. Nothing is going to ruin this special day.*

Just then, the best man, a buddy of Greg's from the accounting firm, barged in to inform them that Greg had gotten a flat tire on the way to the church, and he would be delayed.

*Okay—that might ruin my special day—one has to have a groom to have a wedding.*

He must have seen the panic in Sheri's eyes because he added, "Greg insists he'll be here in forty minutes, max."

*If he can remember how to use a lug wrench.*

Sheri had no idea if Greg knew how to change a flat. Could a nerdy accountant who quoted Shakespearean sonnets metamorphasize into a grease monkey? For all she knew, Greg might decide to call Triple A so he wouldn't get his tuxedo dirty. If so, how long before they would show up to rescue him?

Sheri overheard Matilda whisper to Uncle Max, "He probably got cold feet and ran for the hills." The dastardly duo snickered.

Sheri wanted to punch the smugness right out of them, except it might break one of the nails Roxie had toiled on so painstakingly. Besides, the new, improved Sheri Morris refused to let Matilda, Max, or anyone else rankle her. She was above such petty shenanigans, right?

Wrong! Right now, she wanted to jam an IV pole right down Matilda's backbiting throat. She glared at the family's Botoxed Brutus and forced herself to unclench her fists.

Why was Matilda back here with the wedding party, anyhow? The badmouthing traitor should be taking her seat in the sanctuary. She eyed Matilda smoothing a stray hair on Clarissa.

Of course! She's still back here to make sure her darling daughters are the belles of the ball.

*Take captive every thought and make it obedient to Christ.* Last week's sermon topic had become annoying to the extreme. Why couldn't he have preached about tithing?

Sheri sucked in a slow deep breath and forced herself to soak in the scripture one more time.

*You are not going to allow anything to sabotage your wedding day. Let it go.*

She eyed the clock and her stomach somersaulted. Would Greg make it in time? Her frayed nerves were itching to bite off every single one of her newly manicured nails, but Roxie would kill her.

*What if Greg doesn't have a flat tire, and he's skipped town like Matilda said?*

She couldn't help herself — she began to pick at a cuticle. Roxie grabbed her hand and spanked it. "Stop that! Don't you go ruining all my hard work."

Sheri tried to inhale a deep relaxing breath, but that confounded body shaper thingy that Roxie insisted she wear prevented any hope of deep inhalation.

*He has a flat tire and isn't about to wig out on me, right?*

Memories of Greg telling her he'd wanted to run into a corn maze and never come out when he'd contemplated marriage to Vanessa did little to steady her nerves.

As though reading her mind, Tess put a comforting arm around Sheri's shoulders and whispered, "Don't worry, he'll be here any minute. Greg wouldn't have called and *told* us he had a flat, if he was going to skip town."

True. Or he'd call to say the wedding is off.

Her inner fusspot somewhat mollified, Sheri tried to picture herself on her honeymoon two days from now touring the Tower of London and attending *Romeo and Juliet* in Shakespeare's home turf.

Try as she might to distract herself with lofty visions of England, she couldn't erase the image of a frazzled Greg covered in car grease and whacking the ground with a wrench when he couldn't figure out how to remove the tire's lug nuts. How ironic: Mr. Punctuality, the man who despised tardiness in others, was going to be late for his own wedding!

Forty minutes later, the best man dashed in to inform them that Greg had arrived, and the processional could commence as planned. Matilda and Roxie bid them adieu and headed to the sanctuary to take their seats.

The bridal party lined up, and the organist began the "Air" from Handel's *Water Music Suite* for the seating of the mothers. First down the aisle was Greg's grandmother. Then, Grandma Claiborne hobbled down and took her seat on the aisle of the front row. Then Greg's mother strolled to her seat wearing a lovely cobalt blue dress. Sheri couldn't help but smile as Linda, escorted by her new boyfriend, Richard, sashayed down the aisle in a gorgeous, figure-flattering silver sheathe. The body shaper thingy had worked magic on Linda's matronly figure.

As Linda strolled past Matilda, she smiled smugly, her head held high. When they reached the end of the aisle, they slipped into the front row, and Richard draped an arm around her shoulders.

*Way to go, Mom. There's no reason for you to feel inferior to Matilda.*

When Tess noticed Sheri peeking around the door to watch the processional, she pulled her back and whispered, "Get back here! You don't want to spoil Greg's first impression of you."

With the bride's mother now seated, the organist transitioned into the Pachelbel Canon. As expected, the peacock twins, dressed in their forest green cocktail dresses, couldn't help but smile and do everything but wave like the queen in their bid to snatch up as much attention as possible on their stroll down the aisle.

*Why don't you blow everyone a kiss? Or throw candy.*

Okay, that was snide. Remember the sermon theme: *Take captive every thought...* Sheri had vowed last Sunday to become a nicer person with only pure, charitable thoughts—but maybe she'd start that resolution on January first. Who could be nice with that irritating pair of glory hogs lapping up the limelight?

She heard the audience oohing and aahing over little Jacob, the ring bearer, who was dressed in velvet cranberry shorts, a white shirt, and Christmas suspenders as he marched his way down the aisle with a white satin pillow. Megan, the five-year old daughter of Sheri's nurse, looked adorable with her blond ringlets, cranberry dress with white lace Peter Pan collar, white tights, and patent leather black shoes. Her chubby fingers dropped rose petals along the path to the altar.

Sheri heard the guests rise to their feet as the trumpet soloist played a fanfare announcing her entrance.

Uncle Max offered his portly arm. "Let's get this over with—my knee is killing me. I should have put some emu oil on it."

Even in a black tuxedo, Uncle Max looked like a mini Danny DeVito, with his bald head and short, stocky build. Sheri felt like a giraffe in a wedding dress next to her pint-sized uncle. She swallowed a momentary sadness that her wonderful father hadn't lived to walk her down the aisle.

*He's watching from heaven, and he's here in spirit,* she told herself with a smile. *I love you, Dad.*

"Glide, and don't forget to smile," Cyndi whispered, as Sheri rounded the corner to stroll down the aisle.

She wrapped her hand around Uncle Max's arm and made her first tentative steps, praying she wouldn't fall flat on the floor in her three-inch heels like she had on her dinner date with Caleb.

She glanced around at all the happy faces and grinned at the gaggle of nurses, secretaries, and billing clerks who worked with her in the clinic and hospital.

She nodded to a row of colleagues from her Tennessee Women in Medicine group — Libby, Allison, Angela, and Dana — and then to a row of friends from church.

Vanessa and Nicholas smiled and offered encouraging nods. Relief surged through her to see Nicholas's arm wrapped lovingly around Vanessa. After all he'd endured, he deserved to find happiness with Vanessa.

Michael Abington, the civil engineer, sat next to a pretty brunette he'd met online a month ago. After Greg emailed him about the bedbug fabrication, Michael had started joining them for their morning hikes at Radnor Lake. The two couples planned to hike up Mount LeConte when Sheri and Greg returned from their honeymoon.

As she neared the front of the sanctuary, she gazed in Greg's direction eager to see his reaction to her dress.

He grinned at her, his face beaming with love.

When she reached the end of the aisle and neared the altar, she couldn't help but stare at him.

*What was that ghastly streak of black running above his eyes? It looked like — dare she say it — a unibrow! Could the hideous thing have grown up overnight?*

Greg reached for her hand. Uncle Max rose up on tiptoes and Sheri leaned forward so he could offer her a peck on the cheek. He then joined Aunt Matilda on the second row.

With her lips forced into a smile, she whispered to Greg, "Is this your idea of a joke?"

His forehead furrowed. "What are you talking about?" They strolled together to the front of the altar."

"Your unibrow."

Still puzzled he whispered, "Roxie waxed it before our rehearsal dinner last night."

So it wasn't a joke. As she stared at the unsightly black streak between his brows, it dawned on her — car grease! Of course! He'd gotten a smudge of car grease between his eyebrows while changing that blasted flat tire. He'd probably rubbed his forehead and voila!

"Car grease," she whispered. "Right between your eyebrows."

Greg's eyes widened in dismay.

Why hadn't the best man noticed it and retrieved a facial tissue to wipe it off before Greg stood up in front of two hundred people on the most important day of his life? Sheri glanced over at Greg's best man and inwardly groaned. Thick eyeglasses and a botched haircut with a two-inch cowlick confirmed her worst suspicion — sometimes men could be so clueless. This guy made the old Greg look like a fashion statement.

Greg wiped between his eyebrows with the back of his hand in a vain attempt to eliminate the car grease. Unfortunately, all it did was smear it into a large circle that now covered half his forehead.

*Won't our wedding pictures look pretty with Greg sporting a smear of grease all over his forehead? Oh, well — it'll give us something to laugh about when we're old.*

Besides, she would love Greg till "death do us part" — with or without a unibrow.

In a sudden burst of inspiration, she remembered the white lace hanky Grandma Claiborne had given her to wear as her "something old." Grandma had carried the delicate handkerchief at her own wedding seventy years ago. In an uncharacteristic display of nostalgia and charity, she offered to lend it to Sheri for her wedding. Grandma insisted she carry the hanky in case she got teary-eyed. "You don't want people thinking you're soft."

Sheri stealthfully pulled the handkerchief out from her sleeve, and once they were standing with their backs to the wedding guests, she slipped it over to Greg. He wiped and scrubbed the grease from his brow and forehead until Sheri gave him a nod of approval, He tucked the hanky in his pants pocket. The audience chuckled.

*So much for our little secret.*

Before Sheri could lament the embarrassing motor oil mishap, Greg's brother strode up to the lectern and read their favorite Shakespearean sonnet. This was followed by a sermonette based on the "love chapter" found in Second Corinthians. After they recited their vows, the minister asked if they had rings to symbolize their union.

Sheri's hands trembled as Greg slid the wedding band onto her fourth finger. When she attempted to slide the wedding band onto Greg's finger, it seemed to get stuck on his knuckle.

*Had she ordered the wrong size?*

She pulled it off to try again, but in the process inadvertently dropped the ring onto the floor. It bounced down two stairs, rolled down the aisle, and landed directly in front of Grandma Claiborne in the front row.

Without thinking, Sheri dashed after the ring as fast as her wedding dress and body shaper thingy would allow. Tess, Claire, and Clarissa stood, mouths agape, apparently too stunned to help.

As Sheri bent to pick up the flyaway ring, Grandma Claiborne scolded, "I didn't give you that hanky to mop up car grease." She wagged her gnarled finger in Sheri's face. "It's a family heirloom."

Sheri apologized and promised to get it dry-cleaned. After returning to the altar with the rebellious ring, she tried again to push Greg's ring onto his fourth finger. "Where's that motor oil when we need it? It sure would make sliding this ring on easier," she whispered to Greg.

He chuckled, and she would never know if it was from embarrassment or nerves, but she began to giggle and then laugh. Soon, the two of them were laughing so hard their shoulders shook. They literally had to wipe tears from their eyes. The minister began to chuckle as well, though Sheri could see him chomping on the inside of his cheeks in a vain attempt to maintain a professional veneer.

*Was this a wedding or the Greg and Sheri Comedy Hour?*

When Sheri caught a glimpse of Aunt Matilda's disgusted expression and crossed arms, she sobered up like she'd been doused with a bucket of ice water.

*She probably thinks I've shamed the family again with my clownish behavior.*

With renewed determination, she forced the ring past Greg's knuckle, and everyone cheered.

The minister, gaining his composure, cleared his throat and pronounced them husband and wife. He informed Greg he could now kiss his bride.

Greg's face lit up, and after wrapping his hands behind her neck, merged his lips with hers.

Cheers erupted in the pews from a few of Greg's co-workers. Emboldened, Greg pulled her in and planted a full-blown passionate smooch on her lips. The groomsmen responded with a hoot.

*I wonder what Aunt Matilda thinks of this? She no doubt wants to disown me.*

Sheri and Greg marched down the aisle to Handel's "Hornpipe" from the *Water Music Suite*, and after completing wedding photos (*without* a grease unibrow), they retreated to the fellowship hall of the church for the reception. After a delicious catered dinner, they served their wedding cake with—you guessed it— French Silk ice cream.

"I think our wedding counts as an acceptable excuse to splurge on ice cream, don't you?" Sheri said, only too eager to savor the delectable treat.

"Absolutely," Greg happily agreed, spooning in a mouthful. He licked his lips. "Yum! I love this stuff almost as much as I love you." He winked at her when she feigned offense.

"I love you too, even *with* your grease monkey unibrow."

Greg dropped his head. "I'm never going to live that down, am I?"

"I'll tease you about that 'til the day I die."

He touched her nose. "And I'll enjoy razzing you about dropping my ring down the altar stairs."

"Just think—we have a whole lifetime to tease and annoy each other."

His eyes took on a devilish gleam. "I can think of better ways to spend our time. Shall I show you?" He leaned in for a kiss.

"Then come kiss me. Youth's a stuff will not endure."

He pulled back and tapped his chin in thought. "You may have stumped me on that one. *Othello*?"

"Wrong! *Twelfth Night*." Unable to stop herself from gloating she said, "I *knew* I'd eventually come up with a quote you didn't know." She licked her finger and etched a mark in the air. "One for me."

"You now have a whole lifetime to come up with quotes I don't know."

She grinned. "How about, 'I would not wish any companion in the world but you?'"

"*The Tempest*," he said beaming at his correct answer. He leaned in and whispered, "And I would not wish for any companion in the world but you, either, my darling."

# Book Club Questions

1. Sheri Morris is convinced because she is frumpy and unattractive that she will never find a decent husband. How important is physical appearance in attracting a mate? What hope is there for men and women who are naturally unattractive? Why does God make some people beautiful and others unattractive? (Explore Genesis 29:17 and Romans 9:20.)

2. Do you believe in soulmates? Why or why not? Are there Biblical grounds for this concept? (Genesis 2:18-24)

3. If your current spouse/boyfriend was homely when you met him, but he was otherwise everything you wanted in a spouse, would you have married him anyway? How important should physical attraction be when a *Christian* chooses a mate? What can a wife (or husband) do when they no longer find their spouse attractive?

4. How much do we, as a society, judge people by their appearance? How much do *you* judge someone by their outward attractiveness? How can we overcome our tendency to make snap or superficial judgments? (Consider I Samuel 16:7.)

5. Unlike Sheri, Vanessa Bigelow is insecure because she *is* beautiful. She thinks men are only attracted to her because of her looks. What stereotypes do *you* make about unusually attractive men and women? Do you think your life would be better if you were more attractive? If so, how? What would you change about your appearance and why?

6. Can a beautiful woman use her attractiveness to further the kingdom of God? (Read about Queen Esther in Esther Cpts 4-10.)

7. In a society obsessed with outward appearance and slimness, how can Christians prevent themselves from buying into superficial worries about attractiveness? How can we make what *Christ* says about us overpower the negative media messages that we aren't thin or pretty enough? (Read Matthew 6:25-34, Psalms 31:25-31 and Philippians 4:8.)

8. Do you struggle with insecurity? Has anyone ever made unkind remarks about your weight, appearance, talent, or intelligence? How have these cruel words impacted you? How can you rise above such ego-deflating attacks? (Meditate on: I John 4:4 and Romans 12:2.)

8. Greg Palmer gave up on finding love because of a devastating break-up with a previous girlfriend. Have you ever endured a painful breakup? If so, how did it affect your self-esteem? How did you overcome and move on?

9. Later in the novel, Greg procrastinates breaking off his relationship with Vanessa because he doesn't want to hurt her the way he'd been hurt. Is there a Godly way to break off a romantic relationship? Share your experiences. (See Eph. 4:15.)

10. Linda Morris endured a lifetime of sibling rivalry with her sister, Matilda. Do you have a sibling with whom you struggle to get along? When did the friction start, and what is at the root of it? What could you do to fix the rift? (Meditate on Proverbs 17:9, John 8:1-7, and Matthew 7:2)

Sheri and Tess decide to end their feud and become supportive sisters to each other. Are there steps you could take to improve your relationship with your siblings?

What are examples of sibling rivalries in the Bible, and what could have been done to improve these relationships? (Read about Cain and Abel in Genesis 4, Jacob and Esau in Genesis 25-27, Rachel and Leah in Genesis 29-30, and the disciples in Luke 9:46-48.)

11. Linda Morris meddles in Sheri's life so much that Sheri resorts to little white lies to avoid her mother's interrogation. What is your relationship with your mother like? Is she overinvolved? Controlling? Uncaring? Is she an encourager or a critic?

If you have grown children, do *you* meddle and give unasked for advice? When should you speak up, and when should you back off and merely pray? (For an example of a meddling mother, read about Rebekah and Jacob in Genesis 25-27.)

12. In the middle of the novel, both Greg and Sheri are dating other people, yet are attracted to one another. Have you ever struggled to know which of two suitors to choose? Is it "two-timing" to date two people at once if you are not committed in some way?

The TV show The Bachelor glamorizes loving two people simultaneously. In the course of dating, when should a couple become exclusive?

13. So much of dating is now online. Many embellish their profiles or post pictures that show a considerably slimmer or younger version of themselves in hopes of attracting a beau. How has online dating affected the dynamics of finding a spouse? How has it helped? How has it hurt?

Have *you* ever used E-harmony, Christian Mingle, or a similar dating website? How did it go? What advice would you give someone considering it?

14. Throughout the novel, Greg and Sheri are afraid to share their true feelings for one another. Have you ever shared your feelings with someone and had it negatively impact the relationship? If Sheri had told Greg she had romantic feelings for him *before* he had feelings for her, would it have ruined their friendship? Are there times when honesty is NOT the best policy?

15. If, after the wedding, Sheri and Greg slack off their diet, exercise, and grooming habits and return to their pre-Operation Soulmate appearance, what impact, if any, will it have on their relationship? How important is staying attractive to the success of a marriage?

16. One of the glues in Sheri and Greg's relationship is their mutual love of Shakespeare. How important are shared interests to a marriage's success? What interests do you share with your spouse?

# About the Author

Hi! I am a practicing primary care doctor in Nashville, Tennessee by day and a writer by night. Penning humorous stories about woman physicians provides delightful diversion from the drudgery and aggravation of electronic medical records and insurance hassles.

I grew up on a dairy farm in Derby, Vermont, graduated from Montpelier High School, and then Texas Christian University. After earning my medical degree from the University of Vermont, I moved to Nashville with my wonderful husband, Nathan, to complete my internship and residency.

We are the proud parents of two adult children — Steven, an industrial engineer in Denver, and Eliza, a future veterinarian.

Like Dr. Sheri Morris, I have struggled with insecurity about my weight and so-so looks. Before I met my Prince Charming, I was convinced I would never snag up a decent husband. Like Sheri, I was choosy—my Prince Charming had to be smart, funny, kind, musical, *and* he had to share my Christian faith.

Through the characters of Vanessa Bigelow and Dr. Sheri Morris, I have delved into the lies that demoralize women about their appearance, weight, and self-worth. As Sheri and Greg evolve into more outwardly attractive people, they ultimately learn that what matters most is not external, but internal.

I wrote this book about a frumpy woman and her socially awkward accountability partner so those of us who have never won beauty contests can explore finding love and self-acceptance in a world obsessed with outward appearance. I provided study questions to further explore the deeper meaning of this otherwise humorous book with your book club or friends.

My first book, *Patients I Will Never Forget*, is a collection of humorous and inspiring stories from my thirty-year career as a primary care doctor. In addition, I recently released a non-fiction book, *The Alzheimer's Disease Caregiver's Handbook: What to*

*Remember When They Forget,* to assist the families of patients with dementia.

I am currently writing a five-book romance series called "**The Ladies in Lab Coat**s." All five books feature women physicians. *Can You Lose the Unibrow?* is the first book in the series. The second book, *More Than a Hunch,* shares the unlikely romance between a female oncologist and a prosecuting attorney toying with suing her for malpractice! It will be released in late 2019.

Sign up for my email list to be notified of every book release and for signed copies and exciting giveaways. My website is www.sallywillardburbank.com

Thanks for reading *Can You Lose the Unibrow?* If you enjoyed it, please pen a 5-star review on Amazon and Goodreads to let other prospective readers know how much you enjoyed the book. Thanks!

Sally